PRAISE

"If you have ever wondered what life is like 'behind the veil' of Islam in Afghanistan, then *Freedom's Stand* will touch your heart like nothing else. It brings a message of hope for those whose lives are a desperate search for the reality of God."

CARL MOELLER, president and CEO of Open Doors USA

"Absolutely riveting. Move over, *Kite Runner*, because *Freedom's Stand* captures the life and culture of Afghanistan as if you are standing in the middle of Kabul, smelling the fires of rubber tires, listening to the Islamic call to prayer, wrapped in a burqa, while still offering a gripping message of hope and salvation. The deftly drawn story captured me with every word."

SUSAN MAY WARREN, RITA Award–winning author of *My Foolish Heart*

"I've read several books about the terror and tumult in contemporary Afghanistan, but not until reading Jeanette Windle's *Freedom's Stand* did I realize that Islam's honored prophet Isa Masih holds the answer for this bloodstained country. You may know the prophet as Yeshua or Jesus the Christ, but *Freedom's Stand* beautifully illustrates how he brings inner peace by whatever name he is known."

ANGELA HUNT, author of *The Fine Art of Insincerity*

"I have previously only been to Afghanistan once. . . . I have just returned from another, much deeper encounter with that mysterious, complex country— went there with an author who took down the veil so I could see the Afghanistan that visitors don't see. *Freedom's Stand* leaves me richer and more aware of many hurts I have missed. It has made the people of Afghanistan and their struggles part of me."

STEVE SAINT, author of *End of the Spear*

"Jeanette's characters capture the despair of what Afghanistan is and the hope of what it could be. Within the lives of three vastly different souls, she weaves a wonderfully believable tale about the unlikeliest coalition imaginable. But in the end they all seek the answer to the universal question of 'What am I supposed to do now, Lord?'"

JOE DECREE, retired Army Special Forces major and private security contractor

"It's not easy to capture a war-torn, enigmatic country like Afghanistan, but Jeanette Windle expertly places you right there, wooing you to fall in love with people in dire circumstances. This story of redemption and sacrifice will stick to you like Afghanistan dust, not easily wiped away or forgotten."

MARY DEMUTH, author of *The Muir House* and *Thin Places: A Memoir*

"*Freedom's Stand* is a fascinating, in-depth plunge into the cultural and religious struggles of the Afghan people and those who are trying to make a difference there. Jeanette Windle gives us another breathtaking story of love, faith, intrigue, and sacrifice, proving again why she's one of the best storytellers around."

MARK MYNHEIR, homicide detective and author of *The Corruptible*

"My hope is that *Freedom's Stand* will open readers' eyes to the plight of Afghan women and open their hearts to the love of Isa."

CHUCK HOLTON, former Army Ranger and war correspondent

"Windle writes with the power and authenticity of one who has lived on foreign soil and brought back truth we often do not see from our American living rooms. *Freedom's Stand* is rich with the history, politics, and culture of Afghanistan, and [it] brings a people to life whom we are called to love. A rich and eye-opening tale."

T. L. HIGLEY, author of *Pompeii: City on Fire*

"In a time when Afghanistan is in the news almost daily, it is both refreshing and challenging to read a story of courage and candor, adventure and romance among this ancient and passionate people. Only one with a love for the Afghans and an understanding of their culture could bring such a story to life, and author J. M. Windle has done it. This book . . . will challenge us at the deepest level of our commitment and encourage us to stand for freedom—regardless of the cost."

KATHI MACIAS, award-winning author of *People of the Book*

FREEDOM'S STAND

FREEDOM'S STAND

J. M. WINDLE

TYNDALE HOUSE PUBLISHERS, INC.
CAROL STREAM, ILLINOIS

Visit Tyndale's exciting Web site at www.tyndale.com.

Visit Jeanette Windle's Web site at www.jeanettewindle.com.

TYNDALE and Tyndale's quill logo are registered trademarks of Tyndale House Publishers, Inc.

Freedom's Stand

Designed by Beth Sparkman

Edited by Caleb Sjogren

Scripture taken from the Holy Bible, *New International Version,*® *NIV.*® Copyright © 1973, 1978, 1984 by Biblica, Inc.™ Used by permission of Zondervan. All rights reserved worldwide. www.zondervan.com.

This novel is a work of fiction. Names, characters, places, and incidents either are the product of the author's imagination or are used fictitiously. Any resemblance to actual events, locales, organizations, or persons living or dead is entirely coincidental and beyond the intent of either the author or the publisher.

Library of Congress Cataloging-in-Publication Data

Windle, Jeanette.
  Freedom's stand / J. M. Windle.
     p. cm.
  ISBN 978-1-4143-1476-1 (sc)
1. Americans—Afghanistan—Fiction. 2. Afghanistan—Fiction. I. Title.
  PS3573.I5172F74 2011
  813′.54—dc22   2010051556

Printed in the United States of America

17   16   15   14   13   12   11
7   6   5   4   3   2   1

To B. E., whose one desire since I first met her in Kabul was to serve the women of Afghanistan until the day her heavenly Father called her home. That prayer was granted in the spring of 2010. Her courage, sacrifice, and love remain an inspiration to those who come behind. May you dance, sweet sister, in the presence of your Creator until we meet again.

PROLOGUE

Pashtun Territory, Afghanistan

The girl was breathing hard as she climbed steep outdoor stairs, carrying the basin of dirty water in which she'd been scrubbing vegetables. Sliding the basin onto a flat rooftop, she scrambled after it. She was high enough here to see out over the compound's mud-brick perimeter wall. A narrow river gorge ran between two gently rising mountain ridges. The compound sat halfway up one flank, its crenellated exterior fortification curving out from the mountainside to enclose an area large enough for a *buzkashi* tournament, the Afghan free-for-all version of polo.

Above the girl on the highest parapet, a teenage sentry squatted, an ancient AK-47 across his thighs. Catching his eyes on her, the girl pulled her headscarf higher across her face. But she did not stoop immediately to complete her task, stepping forward instead to the edge of the roof.

Today's sun had already dropped behind the opposite mountain ridge, leaving behind a spectacular display of reds and oranges and purples above the sharp geometry of rock formations. Overhead, a rare saker falcon wheeled lazily against the first pale stars. Perched on a boulder across the river, a shepherd boy played a wooden *toola* flute, the rush of water over stones offering harmony to his plaintive tune. Behind him, a herd of mountain sheep scrambled over terraces where crops would grow when spring runoff overflowed a streambed winding through the valley floor.

The girl saw little beauty in the scene. The narrow vista of this isolated mountain valley, varied only by white of winter snow and green of summer growth, was no less a prison than the compound walls. Just as the bright red and pink of poppy blooms within the compound enclosure below meant only backbreaking hours of hand-irrigating and weeding.

But today that would be finished. Before nightfall was complete, the compound gates that had slammed her inside—how long had it been? five winters now?—would swing wide. Perhaps her new home would be a town with markets and people and the freedom to emerge onto the streets. Perhaps there would be womenfolk her own age who would welcome her as a sister.

Perhaps there would be books. Oh, to study again!

Will there be love?

Her searching gaze had finally spotted what she'd been seeking. A single track scratched the baked earth of the valley floor, paralleling the riverbed. A dust devil moving along it was too large and fast to be the wind. A party of horsemen?

Then a vehicle separated itself from the whirlwind. A single-cab pickup, its bed crowded with human shapes, though still too distant to make out whether they were male or female.

One would certainly be male.

Her liberator.

Or new prison warden.

Her bridegroom.

"Worthless daughter of a camel! Will you take your rest while others labor?"

A blow rocked the girl back on her heels. As her uncle's senior wife hurried down the steps, the girl scrambled for the basin. Water was too precious to just be discarded, and she carefully carried the basin over to a row of potted tomato vines. But as she tilted it above the first pot, the girl abruptly dropped the scarf from her face to bend over the water's murky surface.

Would her chosen mate find her attractive like the tales of ancient Persian princes and lovely slave girls her mother had whispered to her at night? If her bridegroom found her to his liking, he would be kinder. Perhaps even buy her gifts. So she'd observed from the younger women, wives of her uncle's sons and his brothers and their sons, who with their children made this compound a small village in itself. Her uncle's own new bride too, a teenager not many winters older than herself, to whom he'd given gifts of clothing and jewelry that made his senior wife scream with rage when he was out of earshot.

Though her mirror was blurry, the girl could make out features thin and pale as moonlight. Food had been scarce this winter for such as she. Wisps of hair escaping her headscarf were only a shade darker than dried mud; long-lashed eyes somberly returning her gaze, the blue of a hot summer sky. At least the face in the water was unmarred by scar or cleft palate, her body under work-stained clothing whole and hardened to strenuous labor. This past winter she'd been touched by the monthly cycle of women.

Still, that wavering reflection was nothing like the smooth black tresses, golden oval features, and almond-shaped dark eyes of her *wali's* new wife, who was the embodiment of captive beauties in her mother's tales. What if her own bridegroom was dissatisfied? What if he beat her? She'd seen the bruises on less-favored household women. Heard their screams through thick walls of their sleeping quarters.

"Where is that girl? Can she do nothing as she is ordered?"

The girl hastily emptied the basin. But her footsteps slowed to reluctance as she started down the dirt stairs. She would miss this view more than the compound's human residents. Though they had not been cruel, neither had they been kind. The raised voices and blows if she did not work hard or fast enough. The constant reminder that her refuge here was only by the most tenuous of blood ties to her guardian or wali, master of this compound. Most of the time she was simply invisible behind handed-down tunic and enveloping scarf.

She'd been too young for a head covering when her mother first brought her to those tall, wooden gates. No more than eight winters, though birthdays or even birth years meant little here. Making this her thirteenth year of life, if she'd calculated right. To the girl's dismay, it was her mother who'd quickly insisted she cover herself. She'd not understood then the fear in her mother's face when male eyes followed her young, lithe form around the courtyard. The fury of household women directed at her and not the watchers. She just knew she'd become suddenly invisible, the quick tugging of her scarf over her face when any male compound member approached now so automatic she no longer consciously registered the gesture.

Her mother had slipped away in the second winter of their refuge here. Of grief, the girl believed, though compound chatter said some sickness of the lungs. By then she'd come to feel that the individual living and breathing beneath her veil was forgotten, her existence no more than an extra pair of hands and feet and grudging portion of food.

That she wasn't completely forgotten, she'd learned only this morning when she'd been informed her marriage was arranged. If sudden, she'd known this day must come. Not only because her labor from sunrise to nightfall didn't compensate for another mouth to feed. Even her ignorance knew the value a nubile and healthy female represented. Her own initial terror and dismay had given way to rising anticipation. Whatever future awaited beyond those tall gates had to be an improvement. At the least, she would be wanted, her husband's valued possession, a member of his family.

Will there be love?

The girl knew what love was. Her mother's hand brushing fleetingly across her hair. The private smile that never banished sorrow when her mother slipped the girl extra food from her own portion. A soft voice murmuring stories into her ear when the day's work was done and mother and daughter could retire to their sleeping mat.

There were other memories, so distant the girl couldn't be sure they weren't imagined. A "before" time and place that held painted walls and smooth tile beneath her feet. A swirl of vividly colored silks and female laughter. Children darting like butterflies in their own bright tunics. A scent of sandalwood and taste of richly spiced food until one's stomach was satisfied. Bearded features and masculine voices that were loud, but not angry. Her father? Brothers? Above all, one smiling youthful face, still beardless, bending close above her as a patient hand guided small fingers in loops and swirls and dots that made up the name that was no longer hers.

But those images she did not like to relive. Not just because of the aching inaccessibility of such warmth and joy and laughter. But because with them came the blackness. Horrible images of torn, scarlet-stained bodies.

Screaming explosions. Running until her chest hurt. Hiding in dark places. Terror that choked her as much as her mother's hand tight over her mouth. Bitter cold, stomach-gnawing hunger and a mouth parched with thirst. So that when her mother had brought her at last to this compound, the girl had been grateful to leave outside that other world, a past life swallowed up by winter's night.

"There you are! Why have you lingered so long? The guests arrive at the gates. Go make yourself decent lest your husband consider we have cheated him."

Meeting the girl at the bottom of the stairs, the senior wife snatched away the basin. Behind her in the dirt courtyard, smoke rose from a cylindrical clay bread oven. Women stirred pots over an open fire. The girl's mouth watered at the aroma of a sheep roasting on a spit. Though this feast commemorated her nuptials, she'd be fortunate to suck the marrow of a discarded bone.

No one glanced up as the girl filled a pail with clean water at the well. Did anybody in this place care if she stayed or left? The girl hoisted the bucket and hurried toward her sleeping quarters, a small, windowless room she'd shared since her mother's death with an ancient female whose polio-twisted limbs explained her unmarried status. At least she'd leave with new clothing, she discovered when she ducked through the door. Not the red and green and gold traditional to weddings, trimmed with sequins, glass beads, bright embroidery. A tunic and drawstring pants lying on her sleeping mat, their matching headscarf, were the sober brown of daily wear, signal that today was less celebration than business transaction.

Stripping dirty clothing away, she dipped a rag in the cold water, shivering as she scrubbed herself clean. She tugged the tunic over her shoulders and tightened the drawstring around her waist. A plastic brush with broken bristles coaxed tangles from her hair. She twisted it up under the headscarf. If her mother were alive, she would not be doing this alone. There might even be festivities such as had accompanied her wali's recent wedding. A henna-decorating party with the compound's women. A ceremonial sauna and bath.

But then if her mother were alive, perhaps she would not be bartered this day to a stranger.

Will there be love?

The answer to that question became so urgent she could not breathe. Sinking to her sleeping mat, she shut her eyes, arms wrapped around her knees as she rocked back and forth in soundless anguish. It took gentle shaking, a worried murmur, to draw her back to her surroundings. She opened her eyes to her elderly roommate's anxious gaze. Some wordless sympathy she glimpsed there gave her strength to push to her feet.

The compound's largest room was the reception chamber. *Tushaks*, the padded mats used for sitting and sleeping, lined the room, handwoven rugs hiding the dirt floor. Whitewashed walls held photos of *mujahedeen* freedom fighters and a tattered poster of Herat's famed blue-domed mosque. The party taking their seats around a vinyl feasting cloth was a small one as befit the insignificance of this celebration. Half a dozen men in turbans, robes, and embroidered vests, their dark, curly beards and hooked noses similar enough to indicate a common gene pool. Her wali's new bride was leading away three female shapes draped in burqas.

None of the men were less than middle-aged, the oldest tall and heavy, his full beard streaked with white. Neither were they the strangers she'd expected. The girl choked down disappointment. She'd glimpsed these men when she'd accompanied the household to a compound at the far end of the gorge for her guardian's wedding festivities. Her new home would offer no escape from this valley. It only remained to see which of those hard-faced men had purchased her for their own. Two male cousins were now bringing in a huge copper tray holding the roasted sheep, stretched whole on a bed of yellow rice. Women scurried in with samovars and tea glasses. As she placed a platter of *mantu* dumplings among piles of naan bread, the girl slid a glance sideways to see which guest had been seated at the head of the feasting cloth.

It was well she'd set the platter down, because horror convulsed her grip. The guest of honor was not one of those middle-aged men, but the patriarch himself.

A once-powerful frame was now soft like uncooked dough, the white-streaked beard spilling over a well-rounded belly. But there was cruelty in his compressed lips, the deeply grooved frown lines. During those scant hours she'd spent among his household women, she'd seen their nervous tension anytime the khan approached, as though bracing for a blow. She had seen the meager leftovers from the men's feasting even on such a day of celebration, the tattered clothing and rheumy-eyed malnutrition among the children.

At the clap of her wali's hands, she reluctantly straightened to move closer. As a twitch at her scarf left her face bare, she stood, eyes lowered, under the khan's leisured scrutiny. The whites of his eyes were bloodshot as well as yellowed with age. An opium smoker. Something hot and avid in that stare, the touch of his tongue—red, moist—to full lips, deepened the girl's nausea. Then the khan gave an approving grunt, and her uncle's sharp handclap released the girl to retreat into the courtyard.

The visiting burqas, now unveiled, were drinking tea with her guardian's young bride. The girl took one involuntary step in their direction, then froze as heads turned toward her. The animosity in their unified glare chilled her to the bone. No, there would be no welcome from the womenfolk of her new family.

She headed instead to where her guardian's own senior wife was supervising the final relay of serving dishes, emotion bursting out hot and choking. "Tell me if it is not true! Did my uncle trade me for his new wife? Is that why she is here, and I—I am to go to that place?"

As her voice cracked, the older woman raised disbelieving eyebrows. "But of course. How else do you think he could afford the bride-price of such a beautiful young virgin? And why do you complain? To be a khan's wife, senior to other women, is more than you could hope. You should be grateful. It was I who insisted your wedding day be delayed until you had become a woman."

Her tone became less brusque as the girl swayed, blood draining from her face. "Now go, wash the fear from your face and eat something lest you faint. When the men have done feasting, they will call for you, and this will be finished."

Call for her as men called for their food! No wedding ceremony such as her guardian's new wife had enjoyed. No bridal canopy or vows taken upon a wrapped Quran. No veil thrown over her and her bridegroom, a mirror thrust beneath so the new couple might "see" each other for the first time in its bright surface.

But then she was no daughter of the household. Just an orphan woman-child tossed as a bonus into her guardian's own dowry bid, now to be handed over like a bundle of market goods.

The cooked food had all been carried inside now, but a stack of naan too charred and hard to serve at the feast was piled beside the bread oven. The girl grabbed a slab, then slipped up the dirt steps to the rooftop where she'd watered the potted tomatoes.

Sunset's flaming colors had faded to night, the stars bright above the far ridge. In the courtyard below, a soft glow of oil lanterns added their yellow light to the cookfires. A staccato of tabla drums and twang of *rubab* strings signaled the evening's entertainment. The teenage sentry had gone to join the feast. In his place crouched a younger sibling, close in age and size to the girl herself so that the AK-47's metallic length balanced awkwardly across his lap.

Retreating into a corner where roof overhang met the perimeter wall, the girl nibbled at the bread. But despite her stomach's hungry twisting, she couldn't eat. Was all of life no more than smashed dreams?

The girl's slight frame shivered, and not because of the icy breeze, as her eye fell on the nearest doorway. The master of the compound's apartment from which he could enjoy the view as well as his new bride. At least those captive slave girls in her mother's tales had in compensation the attentions of handsome, young princes. And always ultimately, in her mother's telling at any rate, their love. While tonight she would be sharing such quarters with—

Her mind reeled, refusing the image. *I can't! I can't!*

But she had no choice. No woman ever did. It was the penalty of being female. The recognition that even before Allah himself, creator of heaven and earth, she held little value in comparison to her male counterparts.

Or was she so completely without choice? The lovely heroines of her mother's tales had with resolute courage shaped adverse circumstances to their own advantage. Just such courage as had propelled a woman with girl child in tow through winter's icy breath with bombs crashing all around and enemies at their heels until they had reached the safety of this compound.

Did her mother's daughter possess less valor and determination?

Heading across the roof, the girl scrambled up a flight of steps.

Her cousin had made himself comfortable in his sentry assignment. A discarded soft drink bottle was refilled with water at his side. One *patu* covered his shoulders; another wrapped his waist against the cold. He was alleviating boredom by whittling a new slingshot base from a forked branch. In those early days before she'd vanished behind a woman's veil, the two had played together, and if not friendly, his glance was tolerant as the girl emerged onto the parapet.

"If you wish, I will watch for you so you may reach the feasting before it is all gone."

Even up here, one could smell the rich fragrance of roasted mutton, fried dumplings, fresh-baked naan. The boy rose with an alacrity that said just such a worry had been on his own mind. Shedding the blanket draped around his waist, he dropped the machine gun and whittling kit onto its folds, then bounded down the dirt stairs.

The girl briefly settled the weapon across her own thighs. It was dark enough now that a casual glance would not note the exchange. She waited only until she saw the boy duck into the reception chamber. She knew her cousin too well to worry he'd hurry back. Unless the older sibling who'd ordered him to sentry duty noted his dereliction.

Suddenly panicked, the girl pushed to her feet. The rooftop where she stood placed her at chest level below the top of the crenellated perimeter wall. She wrapped the abandoned patu around her own shoulders and picked up the water bottle, then shook the whittling knife free of branch and shavings, tucking both along with the naan bread into a blanket fold. The gun she left abandoned on the parapet. Mud brick crumbled under her hands as she braced to pull herself up onto the wall. She hesitated. Was it courage or insanity to commit herself to that barren landscape? to a future no more promising and far less certain than the one awaiting below?

Bloodshot, avid eyes rose sharply to her mind. A cruel mouth with moist tongue flickering out in anticipation. Squat, round-bellied frame. The images were enough to propel the girl onto the top of the wall.

The drop to the other side was farther than anticipated, knocking the air from her with the landing. Using hands and feet like a mountain goat, she scrambled up the mountain flank behind the compound until she could no longer glimpse the light of cookfires and lanterns. Feeling her way along the top of the ridge, she blinked back tears as bare feet caught repeatedly on protruding stones. But she did not slow. She was under no delusion her wali and bridegroom would do nothing to retrieve their property, and once the sun was up, her stumbling trail would be easy to follow.

Only when a rising moon returned some light to her path did she stop briefly. Sheltering behind a stone outcropping, she fumbled for the whittling knife. It sliced neatly through the thick, curly length of her hair. She dug a shallow hole, burying the telltale strands under a mound of earth and pebbles.

The girl was now exhausted and limping badly. But instead of resting, she drank half her water, ate half the naan, then pushed herself again to her feet. If she followed the gorge downstream, she would be retracing the route by which she and her mother had arrived at those gates far behind her now. Which should bring her sooner or later to a real road and town.

Where she would go then, she had no idea. Nor how she would survive. All that counted was what she was leaving behind.

The thought should have been cause for terror. Instead, the smallest flame of anticipation gave the girl fresh strength.

Like my mother's tales, I go in search of a new world and a new life.
But not love.
Love is an illusion.

Kabul, Afghanistan

"Why did you permit him to walk out alive?" Fury vibrated the cell phone's speaker unit.

"I told you of the recording." Afghan Deputy Minister of Interior Ismail swept the smashed DVD player into a waste receptacle beside the police chief's desk he'd commandeered. "Perhaps such ammunition would not damage you. But it would destroy me!"

"And you are a tool I cannot afford to lose at this time. So perhaps you made the wise decision."

Ismail didn't find the other man's chuckle so amusing. "It has not worked out so ill in any case. We have still advanced our objectives. And he is aware the price of his life is silence. He will not speak further of what he knows."

"Which is little enough. Can he have guessed that wreaking vengeance on Khalid Sayef was not, after all, the end purpose of his mission? Could this be why he turned from his path?"

"There is no way he could know. No, it was the girl. To lie was a mistake." Such admission was another mistake. Ismail hurried to fill cold silence. "In any case, he has made it clear his heart is no longer committed to jihad."

"With the right leverage, he may yet change his mind. If only this had arrived in time, we would not have failed today."

The same image filled both speakers' cell phone screens.

"Who could have known it was under our noses all this time?" Ismail said.

"And his. You should have investigated earlier this American tenant and her doings."

"Only chance brought the trail to my door."

"Or Allah's gift."

The photo was not one a decent woman would exhibit outside her own family. But even in Afghanistan, mug shots required that more than a burqa be visible. Escaping, brown curls under a headscarf framed pale, oval features, an expression of combined despair and defiance incongruous in so youthful a face. But it was the eyes glaring at an unseen camera through a fringe of long and curling lashes that drew a murmur of satisfaction from both speakers. Scornful, a sheen of tears discernible even in JPEG, they glimmered the deep lapis lazuli of a Band-e Amir mountain lake.

Kandahar Province, Afghanistan

When Jamil had saved that burned child's life, he hadn't expected to find himself running for his own.

Jamil glanced back over his shoulder. He was pulling away from the mob. No, the mob had chosen to drop back. Though another hail of rocks hissed through the air, the throwing was halfhearted. But then the men weren't trying to kill him. Only to drive Jamil—and his words—from their village.

All had begun so well too. The village was like any other in southern Afghanistan, dirt cubes behind dirt walls on a parched plain. A riverbed that ran full during wet season was now only dry boulders, but a communal well permitted survival year-round. Jamil had been refilling his water bottle when a villager invited him to share the evening meal. The hospitality of the Pashtun tribes was as legendary as their ferocity.

And their poverty. Mud walls of his host's reception chamber bore no whitewash. Threadbare carpet and tushaks covered a dirt floor. A platter set before Jamil and male household members held only rice with a scant topping of lentils. Thin faces and eager eyes of children peeking around a doorway to watch the men eat restrained Jamil's own hunger. An injustice, Ameera would protest.

A reminder that Ameera was gone now from Jamil's world. The woman who'd first introduced him to Isa. He'd heard her voice only once since being expelled from Kabul. When he again reached a place where his cell phone functioned, her own phone was out of service. He'd called Rasheed instead, only to be told that Ameera had returned to her own country and he was never to call again.

A burqa was pouring tea when Jamil heard the scream. Its anguished pain was too great to consider propriety. His host's own distress was such he hadn't objected to Jamil following into the family quarters. The screams came from a boy no more than two years old. Water boiling for tea had been removed from a cookfire onto a nearby stone block. The toddler had pulled the entire pot over himself. Panicked women were yanking off wet clothing, blistered skin sloughing away with it.

Jamil reacted with pausing for thought. Grabbing a pottery jar of water, he elbowed through the shrieking circle to pour its contents over the child. A chill winter breeze made the wetting as effective as an ice pack.

"For such burns, you must cool the victim immediately so the fire does not burn deeper. And you must not disturb the skin." Jamil indicated raw, red flesh where scalded skin had been peeled away. "It will protect the boy while new skin grows."

The boy was moved to a tushak in the reception chamber, and Jamil urged to stay on as guest. Jamil showed the family how to rinse burns with mildly salted water against infection, how to spread petroleum jelly so healing fingers and joints didn't become fused together.

In return, his grateful host not only allowed Jamil to read Isa's words, but summoned the rest of the village to his compound. As news spread of the visiting healer, they arrived with their own aches and pains. An abscessed boil. A poorly set broken arm. An infant with diarrhea. An infected eye. Nothing Jamil couldn't handle. One advantage of these people's harsh lives was that if they survived to adulthood, they were as tough and enduring as cured goatskin.

And they stayed to listen when Jamil spread his patu to read from his Pashto New Testament. After all, did not everyone know that Islam's most prominent prophet beyond Muhammad himself had been a great healer? If not usual, there could be no harm in hearing words purported to come from Isa Masih. Especially when spoken by one gifted with healing hands.

Yes, whether or not Jamil had actually saved the boy's life, he'd certainly saved him from serious infection and scarring. Though not from pain. Which was why Jamil now fled for his own life into the darkening twilight.

By the time Jamil had settled his primary patient that first evening, his host had ended the toddler's moans with a pinch of opium paste. Jamil hadn't been happy, but his own supply of painkillers was long gone. Opium was the only medicine available to poorer Afghans. So Jamil held his peace and kept a sharp eye on his young patient. Though useful, opium paste was harder to regulate than its processed cousin, morphine. An overdose slowed breathing. Every winter across Afghanistan, hundreds died of respiratory failure after taking opium to calm flu or pneumonia symptoms. Within days, Jamil had coaxed his host into curtailing the opium to a single nightly dose. By now he was no longer a stranger but a favored community member. So much so that his host had invited Jamil to tour the commercial venture that fed the village during harsh winters.

The carpet-weaving workshop was a dark, dank place, its air thick with dust and the acridity of fresh dye so that Jamil had to smother a cough as he followed his host among the looms. Once created by Afghan peasant women to adorn their own homes, the beautiful patterns were now far too valuable to be wasted on the poorest caste who toiled over them. As long as light slanted through the small windows, these weavers would not stir from their crouched positions. But neither women nor children working as steadily as the adults displayed any objection to the tiresome squatting and repeated motion.

Then Jamil took in pinpoint pupils. Quickly, he searched faces around him. Yes, that slow, easy breathing. The slumped relaxation even while fingers never stopped knotting those endless threads. All these workers were under influence of opium, even the children. Along the walls lay babies wrapped in patus. Not just small ones, but well up into walking age. Every one so limply asleep, Jamil had to lean close to assure himself they breathed. Here was a face of Afghanistan Jamil had never known in his own earlier, privileged life. Now in each dreaming, vacant face, Jamil saw his own mother and sister. If they still lived, could it be they might find themselves in just such horrific circumstances?

To Jamil's concern, his host shrugged. "It is difficult labor. They cannot work well and long without the opium. The women cannot work either if their babies demand attention."

"But these women and children are now addicts. These infants as well. Perhaps they will not die from it, but they will not grow as strong nor as intelligent. And they will always need the opium even when they are not weaving."

"They do not need intelligence to weave. Nor to bear children. And they will always be weaving. Tell me, do your words from Isa speak of carpets?"

"Not specifically," Jamil admitted. "But Isa was a healer. He taught kindness to women and children as well as men. If the work is too tiring without opium, there are ways to make it less so. Better air and light so their eyes and breathing are not troubled. To take turns with the small ones so they are cared for and the women too have a rest."

"Those things do not produce as many carpets," Jamil's host answered flatly. "We will not hear more."

And that was that. There'd been a hasty conference of village leaders. His host had at least sent for Jamil's pack while the men gathered around the well with stones in hand. Now, as the mob headed back to the village, Jamil slackened his steps further. He hadn't felt so disheartened since beginning his new quest. Arriving at this village, finding welcome at the well, these past days of healing and reading, Jamil had felt he was truly following Isa Masih's footsteps.

Now here too it seemed Jamil's path emulated the prophet. Hadn't Isa's own neighbors driven him out of town? Hadn't he instructed his own disciples about those who rejected his words? They were not to resist or plead, but to shake the dust from their feet as witness against that town's unbelief.

But Jamil did not want to shake this village's dust from his feet. Despite those hurled stones, he couldn't forget their earlier kindliness and hospitality. If they could only come to see Isa Masih as Jamil had. To understand how following his ways could transform their lives and community.

Jamil found himself wanting this as fervently as he'd once wanted revenge and retribution. Had Isa's heart wept over those who'd refused him as Jamil's heart wept now?

The noise of an engine approaching rapidly from behind whirled Jamil around. A small motorcycle was racing up the mountain trail. Jamil ducked behind a boulder, but he was too late. As the motorcycle drew abreast, it stopped. Jamil heard footsteps as the rider dismounted. "*Salaam aleykum.* I come in peace."

The boulder offered no further retreat, so Jamil stepped warily into the open. "*Wa aleykum u salaam.* And upon you also be peace."

The rider dwarfed his motorcycle, strongly built under his patu, standing head and shoulders above Jamil's slim medium build. Like most in these parts, his speech and coloring were Pashtun. He was also no older than Jamil's own twenty-seven years. "You are the healer named Jamil who has been staying in the village back there? They told me he had come this way."

Jamil's wariness hadn't dissipated, but the stranger displayed no evidence of hostility, so Jamil acknowledged, "I am a healer, and I have been staying in the village."

"And is it true that, like the prophet Isa, you will heal any in need, rich or poor, male or female?"

Was this a trap? an ambush of some kind? Jamil's blood was throbbing in his ears, his heart suddenly racing as he admitted cautiously, "If such need is within my ability, yes."

Stepping forward, the man embraced Jamil with a hearty kiss on both cheeks. "I am Omed. And you are a miracle. When a guest at the *chaikhana* told of such a healer in a village over the ridge, I knew the Almighty had heard my prayers."

His new acquaintance seemed to take for granted Jamil would follow as he headed back to the motorcycle. Gingerly, Jamil squeezed on behind Omed. Twilight had now faded to full night, and the motorcycle had no headlight. But Omed gunned the engine unhesitatingly up ridges and down into ravines until Jamil could not have turned back had he wished, because he'd never have found his way. Then their zigzag trail dropped onto the smoothness of a road, and Jamil spotted a twinkle of lights ahead.

As the motorcycle sped between cubic shapes, Jamil could see this town was much larger than the village where he'd last lodged. Shopfronts and the minaret of a small mosque fringed a dirt commons along with the town chaikhana, a combination tea shop and inn for passing travelers. Lighting came from kerosene lanterns, not electricity. Omed was speaking now over his shoulder, but Jamil could make out only an occasional word above the engine. The motorcycle pulled up in front of a long, single-storied concrete building.

"If you will wait here, I will return immediately." As Omed strode toward the chaikhana next door, Jamil walked along the length of the concrete building. A red crescent above one door, the Muslim adaptation of a Red Cross symbol, identified a health clinic. So the town had its own healer. Then why was Jamil here?

Another symbol marked a schoolroom. But Jamil's attention was drawn immediately through a door that stood open. Inside was a familiar village scene. A carpet-weaving cooperative such as Jamil had encountered in the last village. But here a single large room was airy and dry. Kerosene lamps reflected brightly from concrete walls painted a cheerful sunshine yellow. Windows paneled with translucent plastic would provide ample light during day hours. More strikingly, the looms were not backbreaking floor models but vertical wall units, adjustable so that the section being woven was within easy reach of weavers. Benches permitted sitting instead of crouching on the floor.

Just inside the door was a stall where shoppers sorted through finished rugs. The nearest was not a local Pashtun with his light brown hair and round, sunburned features. Rather than *shalwar kameez*, the tunic and pantaloons of local dress, he wore jeans and a T-shirt, an olive green Army parka instead of a patu. He was also bareheaded and clean-shaven, a fashion becoming popular among Afghanistan's younger urban residents.

In this rural community, he stood out like a jungle parrot among Kabuli homing pigeons.

"Jamil, forgive me for tarrying so long." Omed had returned.

Jamil swung around, exclaiming, "But this is truly wonderful! You would not need opium to work such looms as these. Where did all this come from?"

"Foreign soldiers built the community center. And an aid organization supplies such looms. I—knew some of their people." There was hesitation in Omed's answer. "It was I who convinced the elders to make this change. Though the looms cost the village nothing, they did not at first wish to agree because there are conditions. The women do not weave on Fridays. No opium is permitted. Children may work if their families need them, but only after they attend classes, both boys and girls. Women with small children do not work unless there is someone to watch their child.

"Still with all that, these new looms permit weaving of more carpets than before. The elders have come to see how much better it is for children to be in school and their wives free of the opium. So you see what a terrible thing it is that the accident should happen at this time."

Accident? Just how much had Jamil missed earlier? But the jerk of Omed's head indicated a group of men wandering leisurely over from the chaikhana.

"The mullah and some elders are saying it is a sign we should not have changed to the new looms, that they are too dangerous. The healer has refused to touch her because she is a woman. I begged Haroon to take her to the city, where there are hospitals for women. But he says there is no money. I prayed the healer would change his mind and show mercy. When word came instead to me of you, I knew it was the answer to my prayers."

If Jamil was straining to fill in gaps, the gist became clear as the approaching men swirled around him. A man in lab coat over shalwar kameez pushed open the door under the red crescent. The health clinic was a single room lit by a kerosene lantern hanging from a ceiling hook. Metal shelving and a glass-fronted cabinet held few supplies. On a wooden table a burqa and blanket draped a female shape curled up in fetal position. The woman looked curiously deformed, her shoulder thrusting oddly under the burqa as though a hunchback.

A second burqa was watching over the patient. She retreated into a corner as the men crowded into the clinic. Omed murmured an aside to Jamil. "My wife. The injured woman is her sister."

Then he addressed his wife gently. "Did I not promise you, Najia, that I would find another healer? This is Jamil, the one of whom we were told. He has agreed to make an examination."

Jamil had now caught enough babbled conversation to piece together what had happened. The accident to which Omed had referred was the collapse of a new vertical loom early that morning, wrenching this woman's shoulder from its socket. At question was whether the shoulder was simply dislocated or more seriously broken. For that Jamil would need to examine the injury.

As Jamil reached to fold back pale blue polyester, his hand was struck away. "You would dishonor our women? Omed, what kind of healer have you brought us?"

Jamil's assailant was the man in a lab coat. Jamil paused to look at him. "You are the health worker in charge of this clinic? Then you can tell me. What is the extent of the woman's injury? Are there bones broken? What have you done to treat her?"

The health worker nodded to a small, thin man. "Haroon, the woman's husband, examined her. He said no bones are broken. Only the shoulder has popped from its socket."

Jamil turned to Haroon. "How did you determine whether bones were broken?"

Haroon shrugged. "I raise sheep and goats. I know how to tell when a bone is broken. Besides, I have seen such an injury before. Nabi's shoulder was so hurt when a stone falling down the mountain struck him last winter." The patient's husband nodded toward a bystander. "I helped the healer put it back into its place."

Jamil turned back to the health worker. "If you know how to treat such injuries, why is this woman lying here unattended? To heal well, such an injury must be restored to place as soon as possible."

"But I cannot touch her." The health worker visibly recoiled. "She is a woman. I explained to her husband how it must be done. When Haroon was not successful, I had him give her opium so that she should not injure it further until we see whether it will heal or not. Sometimes if left alone, such injuries will restore themselves to their rightful place. Or so our instructors taught us." The health worker drew himself up proudly. "I studied for three full months to become *dokter* here."

"A dislocation this bad will not restore itself." No wonder Omed had been so frantic for Jamil to come. If Jamil was no true doctor either, he wasn't just a villager who'd taken a few first aid courses in order to man the local medical outpost.

Omed looked anxiously at Jamil. "You can repair her shoulder?"

Jamil didn't answer immediately. He knew the mechanics of fixing a dislocated shoulder, not only from those long-ago studies, but because he'd helped the American medic tend just such an injury after the New Hope bombing in Kabul. But that patient had been a child, the injury fresh. After a full day, this woman's torn ligaments and tendons would be hardened into place, the dislocated shoulder well set into its new position.

"I cannot determine for sure without X-rays. It would be best to take her into a hospital for a proper examination."

The room erupted into speech, some in agreement with Jamil, others in angry denial. Omed's disappointment showed clearly on his face. It was the husband who spoke up. "That is not possible. I do not have money for such a trip nor a hospital. Naveed—" Haroon gestured toward the health worker—"says in time the shoulder will heal enough to work again. If not—" he glanced slyly at Omed—"she can return to her own family. A new bride-price will be cheaper than hospitals."

As chuckles rippled across the clinic, a man standing behind Haroon added, "Besides, who are we to interfere? Does not the Quran state that Allah fastens every person's fate upon their neck at birth?"

The man speaking was not the oldest here, his full, long beard still untarnished black. But he carried himself with authority, and he wore the black turban that the Taliban had made infamous as a sign of Islamic piety.

The village mullah.

Fury swept Jamil. Would the mullah speak out so against interference if one of these men suffered a dislocated shoulder? Were mullah, health worker, even husband, really so willing to condemn a woman to a lifetime deformed and crippled rather than reach for a remedy so easily at hand?

Lowering his bundle onto the table, Jamil undid its knots. There'd been nothing he could do for those women and children working in drugged stupor so their male family members could squeeze out a few more weavings. Here was not the case. Jamil didn't look at Omed as he drew out his Pashto New Testament. If he was about to offend the man who'd brought him here, he'd make his apologies later.

"Does not Allah also send healers to the children of men? And was not Isa Masih the greatest healer of all? Muhammad himself taught that Isa's words and actions are to be commended and imitated." Jamil flipped through the holy book. "I have here the very words of Isa Masih. He was teaching on the holy day when a woman crippled for eighteen years came before him. Having compassion, Isa placed his own hands on the woman, and she was healed. But the mullahs of that village grew angry and demanded to know why he had healed a woman and on a holy day above all.

"I will read what Isa Masih answered. 'You hypocrites! Doesn't each of you on the holy day untie his ox or donkey from the stall and lead it out to give it water? Then should not this woman, a daughter of Abraham, whom Satan has kept bound for eighteen long years, be set free on the holy day from what bound her?'"

The mullah had crowded close to scrutinize the graceful loops and swirls of Pashto script, his black beard quivering with fury. But among other listeners, Jamil's reading drew a murmur of surprise and agreement. Raising his eyes from the page, Jamil saw that his audience had grown, villagers squeezing into the clinic to watch, those who couldn't, jostling each other in the doorway. An olive green arm raised above the sea of heads caught Jamil's eye. It belonged to the outsider from the carpet stall, and Jamil could see in that upraised hand a camera or cell phone angling toward the table.

Jamil's aversion was instinctive, and he turned his back even as he pressed his advantage. "So as you have heard, to touch this woman in order to save her from being crippled is to follow Isa's righteous example. Omed, you are a family member. You and her husband will help me."

11

Omed had said Jamil was an answer to his prayers. If so, then Jamil had not been brought here to fail. His fingertips probed through the burqa's polyester material. Husband and healer were right. The shoulder was not broken, just badly twisted out of location. But the next procedure would still be painful, and Jamil could be thankful the woman had been dosed with enough opium to render her unconscious.

"Ease her on her back and hold firmly. Don't let her move."

The woman's husband helped without protest. It seemed Haroon had no objection to getting a whole wife back so long as he didn't have to pay for it! Wrapping his hand in toweling, Jamil thrust it through the burqa material into the woman's armpit. Then he gripped the affected arm by the wrist, pulling hard even as he pushed against the armpit. The pale blue polyester was slippery, making it difficult to maintain a steady grasp. Sweat had broken out on Jamil's forehead when a moan signaled returning consciousness. *I cannot fail! I must not fail!*

"Almighty Creator of the universe, have compassion on this woman in the name of Isa Masih. Give me strength to heal as Isa Masih healed those in pain!"

Jamil didn't realize he was praying aloud until he felt a sudden pop. A deep sigh indicated the woman's immediate relief. Folding her arm across the burqa, Jamil probed the shoulder cautiously. "It is done."

Show over, Jamil's audience had drifted away by the time he'd rummaged up a sling among the clinic supplies. Only the health worker Naveed and the black-turbaned mullah remained as Haroon and Omed helped the patient down from the table. Omed's wife followed them out the door. Jamil was tying up his own bundle when he heard the motorcycle start.

Naveed and the mullah stepped forward the moment they were alone with Jamil, fury they'd masked from the approving crowd darkening both faces.

"The words you read did not come from the Quran nor any of the prophet's hadiths," the mullah said coldly. "How dare you bring the *kristjen* holy book here. All know the infidels have twisted and changed the truth about Isa. You will take such false teachings from this town before I summon the police."

"Yes, we do not need another healer here," Naveed added even more coldly. "You have made me look a fool. I do not wish to see you near my clinic again."

Jamil made no attempt to argue. His pack shouldered, he exited the clinic into the night. Where to go now? He'd expected at least a night's lodging from the patient's grateful family. He'd no money for the chaikhana, and though he might in other circumstances have negotiated food and lodging in return for treating inevitable injuries and ailments, the mullah's threat discouraged that option. Well, it would not be his first night sleeping in the open with an empty belly.

"My friend, where are you going?" The hand that clapped down on Jamil's shoulder belonged to Omed. He waved a hand toward the noise of the motorcycle receding in the darkness. "I have sent my brother-in-law to take the women home. We will have to walk."

Jamil shook his head. "No, your mullah has ordered me to leave immediately. I do not wish to cause trouble for your family."

"Do you think I care for that? The words you spoke back there . . . I had dared to hope when the visitor brought word. But now I know it is true. You are no spy for the religious police."

Glancing over his shoulder to where the yellow kerosene glow outlined the open clinic door, Omed lowered his voice so it could not be heard even an arm's length away. "You are my brother, for I too am a follower of Isa Masih."

Kabul, Afghanistan

Repeated pounding slid open a panel in the black metal pedestrian gate. Amy Mallory didn't recognize the dark features scowling at her from under a turban. Where was Wajid, the New Hope Foundation compound's elderly watchman?

"Chee gap as?" The snapped question translated loosely, "What's all the fuss about?"

"I live here," Amy answered in careful Dari. "I'd like to be let in."

The scowl deepened in its disapproval. "Then you should not be outside."

Amy had changed into local dress before boarding her final air leg from Dubai to Kabul that morning, headscarf now wound with accustomed expertise. Clearly this new guard had mistaken her for one of New Hope's female residents. The panel slammed shut again, but the gate was swinging open. Amy turned to a large, blond man lifting two suitcases from an SUV. "Thanks for the ride, Hans. I'll see you and Rianne Friday."

Amy had e-mailed her arrival time, so she'd been surprised to find no one waiting to pick her up at Kabul International Airport. Fortunately, a Dutch engineer she'd met at Kabul's weekly expat worship gathering had been on the same flight. As the SUV pulled away, Amy stepped eagerly after the new watchman, a small, underfed man with graying beard who'd emerged to carry her suitcases through the gate.

Though she hadn't made it home to Miami for Christmas, she'd managed a belated holiday mid-January. After months on duty 24-7, Amy had happily acquiesced when her elderly D.C. boss, Nestor Korallis, insisted she add an extra week to her original fortnight. Three weeks of being loved, pampered, stuffed with her mother's Cuban-American cooking. The luxury of hot water. Electricity on demand. Going shopping without worrying about some man glimpsing her elbow, ankle, or hair. Or a suicide bomber blowing up nearby.

It had been a welcome respite. And yet as she'd watched Kabul's crowded, dusty streets flow by, reluctantly stuffed her hair back under a scarf, breathed in the toxic winter smog, Amy had felt excitement welling up inside. *I was home. But I'm coming home too. In a few minutes I'll be hugging my kids again. And Farah, Aryana, Hamida, and the others. Gorg too.*

Amy didn't allow herself to dwell on two people she wouldn't be seeing.

Private security contractor Steve Wilson had departed Afghanistan shortly after the New Hope compound bombing, she'd heard through the expat grapevine. Brusque and uncompromising though he could be, Amy had come to count on the security contractor as an ally she could trust, even a friend. But after their last acrimonious encounter, she hadn't been surprised when he'd left without so much as a good-bye call.

As for Amy's former assistant, she'd heard nothing for almost two weeks after Jamil's departure. The Himalayan foothills through which Jamil had been trekking offered few cell towers and limited electricity to charge his phone. Then one night she'd received a phone call spattered with static.

Jamil sounded at once elated and tired. His medical training had been welcomed gladly among the isolated, rural villages. He'd also been reading to them Isa Masih's words. This trip into town was to purchase more medical supplies with the severance pay Amy had tucked into his bundle. Then he planned to head farther south, where winter's grip was not so harsh. Had Amy found the package Jamil left for her? And she would keep it for him? Good!

Jamil's battery charge was low, so he hadn't been able to speak long, his phone cutting off in midsentence. Nor had he called again before Amy flew home.

The new watchman disappeared into his guard shack as soon as the gate slammed shut, leaving Amy's suitcases on the cobblestone path. A yapping and whining drew her attention downward. The rope around its neck didn't keep a German shepherd puppy from swarming up into Amy's arms, whimpering and licking her face. "Oh, Gorg, you've grown so much. But why are you tied up?"

Gorg—which translated to "Wolf" in the Dari dialect most common in Kabul—had been Steve Wilson's Eid gift to the New Hope children. A dog was an unclean animal in Islam, but not a "wolf." Straightening, Amy looked around with a shock of disorientation. Surely she'd been gone only three weeks!

A sizable compound that had once housed Kabul aristocracy, the property had at some point been partitioned into several rentals, including the two-story villa New Hope Foundation occupied and a mechanics yard. Before flying out to Miami, Amy had renegotiated through the caretaker Rasheed with landlord Khalid Sayef to rent the entire property. She'd expected to find the partitions torn down, the mechanics yard cleared out.

The cinder-block wall to the right of the cobblestone path had indeed been removed. But the mechanics yard beyond bustled with people and vehicles. Men carried market bags, boxes, even a rolled-up carpet through the orchard gate. A pile of burning tires emitted meager warmth for several young boys scrubbing engine parts under a tin-roofed open shed.

And where was the jungle gym Jamil and the children had worked so hard to build? In its place to Amy's left was a second shed where a dozen small girls tramped back and forth across what looked like newly woven carpets.

"Ameera-jan! Ameera-jan!" Gorg's ecstatic welcome had alerted the carpet trampers. Abandoning their task, the girls flocked around Amy. "Salaam! Salaam!"

"Salaam aleykum. Oh, I've missed you all so much." As Amy released the puppy to receive hugs and kisses, she looked over to an older girl who hung back. "What is happening here, Farah-jan? Where is Wajid? Why is Gorg tied up? And why are the children out in this cold walking on those rugs?"

A fair-skinned girl with long-lashed blue eyes and brown curls escaping her headscarf, sixteen-year-old Farah had spent three years in Welayat prison for running away from a forced marriage. She hunched her shoulders. "It is how the rugs are made to look old for the buyers. Miss Soraya's orders are to walk until the bell rings for the midday meal. And Mr. Ibrahim dismissed Wajid. He said he is an opium smoker. He ordered Gorg tied up as well. He says the wolf will not become a fierce and obedient guardian if he is allowed to run free with the children."

Except the puppy had been intended as a playmate for the children. Amy could approve Wajid's retirement. Opium had been the elderly guard's home remedy for his arthritis and other ills, but it made him a poor watchman. As for the carpets, Amy was familiar with this practice intended to yield that antique look tourists expected. But why were New Hope children performing this function?

"Miss Ameera! You came back!" An older boy hurrying by with a bucket of nuts and bolts skidded to a stop.

"Of course I came back, Enayat," Amy said gently. "Did you think I wouldn't?"

Other boys had now dropped their work to hurry over. After greetings, Amy indicated her luggage. "I brought gifts for everyone. We'll unpack them later. But for now, would you take these upstairs?"

The girls returned reluctantly to the carpets, leaving the boys to squabble over who would carry what. Retaining her knapsack, Amy headed up the cobblestone path into the villa. A spacious entrance hall revealed more changes. Salons to Amy's left had been a schoolroom and communal living area. Now they held desks, tables, file cabinets along with a number of male clerks. A large salon to the right had been the site of the bomb explosion. When Amy left, it was being repainted, glass replaced in tall French doors looking out onto the orchard.

Now Amy could see why visitors were coming in and out the orchard gate. The salon had been turned into a shop, handwoven rugs at one end, automotive supplies at the other. A good-looking Afghan man in his thirties waited on customers behind a counter. Ibrahim was her female assistant Soraya's husband, Amy had discovered on the day of the explosion. The entire family had since moved into the New Hope compound.

Amy headed up a corkscrew stairwell. A corridor to her right led to living suites housing Amy and Soraya's family along with infirmary and administrative office. But a murmur of voices drew Amy instead across the landing where double doors stood open onto a single long salon. Like the shop downstairs, this was not part of New Hope's original rental but had been used for storage. With the new contract, Amy had planned an expanded infirmary.

Stepping inside, Amy found the women missing from the masculine stronghold on the first floor. They were hunkered down over looms that covered every inch of the floor tiles. Racks holding colorful skeins of wool yarn filled wall space.

"Miss Ameera! Salaam aleykum!" The usual chorus of greeting broke out, but this time no one moved, deft fingers never pausing as they tied one yarn loop after another.

A plump, middle-aged Afghan man sat cross-legged on a rug, scrutinizing every movement with hawkeyed intensity. Perhaps the reason none had ventured to rise. With stooped backs and bowed heads, it was hard to verify faces. Still, Amy wasn't seeing everyone she expected. "Where are Aryana and Roya and Mina?" The entire Hazara clan, mother and two adult daughters with a dozen kids between them, was also missing. An explanation occurred to Amy. "Are they in the kitchen?"

Lona, a dark-skinned older woman, lifted her head. "But they are gone, Miss Ameera. Did you not know? Their new men have taken them away."

"And would that I could do the same, even if the man is old and fat and cruel." Another weaver flashed Lona a sullen glance. "At least it would be my own home, not breaking my back all day as someone else's slave. How is this different from the Welayat?" The woman broke off at a warning glare from the male supervisor.

Amy could sympathize with her current rebellion. The carpet-weaving process was exhausting. A single floor-size rug took weeks, even months, to finish. Long hours stooped in a single position, face close to the weave, were a strain that eventually ruined eyes and left hands and body twisted with rheumatism.

Amy kept a reassuring smile on her lips until she'd stepped back onto the landing. Down the hallway, Amy's small porters were just depositing her luggage outside her living suite door. Amy called her thanks as she pushed open the door to the New Hope office. *"Tashakor."*

The woman seated behind a desk in the office looked enough like the shop clerk downstairs to be siblings, with the olive complexion, high-bridged nose, full mouth, and black, curly hair of the Pashtuns, Afghanistan's largest ethnic group. In fact, Amy's assistant Soraya and her husband, Ibrahim, were first cousins as well as spouses. She rose swiftly, hurrying forward to kiss Amy on both cheeks. "Miss Ameera, it is good to see you back with us. But I had not realized you were returning today. Ibrahim gave orders for Rasheed to retrieve you from the airport tomorrow morning."

"I sent my arrival time, not my departure," Amy answered evenly. "I'm sure the mistake was mine. How is your family?"

"Fariq has recovered from his cold. And Fatima has now received her final teacher's diploma." Soraya was a tall woman, her cool air of authority not just from being a member of Afghanistan's traditional aristocracy. In a country where most women and more than half the men were illiterate, Soraya was a university graduate, fluent in five languages. Amy had come to admire the Afghan woman deeply and, despite Soraya's innate aloofness, felt they'd established an agreeable working relationship. So Amy pushed back her disquiet until she'd displayed a polite interest in Soraya and her family.

"I'm glad all is well." Amy picked her next words with care. "I hadn't realized we'd authorized a carpet workshop. When did that start? And the children. Why are they not studying at this hour?"

Plucked brows rose sharply. "But classes have ended. Children do not study in these cold months."

A valid point. With most Afghan schoolrooms unheated, only wealthier private schools stayed open during the worst winter weather from January to March. Still, that hardly applied within the New Hope compound.

"And if you speak of the women, Mr. Duane agreed they need beneficial activity to occupy their time. Ibrahim has a cousin with a carpet factory. He is supplying the looms and materials."

"What kind of wages is he paying them? or those kids down there?" Amy heard distress creeping into her voice and deliberately lowered it. "And what is this I hear about men taking some of the women away?"

Soraya looked even more surprised and displeased now as well. "Do these people not receive food and lodging and clothing, even schooling? More than they could hope to earn elsewhere. What other payment should they expect?"

Another valid point. Soraya's tone was cool as she went on. "As to the women of whom you speak, they were not taken unlawfully, but married. The Hazara sisters, Deeba and Geeti, were acquired by two brothers. They are farmers in Helmand, so they were willing to take the mother and her other children as well to work the fields. The others found marriages here in Kabul. A relief now that we no longer have available the main wing salons. With the new Welayat families, the sleeping quarters had grown very crowded."

The Hazara clan had ended up in the women's prison during a sweep of poppy field laborers. Since Helmand was the center of the opium trade, odds were they'd end up right back at that labor. Amy was trying to keep her voice even. "I don't understand. How could they be married just like that? Who arranged this? Their families? No one was even supposed to know they were here. The whole purpose of this place was so that these women couldn't be forced back into marriage against their will."

"They were not forced," Soraya answered even more coolly. "They went of their own choice, as they will tell you themselves, should you choose to ask them. Did you think they would prefer to remain unwed for the rest of their lives? in this place that is not a home of their own? As to who arranged it, all that was needed was for word to spread that there are young, healthy widows here. Many men cannot afford the bride-price for a virgin nor wedding costs. Ibrahim checked to be sure the men were truly seeking a wife and not a servant or concubine. And if to gain a bride, they are willing to take another man's children, then these women should be grateful."

Soraya's tone had turned solicitous. "Miss Ameera, you have been traveling all night, and you must be very weary. Let me send Hamida to your quarters with food and tea. We can speak again after you have taken your rest."

In other words, when you're not so cranky.

Murmuring polite acquiescence, Amy headed down the hall to her own apartment. But not to nap. She dragged her suitcases into the living room, then dug out her cell phone and pulled up a number. "Duane? Please tell me you're somewhere in Kabul."

A pleasant voice answered the phone. "I'm up north in Mazar-i-Sharif. While you were off loafing, I've been busy. Just signed off on a rental I'm planning to make country office for New Hope's Afghanistan operations. None of Kabul's smog. Minimal violence. So what's up?"

New Hope colleague Duane Gibson was why Amy had felt free to enjoy three pleasurable weeks with her family in Miami. He'd arrived in Kabul two weeks after the compound explosion, and Amy had quickly learned why Duane was Nestor Korallis's original choice as country manager. In his late thirties, he was a fifteen-year veteran in relief work, fluent in both Dari and Pashto, Afghanistan's two main languages. He had networked with local nonprofits to deliver more than a hundred tons of school and medical supplies to rural communities by year's end. The audit team had been impressed, their glowing report one reason Nestor Korallis had insisted Amy take that extra holiday week.

"I just arrived back in-country. I've got to tell you I'm a little confused at all the changes I'm seeing. Especially since I don't remember getting any memos." Amy no longer bothered tamping down her frustration as she poured out her disquiet. "Soraya tells me you gave authorization. Is that true? And since when did Ibrahim start calling the shots around here?"

"Actually, I hired Ibrahim on just after you left. What he was making as a city water engineer can't compare with our pay, so he jumped at the job. He's setting up some well projects in communities where we delivered aid."

This at least Amy approved thoroughly. The wages Soraya as an English speaker earned with expatriate NGOs hadn't set well with Ibrahim's Afghan masculine pride. Now that marital strain was removed.

"As to the rest, Ibrahim did mention Soraya was concerned about idleness with school out. He felt keeping the mechanic's shop open would provide job training to the boys. Likewise this carpet weaving. You've told me yourself these women could use some job training, so I saw no reason to object."

Amy ran a tired hand over her face. "It's not just the weaving, though that's hardly the cottage industry I had in mind. Or the kids. Or even the marriages, though I didn't offer these women sanctuary so total strangers could find cheap wives. It's that no one talked to me about any of it! Like signing to rent this whole place. I thought we were on the same page. More room for women and children to be outdoors. Even grow a garden. Now with all those offices and business and . . . and *men* downstairs, they're pretty well trapped inside their own quarters. I mean, we could have at least discussed it. I was on vacation, not the moon!"

"We could have discussed it. I chose not to interrupt your vacation." To Duane's credit, he sounded neither annoyed nor ruffled. "And you seem to be forgetting one minor point. *You* are no longer country manager here."

It was a wake-up slap. No, Amy had not forgotten. Exhausted from the bombing aftermath, an onslaught of new releases from the women's prison, and that whirlwind of auditors, Amy had been grateful to step down to deputy manager, turning over responsibility for the expanding New Hope operations to Duane's far greater experience and résumé.

"But you agreed I'd still have oversight of my Kabul projects."

"So you do. If there are adjustments you want to make, talk to Ibrahim and Soraya. Just keep a few things in mind. For one, you're not in America." Duane's tone was mild but unyielding. "Let me say again what a great job you did saving New Hope's bacon here. Practical quick-start projects. Great emotional impact on donors. Especially with as little as you had to work with.

"But you've also made the classic mistake of a green aid worker—getting personally involved with your clients. These people have to assimilate back into their own society. And in that society, poor children earn their own living and are lucky to go to school at all. Illiterate women are happy to sit all day over a carpet loom just to put food in their children's bellies. Marriage as second wife to some peasant at least puts a roof overhead. Okay, so that doesn't seem fair by Western standards. But our mandate in Afghanistan isn't to change their morality or criticize their society, only to provide some sustainable development so we can walk away."

Amy was glad Duane couldn't see her burning cheeks. Genially, even appreciatively, her new supervisor had laid out all Amy's inadequacies. In truth, her own prior experience in disaster cleanup had involved exactly what Duane suggested. Hand out emergency supplies. Get survivors back on their feet. Then leave.

"As to the Wazir property, New Hope is shelling out a sizable rent. Surely you weren't thinking you could co-opt the whole place for your own pet project."

"No, I suppose not." Amy tried to hold on to her earlier eagerness, but anticipation had drained into deep fatigue. This homecoming was not turning out at all as she'd expected. And yet Duane had reason and logic and every principle of humanitarian aid work on his side. Much though she hated to admit it, Ibrahim and Soraya had acted in accordance with their own customs and maybe even the best interests of New Hope residents.

I did tell Soraya she was completely in charge while I was gone!

It was Amy who'd broken the cardinal aid principle against getting emotionally entangled with her work and charges. She could admit she wanted, not just generic Afghans, but these particular women and children to have a better future. If not a Western living standard, more than allotted by their status in Afghan society.

Can't there be some happy medium that offers a long-term solution as well as a better life?

As Amy rang off, some compromises sprang immediately to mind. No child deserved to work full-time, but maybe Amy had been lax about chores. *I wanted to make up for the past by letting them play and enjoy themselves.* Likewise, Amy could take a realistic look at work hours and conditions for the carpet weavers. But she was so exhausted now, any confrontation was bound to spill over her own frustration and disappointment. *Soraya's right. Just a short nap to sleep off some of the jet lag.*

Amy was asleep as soon as her head hit the pillow. When she awoke, dusk was casting long shadows through the window. A rich fragrance of garlic and cumin and saffron drew Amy to the meal tray Rasheed's wife, Hamida, must have left on the living room table while Amy slept. Even cooled, the dish of marinated lamb chunks on saffron yellow basmati rice was delicious. Amy ate hungrily, then wandered outside onto a balcony.

Below, a colonnade ran around three sides of an interior courtyard. Kabul's capricious power grid was cooperating tonight, and fingers of yellow light filtered with a murmur of women's voices through cracked shutters where a downstairs salon had been turned into a kitchen. Children scampered around a bubbling fountain. Spotting Amy, they swarmed up the courtyard stairs. "Please tell us a story, Ameera-jan!"

Their excited cries drew Farah from the kitchen, drying an enamel plate with a cotton cloth. "I told the children they must wait until you are rested. But if you wish, I will bring the pictures."

"Sure, I'll be right down."

Women were still clearing away the evening meal when Amy entered the kitchen. They gathered with the children on floor mats and cushions while Farah set up the flannelgraph storyboard on a small table. Amy smiled warmly as the sixteen-year-old handed Amy the box of flannel figures. She'd left story time and her flannelgraph collection in Farah's charge while she was gone. The younger girl's mouth twitched in response, but her half smile didn't touch her eyes. What was troubling the girl?

Amy pushed away fresh disquiet to place the first figure on the storyboard. Without Jamil as translator, she'd been uncertain how she could continue the popular story times. But judicious Internet research had uncovered dramatized Dari Bible stories she'd downloaded to her MP3 player, listening to them over and over, hammering the new vocabulary into her mind. Before leaving, Amy had finished the story of Moses, its drama of burning bush, plagues, and Red Sea crossing little different in Islamic versions from the Bible telling. This time she chose Moses' brave successor.

"Do you remember Joshua, one of the two warriors who weren't afraid when Moses sent them to explore their new Promised Land? Now with Moses gone, Joshua was responsible to bring this great crowd of people safely into their new country. And Jericho, the first city they had to fight, was very powerful with tall, thick walls."

As usual, children had crowded close to lean against Amy's tunic and touch a finger to the bright images. Though Amy sorely missed Fahim and Tamana, the Hazara brood, and others, there were new faces, just as expectant and cheerful. Women who'd been working hard all day now looked relaxed, even content. Babies slumbered in their mothers' arms.

Amy found her throat swelling as she picked up the next figure. This aspect of her homecoming, at least, was no disappointment.

Maybe it is breaking the humanitarian code to get personally involved. But is it so wrong? Jesus didn't just shower survival gear from heaven. He came to earth to walk and live with people. He healed them and fed them and laughed and cried with them. He called them his friends. Is that interference?

Or love?

Amy went on, "But as Joshua wondered how he could do all this, God spoke to him. 'As I was with Moses, I will be with you. So be strong and courageous. Do not be terrified; do not be discouraged, for the Lord your God will be with you wherever you go.'"

Wherever you go. Where was Jamil right now? Was he safe? or even still alive? Had he ever uncovered the whereabouts of the vanished mother and sister he so longed to find?

And Steve?

That Thanksgiving outing when she'd spied in Steve's possession the very photo and note Amy herself had once mailed a young soldier years before they first met on the dusty streets of Kabul, she'd had a glimpse of how much past pain underlay the security contractor's own formidable composure and world-weary cynicism. Had Steve ever come to terms with disillusionment and lost faith? Was he still drifting from contract to contract, or had he at last found a new mission worth committing heart and life to?

Jamil. Steve. Two such different men who'd walked into, then back out of, Amy's life. But that did not mean she need banish them from her prayers. *Father God, wherever they are, both of them, keep them safe; grant them peace and a future.*

In her dream she was not cold, but hot and always hungry.

She was hot because even under the blistering sun, she dared not loosen a cotton length bound tightly under her tunic. Thin as her already-slight body had become, the girl's womanhood was unmistakable without the bindings.

She was hungry because her employer was stingy with the single mid-day ladle of rice or noodles. She no longer remembered the taste of meat or fruit nor even the pot scrapings of lentils and oily vegetables over which she'd once grumbled.

During her impulsive flight, the girl hadn't thought further than reaching the nearest town, where she could find food and employment and freedom. She'd seen child laborers and beggars from the safe distance of plenty and security that had been her early life. If they could survive, so could she. For two days she'd wandered the streets. "Please, I will work for food. I am a hard worker. I will do anything."

But this was winter, food scarce enough for the townspeople who slammed doors in her face. At the garbage dump, other scavengers drove her away with curses and stones. Then came the weekly bazaar. Among unsellable produce tossed out behind stalls, she'd stumbled on treasure. A melon still containing good flesh. Half-rotten potatoes.

But the market also brought customers she recognized. Two male cousins. And they were asking questions as they moved among the stalls. Crawling into a brightly painted *jinga* truck, the girl hid under an empty crate until nightfall, when its owners loaded up their remaining produce. As they drove away, the girl scrambled out to rummage a handful of turnips, then fell asleep to the jingling of metal strips and bells hanging from the underbelly that gave the truck its name. She didn't wake until the truckers began unloading at their destination. While they carried crates back into storage, the girl managed to slip unseen into the night.

A gray dawn revealed an urban sprawl large enough to lose oneself in. A bustling commercial zone swarmed with children vying to carry bundles, shine shoes, or wave cans of smoldering incense for good luck against the evil eye. But her juvenile competitors proved as fiercely territorial as a snow leopard. She'd lost her patu in a scuffle when she offered a shopper her services. Without its camouflage, she'd attracted stares that frightened her so much, she'd risked climbing a balcony to pilfer the drying turban that now bound her torso. Ravenous, she'd joined other beggars outside a restaurant, pleading with cupped hands, "*Baksheesh*, kind sirs, I have not eaten in days."

A businessman emerging with a Styrofoam container shooed aside burqas and clutching fingers to offer the girl his leftovers. He watched with an amused smile as she shoveled saffron rice and lamb kebab into her mouth. She was wiping greasy fingers on her tunic when he moved closer. "You are a pretty child and not so dirty as most. Do you have no home? Would you like to come home with me?"

His words were innocuous, but something in his leisurely, satisfied survey reminded the girl of her white-haired bridegroom. Had he somehow discerned she was female? Or even worse, did he actually believe she was a preadolescent boy?

The businessman shouted angrily as she bolted into the crowd, but he did not give chase. Still she'd been frightened enough to stay away from the commercial district. Instead she'd landed a job treading mud and straw to be poured into plank molds for adobe bricks. Filthy as her work left her, at least no one ventured to look too closely. As spring warmed to a sweltering summer, she'd come to believe she was safe from pursuit. Like the half-dozen boys who trod the mud pits with her, she slept at night curled up among the drying bricks. From them she learned to tuck away the slab of naan bread that accompanied their scant midday meal to stave off hunger at night and upon awakening. To chew the straw they trod, swallowing it down with water to fool a stomach twisting with hunger.

Though it was her young coworkers who'd turned precarious and unpleasant survival into nightmare. The brickmaker had promised his underage drudges a real, if minuscule, wage, along with their daily rations. His excuse for failing to pay was that he himself would receive compensation only upon delivery of their product. When after several weeks a dozen large trucks arrived to load the stockpile of sun-cured bricks, the girl was as excited as her male companions. Across the border to the west was Afghanistan's more prosperous neighbor, Iran, a promised land of employment and opportunity, where it was rumored even women worked and studied without the hassle of a burqa. Once she'd saved enough afghanis, she could buy a bus ticket, maybe even return to her real self, leave behind the furtive toilet excursions and other humiliations her current disguise forced on her.

But they hadn't been paid. When their employer retired to his living quarters in a corner of the brickyard, rebellion broke out. That the man had wasted his profits on opium made it easier. Door and shutters were barred, but it hadn't taken long to chisel a window frame from its mud casing. Cautious groping uncovered the money pouch. Their employer didn't stir from his opium stupor. The young burglars divided the takings evenly. The girl hadn't even considered turning her share down. This wasn't stealing, but justice.

In the dark night, she'd scrubbed clothes and body at a communal faucet. A hot, arid wind dried them as she hiked across the city to the bus terminal. Wrinkled clothing and knife-trimmed curls received only a disdainful glance when she'd purchased a ticket. The bus was approaching the Iranian border when a green police pickup filled with gray-blue uniforms pulled up alongside.

Which of her accomplices had laid the blame on her didn't really matter. She'd never have made it anyway, the girl knew now. Border crossings required such things as identification papers. The humiliation of being dragged from the bus was followed by the greater humiliation of a body search. Theft charges were overshadowed by the discovery that a woman, however young and small and emaciated, had been masquerading in the superior guise of a male. A police report matching her lake blue eyes and her curls to a runaway bride earned an added prison sentence for *zina*.

That she preferred prison to being returned to her bridegroom would have infuriated the judge. So she'd remained docile and sullen, eyelashes lowered to hide defiance, as her fate was handed down. Nor was it so bad. There was food, her daily chores less arduous than her former life. As for freedom, she'd known little of it to date. At least within the women's prison, there were no men. With regular feeding, she'd lost her skeletal gauntness and even began to grow again so that the brown tunic was no longer overlarge.

Which was when—

Farah awoke with her heart thudding as though she'd been running a race, her throat raw with silent screaming. The night around her was cold and dark, but in it she could hear quiet breathing, an occasional snore. Outside the barred shutters, her straining ears caught only a murmuring splash of the courtyard fountain.

She was safe.

I will never go back to that world, she vowed into the darkness. *Whatever it takes, whatever I have to do, I will never go back!*

4

Find something I believe in.

When private security contractor Steve Wilson had pledged himself to that undertaking, he hadn't expected two months later would find him back where he'd started in Kabul, guarding the well-fed and silk-clad back of his former *mujahid* ally Khalid Sayef, now Afghan interior minister.

Stepping up to the parapet next to an Afghan security guard, Steve raised binoculars to his brow. Spread out below him from this vista, he could see Kabul's Ghazi Stadium, famed for the executions with which the Taliban had kicked off soccer and *buzkashi* matches, an oval of open concrete bleachers around a grass field. All open, except the elite viewing section beneath Steve's feet.

In a perfect world, Steve's principal would be inside one of those glassed-in theater boxes, surrounded by his protective detail. Instead Khalid stood at a microphone on a platform erected in the middle of the playing field. Despite chill winter temperatures, both bleachers and field were so congested with spectators it would take a firefight to remove platform VIPs if trouble broke out.

Though security was not quite the nightmare it appeared. Looming tall behind Khalid was a burly Russian ex-commando, his single responsibility to get their client under cover if something went down. Which in this case would be under the platform. Its fabric skirting actually draped reinforced steel panels. Behind them, Condor Security operatives, along with event security, kept watch on an array of monitors. If the platform

VIPs did have to take shelter, anything short of an RPG could be held off until backup arrived.

Steve lowered the binoculars as a sudden acrid gust of wind caught at his sinuses. Winter exacerbated the smog that made Kabul one of the planet's most polluted cities, adding kerosene and coal heaters, smoldering tires and other rubbish locals burned for warmth to the perpetual exhaust fumes, cookfires, and diesel generators. Already Steve's eyes were burning, a tickle in his esophagus becoming a dry cough.

And to think I should be on a Jamaican beach right now!

Not that Steve regretted his decision to return. When he'd left Kabul, Condor Security had followed his recommendation to replace Steve as Khalid's security chief with Phil Myers, whose prosthetic foot and partial vision in one eye—souvenirs of a Taliban ambush—in no way diminished a formidable competence. Steve had parked himself over the holidays with his mother, stepfather, and teenage half siblings. Then he'd driven to Indiana to visit the paternal grandfather who'd raised him before heading down to Fort Bragg in North Carolina.

But while it was good to see his former chaplain, Rev Garwood, Steve's past associates were all deployed or back in the private sector. Steve did some desultory job hunting, only to find himself turning down offers from survival instructor to security consultant. Bottom line, none offered anything to which he'd want to dedicate the rest of his life.

Meanwhile, Steve hadn't taken a real vacation in years. He'd accepted an invite from a contractor buddy, now security chief for one of Jamaica's pricier resorts, when Phil called from Kabul. "Got your e-mail on Jamaica. About time you got some decent R & R. And I see you're passing through Fort Bragg. Any chance you could swing over to see Denise and the kids before shipping out?"

Steve knew his friend well enough to catch a distraught note in his level query. Phil and his wife, Denise, herself a former Marine, had purchased a modest home near Fort Bragg when Phil's combat injuries impelled a medical discharge from Special Forces.

"No big deal if you can't. It's just—I don't know if I've mentioned our middle kid, Jamie, has been sick off and on since Christmas. Denise insists there's no reason to worry. But you know my wife, always the Marine."

Yes, Denise was one tough soldier. But when Steve drove immediately over, her warm welcome held the same distraught note. The pallid toddler in her arms was a far cry from the lively boy Steve had glimpsed on Phil's webcam Thanksgiving Day.

"We thought it was just flu, but his white blood cell count's been off the charts. Now they're talking leukemia. But I don't want you worrying Phil. He's only halfway through the new Khalid contract, and you know the penalties for breaking it early. There's nothing he can do here, and we'll need this contract for hospital bills."

Yes, Steve knew the penalties. Private security contracting paid well. But Condor Security wasn't interested in excuses or an operative's personal life, only performance. However, substituting an equally qualified operative was a different matter. Steve made some phone calls before ringing Phil back.

"No, it's not up for discussion. Denise and the kids need you. Hey, you've had my back often enough. It's not like the beach is going anywhere."

Phil hadn't argued further because by the time Steve made travel arrangements, news had come that Jamie would need a bone marrow transplant, Phil the best candidate for a match. Their flights had crossed trajectories over the Atlantic.

God, I know I don't do as much praying as I should, Steve found himself entreating as his binoculars swept the crowd below. *But if you're listening, would you mind dropping in on Jamie right now? He's just a kid!*

What must it feel like to have someone you loved, especially your child, go through this kind of life-and-death trauma? One more benefit in not letting a family wrap their fingers around your heart!

In any case, it looked like Steve was back for the chill, smelly residue of a Kabul winter. If Jamaica sounded better than ever, there was a certain release in having his immediate future settled. He'd stepped off the plane just in time to be handed the day's movement schedule and load up Khalid's convoy for this Peace and Justice Symposium.

Or so it had been billed.

It said much on how completely Steve had pushed Afghanistan from his mind these last weeks that he'd forgotten the country's upcoming presidential elections, scheduled for early April, less than two months away, when spring snowmelt guaranteed reasonable roads for getting to the polls. Just who'd made up Afghanistan's election code, Steve had no idea. Certainly it wasn't based on anything practiced in his own country. Its more controversial provisions included that campaigning was permitted for only thirty days prior to an election.

But those were political banners and placards that screaming, packed mob down there were waving. And one sweep of Steve's binoculars had established that each of those platform VIPs was a presidential contender. The most recent speaker, a slight, black-bearded Pashtun in white robes, wire-rimmed glasses giving him a scholarly look, was Dr. Anwar Qaderi, a prominent cleric and current minister of justice. Earlier speakers had included the ministers of finance, economy, and education.

In fact, the only major cabinet member Steve hadn't spotted was the minister of defense. One stroke of good fortune for the Afghan people since General Abdur Rahmon was a controversial Tajik warlord with an abysmal human rights record. A second was that Afghanistan's current head of state, increasingly unpopular at home and abroad as corruption and ineptitude within his government continued to outpace a growing insurgency, had conceded not to run for reelection.

Maybe they'll have better luck with one of this bunch.

Not that Steve would count the day's final speaker any improvement as occupant of the Gul Khana presidential palace. Khalid's oratory was winding down as Steve turned from the parapet to head across the roof. Less than half those who'd turned up had been able to squeeze inside the stadium itself, but high tech had come to Kabul. Large screens projected Khalid's fleshy features and animated gestures to throngs that crammed the parking lot, spilling out to obstruct traffic for blocks in every direction. At the moment, cheers and catcalls among competing factions held the good-natured rivalry of a sports event. But Steve had seen enough such events turn ugly to appreciate the gray-blue uniforms of police in riot gear encircling the stadium.

Though the crowd was overwhelmingly male, Steve's binocular scan brushed across a knot of burqas and chapans, some carrying children. Excited faces under headscarves brought sharply to Steve's mind other female features, heart-shaped and young. Not as he'd last glimpsed them in that upstairs apartment at the New Hope compound, overwrought with grief and sympathy, hazel eyes brimming with tears. But a more typical snapshot—smiling, earnest, framed by a headscarf that couldn't contain escaping flaxen strands, and always in Steve's memory crowded by a jostling, squirming pack of children.

Was a certain idealistic humanitarian worker still lingering somewhere in Kabul? Or had Amy Mallory finally learned the futility of trying to do good in Afghanistan?

Khalid had now finished speaking. A band struck up the *"Milli Tharana,"* an ode to Afghan pride, tribal diversity, and Islam that was Afghanistan's national anthem. The crowd joined in, punching at the air with their right fists each time the lyrics repeated *"Allahu Akbar,"* or "Allah is great." It was a gesture TV cameras had made familiar the world over. Steve's muscles tautened to alertness. Too many times he'd seen this signal precipitate a riot or worse.

His tension was only a reflex. The crowd was still relaxed, enjoying themselves. As the anthem ended, Steve turned away to head back across the roof to the stadium side. But with the cessation of music, a ripple of angry voices rose abruptly above the merrymaking. Spinning around, Steve spotted what was provoking a flurry of turmoil at the edge of the multitude below. A sizable convoy barreled down the main avenue that ran into the stadium grounds. Nor were these the green police pickups and gray-blue uniforms tasked to augment event security. These were armored personnel carriers with swivel guns on top. Troop transports. Even a pair of Soviet-era T-62 battle tanks. Uniforms manning the guns wore camouflage. Steve spotted a black, red, and green Afghan flag, which meant this exercise wasn't the NATO-run International Security Assistance Force. What colossal blunder brought the Afghan National Army here?

A Russian-built Mi-17 combat helicopter roaring into view answered Steve's question. After years of fighting to drive the Soviets from Afghanistan, it was ironic that much of the new state's military equipment was being purchased from their old nemesis. Tumult became a stampede as the chopper swooped low over the crowd. A loudspeaker blasted, "This is an unlawful election assembly! You must disperse immediately!"

Steve groaned inwardly. The army reported directly to the minister of defense. It would seem a safe bet General Abdur Rahmon had tossed his own hat into the presidential ring after all.

Crossing the roof at a run, Steve shouted above the uproar into the comm piece that curved from his ear to mouth. "Talk to me! Is Khalid secured?"

The combat helicopter was now sweeping over the stadium itself, its loudspeaker still blaring. The downward tilt of a door gun was driving the crowd toward the exits. But the Condor Security team had done its job because the platform itself was empty. Steve's earpiece crackled. The voice speaking belonged to Steve's second-in-command, half-Maori, half-Scot New Zealander Ian Grant, a former SAS paratrooper.

"We've got the minister and others secure. But Khalid's foaming at the mouth. He's ordering his police to stand firm. Says the army has no jurisdiction to interfere with lawful civilian assemblies. What's going on out there, Wilson?"

Just as the army reported to Ministry of Defense, the Afghan National Police fell under Ministry of Interior jurisdiction. Steve was already sprinting back across the roof. Whatever the rights and wrongs of this face-off, with the so-called "Peace and Justice Symposium" for all intents over, a diplomatic resolution would be to follow that helicopter's orders and disband. But such logic didn't include testosterone. The gray-blue line ringing the stadium was now shifting into a mass in front of the oncoming convoy. Green police pickups bumped into place to block the avenue. That first personnel carrier was going to slam into the massed ANP vehicles and uniforms!

Instead it slammed on its brakes. The procession of tanks and carriers following it skidded to a stop as well. But now turret guns were moving into position, camouflage fatigues pouring out of transports. One antsy trigger finger twitching too hard could precipitate a bloodbath.

Nor could Steve do much about it. His defenses were designed to protect Khalid, not intervene between two armed branches of the local government. This time it was his cell phone Steve snatched from his belt. Dyncorp, one of the planet's largest private security conglomerates, ran the current Afghan army training program. During his prior stint as

Khalid's security chief, Steve had worked closely enough with Dyncorp country manager Jason Hamilton to have his number on speed dial.

"Hey, Steve, this is a surprise. I didn't realize you were back in-country."

"Just temporarily. More on that later. But right now I've got a situation." Steve explained briefly. "Tell me Dyncorp's got some ANA embeds out there who can talk sense into these people before World War III breaks out."

"We probably do, but I've no direct line of contact, and there's nothing they can really do but watch. I'll get online to the embassy. Putting pressure on their commander is the only way we'll get the ANA to stand down. Can't you get Khalid to back down and call off his troops?"

"I'll see what I can do, but don't hold your breath. Backing down isn't in Khalid's vocabulary."

As Steve broke off contact, Ian Grant's Kiwi drawl came into Steve's earpiece. "Khalid wants to know if the news crews are filming. He wants the world to see that the people are with him and won't be intimidated by this assault on democracy."

The New Zealander's dry tone echoed Steve's savage thoughts. Around him on the rooftop, news crews, international and local, were gleefully filming the unexpected excitement. But they could hardly be naive enough to consider that continuing pandemonium below signaled any support for Khalid or his fellow speakers. Spectators fleeing the stadium had now collided with the milling crowds outside. A turban stumbled, only to be flattened into the pavement by the panicked mob. But from where Steve stood, it looked as if those riot shields down there were actually forcing back those trying to exit.

Steve was back on the comm set. "Let me talk to Khalid. Does he realize people are getting trampled out there? He's got to tell his police to stand down. Or at least to let people leave."

A pause. Then Ian's drawl returned. "He's on the phone with the minister of defense. Just to let him know he's sending a police unit to arrest him for an unlawful army exercise. It's a real dogfight down here. But don't you worry. Khalid's safe enough, and everything's under control. We won't leave the shelter until we get the all clear."

Except that Khalid's personal safety wasn't on Steve's mind at the moment. Below him, more people were down, the pushing and shoving now a frenzy. Steve headed for a stairwell at a sprint. As he ran, his cell phone rang. "Hamilton, you got anything?"

"The ambassador's on the hotline right to the presidential palace. But there's national pride and sovereignty and all kinds of nasty issues involved. Minister of Defense Rahmon happens to be the current president's white-haired boy as his successor, and he requested proper authorization to shut down what he reported as an illegal campaign event. I've gotten through to a couple Dyncorp embeds. But their ANA colleagues have no authority to issue a stand-down. Nor is this technically any of our embassy's business. We'll just have to hope the ambassador can talk the president around. Then Defense will have to follow suit."

"Except that will take time we don't have!"

Which left Khalid. Reaching the platform was made easier because the playing field had now emptied. Recognizing Khalid's security chief, guards ringing the improvised shelter let Steve duck inside. The minister of interior was on his cell phone—judging by his forceful Dari, still talking with his Defense counterpart. Steve had no qualms about interrupting.

"Minister, if you're really planning to run in this election, I'd suggest ordering your forces to stand aside immediately. Supporters of yours are being trampled out there, and the news crews are filming every bit of it. Do you want all of Afghanistan and the world to see people being hurt, even killed, because your police force is holding them hostage? That's sure not going to win votes."

Steve spoke deliberately in English, which few of the other Afghan officials taking shelter would understand, keeping his tone low and civil. But the authority in it was no longer the glorified security guard he'd become, rather the Special Forces ally who'd once led a ragtag *mujahid* commander to victory.

"On the other hand, if those cameras show the minister of interior being the bigger man, willing to stand down in order to keep Afghan citizens from harm—"

A flicker of black eyes told Steve he'd won even before Khalid snapped his fingers. "Ismail, tell the commander to open the barriers and let the people free."

The minister returned to his phone conversation. "Rahmon, though you have no authority here, I will not risk Afghan lives for your games. The people are now leaving, though at their own choice, not your command. I will recall my police if you will withdraw your forces."

If nothing else, Steve had to admire his client's political acumen. By the time he'd exited at a run again, Khalid was waving over those news crews assigned to platform duty. Back on the roof, Steve saw with relief that gray-blue uniforms had lowered riot shields. Crowds were emptying into side streets. The Mi-17 had banked into a low orbit circling the stadium zone, but it was no longer broadcasting. Even as Steve watched, a turret gun on the front personnel carrier rotated away from the police vehicles. A moment later, weapons were being lowered on both sides.

The sudden drop in decibels allowed Steve to hear his cell phone on the first ring. Snatching it from his belt, he was taken aback to catch sight of the caller ID. Quickly he flipped it open. "Amy, that you? Mind if I call you back? I'm in a bit of an emergency."

There was no answer. That the other line was live, Steve could hear by noises in the background. Screaming and angry shouts. Hard, swift breathing. Then a sound Steve recognized because he was hearing it at the same moment. The roar of that Mi-17 helicopter swooping in low overhead.

Humanitarian aid worker Amy Mallory was not only still in Afghanistan. She was somewhere down in that pandemonium below.

5

"Here, this should do it." Amy tucked the Toyota Corolla hatchback into a tight space between a jinga truck and an elderly cargo van. "I'm afraid we're not going to get any closer."

Scrambling out of the vehicle after Amy, Farah automatically pulled her headscarf across mouth and nose, but blue eyes above the material were wide. "I did not think it possible for a woman to drive as well as any man."

"Even better sometimes." Amy smiled. A good night's sleep had done much to restore her pleasure at being back in Kabul. She'd stepped onto the balcony this morning to find women scrubbing clothes in the fountain basin, children kicking soccer balls among the colonnade pillars, a clatter of dishes and smell of frying floating up from the kitchen.

Of course! This was Friday, the Muslim weekend. Not even Ibrahim's hard-faced cousin could expect the New Hope residents to be working today, if only because this was the carpet merchant's day off as well.

And Soraya's. So when Amy saw her assistant stepping out from the family's living suite, she'd postponed her own concerns, instead thanking the Afghan woman profusely for taking over while Amy was gone. In turn, Soraya had affably dug from their files addresses for those Welayat newlyweds still in Kabul. Visiting family and friends was, after all, a customary Friday activity.

Transport to call on Amy's former charges proved a more difficult issue. Rasheed's ancient Russian army jeep was gone from the mechanics yard before Amy emerged from her own quarters. Soraya's entire family had driven off midmorning in a newish red Mitsubishi Pajero that Ibrahim had acquired during Amy's absence. *Maybe it belongs to a family member because they sure didn't buy it off their New Hope salaries!*

Which left the secondhand yellow and white taxicab Rasheed had acquired for Amy's personal transport, but no driver. Amy had itched to get back behind a steering wheel since arriving in Kabul, especially once she'd discovered that while rare, there were a handful of female drivers.

Amy's own key ring held the spare car key Rasheed had given her. As a sop to a male chaperone, she'd invited along the compound's oldest boy, eleven-year-old Enayat. Catching Farah's wistful glance, she'd invited the sixteen-year-old as well. Maybe the outing would give Amy a chance to probe into what was troubling the girl.

Amy slipped her knapsack over a shoulder and leaned back into the open driver's door. "Enayat, I'd like you to stay here to keep an eye on the car. We may be gone awhile, so be sure to stay inside and keep the doors locked."

Joining Farah on a sidewalk, Amy unfolded a map of Kabul, where Soraya had marked several Xs. The first address had been easy to find. Aryana's new husband proved to be the brickmaker whose compound New Hope rented for their neighborhood literacy project, a dour-faced widower in his forties. The pretty twenty-year-old had been pleased to have visitors and answered Amy's tentative questions readily. She'd been treated well thus far. Her new husband's prior wives had borne him no children, so he was willing to accept Aryana's two-year-old son as his own.

"But are you happy here?" Amy persisted. *To marry a stranger old enough to be your father, make this compound your whole world for the rest of your life?* "I just wanted to make sure you didn't feel pushed into this in any way."

"Happy?" Aryana looked baffled at the question. "I have a refuge for my son where his uncles will never find him. Because my husband has no other child, he will be kind. What else could I ask for?"

Love, maybe? Or was that the romanticism of Amy's very different cultural heritage? For how much of human history had marriage been a social contract between two families where the woman and sometimes the man too had little to say about it? Love could follow. Aryana for one had come to love her first husband and mourn his death.

Sure, then her in-laws accuse her of murder and throw her in prison! The abuse Amy had seen perpetrated against the Welayat women showed how often love *didn't* follow.

Their next visit hadn't allayed Amy's misgivings. Mina's new husband had a welding shop, and Amy spotted Mina's ten-year-old son, Fahim, working there as Mina led her two visitors to living quarters in the back.

Like Aryana, Mina insisted the marriage was her own choice. But her seven-year-old daughter, Tamana, squeezed arms around Amy's neck to beg, "Ameera-jan, please, may we not go back with you? I miss you and Gorg and my friends and the stories. And my new *baba* says I may not study anymore. I must marry my new brother Fareed. But he is not kind to me."

Yes, Mina admitted, such plans had been discussed for when Tamana was older. Her new husband's senior wife, bedridden with rheumatoid arthritis, had a teenage son. Taking Mina as a second wife meant acquiring as well two future spouses who would cost the family nothing.

"My husband does not believe females should learn to read. But if the business does well, he has promised perhaps Fahim may study someday."

Tamana's sobs had made it hard for Amy to tear herself away. Soraya's third X marked a middle-class district not far from the banks of the Kabul River, its chief landmark the nearby complex of Ghazi Stadium. The stadium was why Amy and Farah found themselves on foot. A main boulevard leading into the indicated neighborhood was blocked off for some event happening there, the streets packed with revelers. After several abortive efforts to detour around, Amy had been forced to find parking several blocks away.

Amy traced a squiggly line on the map. "Here's the river. But I don't see where we're to turn. I should have asked Soraya to write out directions in English."

Not trusting her navigational skills, Amy had gone back to the files and photocopied the handwritten sheets in Ibrahim's distinctive scrawl from which Soraya had marked her map. Amy scrutinized the Arabic swirls and dots on the paper she held. "I thought I was getting pretty good at basic Dari, but Ibrahim's wording here makes no sense to me."

"That is because it is written in Pashto." Farah leaned over Amy's shoulder to study the paper. "See? That word means 'river.' And there is *Ghazi* for the stadium."

Amy stared at Farah in astonishment. "I didn't know you read Pashto or even spoke it. I thought your family was Tajik. And that you were just now learning to read and write."

"My father was Tajik. That is why I am so fair-colored. But my mother was Pashtun. They spoke both Dari and Pashto at home, but I first learned to read and write in Pashto. I thought I had forgotten all I learned, because only when I was very small did I go to school. And my studies at New Hope are in Dari. But the script is the same. The directions are simple. From the circle before the stadium—" Farah indicated a traffic circle just ahead—"go right past a school. Turn left at the next corner. The house we seek is five streets beyond."

"Simple to you, Farah. I'm just glad you're along." Amy looked her companion over approvingly. Farah had grown accustomed to leaving off her burqa when she helped with the neighborhood literacy outreach, though she still instinctively covered her face when men were around. Today Amy had coaxed the younger girl into one of her own chapans, a floor-length overcoat of heavy cloth, its full sleeves modestly covering all but the fingertips. This one and its corresponding scarf were a richly embroidered blue that matched Farah's eyes. "You look nice, very professional."

The blue eyes glowed. "Like Soraya? I am your assistant?"

Amy gently tugged Farah's headscarf down to expose her smiling mouth. "Yes, Farah, today you are my assistant."

Ibrahim's directions led past a *madrassa*, an Islamic studies school. A number of adolescent boys were kicking soccer balls around a field. Catching sight of two unescorted chapans, the soccer players abandoned sport to crowd along a chain-link fence, shouting comments Amy was glad she didn't fully understand. Farah looked furious, immediately snatching her scarf over her face.

But they reached the far corner without further incident, a left turn leaving their harassers behind. A distant loudspeaker and cheers of a crowd offered a sound track as they walked. That stadium event, presumably. But presently the roar of an aircraft drowned out those sounds. Amy tilted her head to scan the sky. Just a combat helicopter flying low. In Amy's months here, she'd grown accustomed to military air flights racing overhead, whether ISAF training exercises, American counterinsurgency operations, even the fledgling Afghan Air Force.

But instead of flying by, this helicopter was banking above where the stadium would be if Amy could see through all these buildings. And now even above the whir of rotor blades, she could hear somewhere ahead screams and feel a drumming through her sandals that was thousands of running feet. Amy exchanged an alarmed glance with Farah. They'd heard no explosion of a suicide bombing. A riot? Turning back, both women broke into a trot.

But this move brought them back past the madrassa. As they passed the school, they noticed the teenage soccer players had been drawn out the gate by the disturbance, leaving Amy and Farah no choice but to pass through them. At first they were too occupied talking loudly and pointing at the circling helicopter to offer more than a few sneering epithets that seemed to be their indictment of any female without a male escort.

Then a malicious glare sharpened on Amy's uncovered face. The youth elbowed his nearest neighbor, who called to the others. Amy couldn't catch all their rapid Dari, but she understood well enough the suddenly hostile body language as the entire group closed in, the fear in Farah's eyes above embroidered cloth. Amy snatched her own scarf high across her face. Had some untucked flaxen strand or features even paler than Farah's given her away as a foreigner?

The teen pack didn't try to stop the two chapans but kept pace around them, jeering and calling to each other. Then Amy felt a pinch on her rear. She spun around, furiously slapping the hand away. An angry squeal from Farah told her the girl had suffered the same indignity. Rounding on their tormentors, Farah snapped out furiously, "Do you not fear Allah? Have you no sisters or mothers that you molest decent women? *Be tarbia asti!*"

At its politest, the latter phrase meant, "You are without proper upbringing!"

For a moment, the pack fell away, shame on a few faces. Then one sneered contemptuously, "But you are no decent women. You are—"

The word was not one Amy knew. But Farah's sharp intake of breath told her it wasn't complimentary. The young man who'd spoken was in his late teens, already heavily bearded. A sneer twisting his mouth and hate in his eyes made it easy for Amy to picture him as al-Qaeda or Taliban. "Only daughters of dogs walk the streets indecently exposed and alone."

Encouraged by his derision, others surged forward. As the two girls continued to press forward, huddling together to ward off the groping and pinching, Amy was no longer only angry, but terrified. The iciness of Farah's hand sliding into hers told Amy she wasn't alone.

Then the pack was calling off their pursuit. The girls were now nearing the end of the street, and as Amy stood free again, she saw why the teenagers had retreated. A military convoy had turned onto the main avenue down which she'd parked her vehicle. And like the helicopter circling overhead, it was not just passing through, but slamming to a stop. Men in the camouflage fatigues and berets of Afghan army troops poured from transport trucks, armored Humvees, even a tank. They paid no attention to two female pedestrians, but as Amy and Farah reached the corner, a large man hopped down from a Humvee.

The new arrival was not in army fatigues but sported safari clothing, body armor, and wraparound sunglasses. A flaxen crew cut and ice blue eyes as he pushed sunglasses up on his forehead were definitely not Afghan. An expat contractor involved in training the Afghan National Army? As an M4 assault rifle slid from shoulder to hands, the man called out in heavily accented Dari. "This street is closed. Move back, or you will be shot."

In her own unmistakably foreign Dari, Amy called back, "Please, we are just trying to get around the corner to reach our vehicle."

The assault rifle rose higher, the man's expression as inflexible as the tightening of his trigger finger. Did he think the two chapans could be suicide bombers? Not such an improbable supposition after the burqa who'd assaulted a convoy just like this Amy's first day in Kabul.

The two girls retreated, but that brought them once again into the territory of those jeering young men. As malicious grins spread from face to face, Amy tugged her companion to a standstill. There was no way she and Farah could retreat through that harassment. The army troops had already disappeared at a run toward whatever ruckus was going on down the avenue. But the hard scrutiny of that armed foreigner, large hands caressing the barrel of his assault rifle, made it clear there was no exit that direction.

As the two girls backed against the nearest wall, Amy groped in her knapsack for her cell phone. If they couldn't make it back to the Toyota Corolla, then she'd have to call Rasheed for a pickup, even if it meant dragging the New Hope *chowkidar* from his Friday leisure activities. His tall bulk should be enough to move Amy and Farah safely through this vicious pack of juvenile delinquents. If he wasn't too far away to be of any help.

But the teen pack was closing in again, emboldened by the disappearance of the armed troops. While Amy fumbled with the control pad, the ringleader knocked the phone from her hand, kicking it with a mocking laugh out of Amy's reach. Overhead, the helicopter circled low, the pandemonium of screams and running feet growing louder and closer. Beside her, Amy could hear Farah's quiet sobbing.

But now a running, shouting crowd was erupting from a connecting alley beyond their teen tormentors. As the ringleader turned toward the newest disturbance, Amy scooted quickly forward after her cell phone. Not till she'd scooped it up did Amy realize the phone was live. From its tiny speaker poured a rhythmic whir she recognized as the same helicopter banking overhead toward the stadium, the babble of a panicked crowd. Whatever speed dial number she'd inadvertently pushed was nearby. Then, incredulously, Amy took in the caller ID.

Snatching up the cell phone to her ear, Amy demanded with breathless disbelief, "Steve? Steve Wilson? Is that you?"

Jamil opened his eyes to a murmur of voices, a soft singing that was no music he knew. Last night he'd been too exhausted to decline Omed's insistent hospitality. But he'd planned to be on his way at first light. From a sunbeam slanting through open shutters, the morning was already well advanced. Scrambling to his feet, Jamil pushed aside a blanket that served as a door.

The compound beyond was little different from any other where he'd lodged in this region. Mud-brick rooms opened onto a dirt courtyard. Only the door leading to the street was solid wood. This household was at least prosperous enough to have its own bore pump. An elderly woman scrubbed clothes under its trickle of water. Two more women bustled around cook pots and a clay tandoor oven. A plastic basin set well away from the open fire held a swaddled infant. Older children played tag among grape and rose trellises, currently holding only dried brown vines. Today was a Friday, and from those delicious fragrances, the household was preparing the more elaborate feast of a rest day.

And yet there was something different about this home. The playing children's inevitable dirtiness was the dust of the courtyard, not ingrained filth, sores, and malnutrition distressingly typical of village children. The women too, from whom Jamil kept his gaze discreetly averted, looked well-fed and bright of eye. And though they'd fallen silent at the sight of Jamil, the muted chatter and singing to which he'd awakened had been peaceable and contented.

Jamil saw no sign of his host. In the compound's reception chamber, he found a plastic tray holding naan bread and tea had been placed beside his pack.

First, however, he'd missed the dawn call to prayer. Spreading his patu, Jamil prostrated his face to the ground. But the prayer that rose to his lips was not the automatic repetition he'd raced through five times a day as long as he could remember.

Father in heaven whose name is holy, may your kingdom come soon to my homeland. Help me forgive my enemies as you have promised to forgive me. Protect me from evil and give me courage as I carry Isa's words and healing to my people. Send your blessing on this home which has so generously fed and sheltered me. And may your holy angels spread their wings to protect those precious to me: Ameera, the children, my mother and sister if they remain with breath.

To depart without taking leave of his host would be exceedingly discourteous. Nor was there any real haste to return to his wandering. So Jamil settled himself to savor the hot tea and fresh naan bread, then reached into his pack for Ameera's Eid gift. He'd been working his way through its Old Testament section, a more difficult read than the first volume Ameera had given him. And not because the English words were unfamiliar.

The cataloging of laws, ceremonial duties, and sacrifices was disturbingly reminiscent of the mullahs' endless lists of dos and don'ts. So was the jihad Israel had been ordered to carry out against their Canaanite enemies. The Almighty's ways were not man's, and the holy book made clear these Canaanites were completely lost in depravity. Still, Jamil had found himself rushing uneasily through those pages.

Equally disturbing was how quickly the Almighty's chosen people had sunk into the depravity of the nations they'd displaced. Jamil had shaken his head disbelievingly over chronicles of violence and idol worship, injustice and oppression. No wonder the Almighty had punished Israel with foreign invaders and sent them into exile.

But two things had become increasingly clear. First, the Almighty's chosen people had failed as miserably in following his laws or creating a just and righteous kingdom as Jamil's own countrymen. Secondly, the Creator of heaven and earth passionately, if unbelievably, loved the sinful humans who'd made such a mess of his creation. Loved them as a parent loved a firstborn son. As a bridegroom cherished a dearly purchased bride. These pages sang with that love.

"With the Lord is unfailing love," the psalm writers exulted repeatedly. *"His love endures forever."*

And Isaiah and Jeremiah were prophets as renowned in Islam as among the followers of Isa Masih. So why had Jamil never heard their recordings of love from a Creator to his created?

"I have loved you with an everlasting love."

"Though the mountains be shaken and the hills be removed, yet my unfailing love for you will not be shaken."

As incredible to a man who'd seen family and world swept away were the Creator's promises not to abandon his creation. *"Can a mother forget the baby at her breast? . . . Though she may forget, I will not forget you."*

Jamil turned a page to read again the pledge Moses' successor Joshua had received as he took on the formidable task of leading Israel into their Promised Land. *"As I was with Moses, so I will be with you. I will never leave you nor forsake you. Be strong and courageous."*

If I had only known in the prison that you were there all the time! I was so afraid. So sure only hate and death and hell itself remained.

And yet the Almighty's chosen people Israel had consistently rejected their Creator's love. As had all humanity before and since. Was this why the Almighty had at last sent Isa Masih? Because only in seeing Love himself walk their dusty streets, touch them with healing hands, speak words that were not thunder and lightning, but gentle and kind, could fallen human beings grasp the passion of divine love for them and be drawn back to their Creator?

As Jamil had not understood what love could be until he'd seen it revealed in the person of Isa Masih. And before that, in Ameera, whose own compassion had first opened Jamil's eyes to his Creator's love, turning his heart from hate to his current quest.

A soft chortle drew Jamil's eyes from the page he read. A small face was peeping around the hanging blanket. It disappeared with an excited squeal as firm, quick steps outside were followed by the deep murmur of a man's voice. The face disappeared. "Baba!"

The blanket was lifted aside. Omed stepped into the room, carrying a girl perhaps four years old. Small arms squeezed her father's neck in a stranglehold. "Did I not tell you, Baba, that our guest is awake?"

"Yes, you did, little one. Salaam aleykum, my friend. I hope that you slept well."

Jamil jumped hastily to his feet. "Yes, I have rested and eaten well. Please forgive me. I had not intended to impose so late on your generosity."

"It is a rest day. What is the hurry?" Omed dismissed with a wave. "I have brought lamb from the market. We will be honored for you to feast with us."

Omed's glance fell on the volume in Jamil's hand. "That is the holy book you read to the mullah? the one that holds Isa's words?"

"Yes, though not in Pashto as I read last night." Jamil held up the volume. "You have read the holy book of Isa's followers?"

"No, I never learned to read." Omed's expression clouded slightly, then brightened again. "But my sons and daughters are both studying. Someday they will be able to read to me such a book. And I do know Isa's words."

Omed placed the small girl on her feet, then withdrew from his tunic what looked like the solar-powered transistor radio Ameera had given Jamil and the elderly guard Wajid as Eid gifts. Squatting down, he placed the small, black rectangle in a sunbeam slanting across the carpet. As Jamil hunkered down beside him, Omed pushed a button.

"Blessed are the poor in spirit, for theirs is the kingdom of heaven."

They listened a short while before Omed pushed the button again. As the voice stopped, Jamil stared at him with astonishment. "Those are Isa's words. And in Pashto."

"Yes, all that are in the holy book. It is powered by the sun, so there is never a need of batteries." Omed reached for the button.

"Blessed are those who hunger and thirst . . ."

Stopping the recording, Omed finished the phrase. "'. . . for righteousness, for they will be filled.' See? If I cannot read, I have learned many of Isa's words by heart. It is also a radio. A very powerful one that permits listening to the speech of Isa followers."

Jamil shook his head with growing excitement. "But this is wonderful!

I did not know such an instrument existed. Then your town has already heard the words of Isa?"

Eagerness ebbed from Omed's expression. "No, no, that is not possible. My family came to know Isa during the war years in Pakistan. Isa followers who brought help to the refugee camps gave me this radio. 'Shortwave,' they call its power. But when we returned home—as you have seen, the mullah, the elders, they are very suspicious. If it became known that this radio is not like other radios, it would be taken away, and I perhaps as well. I show this to you only because I now know you are not a spy but truly a follower of Isa Masih. And so that you might worship with us."

The blanket was being lifted aside again. The women and children Jamil had seen in the courtyard filed into the room. Several younger children swarmed around Omed. "Baba. Baba."

Jamil tamped down unaccustomed envy. "Your wives have given you many beautiful sons and daughters."

Omed shook his head. "I have only one wife. Did not Isa Masih command so? Let me make you known to my family. This is my mother, Geeti. My wife, Najia. And my sister Moska. Her husband died two years ago, so she and her children live with us."

Then that baby belonged to Omed and his wife, Najia. The women's glances toward Jamil were shy but smiling. More significant was a lack of any apprehension toward the head of their household. As the new arrivals found places in a loose circle around the radio, Omed slid Jamil an apologetic glance.

"It is because of the women and children that I do not speak openly as you do. If something should happen to me, what would become of them? But as you saw at the carpet factory, I do what I can to encourage my tribesmen to follow the ways of Isa, even if it must be with care. Is that not what Isa would wish, to make a better life for our women and our children?"

"You have done much," Jamil answered with sincere respect, though his host's caution seemed to him excessive. Hadn't Jamil been healing in the name of Isa Masih, speaking the prophet's words openly, for weeks now? *If those who know the truth do not speak it, how shall others learn?*

But then as he'd learned yesterday, there were those who found such truth threatening. After all, who was Jamil to judge when he'd neither wife nor children for whom to be afraid? Jamil took his own place on the carpet as Omed turned the radio on.

"Does worry grip your heart? Then listen to this promise Isa Masih gave to his followers. 'Peace I leave with you; my peace I give you. I do not give to you as the world gives. Do not let your hearts be troubled and do not be afraid.' Yes, this was Isa's promise though he knew in just a few hours he would be arrested and condemned to the cross, his followers fleeing in fear for their lives. You see, peace does not come from the absence of trouble, but the presence of our Savior."

The children were listening as raptly as their parents. Jamil himself listened in stunned wonder. He recognized Isa's promise from the John *injil*. But except for those few cautious discussions with Ameera, he'd never heard anyone explain Isa's words as this voice was doing. And the singing! The Pashto lyrics spoke of a heavenly Father, of the love and compassion of Isa Masih. They dwelt much, Jamil noted, on Isa's martyrdom on the cross, as though this had more significance than all else.

A sacrifice, they called it.

The songs were not new to the household because even the smaller children were singing along. Softly, cautiously, as though there might be hostile ears outside the walls, but with such joy. Then the broadcast ended, and the household drifted away, the women to prepare the lamb Omed had brought from market, the children to their play. The feast was leisurely. By the time Jamil reluctantly bestirred himself to leave, the sun was well past noon zenith.

"You have the food and water?" Omed lifted down the metal security bar from the door leading to the street. His wife, Najia, had put together a packet of dried fruit, almonds, and naan.

Jamil patted his pack. "Yes, it is all here. I only hope I have not caused trouble for you and your household. I had no such thought when I spoke yesterday of Isa Masih. I did not think your mullah and healer would become so angry."

"They were more angry that you did what they were not willing to do. For healing my sister-in-law, I cannot thank you sufficiently. As to the other, the town knows how many things I have done to help it prosper.

Those men would not dare threaten my home." Omed lowered his voice as the rest of the household drifted over to see off their guest, Najia with swaddled infant in arms. "I . . . I could wish I had the courage to do as you have done. Najia and Moska worry for our children's safety, but this town needs to hear Isa's teaching. Perhaps one day."

Omed embraced Jamil, kissing him soundly on both cheeks. "Come again soon. You are my brother now, and you will always have a welcome here."

Stepping through the doorway, Jamil lingered to look back. No, nothing here was so different from any other rural Afghan household. The small compound with its neatly swept dirt courtyard, whitewashed walls, leafless grape arbors and rosebushes. The smoke of cookfire and tandoor oven. The children waving wildly. Omed had turned to lift his youngest from his wife's arms, and Jamil swallowed something in his throat as he caught her adoring glance upward.

It was all a far cry from the upper-class prosperity of Jamil's own upbringing. Yet within these mud-brick walls he'd encountered a difference he would not trade for all of Kabul's new fancy mansions. The sensation was not completely unknown, and suddenly Jamil placed where he'd encountered it before. Nightfall at the New Hope compound, children and mothers gathered to listen in wide-eyed wonder as Ameera told of the almighty Creator of the universe and his sometimes unruly followers, Jamil hunkered at her feet to translate.

Jamil knew now what made the difference.

Peace.

And love.

The peace and love of Isa Masih.

"Amy! Where in heaven's name are you? Are you okay?"

An answering babble of angry male voices and female sobs was not reassuring. That Steve could do nothing was the most infuriating. Picking out individuals in that dispersing crowd below was like isolating a single ant in a kicked-over anthill.

Then Amy's voice returned, composed enough the tears were clearly not hers. "I'm fine; we both are. Farah's here with me. There was this horrible pack of boys, but now a whole mob's pouring down the street, so they're taking off."

Steve let out a lungful of air he hadn't realized he was holding. "The mob you're seeing is from the stadium, which is where I am right now, so you must be close by. Can you give me any defining landmarks?"

"There's a school just down the block where the boys came from. Our vehicle is parked down the avenue. Only there's some kind of army convoy blocking the street. One of your private security types is at the corner, a big, blond guy. I tried to get him to let us through, but every time we move that way, he keeps threatening to shoot."

"Let me guess: you're dressed like a native." Steve relaxed further. "Try calling to the guy in English so he knows you're expat. And if he's really a PSC, tell him you're with Condor Security. Which is true enough because I'll be there in five minutes."

"That isn't necessar—"

"Just stay put!" Cutting off the call was easier than arguing. Amy's mention of a school and proximity of an army convoy identified her position precisely. As he threaded through the parking lot, a blockade of police vehicles still faced off with personnel carriers and tanks, but army fatigues were now climbing back into their vehicles.

Reaching the side street that was his objective, Steve spotted a German commando with whom he'd worked before standing guard beside an armored Humvee. "Heinrich, right? You're with Dyncorp. The ANA training contract."

"*Ja*. And you are Khalid's detail, *nein*? It is well this foolishness is ending, or we might have found ourselves shooting at each other. You are here for the women?"

Beyond the German commando, a pedestrian mob had spilled through connecting alleys into the dirt side street. All were male, many carrying banners and posters proclaiming their favorite candidate. Except for two chapan-draped female shapes, blue and brown, backed hand in hand against a wall. One had her face buried against the other's shoulder. The second woman's headscarf was pushed back, exposing silky strands as flaxen blonde as the German security contractor's.

Heinrich waggled his M4 toward the two chapans. "The American woman tells me she is with your company. So I let them stay instead of shooting them."

Steve let only a tightening jaw betray that he found the jovial remark less funny than the Dyncorp operative did. But now the brown chapan was straightening away from the wall. Steve sloped his mouth into a sardonic grin. "We've got to stop meeting like this, Ms. Mallory."

A flush of red suggested Amy too was remembering their first encounter. "This time it was *not* my fault! Farah and I were just on our way to visit one of the New Hope families when—well, everything started going crazy."

"You're right," Steve agreed peaceably. "If it's anyone's fault, this one's mine. I should have foreseen something like this."

Amy eyed him uncertainly. "I don't see how. Not even you can take responsibility for the Afghan army and an entire riot. And I sure didn't mean to disturb you. I didn't even know you were still in Afghanistan. I was told you'd left. But, well, I was trying to call our chowkidar, and I guess I must have bumped your number."

Steve's right eyebrow rose. "So you still have it on speed dial."

The red flush deepened. "I never even thought about it. There was no reason to take it out. Like I said, I didn't even know you were still on this continent. Anyway, it isn't necessary for you to go out of your way. Especially since you said you were in some kind of emergency. If you can get your blond pal there to let us through, we'll be out of your hair. My car is just a few blocks away."

Was it their last encounter Amy was now remembering that she was so eager to rid herself of him? Steve abandoned diplomacy. "Look, whatever problem you may have with me, you should know me better than to think I've any intentions of abandoning you to that."

Steve jerked his head toward the growing mob behind Amy. The army blockade had turned the street into a bottleneck. Steve was glad he'd arrived when he did because the crowd's mood was turning ugly, not yet a stampede, but a lot of jostling and angry shouts as the men tried to push their way out the far end of the street. "If you think this is bad, there are tens of thousands more out there trying to get out of this mess. This is no time and place for two women to be walking alone. As I intend to make clear to your driver."

Steve braced himself for further debate. But Amy only looked taken aback at his terseness. Her tone was subdued, eyelashes lowered, as she answered. "I don't have any problem with you. I—actually, Farah and I would appreciate your escort. I just didn't want to impose any further."

"You're not imposing; I volunteered."

Falling in at the women's heels as they headed down the avenue, Steve kept an eye out for trouble. But the released spectators were quickly thinning out. The army convoy was now withdrawing by making a U-turn through the emptying stadium grounds. A buzz in his comm set proved to be Ian Grant, reporting all under control with their client.

Steve's satisfaction lasted until the brown and blue chapans stopped abruptly in front of him beside a refurbished city taxi. He eyed with unbelieving disapproval the small boy climbing out hastily from behind the steering wheel. "This is your driver?"

Amy shot him a cool look. "No, I am, actually."

Steve discarded a dozen sharp editorials before responding more calmly, "In that case, I'll drive you home myself."

Amy's chin rose as Steve held out a hand. "Look, I appreciate your help back there; I really do. But if you think I'm going to hand over my keys, not a chance! I drove myself here, didn't I? I can get myself home just fine!"

Gray and hazel eyes locked in brief battle. Then Steve shrugged and headed around the hatchback. "Then would you mind giving me a ride home? Don't want to be any trouble. So just drop me off at your own door, and I'll walk from there."

Steve was already climbing into the front passenger seat. With one disbelieving glance that made clear she was in no way taken in by his mild-spoken request, Amy slid behind the steering wheel. Her two companions scrambled into the backseat. The girl she'd identified as Farah, whom Steve remembered vaguely as a pretty, fair-skinned teenager, huddled into the corner, scarf pulled high over her face so Steve could see only a pair of lowered lashes.

The aid worker was a competent driver, Steve conceded, weaving through anarchic traffic as adeptly as any convoy driver. Though spectators had cleared the stadium, they still swarmed surrounding streets, their earlier conviviality now angry frustration that would take little to tip over into violence, so Steve remained on alert, M4 cradled and ready. Not until Amy had made several turns so that neither convoy, stadium, nor crowd was visible any longer did Steve relax, lowering his weapon.

"For the record, I do not endorse women traveling unescorted in Kabul's current political climate. And, no, those two don't count." Steve gestured toward the backseat. "However, I'll admit you've got the driving part down. Where did you learn evasive maneuvers like that?"

"I grew up in Miami, remember?" The aid worker looked somewhat mollified by Steve's commendation as she glanced his direction. "So what was all that back there? And when did you get back to Kabul? I was told you'd left Condor Security and didn't plan to return."

"I didn't." Wazir Akbar Khan was not far from the stadium, so even Steve's condensed explanation was just wrapping up when a peacock blue perimeter wall appeared ahead.

"Wow, you were serious about being responsible. Though what you could have done differently, I sure can't see." Drawing up to a vehicle gate, Amy leaned on the horn. "I'm just so sorry to hear about Phil's little boy. He's such a nice person. If you talk to him, please do let Phil know I'll be praying."

"That I can do. And how about you? Did you ever make it home to Miami?"

"For three weeks. In fact, I just got back yesterday. It was wonderful. But it's good to be back too." Amy turned her head to Steve as black metal gate panels began swinging inward. "Are you sure I can't drop you off somewhere? Now that you're satisfied I can get myself home in one piece."

Steve ignored her irony. "That won't be necessary." The Condor Security team house was only a ten-minute stroll from Amy's humanitarian project. "Go ahead and pull in. I'll walk from here."

The turbaned guard with gray beard opening the gate was not the elderly opium eater Steve remembered. Amy drew the Toyota Corolla up beside a red Mitsubishi Montero. As Steve stepped out, a wriggling, barking ball of fur on the end of a long rope erupted from a concrete guard shack.

"You remember Gorg?" Behind Amy, her female companion was already scuttling silently toward the villa, though her diminutive escort lingered protectively.

"Gorg? Dari for 'wolf.' So this is the puppy I sent over with Phil. He's grown." Stooping to offer a scratch behind the ears, Steve ran his gaze around the compound interior, taking in a new shed where he'd last seen a jungle gym, the knocked-down cinder-block partition. "You've made some changes."

He straightened up abruptly. "Hey, what happened to the fiber-optic alarm system?"

Amy turned to make her own survey. "You're right; I hadn't noticed. I just got back myself yesterday, remember? It was fine when I left." Her nose wrinkled ruefully. "To be honest, there've been so many changes while I was gone, it hardly feels like my project anymore."

A shrilling interrupted the aid worker's explanation. Amy unearthed her cell phone from a knapsack over her shoulder. From a puzzled line above her nose, the caller ID was unfamiliar. "Hello?"

Then as Steve watched, Amy's expression changed to incredulous delight. "Jamil, is that you?"

Her exclamation came out with far more relief than had been in Amy's earlier greeting of Steve himself. "Where are you calling from?"

As she edged away, cell phone to her ear, Steve slipped away and strode out the gate.

So Ms. Mallory was not only still in Afghanistan but in contact with a certain unsuccessful suicide bomber.

7

Any residual sensation of peace evaporated as Jamil emerged from the narrow dirt lane into the town commons, which was even busier than last night, the open-air stalls of a rest day market buzzing with customers. But not crowded enough to evade an eagerly waving figure in Army parka and blue jeans who trotted down the steps of the chaikhana as Jamil threaded through the stalls.

"Doctor! Wait! Stop!"

Jamil ducked into an alley behind a stack of produce crates, but before he could make a getaway, the young man had placed himself directly in his path. "You are the doctor from last night, are you not? the one who healed that woman? May I ask you some questions? on my camera here?"

The man's fingers were playing across a cell phone as he spoke. He held it up, and Jamil saw his own face on the diminutive screen. The image was not still but moving, a muted static emerging from the unit.

"Your phone takes video as well as pictures?" Recovering himself, he demanded, "Who are you, and why are you taking these images of me?"

The young man drew himself up proudly. "My name is Kareem. I am a journalist from Kabul. Well," he amended, "I am studying to be a journalist. But with this phone, I shall now become one. See? It works off satellites in space and can reach all Afghanistan. The battery will last a week, even two with care. And it is connected to the Internet. I can send and receive images, even watch the television station where I work in Kabul."

Jamil studied the satellite phone with absorption as Kareem pointed out features. "I could wish for such a phone. Though it looks very expensive."

"More than I earn in a year. But I did not have to purchase this. It came from the foreign soldiers."

"Foreign soldiers? They give away such phones?"

"Only to journalists such as myself. You see, their leaders have been angry because many phones now take video as well as pictures, so whenever the foreigners drop their bombs or fight the Taliban, someone is there to film it. With the Internet, images of dead children and women are showing on television and YouTube even before they return to their bases. So—" Kareem's smile grew wide—"the foreigners decided they need images to show instead good things happening in Afghanistan. Girls going to school. Villages that plant food instead of opium. They have given away a hundred of these phones, and they will pay for such good stories. Because I work at the television station, I obtained one."

The young reporter's smile faded. "Though I have not yet been successful. There is a project to restore canals that once brought water to this desert. But the new canals are irrigating opium fields, not wheat. Then I heard of new looms a foreign aid group had given this town. Improving women's lives is a good story. I interviewed the supervisor, some boy children, even a woman, though she was not permitted to show her face. Then I heard you next door and saw what you were doing. An Afghan praying and healing in the name of the foreigners' prophet. Village elders who permit women to be treated as freely as men." Kareem tapped the cell phone screen with admiring incredulity. "This is the kind of story the foreigners will pay to see instead of dead children. Are they not always speaking of freedom of speech and faith and women's rights? *Dee-mo-cra-see.*" Kareem carefully pronounced the English word. "This story will show that the freedoms Afghanistan was promised after the Taliban are not all a lie. And I will earn a name as a real journalist."

The would-be journalist looked so pleased with himself, Jamil didn't even know where to start disillusioning him. How to explain that far from exercising religious liberties, Jamil hadn't even realized his silent prayers had become audible? or that such village leaders as that black-turbaned mullah and health worker were hardly interested in promoting women's rights? More disconcerting, Jamil's face on the cell phone screen had been vivid and sharp even in lantern light. The thought of those images reaching TV and computer screens where they might catch unfriendly eyes was not a welcome one.

"You cannot use this footage. It must be erased immediately," Jamil said urgently, snatching the phone from Kareem's hand. He searched for a reason as he fumbled with the keypad. "You will dishonor the woman, perhaps even bring attention to her from Taliban, who will not approve of a male healer treating her. Do you wish to put her in danger?"

"But her face did not show. How will they know who she is? Besides, I have already uploaded the video."

Something of Jamil's distress had pierced the reporter's self-congratulation because Kareem looked genuinely regretful as he took back the cell phone. "I am sorry you are unhappy. I thought this would be good news, not bad. Do you fear the religious authorities will be angry because you prayed in the name of Isa Masih?"

That particular complication hadn't, in fact, yet crossed Jamil's mind. He considered Kareem's question. There'd been times back in Kabul when he'd wondered if Ameera was aware of the dangers of their conversations about the Christian holy book and Isa Masih. And when he'd started this quest, he'd been prepared for opposition. But the isolated villages to which Jamil had deliberately kept his wanderings possessed little organized law and even less willingness to call on it. Notwithstanding yesterday's events or Omed's caution, Jamil had encountered far more interest than suspicion, especially since his stories and readings accompanied free medical care.

"Why should any care whether I pray in the name of Isa Masih or Ibrahim or any other prophet? It is just . . . I had some—difficulties during the war years," Jamil admitted cautiously. "I have made enemies who are now powerful. So I prefer not to draw their attention to my continued existence."

"Ahh, yes, I know well how it was." Kareem was doing his best to look as wise and concerned as though he had not been a child at the time. "If this is the case, I will not film you further. And perhaps the news service will not use the story. Or only the carpet weaving and not your healing.

Do they not receive hundreds of stories, thousands even, from all over the world?"

"Perhaps." Jamil managed a slight smile. "I could envy your phone in any case. I have not found electricity to charge mine in weeks now."

"Then use mine! No, please, I insist!" Kareem thrust the satellite phone into Jamil's hands. "It is the least I can do for any inconvenience I have caused."

"No, no, there is no one." But even as Jamil shook his head, his fingers were already inputting a number engraved on his mind. Not with any expectation of response, but as had been an automatic reflex in each new region, until his battery died, to check whether he was back within cell phone service. So it was with stunned elation that he heard the call ring through.

"Hello?"

Ameera!

Then Rasheed had lied.

The woman who'd so gripped his heart was still in his country.

"You are back in Afghanistan? Rasheed told me you had returned to your own country."

"I guess he didn't mention it was only for three weeks. I'm *so* glad to hear from you, Jamil. When you didn't answer my calls, I was worried something had happened. Though maybe I was calling the wrong phone because this isn't the number I have for you. Where are you now? And your—uh, quest, is it going well?"

"No, this is not my number. A new acquaintance is permitting me to use his phone. As to my quest, it goes well enough. The people are happy to see a healer, though not all are so happy to hear the words of Isa. Still, today I have met an entire family that call themselves Isa followers."

As Jamil spoke, Amy's peripheral vision took in Steve striding out the gate. *I didn't get a chance to say thank you.* Well, she could always call the security contractor later, even drop a thank-you note by the Condor

Security team house. Seizing on Jamil's rare communication took first priority right now.

Amy listened with pleasure as her former assistant told of his hosts, the woman he'd restored to useful life, the town's revolutionary carpet-weaving industry. "That's wonderful! And your medical supplies? You must be about out after all these weeks. Are you in a big enough town I could send you a box?"

And some funds, Amy didn't add aloud. How had Jamil traveled and eaten all these weeks? She cut into his immediate protest. "No, it's no trouble. New Hope has a project now that distributes medical supplies to village health centers. You certainly have as much right to the stuff as anyone else. Please, Jamil, what you're doing is important. I want to help. Would you not do the same if you were here and I were there?"

"Yes, of course." There was a silence long enough Amy thought she'd lost the connection. Then Jamil spoke again. "There is no postal service, but my acquaintance says the chaikhana will receive packages."

Amy dug out the crumpled paper with Ibrahim's directions and a pen to write down a town in Kandahar province several hundred miles south-west of Kabul.

"And now I must return the phone. I have presumed too long on my friend's generosity." Jamil's tone turned suddenly diffident, but there was a note in it that tightened Amy's throat, it held so much joy and warmth and hope. "Ameera-jan, it makes my heart glad that you have returned to my country. Salaam aleykum."

"Peace be to you too."

Amy headed for the villa as the phone went dead. *I'll ask Farah to help me put together a package. She's always had a soft spot for Jamil, and maybe it'll cheer her up, at least be a distraction from this morning.*

Amy hadn't liked Farah's silent withdrawal since their run-in with those teenage assailants. But before checking on the girl, she had another situation to address. The red SUV in the mechanics yard indicated Soraya's family was back from their holiday outing. Hurrying upstairs, Amy found Ibrahim and Soraya in their suite living room, unpacking a brand-new television they'd evidently just purchased.

Amy exchanged polite greetings before broaching her purpose. "I just learned that our alarm system has been removed. Do either of you know anything about this?"

Dropping the TV's packing box, Soraya slid Ibrahim a nervous glance. But her good-looking younger husband drew himself up to look down on Amy coldly. "I ordered the wires removed when the wall was torn down. Do we not have men here to protect this compound? We do not need the help of foreigners."

When Steve Wilson had installed that fiber-optic wiring, Amy had felt herself very alone with her new Welayat charges and an opium-impaired elderly watchman. With a real guard and his own family living on-site, Ibrahim was undoubtedly right that the system was no longer crucial to compound security. Still, its existence, the knowledge that a trained and willing team of protectors was only a radio wave away, had always made Amy feel safe.

Steve made me feel safe! Amy hadn't had time to process her shock at seeing the contractor again so unexpectedly. And it would have to be in circumstances to reinforce Steve's estimation of Amy as some incompetent damsel in distress always needing rescue.

Even when we argued, I counted him a friend. But as angry as he was the day of the bombing, leaving town without so much as a good-bye, he's made abundantly clear the feeling wasn't mutual. So maybe it's just as well that last connection is gone. In any case, he's only back temporarily, so we'll likely not even cross paths again.

Amy's voice shook a little as she met Ibrahim's cold gaze squarely. "It's too late to undo now, so we'll leave this. But in the future, please speak to me first before ordering changes to my arrangements here."

"I will speak to Mr. Duane or Rasheed! It is for them to give orders here, not a woman."

Apprehension on Soraya's beautiful, oval features unnerved Amy more than the fury of Ibrahim's answer. When Amy had first welcomed the family to live on the New Hope compound, Soraya's husband had voiced profuse appreciation. But Amy hadn't forgotten the abusive language and threats she'd overheard on her first encounter with Ibrahim. Or her composed assistant's tears.

More significantly, Soraya had come here as Amy's assistant. The caretaker Rasheed too, for all his misogynistic attitude, had at least offered Amy the respect owed an employer. Ibrahim, in contrast, had been hired directly by Amy's own new boss. And he'd just made amply clear he no longer considered himself bound to Amy's authority or even wishes on this compound. A consequence Amy had not foreseen in relinquishing her position as country manager.

Drawing herself up to her own slim height, Amy responded calmly, "When decisions impact New Hope projects under my responsibility, then I do expect to be consulted. As Mr. Duane will confirm when you speak with him."

Before Ibrahim could respond, Amy extricated herself with a murmured leave-taking. The last thing she wanted was to contact her new supervisor again. *But if Ibrahim thinks he can treat me the way he does Soraya, does he have a surprise coming!*

Meanwhile, Amy had let Farah slide too long. Heading down to the interior courtyard, Amy found the women and children enjoying their rest day in the kitchen salon watching a Dari cartoon. But Farah was not among them.

Amy tried next the dormitory Farah shared with three other women and their children.

There her search ended. The room was empty except for Farah. Much as Amy had first seen her at Welayat prison, the girl sat huddled on her sleeping tushak, back against the wall, arms wrapped around her knees.

But even in those horrible surroundings of the women's prison, Farah had been smiling and responsive, curious about her foreign visitors. Just as she'd been eager and curious about her new surroundings in Wazir Akbar Khan, her studies, the literacy projects where she'd volunteered, Amy's own life. Over these last months, Amy had come to admire—and depend on—the teenager's cheerful resilience and determination to pursue a new and different life for herself.

Now there was no smile on Farah's fair-skinned, pretty features nor any expression at all, her eyes open wide like a startled deer and focused on the far wall. Amy hurried over, troubled and apprehensive. After all Farah had survived to date, what straw could possibly have broken this girl's indomitable spirit?

She stood naked and shivering.

In her nightmares she always stood alone. But in reality there'd been other girls, younger than she. Not inmates themselves, but prisoners' children, who at nine or ten or eleven years were no longer eligible to stay with their mothers. Young boys too, but those had been led elsewhere. Grinning male guards groped and pinched as the girls were marched past into a large room. Female wardens with whips and batons had ordered them to strip, then turned water hoses as chill as the concrete underfoot on the girls.

In the women's prison, the only *hammam*, or bathhouse, was a bucket for sponging off dirt and soot, used hastily under shroud of a blanket. Not since the humiliation of her arrest had Farah stood completely undressed. Now, even without a mirror, she recognized that the protection of malnourished scrawniness, of rib cage and breastbone protruding through the skin, had abandoned her. Instead, as she scrubbed body and hair with a bar of harsh laundry soap, she encountered rounded limbs and breasts.

When she was clean, a warden turned the chill blast of the hose on her for a final rinse. Then came hands inspecting for defects. Disapproving clucks over scars and calluses of past drudgery. More unpleasant prodding to verify she was still a virgin. Each girl received clean clothing before the shivering group was led to another chamber.

But she'd felt no less naked, for then the men came. Sometimes alone. Sometimes in groups. Now she could wish for a burqa's anonymity to veil herself from lascivious eyes, hands that lifted her long hair, ran themselves over her body through the thin tunic, as though she were a piece of meat or a mare purchased for breeding.

Some of the younger girls disgraced themselves with tears until the female wardens led them out and screams of a beating drowned out sobs. But she'd stood motionless, retreating beyond reach of the groping and prodding and bargaining within the protective shell of her own mind and spirit.

The last man had been the worst, a nightmare clone of the bridegroom she'd fled. Grizzled hair and beard under a black turban. A well-rounded belly and fat fingers that pinched her flesh deliberately in their inspection. Avid eyes that did not smile with the satisfied curving of his mouth.

But his clothing was of finest silk, his fingers and turban clasp a glitter of gold and jewels. Even before the head warden's complacent murmur, she'd known this was the one. Tomorrow the money would be exchanged. She kept her eyes closed during the negotiations, as though by doing so, she could banish her surroundings. Had she not escaped once before in body as well as thought?

Only this time the walls around her were high and strong, the bars unbending.

This time she would not awake from the nightmare.

8

"Oh, here you are, Farah." Crouching beside the tushak, Amy put an arm around the girl's shoulders. "I've been looking for you. Is everything okay?"

"Do not touch me!" Farah lashed out, her arm striking Amy in the chest. The girl's eyes had a wild look that did not even register Amy. But she fell backward, air leaving her lungs with a small gasp of pain.

The sound pierced Farah's withdrawal as Amy's words had not. Farah turned her head, her expression crumpling to dismay. "Miss Ameera, I am so sorry! I . . . I was not thinking. Did I hurt you?"

"No, I'm fine. It's okay." Amy recovered her balance, but this time she didn't reach to touch the girl. "Farah, what's wrong? Is it those boys? They were horrible and rude, but you were so brave standing up against them." Or had something happened beyond the pinching and groping Amy herself had endured? "Did one of them do something to hurt you?"

"No, I am not hurt." Farah's admission was muffled because she'd buried her face against her arms. "It is just . . . I hate them so much! I—I would kill them if I could! Miss Ameera-jan, what will I do? I am so full of hate, I cannot see any light, only darkness."

"Oh, Farah." Amy put her arm again around her. This time Farah didn't push her away. Of Amy's Welayat charges, the sixteen-year-old alone had never actually endured a forced marriage or borne children to an abusive spouse. And because the girl was always cheerful, responsible, levelheaded,

Amy had come to conclude that Farah of all these women was relatively whole and undamaged by her life experiences.

Yet what did Amy really know of this girl's life? of the traumas she'd survived—and perhaps not so unscathed after all?

"I'm so sorry about what happened earlier, Farah-jan. I should never have led us past that school. But it's over, and we're safe. Why do you hate them so much? Is it—has something like this happened to you before?"

The slim shoulders stiffened immediately under Amy's embrace. "Remembering does not change the past, so why speak of it?"

"But sharing it with someone else can make you feel better," Amy said gently. "Please, Farah, I know so little about you, and I'd like to know you better."

Amy did not let Farah pull away as she coaxed, "We have the rest of the day and nothing to do. Won't you tell me some of your story? Where did you live when you were little? Who taught you to read Pashto? You must have had parents who cared about educating their daughter."

Farah raised her head, but her expression was stony and unrelenting, and for the space of several heartbeats, Amy thought she'd lost. Then with a whoosh of released breath, resistance left the girl's body. "I . . . I do not know where I lived when I was small. But there was a house with painted rooms and many people. I know I had a father and brothers. I remember one teaching me to write my name. But I cannot remember their faces. Only my mother. There was a truck. We drove through the night. After that—" Farah's taut frame shuddered against Amy's arm. "What came after that I do not want to remember. There was darkness and shooting and dead bodies. My mother and I, we were running and hiding and hungry. The others we never saw again. Then we came in the night to tall gates."

As though a dam had been unleashed, the words kept pouring out. Amy did not stir, though her arm was growing cramped, afraid if she moved, the pent-up flow would stop. This story was too terrible for comment and too vivid to be fabricated. Amy shuddered through a twelve-year-old Farah's escape from her wedding. The months of slave labor in the brick-making troughs. Her flight and arrest. The green metal gate of the Welayat women's prison clanging shut.

"I knew the male guards came in sometimes to find women. The police too. Some women did not mind because then they received better food. And what choice did they have? But I was too ugly and thin to attract their eyes. I knew too that girl children were removed from the prison when they began their woman's cycles; their mothers screamed and cried when they were taken away. And boys too. But I thought they had gone back to their families.

"Until I too was taken away. Virgins are of value, even virgins of such lowly origin. And young boys—there are always men who will pay for such. Because I was unblemished and still a virgin, a good price was negotiated for me, the warden said. I could have wished then I was covered with scars like Najeeda and Parvati."

"But you're here," Amy prompted gently as Farah wound to a halt. "So the man didn't take you after all. What happened?"

"You saved me!" The passionate gratitude in that exclamation touched and embarrassed Amy. "The day you came with Miss Debby was the same day the wardens first took me apart with the other girls. But the very night I was sold, word came that I was chosen to come here. I think perhaps those who run the prison do not know all the wardens and guards are doing, because even though they had been offered much money, they were afraid and returned me with the others to come here."

Amy tightened a numbed arm around Farah's shoulders. "I'm so thankful you did come here, Farah-jan. And I can see now why those awful boys would be so upsetting. But I hope you will believe me that here at New Hope, you'll never have to worry again about any man marrying or touching you against your will."

A sudden troubling thought came to Amy. "Farah, I've been wanting to ask you—Aryana and Mina and the other women, they do understand there is no time limit on living at New Hope. These marriage offers, they don't have to accept them just to find a place to stay. Or marry at all, if they choose."

"So you say. But you are not wali here. And in time, like all foreigners, will you not return to your own people? Then who among us will dare refuse when Mr. Ibrahim summons one of us from our work to be sent away before the day is out? Which is why I . . . I am afraid."

The girl's long eyelashes were downcast, her lips quivering until she pressed them tightly together, then admitted, "Aryana and Mina, they are right to accept such arrangements. They have children to feed and clothe. But me? I wish to be like you, unmarried and free. To have a profession and money so I need never again be under the command of any man. You said I was a good assistant. Perhaps we can live together, and I can be your assistant instead of Soraya. Please promise you will take me with you if you go. For I would rather die than remain here to be given in marriage to one I do not know or choose."

Wali. A term used for the male guardian, whether husband, father, brother, or other close male relative, that sharia law appointed over every Muslim woman from birth to death, to control her finances, movements, the very air she breathed.

And her marriage.

Was this why Farah had seemed so troubled? Did the girl somehow think that Soraya's husband was the New Hope compound's wali with legal authority to dispose lives and futures of its residents?

"Farah, I can't make promises I'm not sure I can keep. But I can assure you Ibrahim has no authority as your guardian to force you to marry or anything else. And I don't want you to get the wrong idea. If I'm still unmarried, it's because I haven't yet found the right person to spend my life with. In my country, women are free to stay unmarried. But they're also free to marry someone they love. When I find the man I love and who loves me, I'll be happy to give myself to him in marriage."

Farah's head shot up, her expression again stony and cold as she spat out, "Love? Love is an illusion. At least between a man and a woman. A mother loves her child, yes. Because a child is part of her own body. My mother would have done anything for me. But a man? A man wishes to own a woman, not to love her. If I remember little of my own father and brothers, I saw other fathers and brothers where my mother took me to live. They sold their daughters and sisters for the highest price without any thought of their wishes, just as they did me. My wali's new wife was no older than I am today when I was traded as part of her bride-price. So if my father and brothers had lived, would they not have done the same? No, love is for a storyteller's tales. I do not ask for love, but freedom."

Farah's head dropped suddenly back to her arms, her body rigid so that only the dampness on her sleeve gave away that she was crying, her voice muffled. "But I do not wish to hate either. I . . . The hate is such a stone in my chest."

Amy hugged the younger girl tight, feeling completely helpless to speak or do. *What can I say to this beautiful child? What do I have any right to say to her? She's been hurt so deeply. And me? I've been so unfairly, fortunately whole! Oh, sure, I've had life's normal ups and downs, a broken dream or two. But I've always had my faith in God to fall back on, loving family and friends, anything I've ever really needed.*

So how can I possibly understand what a girl like Farah has gone through? how deep the scars must be?

I can't! But I can love her. I can empathize as much as is in me. And I can promise not to abandon her. Except I can't really guarantee that promise.

Amy straightened up suddenly. She debated only briefly before making her decision. Her numbed arm came to life painfully as she removed it from around Farah's body. "Farah-jan, I'm going to be right back, okay?"

It took only minutes to retrieve the MP3 player from Amy's own apartment. The girl hadn't moved or lifted her head when Amy returned. "I wish I could promise to let you stay with me always. I *will* do whatever I can, but I don't have the authority to make such a promise. But just as the Lord Almighty promised Joshua in last night's story, there *is* someone who will never leave you or forsake you. Someone who showed love and kindness to women as well as men. His name is Isa Masih. I don't know the Dari words to tell you his story properly. But I have it here on this little machine. I'm going to leave it with you to listen."

Farah didn't cooperate, but neither did she protest as Amy found an ear in which to tuck the earpiece. In the kitchen salon, she dished up some of the lentil and eggplant stew the Welayat women had simmering for supper, then added a small pot of tea to a tray. Upstairs, Amy found Farah no longer hunched against the wall but stretched out on her tushak, a blanket pulled over her shoulders. Amy couldn't tell if the girl was asleep or simply had her eyes closed. But the earpiece was still in place, the MP3 player clutched tightly in one hand.

Setting the tray on the floor beside Farah's tushak, Amy slipped quietly away.

"Thank you again for your kindness. And now I must be on my way. *Khuda hafez.*"

Kareem had insisted on accompanying Jamil to make arrangements for the package delivery, offering his own phone number when the chaikhana owner demanded contact information. But as Jamil turned away to head once more toward the dirt track leading out of town, Kareem hastened his own steps to keep pace beside him. "Where do you go now?"

"I do not know yet," Jamil admitted. "Away from here."

"Then perhaps you would like to come with me." Kareem patted a bulging pack over his shoulder. Like his clothing, this was a foreign-made knapsack rather than a tied-up patu. "I have food and water enough for two."

Jamil slowed his pace fractionally. "Where would we go?"

"I heard a story in the last town that three Isa followers can be found in a village beyond those hills." The mountain flank Kareem indicated was the same Jamil had descended with Omed, but in the opposite direction. "I did not give the story much mind, since how could Isa followers live openly in Afghanistan? Yet here you are. And since I am sworn not to film you again, I thought I would look for these others. Such a story of freedom might indeed pay well. If you have no destination, I thought you might wish to meet others like yourself."

Jamil was torn. His heart had leaped within him at Kareem's words. Then there were others who'd come to see that only Isa Masih's teachings of love and peace and forgiveness could truly transform Afghanistan. And unlike Omed's household, these men were following Isa openly. The movement Jamil had hoped to start was already happening.

But he hesitated. What did he really know of Kareem? Suspiciously Jamil demanded, "How do I know you are what you say? You speak so easily of Isa Masih and freedom and *dee-mo-cra-see.* How do I know you are not a police spy who wishes to find these men only to make trouble for them? and me?"

Kareem seemed not at all perturbed at the accusations. "I am no spy, only a believer in freedom. My father was an educated man, a university professor. After the Taliban came, he took our family to New Delhi to live. It was a foreign Isa follower who helped us find refuge there. Christians, they call themselves. I have even read their writings of Isa. To love your neighbor. To do as you would have others do to you. They were good words I could wish to read again. But jobs are few for Afghans in India. And Kabul now has many free study programs paid for by the foreigners. So I returned here to become a journalist."

Jamil's suspicions were ebbing. "Then you too are a follower of Isa Masih? You understand how Isa's teachings alone can bring freedom to our country? true freedom that changes men's hearts from hate and war to love and peace and forgiveness?"

But Kareem's glance toward Jamil was almost pitying. "To bring such transformation requires that people not only hear these teachings but follow them. And that will never happen. People would rather hate and envy and seek power and riches for themselves. Was not Isa Masih himself killed because his countrymen did not wish to obey his teachings?"

Kareem made a dismissive gesture. "No, however good their sound, it will take more than beautiful words spoken long ago to change a people. Still, if those stories are but impossible tales, I believe you should have freedom to share them. All men should be free to seek knowledge where they wish. Which is why I wish to be a real journalist like those in other countries who know this freedom. And why I wish to interview these men who have found courage to proclaim themselves openly as followers of Isa."

"As would I," Jamil admitted. "I would be pleased to come with you. And if you truly wish to read Isa's words again, here." He drew a tiny, olive green volume from his pack. "This does not contain all of the holy book, but it holds the injils of Isa. It was given to me by an Isa follower, a foreigner like those you met who helps people in need."

"A woman, I am guessing?" Kareem's eyebrows rose knowingly. "The same whose voice brought such joy to your eyes?"

Jamil's mouth gaped. "How did you know?"

"I learned English in India," Kareem answered complacently. "You spoke of Isa and referred to her distant country. But if this is from such a friend, I would not take it from you."

"No, no." Jamil pushed the volume into Kareem's hand. "I have other copies now that contain all the holy book. I know she would be pleased if I gave this one to you. Only we must go now before we draw more attention."

The smallest jerk of Jamil's head indicated two men emerging from the market stalls to stare after them. One wore a black turban. The other was the health worker, Naveed. "Do you know how far this place is, and are you sure of the way?"

Without further protest, Kareem slid the olive green volume into his parka. "I will treasure your gift. As to the village we seek, I know only that it is this direction. But it cannot be too far if so many have heard of these Isa followers. We will ask along the way."

What's with you? Steve sternly asked himself yet again as armed guards waved his Pajero utility vehicle through the gates of a three-story mansion festooned with turrets, gables, balconies, and one tall, onion-domed tower. An array of reinforced Hummers, SUVs, and an armored BMW confirmed that the minister's convoy was back from the stadium. *It's hardly your business what Ms. Amy Mallory chooses as to perimeter defenses or associates!*

After all, Steve had neither expected nor planned to cross paths with the humanitarian aid worker again. He hadn't forgotten the look on Amy's face when he'd arrested her Afghan assistant. Nor her tears on their last encounter that made clear her concern for the failed suicide bomber was far more personal than Steve had assumed. He'd only been doing his job, both that day and on his first long-ago run-in with Jamil, which had set the whole nightmare in motion. But it was perhaps inevitable Amy wouldn't see it the same way. Which was why Steve had resisted every impulse to renew contact with the aid worker once he'd left Afghanistan.

So what had dropped Amy right into Steve's path after he'd finally succeeded in banishing her from his thoughts? *Hey, you're only back temporarily. Odds are you won't even see her again.*

Which didn't keep Steve from demanding as he entered the Condor Security command suite, "Bones, what's the status on that fiber-optic system over at Khalid's Wazir rental?"

Condor Security pilot and mechanic, Timothy "Bones" Bonefeole had helped Steve install the leftover fiber-optic fencing at the New Hope compound. He glanced up from a computer screen. "You didn't know that was down? Yeah, I guess you were out-of-country. It went off-line a couple weeks ago. I went over personally to check on it. But some local aristocrat type said Ms. Mallory was no longer in charge and that he'd ordered the wiring pulled out."

So Amy was no longer New Hope's country manager. Was that why she'd looked so unhappy when Steve mentioned changes? Not that it was any more Steve's concern than the aid worker's perimeter defenses or associates. Still, now that Steve was again Khalid's security chief, it *was* his business to check out the movements of any man who'd once tried to blow up his client.

"Wilson, you there?" Ian Grant's Kiwi drawl demanded over the intercom. "The minister's next appointment just showed. They've specifically asked for Khalid's head of security to sit in. With Myers gone, that would be you."

Steve pushed himself reluctantly to his feet. Jet lag and a long day were kicking in, and he took time to chug a can of Red Bull before heading down the hall. Three men were just emerging onto the second-floor landing from a broad, marble staircase. The tall, lean man in silk caftan and turban was Ismail, mujahedeen liaison and translator for Steve and Phil's Special Forces team back during the 2001 war of liberation, now Khalid's deputy minister. Steve had met both his companions. The heavily built man with iron gray hair and piercing blue eyes was Carl Bolton, deputy chief of mission to the U.S. ambassador. The fortyish blond crew cut with the muscled fitness of a soldier had been the speed dial Steve hit during the stadium riot, Dyncorp country manager Jason Hamilton.

As Ismail steered the embassy official toward Khalid's reception suite, Jason hurried down the hall to meet Steve. Shaking hands, Steve eyed the Dyncorp operative quizzically. "Great to see you again, man. I sure appreciated your help with our little situation this afternoon. Though I hadn't expected a personal report."

"Don't flatter yourself. This meeting's been on the books awhile. As you're aware, security for the upcoming elections falls under Ministry of Interior. And since our government's footing the bill—"

Jason gestured toward Bolton, disappearing with Ismail through a door ahead. "I'm tagging along because Dyncorp scooped the bid for training police and poll workers as well as general campaign security. With forty-plus candidates announcing their bid to date, we're counting on one major free-for-all."

Was there any pie in which Dyncorp *didn't* have a finger? Steve let out a small groan. "I picked the wrong time for a comeback. Just promise me Khalid isn't a serious contender."

"Are you kidding?" Jason grinned at Steve's sour tone. "Khalid's the favored front-runner."

Steve had no chance for response because Ismail was approaching to usher them into the reception suite.

Khalid hurried forward to welcome his guests with a hearty kiss on each cheek. As the group settled on leather sofas, servants passed around tea and pastries. DCM Carl Bolton waited for them to depart the room before broaching the meeting's agenda.

"Minister Khalid, I am pleased to bring good news that my government has just approved funding to add an additional twenty thousand police to your forces by election day." Bolton indicated his companion. "Dyncorp will be working with your ministry to provide the necessary trainers and equipment."

The following discussion didn't take long. Steve spotted Bolton slipping a discreet peek at his watch before the DCM cleared his throat. "I have a pressing engagement for which I'm running behind, so will need to excuse myself. But there is one final matter I've been instructed to address. First, let me say that my government congratulates you on your candidacy, Minister Khalid. Your success since taking over the interior ministry last year has not gone unnoticed. Your continued arrests and drug seizures are impressive. Afghanistan needs that kind of strong leadership if security and peace are to be achieved. As this afternoon's events demonstrated yet again. Your swift thinking and action in bringing about a peaceful resolution saved a lot of lives."

Khalid's swift thinking? Steve did not permit sardonic incredulity to touch an impassive expression as his client beamed gratification.

"However—" The deputy chief of mission cleared his throat again. "Favorably though my government views your candidacy, you will understand we must maintain a neutral stance toward the execution of Afghanistan's elections. At issue is our State Department funding of your security detail. Complaints of favoritism have already been lodged."

Yes, Steve could see how Khalid's oft-televised muscular expat bodyguards with their wraparound glasses and body armor might scream favoritism to opposition candidates. The minister abruptly lost his smile. His tone was aggrieved. "Who would dare complain that a servant of the Afghan people who has survived so many attacks on his life be afforded protection? Besides, is it not a good thing for the voters to see how our foreign allies value me?"

How to explain Western notions of democratic protocol and election fair play? Bolton made no effort. "Your main challenger, Anwar Qaderi, does not see it that way. You must be aware he's running on a platform of restoring respect for law and ending government corruption. As minister of justice, he's already made formal representation to our embassy that your expatriate security team constitutes both campaign fraud and intimidation of other candidates."

"Qaderi!" Khalid stiffened instantly. "Is this man not cause of enough insult?"

Steve knew exactly why the minister was so outraged. Shortly before Steve's departure from Kabul, the Afghan president had abruptly removed oversight of the country's prison system from its longstanding MOI control to the Ministry of Justice. Ceding to Qaderi a sizable chunk of his own power base had left Khalid livid.

"Have I not also pledged the Ministry of Interior to fight corruption?" Khalid went on angrily. "Do crowds not cheer when I appear? Do the world's cameras follow Qaderi around as they follow me? Or does Qaderi think to win treacherously by forcing you to abandon me to my enemies? If they tried to kill me before, what will they do now?"

The DCM raised a calming hand. "My government made a commitment to your protection when you had the courage to lead the Ministry of Interior after the tragic death of your predecessor. And we're aware the police still haven't determined who was behind those bombing attempts. Which is why we've chosen *not* to cancel your Condor Security contract. However, my own superiors insist any visible expatriate presence be removed from the political arena."

Bolton swung around to Steve. "I'm assuming this is doable, right, Wilson?"

So this was why Khalid's security chief had been asked to sit in. Steve took time to marshal his thoughts. Since his earlier exchange with Jason Hamilton, he'd been fighting to tamp down growing dismay and anger. If his client truly was a front-runner in this campaign, that was unfortunate enough. But for his own embassy to be offering Khalid such an enthusiastic green light?

Steve hadn't forgotten the shock of finding out just what sleight of hand had produced those impressive results to which Bolton referred. And Jason Hamilton at least, nodding solemnly beside Bolton, had seen a certain surveillance tape where a seizure of several thousand kilos of opium and hashish was revealed as a setup between Khalid, a district police chief, and an Uzbek warlord!

"Anything's doable," Steve answered slowly. "We've been running security training exercises for Khalid's personal militia since day one. And we've got Latin American and Nepalese hires who can pass as Afghans. Mixing them in with the best of Khalid's men would provide decent out-front coverage. What do you think, Ismail? You handle the militia. Can they do the job?"

Khalid's deputy had been listening in silence to the discussion till now. He spoke up smoothly, "But of course. Our men are fierce fighters, and you have trained them well. They will protect the minister with their lives."

"Then that settles it." Steve looked at Jason Hamilton. "And since Dyncorp has the overall campaign security contract, I assume there'll be no difficulty tucking behind-the-scenes expat personnel in with yours?"

"No problem," the Dyncorp operative agreed cordially.

The meeting didn't linger. Steve's mind was still seething as he accompanied the visitors down to their convoy. As a State Department security hireling, he'd been forced once already to bite his tongue while Khalid got away with the very corruption he'd just denounced. And speaking out now undoubtedly involved some conflict of interest. On the other hand, this time Steve was only a stand-in, and he'd never been one to back down from a fight.

Steve kept his tone quiet as they stepped through the pedestrian gate. "Look, Hamilton, I'm on board with the security revisions, but I've got problems with the other, and you know why."

His two companions exchanged glances. It was Bolton who gestured with grim authority toward a black SUV with red and white diplomatic plates. "Seems we need to have a talk. Would you mind stepping into my office?"

The SUV's backseats faced each other limo-style. Bolton leaned forward as soon as the three men were seated. "Let me guess. You've got intel on Khalid you wrongly assume I don't possess. So let me just lay it on the line. I've read your file, Wilson. Special Forces. Tours on the ground in Afghanistan and Iraq. So you must have studied the history books. Sure, it'd be nice to always deal with Mr. Pure-of-Heart in places like this. But we don't always get that choice. Sometimes pragmatism necessitates choosing allies who are at least strong enough to maintain order and security. Not to mention favorable to our own people."

"Khalid, you mean?" Steve demanded. "Surely the Afghans deserve a better alternative than a leader who's shown already he'll do whatever it takes to achieve his own ends."

"And that's a bad thing?" Bolton asked calmly. "What are the alternatives? Minister of Justice Qaderi? He's been growing in popularity, especially as rumblings of corruption and ineptitude in the current administration get louder. He's seen as a devout religious leader. He lives simply, no unaccounted income we know of. His family's well-known, and he's making lots of noise about reining in the warlords and fat cats in office getting rich off foreign money and bribes."

"And that's a bad thing?" Steve echoed.

"Maybe not. But let's not forget that same scenario pushed the Taliban into power. Qaderi is a fundamentalist mullah who's determined to roll back even modest gains in personal freedoms and enforce strict sharia law. More troubling, he's not favorably disposed toward the West, which he considers a morally corrupting influence in Afghanistan. The other candidates are mostly nonstarters. But now we've got Minister of Defense Rahmon jumping in with guns blazing. However atrocious his human rights record, he's still popular as a mujahedeen war hero against the Soviets.

"At least Khalid is solidly pro-West. He's popular with the press and the Afghan people, who are screaming for someone to restore order so they can go about their daily lives without getting shot or blown up. However he does it, Khalid has the strength of character and will to get things done. Given a free hand and his connections, he just might be able to enforce a reasonable stability. Which means, for one, we might be able to bring our troops home. I hope you've got enough soldier left in you to care about that."

Sure, and at what cost! Hadn't Saddam Hussein done that much? Hadn't he too been a favored American ally in his time? And yet Bolton had a point. The worst self-serving despot still offered more freedom than an Islamic theocracy. And wasn't it better to see in power a leader favorable to the West? Maybe even strong enough to enforce law and order around here?

Except how can anyone guarantee Khalid would turn out to be better? Again like Saddam Hussein. Or Chile's Pinochet. Panama's Noriega. All in their turn once favored American allies.

Steve was suddenly and intensely weary, and not just because he'd been up for over twenty-four hours, most of them squeezed into a coach airplane seat. This was a reminder of why he'd made the choice to leave Afghanistan.

If he'd been hoping to find something to believe in, he sure wouldn't find it here!

9

"We've divided the women and children from one dormitory among the others. So that salon will be available for Fatima to start classes again tomorrow. The children will continue chores in the afternoons. And I've talked to Ibrahim about vertical looms for the carpet workshop."

"All sounds good. Our Kabul station would appear to be in excellent hands, wouldn't you agree, Nestor?"

"Excellent! Excellent! Then you're definite about remaining up in Mazar-i-Sharif?" Though the three-way call was a convenient late afternoon for Amy in Kabul and Duane Gibson in northern Afghanistan, it was the crack of dawn for their mutual boss Nestor Korallis in D.C. But the elderly New Hope CEO sounded wide-awake and excited. "The board will be thrilled to see well-functioning centers in two sectors of Afghanistan."

"No point in tying Ms. Mallory and myself both down in Kabul," Duane agreed genially. "Not when we've got outstanding Afghan staff like Ibrahim and Soraya to pick up the slack. By the way, Amy, I've just signed off on one more change. You know I haven't been excited about depending on your prison parolees for the neighborhood literacy project. Especially now that Ibrahim needs them for the carpet workshop. I've been networking with a Swedish nonprofit that does similar projects. They have ample Kabul personnel, but no funds for school supplies and teacher salaries. They've agreed to take over our literacy outreach if we'll cover the resource end. A win-win for everyone."

Except that once again, a decision had been made concerning Amy's own project without consulting her. Nestor's presence on the line kept Amy's tone sweetly reasonable. "So did you have plans for the time I was investing into that project?"

"We've got plenty to fill your time, Amy. For one, I need on-site verification of those medical and school supplies before we send out another consignment. And an audit of inventory and funds. We don't want a repeat of our predecessors siphoning off resources into their own pockets."

Amy slapped her cell phone shut with unnecessary force as the conference call ended. She'd longed for another expatriate coworker to alleviate her load. Now that she'd gotten exactly what she wished for, she was less and less sure she wanted it.

Not that there was anything intrinsically wrong with Duane's decisions. His superior experience showed in everything he said and did. But Amy's vision for New Hope Foundation in Afghanistan was clearly very different from Duane's. Could Amy see herself for the foreseeable future checking off supply lists and accounting ledgers instead of working with living, breathing human beings?

At least there's still my Welayat women and children.

And speaking of supplies, Amy had been trying to find time all day to put together that package for Jamil. A box filled with medical supplies New Hope had been shipping to health outposts already sat on Amy's living suite table. Now she tucked in an envelope of afghanis that was her personal contribution before swaddling the package in brown wrapping paper and duct tape. Amy was struggling with the address when she heard soft noises outside in the hall, then a stealthy scrabbling at the base of her door.

Amy yanked open the door, expecting to find some of the children escaped from their chores. Instead she surprised Farah trying to slide the MP3 player under the door. The younger girl straightened up hastily. "I . . . It is my turn in the kitchen. I was carrying in market purchases for the chowkidar, and . . . and I did not wish this to become damaged or lost, so I came up here to return it."

"Well, thank you." Amy accepted the gadget as Farah pushed it at her. "But there's no hurry if you're still listening to it."

"No, no, I am finished." Farah shook her head with agitation. "And I must return to the kitchen before it is asked where I have gone."

The teenager was turning away when Amy had an idea. "Wait, Farah, maybe you can help me just a moment. If I give you an address, could you write it out for me? I'm trying to mail a package."

Farah's agitation gave way immediately to a pleased smile. "Be your assistant again? It would be my delight."

If the teenager felt curiosity at Jamil's name, she said nothing as she spelled it out in exquisite Arabic calligraphy, followed by the town Jamil had given on the phone. When Farah laid down the fine-tipped marker, Amy nodded toward the MP3 player sitting beside the package. "So what did you think of the stories?"

Farah's shrug was noncommittal. "Are they true? these tales of Isa?"

"Yes, they are true. Like the story of paradise. All the stories I have told you are true."

"Then your Isa was indeed a good man and kind to women and children as well as men. It is too bad he should have been killed. If such a prophet lived today, perhaps our world would be different."

"But he is alive. That's why—" Amy broke off at a knock on the doorjamb.

A stooped figure draped in a black chador—the chowkidar's wife, Hamida. Farah slid hastily past her as the woman murmured timidly, "Rasheed says to inform you there are foreign women at the gate asking for you."

Amy was not expecting visitors. Who could it be? She hurried downstairs and along the cobblestone path. The guard had already ushered through the gate a quartet of women in headscarves and winter chapans. One was much taller than the rest, and her headscarf was pushed back, revealing a tawny brush cut.

"*Guten Tag*, Amy Mallory."

"Elsa! How good to see you." A German anthropologist, Elsa Leister had been a fellow boarder in the expat guesthouse during Amy's first days in Kabul. "But I thought you'd gone back to Germany."

"I am back for a short time. My government approved my study on the continuing sad plight of Afghan women. I have now been assigned to administer a foreign aid grant for advancing women's rights in Afghanistan. Perhaps you've heard of the organization with which I am partnering, AWR?"

Elsa indicated the three women with her. Two were youngish, though ages were hard to judge in Afghanistan, where girls were mothers before they were teenagers and life expectancy was little more than forty years. A third was wrinkled, stooped, and white-haired with age. "If you permit, I wished to show them what you have accomplished here."

"I would be delighted." Amy offered her guests the traditional Afghan greeting of a kiss on each cheek with as much awe as pleasure. The Afghan Women's Revolution was a legendary underground movement of Afghan women who'd kept alive clandestine girls' schools, women's clinics, even beauty salons during Taliban years. Since the fall of Taliban rule, they continued to battle for an end to such cruel injustices as had put Amy's own New Hope residents in prison. In Dari, Amy added, "I am honored to have you here."

Behind Amy, wild yapping was making conversation difficult. With classes not yet resumed, the older children were taking advantage of having finished daily chores by kicking soccer balls around the sawdust that had held the jungle gym. The half-grown puppy's antics as Gorg dashed from one ball to another were so funny that the children were laughing as hard as they played. The oldest Afghan woman nodded toward the giggling children.

"I approve the utilization of the young wolf. A small investment to bring such joy. My countrymen much underestimate the power of laughter and a pet such as this to heal emotional trauma."

The elderly AWR leader's English was perfect and American in accent. Amy was startled enough to catch her sandal on a cobblestone. As the old woman put out a hand to steady her, Amy caught a twinkle in her shrewd gaze. "You look surprised to hear your language. I graduated from the American University here in Kabul before the Soviets came. I was the first woman to earn a medical degree."

"Dr. Amrita is founder of AWR," Elsa put in. "She is among those who risked her life giving medical treatment to women here in Kabul when the

Taliban closed down the women's clinics. Faiqa and Masooda both taught underground girls' schools."

The two younger women clearly spoke no English, but they'd caught their own names, smiling and nodding as Elsa gestured toward them. As they continued along the path, Dr. Amrita handed Amy a dog-eared, black-and-white photo. The snapshot was of a group of girls strolling a street Amy recognized as central Kabul. Their heads were uncovered, and they wore short black skirts, nylons, and high heels.

Dr. Amrita tapped one of the girls in the photo. "Myself when I studied at the university in 1965. Too many say it is acceptable to lock our women away and treat them as less than human because this is the Afghan way. But you can see we were once free, at least the educated people in the cities. Did we not worship God? Were we atheists and Communists? No! But then it was our choice to pray, to live, to study.

"The Taliban took choice and made it force. But these men your own government has put into power, the warlords and corrupt politicians, are they any different? If within my lifetime, we once knew freedom under Afghan rule, how is it that with all the weapons and might and money your government pours into my country, you cannot give my granddaughter the freedom I had as a young woman? This . . . *this* is the new Afghanistan!"

The elderly AWR leader passed Amy more photos. All of young girls, they were horrible enough Amy could barely glance at them. Dr. Amrita tapped one. "This is Shiquiba. She was seven years old when she was raped by young men in her village. They said it was her fault because she walked with uncovered hair. This girl Bashira was twelve when her brother was spied conversing with a young woman of prominent family. The young woman's brother slit Bashira's throat after he and his friends raped her. But his father is a member of parliament, so he was not even arrested. And this girl set herself on fire to escape the beatings of her mother-in-law and husband. She was thirteen."

Like Parvati and Najeeda, the girl in the last photo was a mass of scar tissue. Amy discovered that her hands were trembling as she passed the photos back to Dr. Amrita. Was there no limit to the brutality one human could inflict on another?

Dr. Amrita tucked the photos back into her tunic. "All these pictures were taken within this last month. Elsa tells me you have given refuge to many such Afghan women who were prisoners. AWR has long desired to see such a sanctuary in every city. Now with Elsa's partnership, this will be possible. And if we begin with released prisoners, perhaps some of those women abused at home will find courage to escape to us before they end up in prison or dead. But come, let us see what you have done here."

Since Elsa spoke no Dari, Amy gave an overview in English as she walked the group through dormitories, infirmary, carpet-weaving workshop, letting Dr. Amrita murmur a translation to her two colleagues. The AWR delegation offered no comments, but Amy grew increasingly conscious of the male clerks and mechanics and customers crowding downstairs salons and yard, Ibrahim's cousin squatting among the carpet weavers so they had to keep scarves drawn even as they bent over their looms.

"Originally, we had . . . ," Amy found herself explaining over and over. "But now with the changes . . ."

Dr. Amrita looked thoughtful as Amy led the group back down the cobblestone path. At the gate, she turned to Amy. "Ms. Mallory, what you have done here shows a good heart. But I must tell you it is evident this place is no longer a sanctuary for women and children, rather a stronghold for men's doings. And property in Wazir Akbar Khan is expensive to maintain. We are negotiating now for a property outside the city. The house is not so large as this, but within its walls are more than ten acres with fruit orchards and a well to water a garden. We will have a school, at least for the lower grades. And a clinic."

"What are you suggesting?" Amy responded slowly. "That we not take in any more prisoners here, but send them to you?"

"Not only that. If you wish, your women and children can be the first of its residents. If all goes well, we will be ready to receive them within a few weeks. I can guarantee your residents would find a home and refuge, not a place of business." With a smile, the elderly doctor added, "And your *gorg* as well, if you would like him to come."

Dr. Amrita's offer was exactly the kind of self-sustaining, locally spearheaded project that had been Amy's original vision. For Farah too, this could be an answer. Here were independent, educated Afghan women standing up for other Afghan women and working together for the future of their country. Surely they were far better role models for the sixteen-year-old than a foreigner like Amy could hope to be.

So why was Amy hesitating now? *Because it wouldn't be mine! I've poured my heart and soul into this place. And now I feel it's being taken away from me, one piece at a time.*

Amy summoned up an appreciative smile. "I'll have to run this by my own superior. I'll get back to you as soon as we've made a decision."

In the end, it took four days of arduous hiking. Each additional ridge over which Jamil and Kareem scrambled led higher into the Himalayan foothills until they were back in the chill bite of winter Jamil had eluded by heading to the southern plains.

The few men Jamil and Kareem encountered on narrow, crisscrossing trails were hard-faced, their wary gazes patently suspicious of strangers wandering their hills. This was mujahedeen country, and it would seem not all had declared a cease-fire.

Jamil could be thankful now for the worn shabbiness of his shalwar kameez, the untrimmed growth of hair and beard. But not even rubbing dust over Western clothing and parka could transform his companion from a well-fed urbanite. The third time Kareem introduced himself as a journalist, showing off his phone's video capacity as proof, Jamil had intervened. The shepherd herding winter-thin goats didn't know what a journalist was, but covetous eyes on the satellite phone made Jamil uneasy. By good fortune, he'd carried no weapons, and though he'd trailed Jamil and Kareem for a distance, the scattering of his flock eventually turned him back.

On the fifth morning, they'd come across a small boy who'd insisted he knew the village in question. By then Jamil's and Kareem's water bottles were empty, only crumbs left of their food. So it was with relief that the pair crested the next rocky ridge to discover their latest guide had not been spinning another tale.

A shallow gorge below held orchards of almond and apricot and mulberry trees while tilled fields along a meandering stream promised a generous poppy crop. All enough to sustain a sizable village as well as a chaikhana. The two travelers found the chaikhana's single large room busy with customers lounging on tushaks with tea glasses and a hookah. A whiff told Jamil it was hashish the smokers were passing around, not tobacco. While Kareem purchased food and refilled their water bottles, Jamil made inquiries. The hashish smokers responded without hesitation.

Yes, it was true there were three Isa followers in this village.

No, it would be no problem to take the new arrivals to see them.

Jamil could hardly contain his excitement as he and Kareem followed a knot of village men through a mulberry grove. Only now that the prospect was before him to meet other Isa followers could he acknowledge how alone he had felt. Though Ameera had taught him much about the prophet she followed, she was from another world. But these Isa followers were of his own people. Isa Masih's "kingdom of the heart" that had so fired Jamil's imagination was indeed coming to pass. Maybe he could stay with them awhile. Learn from them.

The grove petered out into a slope that marked the boundary of the mountain gorge, too rocky for cropland. Mounds of whitewashed stones studded the slope. Green flags thrust among the stones fluttered in the wind. A cold lump was growing in Jamil's breast as he recognized where he stood. This was a graveyard.

Before Jamil could force a question through dry lips, one of their guides waved a hand at the mounds, his laughter the silly giggle of too much hashish smoke. "Did we not say they are here? We knew when three of our village became Isa followers that one day the authorities would come to demand account. To save trouble from descending upon our families, we have dealt with the matter ourselves. You may go back and report that all of us here are faithful followers of Islam, and none dare accuse us otherwise."

It was only as the man's appalling statement sank in that Jamil realized all the mounds were not the same. Three of them, laid out in a row, bore no green flag but a pair of sticks lashed vertically to each other.

Three crosses.

10

"Sorry it's taken this long to get back."

Steve scanned a single sheet the Condor Security command suite fax had just spit out as the embassy techie on the phone line went on.

"You did say it wasn't high priority, and as you can guess, monitoring warlord phones for the Kandahar offensive has taken precedence over civilian contracts. Anyway, we traced the receiving number and time frame you specified to a call made down south in the Kandahar area."

The fax included exact coordinates. So Jamil had not left Afghanistan. What had he been up to these last weeks? And in a region currently a hotbed of insurgent unrest?

The easiest way to find out would be simply to ask the person Jamil had bothered to call. Steve hadn't spoken with Amy Mallory since the stadium riot. He'd been on an urgent call when she'd left a polite thank-you on his voice message service. When Steve eventually called back, he'd gotten Amy's own voice mail. He'd opted not to leave a message. After all, her thank-you had been courteous but final.

The techie was still talking. "The call in question came from a sat phone, top-of-the-line. The billing is an American expense account. State Department, in fact. Some kind of Afghan media project they're sponsoring. The phone log reveals several video segments uploaded from the same location around the same time frame. I tracked them to YouTube, if you think they're relevant. You've got the links on the intel sheet I faxed over."

A media project? Before the techie had rung off, Steve was pulling up

Internet access at the nearest computer station. Had he inadvertently given wrong data to the embassy technician?

The first link would seem to confirm that. Some local news story of a rural carpet-weaving co-op. But the second—

Steve frowned. Even with the scant night-lighting of a kerosene lantern, there was a definite familiarity about a slimly muscled Afghan male with dark, curly hair and beard dominating the news clip.

Steve watched the YouTube entry run its entire course before hitting a speed-dial number.

"Amy, is everything okay?"

Startled, Amy looked up from the meatballs she was scooping onto her plate. She'd thought her inner turmoil was under enough control not to show. But then Becky Frazer knew Amy better than anyone else at this potluck dinner.

Since her return to Kabul, Amy hadn't seen the American nurse-practitioner who'd been so helpful with her New Hope residents. Last Friday she'd been too caught up with visiting Mina and Aryana, then the stadium riot, to make the expatriate worship gathering, hosted this week by the humanitarian mission with which Becky worked. Tables set up for potluck in the compound's main assembly hall would be replaced with chairs for the following worship time.

Amy dredged up a smile. "Sure, everything's fine. Why do you ask?"

Certainly the remainder of the week since Elsa brought her AWR colleagues to visit had gone smoothly enough. Classes and the reduced work schedule were going well, despite some grumbling from Ibrahim and his cousin. Amy had tracked down the aid organization distributing vertical looms and scheduled a demonstration at New Hope. She'd spent countless hours checking the paperwork against actual delivery on those medical and school supplies Duane had referenced.

She'd also mailed Jamil's package. Had he ever received it? Amy had used the shipping service that delivered New Hope supplies, so the package should have arrived at least two days ago. But though Amy had kept her cell phone close, Jamil hadn't yet called. Soraya had confirmed Farah's careful penmanship, so mislabeling wasn't the problem.

Farah.

After returning the MP3 player, the teenager had reverted to her usual cheerful, hardworking self. The last several evenings since finishing the Joshua story, Amy had turned the flannelgraph over for Farah to work her way through Creation and paradise, always favorites with the New Hope residents. Amy had once smiled to see the younger girl mimicking her own exact facial expressions and gestures. But now Farah had made the stories her own, narrating them with such grace and dramatic imagery Amy was happy to abandon her own stumbling Dari. Each day Amy found herself more impressed with the Afghan teenager's abilities and potential. If only she could believe this current smiling, confident veneer was the real Farah and not a protective shield hiding a frightened, unhappy little girl.

Becky Frazer was still eyeing Amy with a quizzical expression. So Amy added quickly, "Two more women left this morning and five of the children."

Both brides had satisfied Amy they were leaving willingly, so there was no reason why Amy had to blink to clear a sudden mist from her eyes. Setting her own plate down on the buffet table, Becky lifted Amy's from her hands.

"Come with me, dear. No one's going to miss us if we disappear for a bit."

Staff quarters were a motel-style row of apartments across a paved courtyard. Becky unlocked her own door and ushered Amy into a minuscule living room. "Okay, dear, I know you well enough to see something's eating at you."

Amy slumped onto a sofa. "Oh, Becky, I don't know how much longer I can do this. I don't see how you've done it all these years."

The older woman dropped down beside her. "Do what, exactly?"

"Keep pouring yourself into people, only to have them taken away. The children especially. I know we're not supposed to become emotionally involved. And when I was doing disaster relief, that wasn't a problem.

I never got to know the people. But here. These precious, beautiful children. And their mothers. I've come to care about them so deeply."

The tears were pouring down Amy's cheeks now. "It would be easier if I thought they were all okay. But they're not! Little Fahim and Tamana, I know they're not happy. Nor Mina, though she'd never say. Fahim wanted to study. Now he has to work instead. And Tamana. How long before she's handed over to her own stepbrother or whichever man offers her new stepdad enough money? And the ones still left at New Hope. They need a better living situation. I've even got a group willing to receive them. But how do I just turn my Welayat women and children over to strangers who may not care for them as much as I do? Like Farah. She's so smart and eager, and she seems to believe I'm some superwoman who can whisk her away from the awful life she's had and guarantee she'll never have to go back. Except I can't give her that promise!"

Amy wiped a hand across her eyes. "What I want most is to let them know that the Creator whose stories they've been hearing really is there for them. That he loves them enough to send a Savior who gave his life for them. But I'm not allowed to do that. And now they're leaving me one by one. It's breaking my heart, especially to think of the children out there, maybe afraid and unhappy, and too far away to ever let them know how much I still love them. Or even to find out what happens to them. Which maybe shows I'm not right for this kind of work. I don't know how you've kept doing it all these years when I'm ready to throw in the towel after just a few months."

Becky's arm came around Amy's shoulders. "Oh, honey, do you think my heart hasn't broken a time or two? That doesn't mean you're wrong for the job. It shows how much you care. And what better quality for a job like this! But you need to keep in mind just whose love you're here to show these people. Yes, your New Hope children may move beyond your reach. You may never in this lifetime find out what's happened to them. But do you think your heavenly Father loves these children less than you do? And he knows exactly where they are. He sees every moment of their day and night. Let me tell you a story."

Becky pulled a tissue from a box sitting handily on a coffee table. As Amy mopped her cheeks, the nurse-practitioner went on musingly. "I'll never forget the first little boy I ever lost my heart to here in Afghanistan. His name was Sami, maybe seven years old. This was back before the Soviet invasion, when Kabul was full of expat hippies looking for cheap heroin, girls went to school in miniskirts, and no one cared what you taught to a bunch of street orphans. That building where we now have the vocational institute was a boys' home. As a brand-new medical volunteer, I practiced my Dari telling stories of Isa Masih. I'd walk in to find little Sami with the smaller boys, repeating those stories just as I'd told them."

Like Farah.

"Then came the Soviet invasion. We were all evacuated. I cried the whole flight home. I felt I'd betrayed those kids, especially Sami. But I never stopped praying for them. Or loving them. I didn't make it back to Kabul until the Soviets pulled out. By then the mujahedeen were smashing things up. Then the Taliban. I couldn't find out what had happened to those boys. Until one trip home, I met an Afghan refugee at a church where I was speaking. His name was Sami."

As Amy sat up abruptly, Becky nodded. "That's right, the same Sami. He'd ended up in a Pakistani refugee camp, where he met Christian aid workers. He eventually came to know Isa Masih, made his way to the States, married an American. But he still remembered the stories I told in the boys' home. Now he's got a ministry producing dramatized Dari Bible stories."

"I think I have some of them," Amy said slowly. "What an incredible coincidence."

"In God's economy, there are no coincidences," Becky said definitively. "All those years I'd thought Sami lost, maybe even dead, God was working out his own plans in Sami's life. I've never tracked down any of those other boys. But I'm so thankful God allowed me to find out what happened to Sami. Because it helped me grasp that I can love people for however short or long a time God puts them into my path. But I can also let them go. Because even if I don't know where so many lost children like Sami have ended up, they have a heavenly Father who loves them more than I ever will. And who can make it possible for them to come face-to-face with Isa Masih's love, even if I'm not there."

"Like Joshua." Amy repeated the words she'd taught in Dari to the New

Hope children. "'Do not be terrified; do not be discouraged, for the Lord your God will be with you wherever you go.'"

Little Tamana, Fahim, all the others, you know those truths. You've heard the stories. David with Goliath. Daniel in the lions' den. Joseph frightened in a strange land. Adam and Eve with paradise lost being promised a Savior. Hold on to them tight. May your Creator God bring them to your mind and bring into your path those who will love you and point you to him.

"Is that all that's bothering you, dear?" Becky's kindly blue eyes were still sharp on Amy's face. "You seem very . . . alone."

The understanding in Becky's tone broke down Amy's remaining defenses. "I . . . I do feel alone even with Soraya's family and all the women and children. I thought it would be easier now working with another American. But we just don't think alike. I want to help change people's lives. Duane figures Afghan lives are none of our business, only their physical needs. And of course he is the boss now."

"Maybe you should consider changing employers," Becky offered sagely. "We could always use your skills here. The salary isn't a lot. But we have each other for fellowship and support. We pray together. Share our struggles. Laugh and cry on each other's shoulders."

"You don't know how much I'd like to say yes," Amy said. "But I can't leave New Hope now. And not just because I still have a contract and school loans to pay off. No matter how frustrating, I can't simply walk away from the Welayat women and children. Or Farah. Especially Farah."

"Well, you do what you feel God is calling you to do. Meanwhile, there's no reason to be alone. And I don't mean hanging out with an old spinster like me. Whatever happened to your American soldier friend I met that day at New Hope? He seemed such a sweet person, so helpful in the situation."

"Sweet?" The image brought a wry smile to Amy's mouth. "Steve Wilson is a lot of things, but sweet isn't an adjective I'd have picked. Actually, he is back in Kabul, though I don't expect to see him again."

Spilling her guts on Becky's shoulder had banished Amy's earlier fidgeting for her phone to ring, so when it did, she was taken by surprise. She snatched the phone from a side pocket of her knapsack.

But the caller ID was not the one she'd been hoping for.

"Amy? We need to talk."

After her initial disappointment, Amy wasn't sorry to hear the security contractor's abrupt tones. As she'd resolved, she'd called Steve the evening of the stadium incident to reiterate her thanks. Drained from dealing with Farah, she'd been relieved to get his voice mail. When she'd heard nothing back, she'd debated calling again to thank Steve personally. The memory of that swarming mob, Steve in full security gear and machine gun, the soldiers and tanks and personnel carriers, had deterred Amy. The contractor was occupied with far more urgent matters than rescuing stray aid workers.

Still, here was an opportunity to satisfy Amy's personal standards of courtesy. "I'm glad you called. I've been wanting to thank you properly for intervening at the stadium the other day. I left you a voice message, but I did want to express in person how much Farah and I appreciated it."

"Yes, I got the message. No big deal, really." Steve's baritone drawl sounded uncomfortable with her thanks. "But that's not why I called. Have you *any* idea what your suicide bomber pal Jamil is up to this time?"

"Jamil? I don't understand. What do you have to do with Jamil? Have you actually seen him? Wait, you haven't—?" Sudden suspicion cooled Amy's tone. "You did say you wouldn't bother Jamil anymore. That he was free to go."

"No, I did not arrest your pal again!" Now the drawl sounded exasperated. "Nor have I seen him. Except all over the news."

"The news?" Amy repeated blankly. "But . . . I talked with Jamil just last week. He's been out in the middle of nowhere minding his own business. Why would he be on the news?"

"It's not something I can explain over the phone. I'll need to show you. Are you at your compound?"

"Actually, I'm over at Becky Frazer's. You remember her, the American nurse who's been helping me at New Hope? She's with the Afghan Relief Mission, if you know where their compound is over by the main market."

"I know it. I'll be right over. Don't leave before I get there."

"I'm not going anywhere. We're about to start the expat wor—"

But Steve had already hung up.

"—ship gathering," Amy finished to herself.

It had taken only two days to make it back to Omed's town, an indication of how far astray they'd wandered. Jamil spoke only to discuss their route. Kareem hadn't tried to intrude on Jamil's dark mood, his own cheerful effervescence vanished. The young journalist had seemed stunned, even dazed, at the outcome of their trek. He'd made no attempt to pull out his cell phone to shoot footage or conduct interviews. Nor had he objected to Jamil's insistence that they leave the village without taking advantage of the chaikhana's lodging for the night. Leading the way out of the gorge, Jamil had set a breakneck pace down the mountain until it grew so dark they were in danger of wandering over a precipice.

By the next night they were far enough down the mountain, Jamil no longer shivered under his patu. But the turmoil of his thoughts remained no less chilled. Had Kareem been right, then? Was Jamil's dream of a "kingdom of heaven" spreading across the country he loved only that— a dream? After all, how long had it been since Isa Masih had walked dusty roads, healing and preaching his message of peace? If all these centuries had not produced the peace and love and kindness of Isa's kingdom, maybe it was futile to dream of men changing their minds and ways.

The sun's climb into the sky was past its midday apex when Jamil and Kareem scrambled down the last ridge to drop onto the track leading into Omed's town. Jamil had no desire for a confrontation with the village leaders who'd demanded his departure, so he led his companion around the perimeter of the town to come in on the opposite side near Omed's compound.

"Unless you have other lodging, I am confident Omed will give us both hospitality for the night," Jamil was saying over his shoulder to Kareem as they threaded through a narrow dirt lane. "If the package I am awaiting is here, I will leave in the morning. Otherwise, I must wait. And what of you? It is Friday market again, so transportation will be easy enough to find."

"Yes, I need to start back to Kabul, tonight if possible." Kareem had unearthed his cell phone as soon as they'd reached the town, and he lingered several steps behind Jamil, fingers flying over the keypad. His tone turned somber. "I do not think the story of these past days is one I will choose to report."

It was the younger man's first comment on what they'd encountered. Jamil didn't answer. The alley he'd chosen did not, as he'd estimated, lead directly to Omed's front door. Instead the far end opened onto the town commons. Though this was market day, its buzz of activity was not from shoppers. Jamil counted at least a dozen gray-blue uniforms and two olive green pickups. What in this small town could prompt such a sizable incursion of the Afghan National Police? Outside the carpet workshop, the uniforms held at least one man captive, down on his knees in the dust, hands bound behind his back.

Kareem hurried up on Jamil's heels, his round features draining of blood as he took in the police activity. "I checked my messages. My employers say the story I sent on the carpet weavers was so well-received by the foreign media, they chose to use it as well as the story on you. I . . . Surely all this could not be related. Perhaps they seek opium growers. Still, it might be wisest to leave."

But it was too late for retreat.

"There he is! That is the man! The healer who was here."

A dozen uniforms were now running their way, raised weapons discouraging any thoughts of flight. Though Jamil would not have fled if he could because he'd now identified the captive kneeling in the dust across the common area. The man who'd brought him here and offered such warm hospitality.

Omed.

11

Steve knew the Afghan Relief Mission compound, as he'd committed to memory every major expat and government facility in Kabul. Slowing to a crawl, he eased the Pajero through a congestion of stalls, foot vendors, and shoppers. Kabul's biggest open-air market was always busy, but especially on the Friday weekend when residents had the day off. Turning down a side street, Steve had no difficulty determining which compound harbored an expat organization. A line of SUVs and minivans was inching forward to enter the gate, a tall, rawboned man with graying blond hair waving them through one at a time. Was Steve crashing some humanitarian social event?

Nor was Steve the only one wondering. Shoppers from that busy market had drifted down the dirt lane to check out the commotion. Steve didn't care for the warring inquisitiveness and hostility he saw in their faces. More observers lined balconies of an apartment building across the street.

The Pajero rolled up to the gate. At a sharp rap on the glass, Steve lowered his window. The graying blond man peered inside. Evidently satisfied, he waved the vehicle forward, saying with a strong Scandinavian accent, "Welcome. The worship gathering is about to start. Follow the crowd to that building."

The worship gathering. Steve's mouth twisted wryly as he followed a Land Cruiser to park in a grassy area. That was what Amy had started to say just as he'd hung up. In Kabul, where Sunday was a workday even for expat aid organizations, it made sense they'd hold it on the local weekend.

I'll be in and out as quick as I can get some answers.

The compound was a large one, its main building a three-story brick cube. Stragglers milled around in front, their cheerful conversation a babble of English, German, French, even what sounded like Korean. Steve scanned the yard in hopes of spotting Amy. Though as he did so, he knew it to be futile. Through an open door, an electronic keyboard was already playing, latecomers hurrying that direction. With resignation, Steve trailed an Asian couple with three small children into a sizable assembly hall filled with folding chairs.

In all his years overseas, Steve had rarely visited an international church. The armed services had their own chaplains, and as a private security contractor, he'd usually been attached to some American military operation. This group was bigger than he'd expected and of varying nationalities. Most of the women wore the loose tunic over pantaloons that Steve had seen Amy wearing, a practical adaptation considering local dress restrictions for even Western women. Though here they'd thrown off headscarves. Many of the expat males also wore native shalwar kameez.

Afghan clothing wasn't the only difference. Whether military, embassy, or private contractors, most expats Steve encountered were youngish and unattached, overseas for too short a time frame to justify bringing family. Here were all ages from babies to white hair. The Asian kids Steve had trailed were now joyously hailing a pack of redheaded siblings. Scottish and Filipino, from their parents' calmer greetings. What kind of people brought children to live in a place like Kabul?

Steve hadn't yet spotted Amy when a guitar joined the electronic keyboard and the congregation rustled to its collective feet. The singing was in English, lingua franca of the expat world. "Our God is an awesome God."

So much for pulling Amy aside for a quick exchange! Steve could retreat, but he'd just spotted a platinum spill of hair halfway down a row. Besides, when had *retreat* entered Steve's vocabulary? This might even prove educational. These civilians in local dress singing with such sincerity of a faith they were forbidden to mention outside these walls represented

Ms. Amy Mallory's world. A world Steve found baffling, infuriating, and yet, however reluctantly, of curious fascination.

Resigning himself, Steve stepped to an empty chair at the end of Amy's row. An older woman Steve recognized from the day of the New Hope explosion was singing energetically beside Amy. The American nurse Becky Frazer. Had Amy even noticed Steve's entrance?

That question was answered as the aid worker turned her head. A hazel gaze met Steve's eyes squarely, and her mouth curved fractionally. Chuckling inside no doubt to witness Steve trapped by his own hastiness in the very kind of crowd he'd told Amy he avoided at all cost!

But Amy's smile curved further to diffident welcome, and her female neighbor's nod of recognition held unabashed approval. Steve's own mouth tilted in a reluctant grin. Then he remembered what errand brought him here, and his grin evaporated. Down the row, Amy's mouth immediately lost its curve, and she turned her head away.

The music stopped, and the congregation sat down. The guitarist, a slim, sunburned young man in shalwar kameez, handed his instrument to a brunette woman who'd been playing the keyboard. As he opened a Bible, Steve surreptitiously keyed his iPhone. Cougar, the CS logistics manager, was paging him. Steve sent a text message before returning his attention to the speaker.

"So just why are we here? Oh, I know the vocations that bring many of you to Kabul." The speaker's accent was American Midwest. "We've got here today surgeons." A gesture indicated the Asian couple, then moved on to the Scottish family. "Bush pilots."

He nodded toward the tall Scandinavian who'd manned the gate. "Engineers. Some of you are medical personnel or literacy teachers. Some have been here longer than I've been alive."

From the laughter, his audience knew well the indicated white-haired couple. The speaker turned to a college-age knot. "And some are new to our community and maybe not sure why you're here at all. I can tell you that if you came thinking your services can fix Afghanistan, you'll be sadly disillusioned. Those who've been here longest know what I'm talking about. This very facility where we're sitting has served the people of Afghanistan for more than fifty years. And yet for all their decades of hard labor, do we see today one whit less poverty, violence, drug addiction, injustice, or corruption?"

Steve straightened up, resignation giving way to downright approval. Steve himself had once tried to offer these very truths to a greenhorn aid worker. And been slapped down hard for his honest assessment. Steve's glance slid to Amy. Her eyes were on the speaker, and in her profile Steve detected nothing but thoughtful interest.

"So why are any of us still here? Why *should* we be here? Why expend our lives, our families' comfort and security, the generous donations of churches and individuals, on a country, a people whose problems can be ascribed as much to their own bad choices as to outside aggression or catastrophe?"

Yes, why? Steve wouldn't have expected a civilian to get it so right, if this seemed an odd sermon for a bunch of humanitarian workers.

"Except we might ask the same question as to why our Creator should look down at a violence-racked, greedy, self-centered human race and still bother to clothe himself in human flesh, stepping into our midst in the person of Isa Masih, Jesus Christ. To walk our dirty streets, not as a king but as a servant. To heal our hurts and grief with his compassionate touch. To lay down his own life on a cross for our redemption. What could motivate such a seemingly absurd, irrational act?

"Romans chapter 5 answers that question unambiguously. 'You see, at just the right time, when we were still powerless, Christ died for the ungodly. Very rarely will anyone die for a righteous man, though for a good person someone might possibly dare to die. But God demonstrates his own love for us in this: while we were still sinners, Christ died for us.'

"Love. It's that simple. Unconditional, undeserved, and utterly unimaginable love."

Steve was no longer mentally tapping a foot for this to be over but was caught by the passion in this speaker's words.

"Aren't you glad our Creator didn't wait until we deserved it to offer up his life for us? I know I am. And right there's why I'm still in Afghanistan. Why I know many of you are here. Christ's love burning in us, vessels as cracked and undeserving as any Taliban, for the Afghan people.

"You see, it's not our responsibility to change this country. It isn't even our responsibility to change hearts. We're called simply to be a channel of Isa Masih's love to a lost and broken people. To be his hands and feet in this difficult place. Because if we aren't willing to do it, who will?"

Reaching for his guitar, the speaker ended the service with a song familiar to Steve because it had been one of Rev Garwood's favorites in the days when he'd dragged a Special Forces recruit to sing in his choir. A song that held a special meaning for a team of young warriors heading into danger. As it clearly held for these people as well.

Steve held himself completely rigid as the chorus rose around him. "'There is no greater love than this, no greater love than this, that a man should give his life to save another.'"

The congregation stood for the second verse, the words somewhat different from what Steve remembered. "'In going or in giving, in dying or in living, I'll show Afghanistan it has a friend.'"

Steve rose with them and took the opportunity to step unobtrusively to the door, then stride swiftly out of the building. But the chorus followed him across the yard. "'There is no greater love than this . . . that a man should give his life to save another.'"

Steve was back in the mountains of Spin Boldak on the Pakistan border, kneeling in dirt made muddy by blood. Beside him, Phil as unit medic worked frantically to load intestines back into a fellow soldier's stomach. It was Private First Class Devon Archer's first combat mission. The evening before, they'd celebrated the young Army Ranger's birthday. Then came the patrol and a surprise ambush. If Devon hadn't stepped into the salvo of AK-47 rounds to toss a grenade, the whole unit would have been goners.

He'd gripped Steve's hand tight as they waited for the medevac chopper. "Sing that song of Rev's, Willie. You know the one."

And Steve had sung it, softly in case any more insurgents waited nearby to draw a bead on them. Before he'd finished the chorus, Phil had reached a hand to close wide-open eyes. At age twenty-one and a day, Private Devon Archer had earned himself the Medal of Honor for conspicuous bravery in the face of enemy fire. Like so many such awards, its granting had been posthumous, a meager consolation to the parents who'd received it in place of their son.

"'There is no greater love than this, no greater love than this; make me willing, Lord, at least to help my brother.'"

As the song ended, worshipers poured into the compound yard. Steve's first impulse was a hasty retreat out the gate. But he'd not yet carried out his errand, and Steve wasn't about to waste more time abandoning it for later. Amy hadn't emerged, and the last thing Steve wanted was to be drawn into conversation by some stranger trying to be courteous. So he stepped over to the perimeter wall, tilting his head back to study its defenses while keeping a peripheral eye out for Amy.

"PSC or active military?"

Steve spun around. Standing a few feet away was the young man in local dress who'd been guitarist and preacher. Though not so young as Steve had calculated at a distance. Care lines radiated from steady, blue eyes. Grooves deeply etched from nostrils to mouth bespoke of some hard living. More like Steve's own age of thirty.

"Excuse me?"

"It's the walk. And the way you're staring at that wall like you're assessing threat level. Special Ops, I'm guessing. I ran into enough of you guys during liberation when you were dropping in all around us. By the way, if you've got some suggestions, I'll be grateful to hear them. I recently found myself responsible for security around here."

The man grinned as he thrust out a hand. "Guess I should introduce myself. John Atkins, American. I was in the Panjsheer Valley doing food relief during Operation Enduring Freedom. Been down in Kandahar the last few years. After a colleague was kidnapped and killed a few months back, the rest of us were relocated here. If we've already met, forgive me. I'm still sorting out the congregation since I was asked to lend a hand."

"Actually, it's my first visit." Despite his initial annoyance at the intrusion, Steve found himself returning the other man's grip readily. "I'm Steve Wilson. And you're right. I was with Special Operation Command during Enduring Freedom. Spent some time in the Panjsheer. So maybe we have met."

Steve studied the other man as he spoke. Taller than Steve, a wiry build, brown hair overdue for a trim, the guy could have been a lot of people. But Steve took away a decade, added an untrimmed beard, the same local dress.

"I only remember one American when we dropped into the Panjsheer. A young aid worker doing food relief right on the Taliban front lines. The embedded journalists went nuts because they finally had an English speaker to interrogate. Especially since Special Forces weren't giving out interviews."

"Yeah, well, that was fifteen minutes of fame I'm glad are long over." The other man made a rueful grimace. "I'll admit I don't recognize you. But then you guys didn't exactly let civilians get too close. So what brings you to Kabul? And, hey, while I've got the chance, I'd like to thank you. A lot of those people we were trying to feed would have starved that winter if you hadn't arrived when you did."

"Yeah, well, only doing my job." As always, the thanks made Steve squirm. But he found himself liking this John Atkins. Liked the firmness of his grip. The calm appraisal in his gaze that held neither the hero worship nor the condemnation Special Ops usually drew, just approval and respect from one man carrying out his mission to another. And if this thin, sunburned man in shalwar kameez was really that kid Steve's A-team had come across handing out bags of wheat to starving villagers with bombs dropping within earshot, here was one aid worker who deserved all the respect Steve usually doled out only to another combat-experienced warrior.

"These days I'm just a civilian," Steve added. "I'm with Condor Security heading up Minister of Interior Khalid's personal detail."

"Then I've likely seen you on the news. Your client spends enough time there." John's gesture encompassed the crowded yard, the vehicles inching out the open gate. "So what do you think? Anything we can do to tighten things up? As a humanitarian organization, we've been reluctant to project the image of some military fortress. But with the upsurge of violence, I'll admit I'm concerned whether we're taking enough precautions. Especially when we're hosting an event like this."

"Actually, a few things do jump to mind. For one, those spikes topping your wall are decorative, but you might want to add some concertina wire. And you've got a serious line-of-sight problem for gunfire or RPGs." Steve gestured toward those balconies filled with interested viewers.

"But your biggest choke point is that bottleneck of vehicles coming and leaving. For one, a backup at the gate offers hostiles a soft target. But the gate itself is a weak point. Ramming it with a car bomb is the easiest way to penetrate your perimeter. Barrels filled with concrete or sand with a pole across them make an easy checkpoint. Keeps your bottleneck at the end of the block, not your open gate.

"And while you're at it, you need an ID check. I drove right in this morning. Sure I look expat. But I could dress up a mujahid so you couldn't tell the difference. There's plenty with my coloring. For that matter, even if you know the family, you can't know if someone's inside their car with a gun on them. You should do a full inside and underbelly eyeball of every car before you let it down your street. There's plenty I could add, but that's probably already more than you were asking," Steve finished dryly.

"Actually, it's just what I wanted," the other man said quickly. "And you're right; I guess we've been a little trusting. Any chance you'd have time to sit down and go over this in detail?"

"I'd have to check my schedule, but I don't know why not."

"Then let's set a time at your convenience. Here's my contact info." John Atkins produced a business card from his shalwar kameez. "Now that concertina wire, we don't have the budget of a security company. Would ordinary barbed wire do?"

"Sure, so long as you've got a solid base for stringing it. Take those spikes up there."

Both men had tilted their heads to scrutinize the top of the wall when Steve heard a soft chuckle. He didn't need to turn around to know who stood behind him.

"Go! Go!" Jamil hissed over his shoulder. "They must not know you are with me! There is no reason you should be taken prisoner too."

Kareem needed no further urging. He'd already melted into the shadows. Jamil strode out onto the commons, hands spread wide. To his relief, the police unit closed around him with hardly a glance down the alley. It seemed obvious now what had brought the uniforms, the reason Jamil had been perturbed since he'd first glimpsed the capacity of Kareem's elaborate camera phone. Either Khalid or Ismail must have recognized Jamil's face on a news screen and decided it was no longer expedient to leave him at liberty.

How they'd tracked Jamil so quickly was more astonishing. But then, Kareem's carpet-weaving story would have included the town where it was filmed. If Ismail was behind this raid, it was well Jamil still had an incriminating DVD as leverage over him. While if it was Khalid who'd ordered Jamil's arrest, once again Ismail's cooperation would be useful.

In either case, Jamil had no reason for panic. Assuming the packet he'd made was still safely in Ameera's care. Jamil had been so joyful at her return, he hadn't thought to inquire.

No, he must assume it was. Jamil drew himself up composedly as his pack was snatched away. "What is the difficulty here? I have done nothing unlawful. And this man, why have you arrested him?"

A uniform stepped away from their kneeling captive. At his order, plastic flexicuffs twisted Jamil's arms behind his back. "You have been identified as a wanted criminal. Is this not your name written here?"

Ameera had been generous because the parcel thrust into Jamil's face was a large one. Neat Dari script spelled out Jamil's name as well as the town. "As to this man, he is under arrest as your accomplice. Did he not bring you here? These men inform us you have been inciting trouble in this town as well, agitating the people with unlawful speech and interfering with their traditions."

A cluster of sullen-faced men to which the patrol leader gestured included the health worker Naveed and the mullah as well as the chaikhana owner. Conspicuously absent was Omed's brother-in-law Haroon. Decency or cowardice?

Jamil shook his head decisively. "This man is neither an accomplice nor even a friend. I am a healer, as was stated. The man had a family member in need of care." Did they know Omed had provided Jamil lodging? "The package contains only medical supplies to replace those I had expended."

The truth of which the unit leader was aware since the brown wrapping paper was ripped open. Pilfered bottles, alcohol containers, packaged bandages protruded visibly from uniform pockets.

"If you are to arrest a man for utilizing my services, then why not the health worker whose clinic was used to treat the patient?" Since his hands were bound, Jamil used his chin to point out Naveed, who flushed angrily at the identification. "Or the town leaders who were there and gave willing assent?"

If the mullah and Naveed were both now scowling, the chaikhana owner stepped forward. "It is true many of us observed this stranger perform his healing. I heard no agitating speech, only talk of kindness and compassion. Nor did our own healer Naveed nor Mullah Zakir offer any objection. As to this man you have arrested, I cannot conceive who would have cause to speak ill of him."

The chaikhana owner shot Naveed a darkling look as he indicated the kneeling prisoner. "Omed is an honest neighbor and has done many good things for our town."

The health worker and mullah offered no rebuttal, but a supportive murmur was sweeping through a rapidly growing crowd. The gray-blue uniforms huddled for a muted discussion. Then a knife slashed through the flexicuffs binding Omed. But not Jamil's. Instead as Omed slipped away, assault rifles prodded their new captive over a tailgate of a police pickup.

Even kneeling awkwardly in the pickup bed, Jamil could see from this vantage across the crowd. On its far edge, Jamil spotted Kareem. So the journalist hadn't capitalized on his opportunity to escape. Round, sunburned features showed distress, but a hand was raised to shoulder level, a parka sleeve pulled discreetly forward. Kareem was filming Jamil's arrest. This time Jamil had no objection at all.

Beyond Kareem stood another man head and shoulders taller than the journalist. Omed too had declined to flee when he'd been freed. Gratitude warred with anguished remorse as his gaze met Jamil's above the crowd. In sharp contrast were gloating smiles that had replaced Naveed and Mullah Zakir's scowls.

But among the rest of what was now a sizable mob, Jamil saw more bewilderment. Anger too reflected in dark glances and agitated murmurs. Whatever the townspeople might think of Jamil, no one in Afghanistan drew more ire than the Afghan National Police. Jamil caught a hand stealthily scooping a stone from the dust. Other fists were clenched or hidden from view. And was that the outline of an AK-47 under a patu hurrying over from the chaikhana?

Jamil wasn't the only one absorbing the crowd's mounting displeasure. The gray-blue uniforms were falling warily back toward the pickups, assault rifles sliding from shoulder straps into cradling hands. A vision of bloodied, tumbled bodies propelled Jamil to his feet. As he faced the crowd, the anguish on Omed's face shaped Jamil's words even more than his desire to stave off violence.

"Please, my countrymen, do not be angry or disturbed. Though I am no criminal, nor have I broken any laws, I am happy to go with these men to set matters right. Do not fear I will be mistreated. I have friends in high authority who, when called, will swiftly settle this matter and arrange for my release."

Jamil was looking straight to the back of the crowd as he spoke. Had Kareem caught that the last statement was for him? Was Jamil imagining a slight assenting nod from the young journalist?

Jamil turned to address himself directly to the patrol leader. "Let us leave here then so I may face my accusers. I demand to speak in person to Minister of Interior Khalid. Or to his deputy, Ismail. They will attest to who I am. And I think you will find there has been a very great mistake concerning the orders for my arrest."

It was a bluff Jamil could only hope held some truth. But the patrol leader was staring at Jamil with baffled incomprehension. "I do not know of what you speak. It was not the minister of interior, but Minister of Justice Qaderi himself who commanded your detention. As to the accusations against you, there is no mistaking. My orders read that you are charged with the capital crime of apostasy."

12

"Why am I not surprised to find you out here checking security?" Amy hoped uncertainty didn't show in her smile as the contractor spun around on a heel. She'd spotted Steve's tall, powerful frame the moment he strode into the meeting area, and she'd been pleased to see Steve settle into a chair. Despite all that came later, Amy hadn't forgotten her delight in that Thanksgiving celebration to which Steve had invited her. Maybe here was an opportunity to return the contractor's kindness.

But when she'd offered a welcoming smile, Steve's mouth had tightened immediately into a stern line. Was Amy herself the problem? Or did that chilly reserve have anything to do with whatever brought him here searching for Amy?

She'd seen Steve walk out before the meeting ended. When he hadn't returned to seek her out, she'd been tempted to simply ignore his earlier brusque command. But curiosity as well as worry had changed her mind. Could Steve have some news that would explain Jamil's silence? The contractor did have intel sources not available to someone like Amy.

"And I see you've met one of my favorite people in Kabul. Or two of them," Amy amended as the keyboard player stepped up to slide an arm around the speaker's waist. The heavy winter weave of the other woman's tunic didn't hide an advanced stage of pregnancy. "Hi, John, Ruth. How much longer?"

"A month," Ruth said happily. Her accent was British. "If Junior doesn't get too impatient."

She smiled at Steve. "So are you going to introduce us, Amy?"

"Sure, of course. Ruth, this is Steve Wilson, a security contractor who works with my landlord, Minister of Interior Khalid. Steve, Dr. Ruth Atkins. Ruth is a pediatrician with ARM. And you've met John. They've both been in Afghanistan for years. In fact, you met here, didn't you?"

"That's right, down in Kandahar. I'd just arrived from London. His relief team couldn't figure out what to do with a shipment of protein supplement, so John brought it over to our clinic. We were married two months later."

Amy swallowed envy at the contented glance the couple exchanged. *They seem so—so one!*

Steve shook Ruth's hand, his smile holding an approval he'd never wasted on Amy herself. "A pleasure to meet you. I must say I hadn't realized Kabul had so many expat families. Are you planning to stay on with a baby?"

"Definitely." Ruth's response was unhesitating. "John and I are excited to have our child born here in Afghanistan. And so are our many Afghan friends. It means a lot to them that we believe in their country enough to stay here for the birth of our firstborn. And of course we've got great medical personnel right here in our congregation."

"There you are, Ruth." A newcomer bustling up was Becky Frazer. "I've got a Swiss couple wondering if you'd look at their two-year-old. They're new in town, and I'm thinking Kabul throat, all this dust and smog, poor baby. But I'd rather you gave your opinion."

"Sure, I'll take a look."

"I'll go with you. Steve, it was good to meet you." John Atkins offered Steve a parting handshake. "I'll definitely be in touch on those security tips."

As the couple drifted away, Becky lingered, her gray head tilting to eye Steve meditatively. "May I add it's nice to see you here today? Do join us again." Shrewd blue eyes went from Steve to Amy. "Though I'm sure you didn't come here to look over our security setup. Amy mentioned you had something to discuss with her, so I'll leave you to it. Amy, I'll be in the clinic if you need me again."

Then Amy and Steve were alone. Or as alone as was possible with dozens of people still milling around the yard, children racing in excited circles. Steve lounged against the perimeter wall, shoulders resting against whitewashed brick, hands sliding into his pockets. The smile Amy had maintained for John and Ruth faded as she lifted her gaze up the long, hard length of his body as far as the taut line of his jaw. "You said you had something to show me?"

Steve's wraparound sunglasses had turned to follow the group of three hurrying across the yard. Abruptly, he said with unmistakable sincerity, "You told me once you liked my friends. Well, I can say honestly, I like yours too."

Amy's uncertainty gave way to a genuine smile. "Does this mean you've changed your mind about aid workers? Maybe what we're doing here isn't quite so useless as you figured?"

Steve pushed up his sunglasses so Amy could see his gray eyes hard on her face, his jawline relaxing to a suggestion of amusement. "I'm still reserving judgment. Like your preacher said, what difference has fifty years of handouts done for Afghanistan? But that doesn't mean I can't have respect for commitment. And courage. Your friends aren't like any humanitarian crowd I've run across before. Excepting yourself, of course."

Steve's mouth curved to full amusement as Amy's cheeks grew warm. "Then you've been running around with the wrong crowd," she retorted. To cover her embarrassment, she added quickly, "You said you had news of Jamil?"

"Ah, yes." Steve's mouth went straight again, and he withdrew his long frame from the wall. "Is there somewhere we won't be interrupted?"

"The meeting hall should be emptied out by now." That brief flash of camaraderie was gone again as Amy led the way back into the assembly hall, where chairs and tables were now stacked neatly against a wall. "So what's this news about Jamil? I've been expecting him to call, and I'm a little worried he hasn't."

"I never said I had news. I said your bomber pal was *on* the news." Any hint of friendliness had left the security contractor's tone. "Here's the entire clip posted on YouTube."

Steve turned his iPhone so Amy could watch it. There was something eerie about seeing Jamil's face, hearing his voice, on the tiny screen. But to Amy's disappointment, it quickly became clear the YouTube clip was not recent footage.

There was Jamil reading to village men gathered around a table. Though Amy didn't understand the dialect, she recognized the name Isa Masih as well as the Pashto New Testament she'd given Jamil. Then came Jamil bent over a motionless burqa. Appreciative murmurs greeted a pop as the dislocated shoulder slid back into place, but Amy saw storm clouds in the faces of a man in a black turban and another wearing a dingy white medical jacket. As the video ended, Amy raised her eyes from the screen.

"I'm not sure what you're wanting me to see. Jamil told me about this when he called. How he was able to help that poor woman when the village health worker wouldn't touch her. And how he read them the story of Isa Masih healing a woman."

"And you see no problem with this?" Steve's fingers were playing again across the screen. But now he was pulling up headlines. CNN. NBC. FOX News. BBC. The headlines were almost identical. *YouTube Phenomenon Indicates Unexpected Level of Religious Tolerance in Afghanistan.* One subtitle demanded, "Does this signal hope for true democracy in the Muslim world?"

But the next headline Steve pulled up was the English edition of Al Jazeera, and its headline was not so approving. *Christian Convert Practices Unlicensed Medicine to Proselytize Muslims.*

"As if he doesn't have more credentials than any village health worker!" Amy said indignantly. "As to a problem, I think it's wonderful! And I'd think you would too. You said Afghanistan will never change except from within. And that it wouldn't happen until Afghans themselves are willing to make a stand, risk their own lives, for change. Or are you thinking Jamil is just faking it all? that he's really hanging around some village clinic planning a suicide mission? Because if so, I can tell you you're wrong!"

"Like your vocation, I'll reserve judgment on that," Steve answered coolly. "But say you're right, and your pal's had a genuine change of heart. It's one thing to be wandering around offering first aid in the name of Isa Masih. It's another to do it on international television. If you think democracy has come to Afghanistan to that extent, then you're crazy. And so is he! Especially when the smallest background check will turn up the fact you were his last employer. I'm just trying to think rationally here."

"And I'm not?" Amy demanded hotly.

"Maybe you're letting personal feelings cloud your judgment," Steve answered impatiently. "For the sake of your own mission here in Kabul, not to mention Jamil himself if you care so much about him, the least you can do is tell him to keep his head down and off the news. Maybe even drop out of sight for a while."

"I'd do that if I could just get ahold of him!" Amy cried. "I sent a box of medical supplies to the town in that video. Jamil was supposed to let me know when it arrived. Which should have been at least two days ago."

As though on cue, Amy heard a jangle. Grabbing her cell phone, she saw on its screen the number from which her former assistant had last called. "Jamil?"

But the voice on the other end was not a familiar one. And it was frantic enough Amy could hardly understand it. "I'm sorry; can you repeat that?"

The unknown voice switched abruptly from Dari to English. Amy felt the blood receding from her face as she listened. "Yes, please call me again when you know more."

"What is it?" Steve's tone was no longer cool or impatient.

Amy raised her head. "Jamil's been arrested."

If Steve had doubted how strongly Amy felt about her former assistant, the anguish in her hazel eyes would have convinced him. The blood had drained from the aid worker's face, leaving it chalk white, and Steve saw her rock on her heels. The girl was going to faint!

Steve reached swiftly for two folding chairs. Slapping them open, he eased Amy down into one before straddling the other, arms propped on the chair back. "Okay, tell me what happened."

Some color returned to Amy's face as she sank into the chair. "The man who called says he's a journalist named Kareem. He's the one who videoed that YouTube footage."

As Amy related her conversation, a single detail shot Steve's mental antenna to alert. His initial inference from her shocked proclamation was that Khalid must have chosen to rescind his quixotic pardon of the erstwhile suicide bomber. Jamil was, after all, a criminal by the standards of Steve's own nation as well as Afghanistan.

But the arrest was ordered by the minister of justice? For Qaderi to order Jamil's arrest was an unexpected twist. Not long ago when Qaderi had ordered a death sentence for an Afghan Christian convert who'd returned from abroad, the international press had been all over the case. Massive negative publicity finally forced a face-saving resolution for all parties, wherein said convert was declared mentally incompetent and exiled to Italy. But with Afghanistan's claims to democracy on the line right now in front of an avidly watching world and Qaderi's own presidential bid hanging in the balance, why would the minister of justice want to stir up new controversy by arresting Jamil?

Except that Jamil had managed to get his face and activities plastered all over the Internet and cable news. And Qaderi was running on an Islamic fundamentalist platform of restoring Afghanistan to strict sharia law. Perhaps he would have ignored an itinerant rural healer with unorthodox teachings, at least until the elections were safely past. But once the issue was thrust into the public eye, Qaderi's own followers would be demanding a response. What idiot at that news service hadn't foreseen these consequences? Did someone over there really believe that YouTube clip heralded religious freedom in Afghanistan?

Or did they care? However it turned out, the story promised high ratings. In fact, the more controversy the better, from a news standpoint.

Amy had fallen silent, her eyes fastened on Steve, hands entwined tightly in her lap, the shining flaxen length of her hair spilling over shoulders without the customary headscarf to hold it back. When Steve didn't speak, she bit her lip, then dropped her gaze so that her hair became instead a curtain veiling her face as she asked in a low voice, "Do you think they'll hurt him? or try him for apostasy like that other man?"

Steve made an impatient gesture. "What do you think? The precedent is already there. And I don't think they'll be able to write off your pal as a mental incompetent like that other man either. That video footage was pretty persuasive. Why do you think I came over here? The moment I saw it, I knew there'd be trouble."

"Saw what?" Pushing the hair away from her face, Amy raised her eyes to flash hazel fire. "Jamil helping a village woman because their own medic wouldn't? That's what gets me! They let him go after he plotted to blow up the minister of interior, but they're going to arrest him for this? for speaking of Isa Masih? It's all so ridiculously unfair!"

"Of course it's unfair," Steve said evenly. "Since when is that news to you, Amy? You've been crusading against this very thing since I've met you. Jamil had to have known the risks."

"Maybe. I don't know. It's just—it was never personal before."

Steve's mouth tightened sardonically. *Well, it's certainly personal now!*

"I . . . I can't even think what to do." Abruptly Amy rose to her feet. "In any case, this is hardly your problem. I do appreciate your stopping by with that video. Especially the way I know you feel about Jamil. At least now I have some idea what all this is about."

Her chin went up, and ice edged her tone as she added, "I won't take any more of your time. I'm sure you've got some more urgent crisis to resolve. And with all that study of the perimeter, I'm sure you can find your own way out. So if you'll excuse me, I'm going to start tracking down just where they've taken Jamil."

Steve's mouth twitched with involuntary appreciation. Ms. Amy Mallory might be irritating at times, not to mention headstrong and impulsive. But Steve had always approved of courage and determination, and those the aid worker definitely possessed in abundance. Despite her clear dismissal, he made no move to get to his own feet. Instead, he commented mildly, "Actually, checking out Jamil's whereabouts is something I can do. In fact, you should figure I'd be too nosy to forgo that."

There was gratification in watching suspicion and hopefulness war on her face. "You're serious about that? I don't know what to say except thank you. Or . . . I'm assuming you'll let me know what you find out?"

"That was the idea. And don't thank me yet. I'm not sure how much I can do." Now that it was on his own terms, Steve rose to his feet. "By the way, if you're wondering how you can help your pal Jamil, you might try getting ahold of his journalist friend. And any other media contacts you can scare up. See what you can do to get the details of Jamil's arrest on the evening news."

"I thought you said getting on the news was a bad thing."

"That was before. Now that his name's already out there, safety isn't in trying to avoid attention but seeking it out. With Jamil's arrest coming right on top of that earlier story, the press should jump on it. Which is what you want because Qaderi is going to want to make this go away as quietly as possible. And so will the rest of the Afghan government, not to mention our own. Especially during this election season. They won't have forgotten the uproar last time around. The easiest will be a quick trial behind closed doors. There are no public hearings for prisoners in Afghanistan, unless you can get the media and human rights organizations involved. That's what saved that other convert—having an international spotlight on him so Qaderi and the rest didn't dare pull a vanishing act."

"And you think that might get Jamil released too?"

"I don't know about getting him released. But it just might be enough to keep him alive."

13

It's all my fault. It's all my fault.

The anguished refrain pounded furiously at Amy's temples as her deft maneuvering of the Toyota Corolla around a traffic circle left the market district behind. During the last week, Amy had submitted to Rasheed's convenience the few times she'd needed a driver. But today was again the chowkidar's day off, and the ARM compound was not far from Wazir Akbar Khan. The convenience of being her own chauffeur more than outweighed hostile glares and angry honking.

A peacock blue perimeter wall was now visible on the next corner. As Amy slowed for a speed bump, Jamil's terrible narrative about those undeserved years in prison rose sharp to her mind. *I can't bear it that my doing should put Jamil back into that horrible position! Is this how Steve felt when he discovered his own role in Jamil's capture all those years ago?*

And yet what could Amy have done differently? What *would* she have done differently if she could have read the future? If she hadn't given Jamil that New Testament, if the love of Isa Masih hadn't changed his heart, Jamil would be dead right now instead of under arrest. As would countless others with him. And Jamil was a man, not a child to be protected from his own decisions. He'd understood the risks better than Amy ever could. And he'd felt what he'd chosen to do worth those risks.

No, it's not my fault. Or anyone's. It just—is!

More urgent was not affixing blame but what to do next. Steve Wilson had suggested contacting the media, getting them on board. But Amy had no media contacts. And she cringed at the thought of trying to explain her own connection to Jamil. Friendship with an unmarried Afghan male, Jamil's exploration of Amy's faith and holy book, his dismissal from New Hope were all innocently explained. But Amy could see how easily they could be twisted into something ugly and sordid and controversial, her own motives and involvement brought into question.

An anonymous news tip?

No, the Ministry of Justice could simply deny the arrest had ever taken place. And once Jamil disappeared into some dank cell in one of Afghanistan's notorious prisons, how could Amy or anyone else ever prove he was there? Unless . . .

Amy waited only until she'd parked in the mechanics yard before retrieving her last received phone call. "Salaam aleykum, Kareem. You called me earlier about Jamil."

Kareem's cautious English reply held the same Pakistani lilt as Jamil's.

"Kareem, I . . . I don't want to cause any trouble for you. But you said you were a journalist. That was your video on the news, wasn't it? I was hoping you might have taken more video, maybe Jamil's arrest? Is there any way to get that on the news like the other? I'd be happy to purchase the footage if—"

"I do not want pay." The Afghan journalist sounded stiff with indignation at her offer. "And yes, it will cause trouble. But I count Jamil as a friend. He is not the heretic they say. And no matter what his beliefs, he should have the right to hold them and speak them. At least such is the Afghanistan I hope to see. Nor am I the only Afghan to think this way. If I can persuade others also to speak out, then perhaps the world will listen. This is what your people call a 'free press,' is it not?"

Kareem would not arrive in Kabul until the next day. But the arrest video had been uploaded to the news service.

"The minister of justice will not listen to such as I nor my fellow journalists here in Afghanistan. But Qaderi is a candidate for president and so must consider the goodwill of other governments who help our country. If the foreign media ask enough questions, Qaderi may at least be forced to produce Jamil to prove he is unharmed."

"I've got someone working to find where Jamil's being held," Amy contributed. "For now, I guess there's not much else we can do but pray."

"Yes, we can pray." Kareem's agreement held sincere fervor.

Amy's heart was fractionally lighter by the time she'd stowed her cell phone. *I know it's going to be all right, Father God. You won't let anything happen to Jamil! Not when he's just trying to show your love to his people. Maybe this is even your way of focusing world attention on freedom of worship and speech over here.*

Amy made her way toward the villa. Free of chores or school, the children were racing around orchard and interior courtyard. But as she'd expected, open shutters along the veranda revealed the women enjoying their own Friday leisure within the warmth and comfort of the kitchen. Two of them idly stirred pots simmering on the gas grill for supper. The others were congregated on tushaks and rugs that converted the far end of the salon into a sitting area, several with babies and toddlers resting in their arms.

Less expected was to see the TV muted, a silenced Bollywood soap on the screen. The women were instead listening intently to Farah, the girl's voice rising and falling in the dramatic timbre of storytelling. As Amy listened from the veranda, she recognized with astonishment the narration to which she'd once cued her MP3 for the Afghan girl. The Dari dramatization of Isa Masih's life. At her side, Farah had set up the storyboard, and though the flannelgraph instructions were in English, she'd managed to match figures to Isa's healing of a blind man.

Amy's initial reaction was dismay. What had she started in giving that MP3 player to Farah? Hadn't Amy herself refrained from telling these stories because the life, death, and resurrection of Jesus Christ could not be so easily explained away as the Old Testament stories Islam shared with Christianity? Especially after today. The last thing she wanted was to bring down on these women the kind of trouble that now engulfed Jamil.

Then rebellion rose hot and furious inside Amy. *I gave that MP3 player to Farah because I wanted her to know love isn't an illusion. That there really is someone who cares enough about Afghan women to give his own life for them. Why shouldn't Farah have the right to pass that along to anyone she wants? or these women to listen if they choose?*

Despite her inner turmoil, Amy found her mouth curving in a rueful smile as she headed upstairs to her own quarters. *And now you're starting to sound like one of Dr. Amrita's women revolutionaries!*

14

What am I doing letting myself be pulled again into Amy Mallory's life and love? Steve asked himself savagely as he headed the Pajero toward the mounted MIG fighter that marked the airport entrance. Cougar's page had been a request for Steve to join him in the cargo hangar Condor Security shared with a coalition of private security companies. By now the logistics manager would be chafing at Steve's delayed response.

Not that Steve regretted this morning's side trip. If nothing else, it had proved an eye-opener. Steve's opinion of the humanitarian crowd had never been high. He'd considered them sentimental and spineless, if admittedly well-intentioned, with their misguided conviction that humanity was basically good and needed only enough handouts to exchange all enmity for goodwill and peace on earth.

But in John Atkins, Steve had encountered an immediate and unexpected meeting of mind and spirit. A like-minded toughness and willingness to risk life and limb on the front line of battle Steve had known before only in Special Ops colleagues. Except the battle John Atkins and others in that worship gathering fought was never-ending and probably held more daily risk threat than Steve experienced. And they fought it without body armor and weapons. Or any expectation of medals or reward. That took guts!

Maybe Amy Mallory wasn't so unique as Steve had thought.

They've certainly got something I don't. Something I once had. Something I didn't want anymore because it hurt too much. Devon gave his life for the rest of us. But he shouldn't have had to. If our local allies hadn't lied through their teeth that the village was friendly. If the militia leader stuffing his pockets with American dollars hadn't tipped off the Tallies we were coming.

Had Devon's needless death been the last straw for Steve or just one more on the pile until it was easier to shut down, to stop caring? *Do your job. Don't get involved. Maybe you don't feel much, but you don't hurt as much either.*

And now Steve had broken his own cardinal life principle. Not for the first time either when it came to Ms. Amy Mallory. Steve still wasn't sure why it had seemed so urgent to inform the aid worker personally about that YouTube clip instead of leaving a voice message. Or simply minding his own business. After all, what difference did it make what Jamil was doing with himself, so long as it didn't include blowing up any more of Steve's clients?

Okay, be honest with yourself. You jumped on the excuse to look Amy up. Though if Steve was pursuing honesty, he'd have to admit as well some curiosity as to what Amy's former assistant was up to with the new lease life had granted him.

Find something you believe in. Steve had left Afghanistan with Phil's challenge ringing in his ears. And yet from that YouTube video, it seemed their former antagonist was the one who'd made good on that challenge. That Jamil had once been a medical student, Steve knew from Amy. That he was a competent medic, Steve knew from Phil's own assessment working together with Amy's assistant in the aftermath of the New Hope explosion.

An explosion for which Jamil himself was responsible, however unwittingly, if one believed his story.

And there was the dichotomy. Steve would have expected Jamil to take his new lease on life and flee as far from Khalid's reach as he could, back into Pakistan perhaps, where he'd spent most of his early years. He'd been as stunned as disapproving when he'd seen that video clip of an itinerant paramedic spouting off biblical passages while practicing village health care. Was this for real? or the kind of scam that had led Jamil to work at New Hope while plotting mass murder?

Or was it simply an attempt to stay close to Amy? to convince the aid worker Jamil shared her passion and vision? Steve had always assumed Jamil's undisguised personal sentiments toward the aid worker were what had deflected the suicide bomber from his original mission. Sentiments Amy had again made clear she shared.

Yes, that was far more likely than some foolhardy, if courageous, mission to emulate the life and teachings of Jesus among Afghanistan's die-hard Islamic fundamentalist rural populace.

Steve strode into the cargo hangar to find the CS logistics manager and Khalid's deputy minister Ismail standing with a pair of customs officials beside an open shipping container. Cougar swung around as Steve strode up, his round face bright red with pent-up fury. "Would you take a look at this mess?"

If the CS regional depot in Amman, Jordan, had filled Steve's order correctly, the shipping container should have held surplus M16s, body armor, night vision goggles, and other equipment he'd requisitioned to outfit Khalid's militia for their new duties. One glance inside explained Cougar's agitation. Cartons slashed open for viewing held only stack after stack of meals-ready-to-eat military rations.

Cougar waggled his cell phone. "I've got Amman on the line. Paulson insists this was your order. And that he's responsible neither for replacement nor wasted shipping."

"Is that so?" Steve's teeth gritted. A certain pencil pusher was overdue for a taste of real hand-to-hand combat. "In that case, inform Amman that Afghan customs will not permit processing of this shipment until it matches the manifest we submitted. I'm afraid it's going to have to be sent back on the return flight. Isn't that right, Ismail?"

Considering the missing gear's intended destination, Steve had little doubt of the deputy minister's support. Ismail's grin was as savage as Steve's own as he spun around to give orders to the customs officials. As the two men immediately began closing the shipping container, Cougar retreated several meters to continue a heated phone conversation. Which presented Steve an unanticipated opportunity to carry out his promise to Amy.

"Thank you, Deputy Minister, for your intervention. I assure you this matter will be quickly resolved, and your men will receive their equipment. Now just one other matter that has arisen. You remember the suicide bomber we picked up a few months back after the explosion on Khalid's Wazir property? Jamil, the man's name was."

Ismail's eyebrows shot high. "But of course. After Khalid so mercifully pardoned him, he was released."

"Yes, well, I have only now been informed about your police force arresting him again. Since this is a matter of obvious concern to Khalid's security, I was hoping you might have more details for me. Where he's been taken, for instance. Just to make proper security precautions, of course, considering our past history with this man."

"Arrest?" Ismail looked genuinely startled. "But that is impossible! I have heard nothing. No, such an action would not have been taken without authorization. And if so, it would have been reported to me immediately. I have given strict orders concerning this man."

"I'm told the minister of justice actually gave the arrest order," Steve murmured diplomatically. "You might want to take a look at this."

Qaderi.

Ismail's mind was churning furiously as Khalid's infidel security chief called up a video clip on his iPhone. The minister of justice had no occasion for direct contact with Ismail's former protégé. Ismail, if anyone, should know! So what had triggered Jamil's arrest? What did Qaderi know that Ismail didn't? What *could* he know?

Or was this some election ploy designed to boost the justice minister's lagging popularity in the polls? Though what use was arresting the man who'd failed to assassinate Qaderi's chief rival?

The video clip offered some illumination but left Ismail even more appalled. *This* was the new mission to which Jamil had referred when he'd turned his back on his oath and Ismail himself?

When Jamil had first fled Kabul, Ismail had anticipated no difficulty keeping track of him since the deputy minister had deliberately kept the cell phone he'd provided Jamil activated and paid up. The single call he'd monitored weeks ago to Jamil's foreign employer confirmed the fugitive was heading south toward Pakistan, where he'd spent his growing years and undoubtedly still could find acquaintances and relatives.

But the phone log Ismail as subscriber received each month had registered no further calls. If sold or stolen, *someone* would be putting it to use. More probable was that Jamil, along with his phone, had met some adverse end.

Which suited Ismail well enough if not for that video footage and photos the traitor had so deceitfully taken. And deposited somewhere as life insurance.

Now Ismail had a viable, if less welcome, explanation for Jamil's silence. So he hadn't taken refuge in Pakistan but was wandering a region that offered minimal cell phone service or electricity for keeping a battery charged.

So why would a scion of Kabuli aristocracy, who until his prison experience had lacked none of the luxuries and privileges of his class, take refuge in one of Afghanistan's poorest and most isolated regions instead of the comfort and safe distance of Peshawar or Islamabad? Had he chosen to join the Taliban? maybe put to use the bomb-making skills Ismail had taught him? An itinerant health worker would make a perfect cover.

Still, if Jamil remained committed to a mission of vengeance, why had he reneged on his original mission to eliminate the family friend and business associate whose betrayal had destroyed Jamil's own family and life, Ismail's current employer, Minister of Interior Khalid Sayef?

As for the minister of justice, had he thought through what he was unleashing in this latest move? Did he care?

Ismail would make it his business to remedy that. Meanwhile, it would be wise to quickly find out exactly where Jamil had been taken before others had opportunity to interrogate Ismail's one-time coconspirator. Which should be simple enough. Ismail himself had been responsible for appointing the current superintendent of prisons back when Afghanistan's penal system was still under MOI rather than MOJ management.

By the time Ismail finished a series of phone calls, his habitually forbidding expression had relaxed into a gratified smile. If Jamil had thought his last prison experience was unpleasant, he would soon be learning just how much worse it could be.

Which made this the perfect opportunity for Ismail to reintroduce himself to his erstwhile tool.

But not too soon.

Apostasy! Astonishment, more than fear, twisted at Jamil's gut as the green police pickups jolted from the dirt track onto pavement. Had he not, after all, once steeled himself to death? Was not every breath he still drew into his lungs an unexpected gift?

If unwelcome, an arrest order from the powerful Ministry of Interior to whom the Afghan National Police reported at least made sense. Khalid had eyes and ears in every corner of Afghanistan. Though the bullet Jamil half expected when he'd turned his back on Ismail to walk out of the police precinct had never come, he'd braced himself for weeks for a tap on the shoulder from gray-blue uniforms like these. Yes, he'd arranged the insurance of that DVD and those photos in Ameera's safekeeping. But Jamil had been less certain than he'd claimed that those scanty images would be an effective deterrent.

So Jamil had been as surprised as relieved when weeks became months with no sign anyone was hunting him down. By the time Jamil had called Ameera on Kareem's satellite phone, it was with growing confidence that his current course was no temporary reprieve, but a future. Even such a future as might hold a beloved wife, a family such as Omed enjoyed.

But apostasy charges?

Jamil remembered well a case not so long ago when Minister of Justice Qaderi had levied such charges against a returning Afghan refugee. But that man had been an open Christian convert. Jamil had never spoken against Islam nor even encouraged others to do so. Did he not pray five times a day? fast in season? show *zakat*—charity—to those less fortunate? As to following Isa Masih's teachings of peace and kindness and forgiveness, did not these make Jamil a better Muslim, not an apostate?

Yes, there were those who seemed to equate Isa's teachings with the infidel foreigners. But to heal in the name of Islam's own greatest healer, to urge Jamil's countrymen to follow the prophet's example of peace instead of hate broke no laws. When Jamil had assuaged Ameera's concerns about his new mission, it was bandits and Taliban and Ismail's own vengeance that had come to mind, not sharia courts.

Still, it was one thing to speak confidently about setting things right and being innocent of crime. Did not Jamil above all men know how little innocence or guilt mattered when it came to justice? He'd spoken bravely of calling friends in authority. But even if Kareem understood this reminder that his phone now held Ameera's number, could Jamil hope the journalist would bestir himself to call some foreign woman on behalf of a virtual stranger? And yet if he did not, who beyond his captors and a few villagers would ever know of Jamil's arrest?

Once again, Jamil would disappear, perhaps this time forever.

The police convoy didn't make camp at a roadside chaikhana, climbing instead through the night up a narrow, winding highway edged with stark precipices and no guardrails at all. Jamil's captors dug out blankets to wrap around their padded winter jackets. But Jamil's belongings had not been returned, and he was now so chilled, a plunge over one of those precipices would be almost a relief.

Then he was no longer cold. Jamil had fallen asleep or lost consciousness because when he was next aware of his surroundings, his body no longer rested against metal but dirt. Numbed flesh barely registered repeated slaps across his face. With a groan, he rolled to a sitting position and forced his eyes open.

Floodlights illuminated a graveled track that ran between two high walls as far as Jamil could see in either direction. Double coils of concertina wire topped the walls. Massive, square watchtowers hemmed in the tall, barred gates through which Jamil had been dumped. Beyond them, Jamil's arresting detail was driving away, but guards now slashing flexicuffs and hauling Jamil to his feet wore the same gray-blue. Above the interior perimeter wall rose a colossal concrete structure pocked with long, barred slits that were windows. More gray-blue uniforms swarming catwalks were heavily armed, and huge machine guns mounted atop the gate towers were directed inward against facility residents, not outward attack.

It was a prison. If not the one where Jamil had spent so many years, then similar enough to be its prototype.

Painful twinges as the guards propelled Jamil through a steel door into the concrete fortress indicated he hadn't just been slapped into consciousness but kicked as well. The floodlights filtering through window bars did little to leaven the gloom of narrow, dank corridors. A reek of urine, sickness, and despair was as familiar to Jamil as the low moans, shouts, banging on walls. A single bloodcurdling scream was quickly stifled.

Rape or torture?

The corridor into which Jamil's new escort thrust him was untenanted, perhaps because its walls were crumbled, floors littered with fallen plaster, windows boarded over, cell bars rusted or broken away. But the flashlight one guard produced illuminated a metal grate sealing off the far end of the corridor. Here several cells had been swept clean, their bars shiny new and depressingly solid. As Jamil's escort thrust him into the first cell, the flashlight played over a concrete floor, walls mildewed with damp. One corner held a tattered tushak, another a bucket. A foul stench explained the bucket's purpose.

Though not so cold in here as outdoors, it seemed more so now that Jamil's numbed limbs were recovering life. His belongings had not reappeared, but a guard tossed Jamil a blanket. He'd had no food or water either since arriving back to Omed's town, but these his escort didn't offer. The cell door clanged shut, followed by the metal grate. Then the flashlight retreated down the corridor, and night closed back in on Jamil.

With darkness came a too-familiar wave of rage and despair. These recent months of freedom might have been only a brief hallucination born of his yearning. Jamil was right back where he'd started. Where he'd sworn he'd never allow himself again to be ensnared.

Breathing deeply, Jamil groped frantically for some flicker of sanity. Some assurance that beyond these thick walls and dark night really existed a world that held light and life. That all for which he had renounced vengeance and death was real, not merely an illusion to vanish upon sober examination like a heat mirage on a Helmand salt flat.

"Be strong and courageous. Do not be terrified; do not be discouraged, for the Lord your God will be with you wherever you go."

Had Joshua, Moses' successor, known such fear and doubt as Jamil felt now? He must have to be offered such instruction.

If this Joshua had ever really existed. Was it possible that here too Kareem had been right? that the stories in Ameera's book were no more meant to be accepted as true than the Arabian Nights tales Persian invaders had long ago introduced to Afghanistan?

But if those stories were not truth, neither was Isa Masih himself. Nor the words he'd spoken.

Then was Jamil truly alone. Alone as he'd been for so many long years before fate—or Ismail—had set him free to pursue retribution and revenge. Years when only hate and bitterness and fury had given him strength to endure.

A shudder went through Jamil's body. No, to let such doubts consume his mind would be worse than prison itself.

Jamil tugged the tushak from its dank corner and shook it out, ignoring dampness as he knelt. It at least gave protection from the cold concrete. Pulling the blanket over him so that his entire world was reduced to a snug, enveloping tent, he bent flat so that his forehead touched the cushion in attitude of prayer.

Our Father in heaven . . .

But this time the prayers did not come.

It must have been the retelling to the other women that thrust the story from Ameera's tiny machine so vividly into her dreams. Farah was walking the dirt road of the storyboard backdrop. Yet it was also a dusty trail of her native Afghanistan. In front of her, she could see the one she sought. But his back was turned to her, and there were too many people between to approach closer. A whole multitude jostled around her, reaching out seeking hands, their faces poignant with yearning. Some were blind or crippled. Others were small children who shook with sobs because they too could not push through to that turned-away figure.

Suddenly, reaching the front of that mob was the most important thing in her dream. Dropping to her belly, she squirmed forward through a jungle of legs and robes and sandaled feet. One of the weeping children caught her action and dropped down to crawl beside her, its small, dirty face now alive with hope.

But the farther she advanced, the tighter the packed crowd. And now she could no longer tell which way to crawl. Her diminutive companion had faded from the dream. Only her own yearning and desperation propelled her onward.

But at last she could move no farther. Sick with despair, she capitulated, pushing herself back to her feet.

Then she saw him, no longer turned away, but looking straight at her. Somehow in her dream, the crowd that separated them had become hazy, almost transparent. She could not see his features clearly, only his clothing, the shalwar kameez and enveloping chapan as dazzling white as new-fallen snow under a midday sun.

And his eyes.

They were Ameera's eyes, she thought with confusion, green-brown and soft with compassion.

No, they were her mother's eyes, dark, sorrowful, filled with tenderness.

They were neither. It was the love blazing down from them that had confused her.

Only, the love in these eyes was greater than she'd ever known, than she'd imagined could exist.

She realized the sobbing child who'd crawled beside her now rested in strong, gently cradling arms, a joyous smile lighting up tear-streaked face. She took a step forward. Then another. One more step, and she too would be in his embrace.

But now the scene was dissolving into darkness. First the crowd. Then the dust under her feet. The blinding-white clothing. The cradled child.

Those loving eyes were the last to go, and as they faded into the darkness, she found herself reaching out a pleading hand. *Don't go! Please don't leave me!*

She awoke to find her arm outstretched, groping at the night. It had only been a dream. A beautiful illusion like Ameera's stories.

Like love itself.

But if only it were not!

The vivid images were now slipping from her memory, and when she tried to conjure them back up, she could not. In their place were such longing and desolation, she felt a physical pain in her chest. When she touched her face in the dark, it was wet.

If only it were not just a dream, a story, an illusion.

Burying her face in her tushak so that she would not awake her room-mates, Farah wept until she felt her heart would burst within her from grief and loss.

15

"Rumors of improved freedoms in Afghanistan appear to have been exaggerated. Just days after reports of an Afghan medical worker openly sharing personal faith in Isa Masih—Jesus Christ—his arrest . . . What will this mean for Afghanistan's current election campaign? Where do the candidates themselves stand on the issue? Minister of Justice Qaderi . . ."

The BBC commentary droning from Amy's TV set was superimposed against video of Jamil being shoved into a green pickup by gray-blue police uniforms. However Jamil's journalist friend had managed it, within twenty-four hours of Amy's call, indignant reports had swept international news channels as well as the Internet. Like any negative news, Jamil's arrest was playing out much bigger than the original story.

Yes, Kareem had kept his promise superbly. Which was more than Steve Wilson had managed. Though two full days had gone by and half a third, Amy had heard nothing from the security contractor. Nor did the news coverage offer any hint as to where Jamil had been taken. The Ministry of Justice had as yet released no statement. And though both international and local news services were clamoring for access to the prisoner, none seemed sure even as to whom their demands should be directed.

When the BBC news shifted to cyclone casualties in India, Amy reached to turn off the TV. Silence allowed her to hear a quiet cough nearby. Turning, Amy saw Farah standing hesitantly in her living suite doorway.

Amy had seen little of the teenager since her glimpse of Farah's clandestine storytelling. Duane had now assigned Amy to document in person the clinics and schools around Kabul listed as receiving supplies from New Hope. While Rasheed was still filling in as Amy's driver, she'd needed a female companion, and with Soraya so busy in the office, Amy had considered initiating Farah officially as her assistant. But she'd been reluctant to pull the girl from her studies, now that these had recommenced. Instead various Welayat women were taking turns accompanying Amy. They'd been happy for the break from weaving.

Amy was less enthusiastic. The impoverished neighborhoods and outlying towns on her list were widespread, unpaved roads horrendous, so that Amy was out of the compound early each morning, not returning until too late at night for story hour with the children. And while she'd verified several dozen projects, at least five didn't exist. Someone in the local NGO with which New Hope now partnered was siphoning aid into their own pockets. Well, that would be Duane's problem to deal with.

At least her hectic pace kept Amy distracted from brooding. She was back at New Hope now only because her Toyota Corolla had developed a rattle Rasheed didn't like, and the chowkidar had insisted on stopping by the mechanics yard before heading to their next destination. Amy dropped her eyes to a tray in Farah's hands. "You've brought me lunch. *Tashakor.*"

"I saw Hamida when I finished classes." Farah entered the living suite to set the tray on Amy's table. "She said you would want to eat before leaving again. Rasheed is eating now. Since I wished to speak to you, I asked if I could bring it up."

"You want to speak to me? Of course. In fact, if you haven't eaten yet, why don't you have lunch with me. Hamida always sends up far too much food for one."

Amy broke off. Farah was removing a heaping plate of *mastawa* from tray to table, but her lake blue eyes were on the now-dark television screen. Were those signs of recent tears Amy saw there?

"What is it, Farah-jan?" Amy asked quietly.

Farah's gaze drifted from TV to Amy's face. "I . . . The man that was shown being arrested. I saw the same on the television in the kitchen last night. He looks like Jamil, and the other women who knew him say that it is. Is it really Jamil? After the explosion, some said it was Jamil's doing. Is that why he was arrested?"

This was all Amy needed! If only she'd been able to banish TV from the compound. Or at least the news programs. Amy hadn't forgotten Farah's distress when Jamil first left. Amy's former assistant was a good-looking man by any standards, with the slimly muscled build, aquiline features, dark curls and beard that made him a cinema stereotype of the Healer he'd chosen to emulate. If those intense dark eyes could admittedly affect any woman's heartbeat, what had been their impact on a girl who'd spent adolescence in a women's prison and been sold off as a mere child to a vile, old man? Introducing an unattached and attractive male into the tightly proscribed female world of her Welayat charges was one more lapse of judgment Duane would have undoubtedly never made.

"Yes, Farah, that was Jamil on the news," Amy said gently. "And yes, he was arrested. But not for the explosion. That wasn't his fault, as I told you, remember? I'm sure it's all a mistake, and once everything's been straightened out, Jamil will be fine."

Farah was too well acquainted with Afghanistan's justice system to look convinced. "Then it's true what Geeti says. That Jamil was arrested because he spoke of Isa Masih. She says I too could be arrested for telling such stories to the other women."

Amy went cold at Farah's statement. Searching for the right words, she said carefully, "I'm afraid it's true an accusation was made against Jamil. But I don't think anyone will want to arrest you simply for repeating these stories. But perhaps it would be better not to do so again. I'm sorry. I wouldn't have given them to you if I'd known they would cause you any trouble."

Farah shrugged. "All here know you are an Isa follower. But you are a foreigner, and it is so permitted for you. Geeti is new, and she likes to cause trouble."

Amy shook her head, taken aback. Beyond those brief—and private—exchanges with Jamil, she'd never referenced her personal faith here at the compound. "How do you say all know I am an Isa follower? Or is it just because I am a foreigner? Not all foreigners are Isa followers, I hope you understand, even if people call them Christian."

"But of course. It is easy to distinguish those who come here only to heap up wealth and power from the troubles of my country," Farah agreed sagaciously. "Just as not all are good Muslims who claim to be. But you pray, even if not in the way of Islam, as Mr. *Du-ane* who was here does not. And some of the women have known other foreigners like you who help the poor and widows and sick. They say those who showed such kindness were known as Isa followers. Some had heard the Isa story before from these other foreigners. That is why they quickly told Geeti to be silent.

"Me—I am not afraid of her threats. Though I do not understand why anyone should care about such stories. Isa showed kindness to women and children as well as men. I could wish there were such men today. But he is dead. The very people who received his kindness put him to death. And for all the miracles he did, Isa could not stop them. Besides, it was all so long ago. So why should anyone care now if his story is told? or arrest Jamil for speaking of this Isa?"

"Oh, Farah! But that is the point. Isa Masih isn't dead!" Amy was getting into deep water again, but the words burned in her chest so she couldn't have stopped herself from speaking if she'd wanted. "Isa let himself be put to death, not because he couldn't prevent it, but because he loves us. But like you heard on my player, he did not stay dead. He's alive! In giving his life for us, he defeated death forever. He watches over his followers. I am never alone because I know he is with me and that he loves me. And someday I will be with him in paradise. That's why I wanted you to hear his story. So you would know you aren't alone. That there is someone who loves you so much."

"But I wish to be alone. And I do not wish to think again of this Isa. Or to speak of him. You say he is not dead. I do not know why it matters. Are men not still cruel, do bombs not still fall, do people not still know hunger and pain, whether this Isa is dead or alive?"

The set of Farah's chin was mutinous, and any traces of tears were banished by the stony chill of her gaze. "As to love, I once wished to be like you, Miss Ameera. To know the freedom you possess to marry and work and travel as you please. But now I see that you too know worry and fear and pain. Only it is for others you feel them. For the women and children from Welayat. For Jamil. For me even. Because you have allowed your heart to care.

"But to set one's heart on another means only pain and fear when they are taken away or prove cruel. Me, I have now no family, no husband, no children. And so I stand free with only my own next meal and task to concern me. To love means one is never truly free."

Amy's heart ached for this beautiful, defiant, *lost* girl even as she cried softly, "Oh, Farah, I wish I knew some way to show you how backward you have this. It is because I am free that I can love."

"So you say. And perhaps there is something I do not yet understand, or why would these Isa followers leave behind their freedom and riches to come to Afghanistan? Why should Jamil offer healing in the name of Isa, as the television accuses, to villagers who cannot pay and would turn him over to the police? But for me I think it is better for a woman to stand alone. I do not wish to depend on a husband who might be cruel and beat me. I do not wish even to depend on such as you, because you too will leave someday. No, what I wish—"

"What is it you wish for so greatly, Farah?" a cool voice demanded. Soraya stepped into view in the doorway.

As Farah whirled around to face the tall, stately Pashtun woman, defiance drained from her face and tone, but it lingered in lake blue eyes. "I wish to order my own life and future, not bow my head to the will of any man. Then I will be happy."

Soraya's dark eyes flashed as though she'd taken Farah's statement as a personal affront. "A woman is designed by Allah to be under the will of a man. How do you think one like you will ever find such a life?"

Farah dropped her eyes under the older woman's scorn, but she muttered, "I did not say it was possible, only what I wish. I am not foolish. I know it is but a dream, an illusion. Like love."

"Then you should think of your work, not dreams. Why are you lingering here? You are causing Miss Ameera's food to get cold. Go at once to your own meal and then to your work."

As Farah scurried out of the room, head down, Soraya turned to Amy. "You should not permit the girl such liberties. Dreams are not for Afghan women! One must learn to be content with the life Allah has appointed. And if the girl remains unwilling to bend her will to a man, I do not know what will become of her. She has been too long without a proper wali to arrange her future."

In no mood for an argument, Amy was grateful for the interruption of a shrilling from her knapsack. Soraya followed Farah down the hall as Amy retrieved her cell phone. Amy's heartbeat quickened as she saw who was calling, and the first words on the line banished any lingering worries over Farah from her thoughts.

"I found Jamil!"

"Kareem, that's wonderful! At least—" Amy faltered. "Is Jamil okay? Just where is he?"

"He is right here in Kabul. At Pul-e-Charki. And he was alive when last seen."

Pul-e-Charki! Amy had been in Kabul long enough to have heard horror stories of Afghanistan's most notorious maximum-security prison. "But how were you able to find out?"

"I am a journalist, am I not?" Kareem's voice held pride. "My colleagues and I have been investigating. A guard at Pul-e-Charki recognized their newest prisoner on the news. He contacted the television station to sell Jamil's location. Once it was no longer secret, the Ministry of Justice could no longer ignore the clamor of the media and human rights organizations. It is because of the elections, of course. All the candidates wish to please the journalists. Just like America, no? Minister of Justice Qaderi is making a public statement right now. He has agreed to let representatives from the Red Cross in to inspect the prisoner. And he will permit one journalist to come to make a report for the news."

The expectancy in his pause made Amy's question unnecessary. "Who?"

"Myself. I was sure at first it must be a mistake. But it seems that because my video caused Jamil's difficulties, Minister Qaderi considers I am favorable to him. The Red Cross director is German, so we are meeting at his embassy to go to Pul-e-Charki this very afternoon. I am on my way there now."

"This afternoon! You mean, you're actually going to see Jamil?" Amy didn't even pause to deliberate. "Is there any hope I could go with you? To . . . to see Jamil myself?"

Immediate silence on the phone drove home the enormity of what she'd just asked. Amy was already phrasing her retraction when Kareem spoke up cautiously. "Perhaps it is possible. Jamil was most anxious for you to know of his arrest. I think there is no one he would wish more to see. And who knows if there will be another such opportunity. Let me see what I can arrange."

The phone went dead. Amy turned to her food. Hamida's *mastawa*, a savory rice dish with dried lamb, chickpeas, and yogurt, was indeed cold by now. But Amy was hungry enough to eat heartily. Hamida appeared to carry the tray away before Kareem called back. "It is arranged. But you must come quickly. Do you know where the German embassy is?"

"Yes, I do," Amy answered with relief. Wazir Akbar Khan was home to any number of foreign embassies, and the German embassy was only a few blocks away. "I can be there in about fifteen minutes."

"Good. But there is another matter. You must come as an Afghan woman. Your papers do not matter because many females do not possess such. But the prison guards must not discover that you are a foreigner. Do you speak Dari or Pashto?"

So there was a catch to this invitation! But to see for herself that Jamil was all right, maybe even have a chance to talk to him, was worth any amount of trouble—and risk. "I can dress as an Afghan woman. And I do speak Dari, though not perfectly."

"Then we will say your native tongue is Tajik or Uzbek. Only make haste. The Red Cross doctor is an impatient man, and he says he will not wait long."

Amy's usual chapan and headscarf were not adequate disguise for close scrutiny. Hurrying to the infirmary, Amy dug through a sack of tattered garments. Near the bottom she found what she was looking for, a black chador like the one Hamida wore. If threadbare and frayed at the hem, it would cover all but Amy's eyes, and their green-brown shade drew no particular attention in Afghanistan.

If anyone realized the black chador wasn't Hamida as Amy slipped out through the mechanic yard's open gate, they gave no sign. The white SUV with Red Cross markings was idling at the curb when Amy reached the German embassy, its passengers aboard except for a clean-shaven youth in

Western clothing, a camera bag over one shoulder. An anxious expression turned to relief as Amy hurried up. "Salaam. You are Ameera?"

He'd spoken in Dari, his tone warning. Amy answered in the same. "Yes, I am Ameera. You're the man who called me earlier?"

The trick to speaking in a chador was to pull the face veil slightly away so the material didn't suck in and out of the mouth. Even so it was already getting damp and clammy.

"Yes, I am Kareem. But we must go quickly." The cameraman gestured toward a large, blond man watching from the front passenger window. "The foreigner is in a hurry. He would have left already had I not insisted it was you coming down the street. And because he needs my camera."

Amy's first qualm came when she glanced inside the SUV. Along with the German doctor were three Afghan men plus a driver. It was just sinking in to Amy that she knew none of these men and was taking the word of a total stranger whose only credentials were lending Jamil a phone. And getting him thrown into jail!

The German doctor looked even more impatient as Amy swung around to whisper to Kareem in low, fierce English, "How do I know you're really who you say? or a friend of Jamil's at all?"

The cameraman reached into a pocket. Amy recognized immediately the small, olive green volume he pulled out. "Jamil gave this to me. To read about Isa Masih. He told me he did not need it because he'd received another better one from the foreign woman who is his friend."

The pocket-size Bible Amy had given Jamil for Eid was not a detail this man could have known unless Jamil had freely told him.

"I am his friend," Kareem added in the same low, fierce whisper. "And I would do anything to help him."

"So would I." Amy was obeying the journalist's gesture to climb into the Red Cross vehicle when her cell phone rang again. This time as Amy dug it out from under her chador, it was with no enthusiasm that she took in the caller ID.

16

"I should have killed him when I had opportunity. He should have been slaughtered like the dog he is. This is all your doing, Ismail. Had you not urged mercy!"

Steve took an unobtrusive step back as Khalid's angry pacing threatened to hook his flapping Italian suit coat on the muzzle of Steve's M4. On the wall behind the minister, a muted flat screen displayed a bearded face with wire-rimmed glasses and black turban. But the visitors scattered around Khalid's reception suite were under no delusion their host was urging a precipitate assassination of Afghanistan's minister of justice. These included a dozen Afghan males ranging from a youthful computer expert in suit and tie to a white-robed patriarch Steve had known during liberation days as a prominent Northern Alliance warlord.

Khalid's campaign team.

Ismail threw his employer a cautionary glance as he murmured diplomatically, "You remember this arrest was not the doing of our ministry, but Qaderi's. Perhaps you are thinking of another delinquent?"

Khalid dropped abruptly into a leather armchair. "Yes, of course, I was speaking of something else. But you are all paid to have my face on this screen, not this delinquent's or Qaderi's. And since this man's arrest, where have I been? Nowhere! Even the radio stations speak of nothing else."

As Khalid's furious glare swept the suite, Steve concentrated on keeping an amused twitch from his lips. *Good for you, Amy Mallory!*

Assuming the aid worker was responsible for video footage that had been alternating with Minister Qaderi on the screen. Steve had not expected to leave Afghanistan immediately after his encounter with Amy. But when that Amman pencil pusher finally admitted he'd inadvertently shipped Steve's order to Nepal, he'd compounded the mistake by insisting they'd just have to wait until he got around to reordering. Instead Steve had personally escorted the shipping container back to Jordan. By the time he'd ransacked the warehouse, unearthed a satisfactory assortment of automatic weapons and body armor, and shepherded his plunder back through Afghan customs, images of Jamil's arrest were all over international news.

And local news, the reason for Khalid's current ire. The topic was dominating TV and radio, both Dari and Pashto channels, pushing the upcoming election to a back burner. Nor was coverage as uniform as Steve might have expected. Yes, some mullahs were already demanding an immediate verdict of apostasy. But others, especially the local Afghan journalists and human rights organizations, were calling for an impartial investigation. In this new democratic Afghanistan, should there not be irrefutable and public evidence before declaring a man guilty of such a heinous crime as apostasy?

What received no discussion at all was the legitimacy of apostasy itself as a crime. Steve had heard some animated talk show chatter as to whether a devotee of Isa could also be a devout Muslim. But not one voice had been raised to suggest it might just be Jamil's own personal business and choice as to which religious figure he followed or how he worshiped.

"We can hardly control the entire news network, Mr. Minister," the computer expert spoke up. "But according to our polling, last week's coverage of the peace summit has marked you as a clear front-runner. And this story will soon die. Then we can see how to get you back in front of the people."

"Khalid, you worry too much," the former warlord contributed. "Do you not have the police at your command? And they reach every corner of Afghanistan. They will be your eyes and ears and mouthpiece where you cannot reach. What other candidate can match that?"

"But Qaderi has the mullahs and judges," another guest contradicted sourly. "Do you think he will not have them singing his praises in every mosque?"

Steve stifled a yawn. He'd spent most of the night in a too-small airplane seat. But when he'd stopped in upon his arrival from the airport, Khalid had insisted on Steve's personal appearance as bodyguard for this campaign strategy meeting.

"But Qaderi does not have the foreigners behind him. Nor such protection." The former warlord slid a glance toward Steve before adding slyly, "The Taliban have threatened to eliminate any Afghan who runs in this election. Perhaps we can arrange for them to reduce some of the competition."

"Yes, as long as my Willie is watching over me, I do not fear for my safety. He speaks our languages too, unlike so many who come here." Khalid's reply held warning along with satisfied complacency as he gestured over his shoulder. The conversation became immediately more general, allowing Steve to return to his own thoughts.

Khalid's rant was a reminder that though Amy had carried out her own objective concerning Jamil, Steve had not been so successful. After showing that YouTube video, Steve hadn't spoken again with Ismail before flying out to Jordan. A single voice message from the deputy minister had said only that Ismail had not yet located Jamil.

Now that Steve was back in town, he'd make tracking Jamil down more of a priority. Meanwhile, it was only fair to let Amy know of his search progress—or lack thereof. The computer expert wrapped up the campaign strategy meeting with a demonstration of Khalid's new Web site. That only one in fifty Afghans had access to the Internet was not reflected in admiring oohs and aahs. Steve called Amy as soon as he'd turned Khalid's protective detail back over to the day's assigned leader.

"Hello, Steve. Is there something I can do for you?" Amy's voice was frosty and little above a whisper.

"No, just wanted to touch base. And apologize for not getting back to you earlier. I've been out-of-country the last couple days. But I did forward your request to appropriate channels. I haven't received any solid intel yet, but now that I'm back in-country, I'll be pushing more aggressively."

"Oh, that won't be necessary." The chill in Amy's voice eased fractionally. "I've already found out where Jamil is. He's right here in Kabul. A prison called Pul-e-Charki. Excuse me; I can't talk right now. I've got someone waiting for me. In fact, someone who's working to get Jamil out of prison."

Then she was gone. Steve's thoughts were meditative as he headed downstairs to his Pajero. Pul-e-Charki! Steve knew the high-security complex well enough. Used by the Soviets to hold political prisoners, the prison was laid out from an aerial view to look like a massive concrete wagon wheel. Spokes and connecting rim provided four stories of prisoner housing, the pie-shaped spaces between paved over as exercise yards for the inmates. The concrete wheel was itself set in a high-walled square that separated it from administrative offices and staff quarters. Another high exterior wall surrounded the whole layout, creating a no-man's corridor where, during Soviet times, killer dogs had roamed.

These days Pul-e-Charki was reserved for terrorists, opium dealers, and other serious lawbreakers. That Jamil had been sent there instead of the Welayat, Kabul's regular city prison, was not an encouraging sign. And how had Amy come up with that intel while Deputy Minister Ismail, to whom the Afghan National Police reported, had not?

Questions to explore, but not until Steve tucked a few hours' sleep under his belt. In any case, Ms. Amy Mallory would appear to be handling matters quite competently without Steve's input.

Jamil knew when it was day only because a careless nailing of planks over the window slit opposite his cell permitted entry to a single shaft of light that crept over the corridor floor as morning advanced, to retreat before ever reaching his cell bars. He'd given up straining his ears for footsteps along the corridor. Just how long he'd been in this cold, dank cell, he had no way of judging, but that stray sunbeam had dwindled to night at least twice since his arrival, perhaps more.

Rolling over, Jamil noted dully that the angle of shadows signified afternoon. Had he been asleep or unconscious that he couldn't remember the day's passage? Jamil could wish for either again. Lack of food he could dismiss. He'd gone hungry often enough. And the stiff ache of his body where kicks and blows had landed was nothing new. But his thirst had now become unbearable.

No, that wasn't true. If there was anything Jamil had learned, it was just how much the human body could bear beyond the point where it seemed intolerable.

The clink of a key in the metal grate down the corridor allowed Jamil to scramble to his feet by the time footsteps approached his cell. A tall, lean silhouette carried his memory back to a broken-walled aerie in an abandoned building. "Salaam, Jamil."

Weakness and thirst were not enough to keep Jamil from lunging to reach through the bars. "Then it *was* you! They told me Minister of Justice Qaderi ordered my arrest. But I knew it had to be you."

Only the distinct click of a trigger mechanism sliding back on an AK-47 released Jamil's grip on a silk chapan. A burly man in uniform resplendent with medals and ribbons, a single white streak splitting a full, brown beard, strode forward, a cluster of prison guards at his back. "Comrade, are you sure you will be safe here? Would you like me to order the prisoner immobilized before you speak with him?"

"No, you need not concern yourself. I have brought my own protection." As the prison official and his escort retreated through the metal grate, Jamil's visitor stepped closer so that the sunbeam sieving through the broken plank illuminated sharp, beak-nosed features. The man who'd liberated Jamil from that other prison and set him to the mission of destroying his own employer.

Ismail, deputy minister of interior.

The shaft of light glinted too off a handgun aimed unwaveringly at Jamil's midriff. But Jamil's attention was given only to a translucent cylinder glistening like the priceless treasure it was in Ismail's other hand. A bottle of water. As Jamil's tongue involuntarily touched cracked lips, a slight smile flickered over the deputy minister's own mouth.

Tossing the bottle to Jamil, he said calmly, "I am not responsible for your arrest. On the contrary, I do not wish you here at all."

"No, you wish me dead," Jamil answered flatly. His glance dropped to that unwavering handgun. "Is that why you are here?"

If so, at least Jamil would die with his thirst quenched. Already he had the cap twisted off. A rush of cool liquid down his throat was as reviving as spring runoff. Jamil made a brief effort to save some for later, but his thirst was too great.

"That would be one solution," Ismail acknowledged as Jamil tossed the empty container aside. "Unfortunately killing you here and now would cause more difficulties than it would solve."

"Because of the threat I leave behind?"

"That too." Ismail took a step closer to search Jamil's face. "What I do not understand is why we are here. I let you walk out that door. In part, yes, because of your threats. But also because there seemed little benefit in your death. Nor, though you betrayed the mission, did I wish you any real ill. All that was required for you to walk away to a new life was silence. Instead—" his head's motion back and forth held genuine perplexity— "I have seen this YouTube video, so I know now what you have been doing all these weeks. Tell me, this new mission of which you once spoke, has it proved what you sought?"

The question, skeptical, touched with contempt, brought sharp images to Jamil's mind. Grateful relief on a patient's face. A throng of villagers listening with absorbed wonder as he read. A family's voices joined in song.

Then other images rose more sharply to blot out the pleasant ones. Furious faces and a hail of stones. Three mounds marked with twig crosses.

"It has been more difficult than I thought it would be," Jamil admitted. "I believed my countrymen would be glad to hear Isa's teachings of love and forgiveness, to learn his way of peace, not hate and violence."

Ismail's dark eyes narrowed in disbelief. "You are in earnest! Which means you are a greater fool than I deemed. Have you not learned men are evil by nature? They will not choose good unless they are forced to. That is why it was necessary for Allah to send Muhammad. Because only at the edge of a sword will men make peace. Evil must be destroyed, not forgiven. Which is why the mission you betrayed would have done more by wiping out corrupt and evil leaders to bring true peace to our people than all your bleating of love and forgiveness."

"If you think I will change my mind—"

"I would not be so foolish as to trust you again. Besides, it is now too late for that mission." Ismail looked Jamil over contemplatively. "Tell me, if I should open again the doors of your prison, would you leave

Afghanistan altogether? go to Pakistan or India? They have many villages that would be grateful of a healer's services. I could even provide you the funds to begin a new life there."

"And why would you do that?" Jamil stared at Ismail suspiciously. "And you? If you come here today with such authority, then you still serve my enemy and yours. Nor do you speak like one who has changed his own mission. What is it you are planning?"

"That is none of your concern," Ismail answered sharply. "But though your present mission is pointless, this charge of apostasy is causing trouble for far more important men than yourself. Especially now that your allies have agitated the foreign media on your behalf."

Jamil's heart leaped at Ismail's last statement. Then Ameera had indeed done what he hoped, and so presumably Kareem as well. "Why then did Minister of Justice Qaderi arrest me?"

His visitor shrugged. "Qaderi aspires to be Afghanistan's next president. But all eyes and ears have been on Khalid. The minister, or more likely some imprudent subordinate, must have observed your performance on this video and saw opportunity to draw notice to his own campaign. A successful maneuver. Only you are now proving more trouble than benefit. So if you will go away quietly, I can assure you the minister of justice will be happy to forget your existence."

Just how Ismail could make such a promise, Jamil didn't question. Hadn't he witnessed how far-reaching were the tentacles of his former mentor's command and knowledge? "You will open these bars and let me go?"

"Not so easily. As your arrest was public, so must be your release. You are not accused of following the prophet Isa's example in tending the sick and poor but of abandoning the faith to become one of these infidel heretics who worship not one true God but three or even more. If you have grown soft and weak in abandoning jihad, I cannot believe you foolish enough to swallow such absurdities."

Jamil was no longer so thirsty, but hunger still weakened his limbs, which must be why his mind swam so with bewilderment. By now he'd read the injil accounts of Isa Masih's life numerous times and worked his way through most of the complete holy book Ameera had given him. If there were things that still confused Jamil about Isa's birth and life and martyrdom, nowhere did he remember any teaching that the almighty Creator of the universe was not the one and only true God.

"Of course I believe God is one and not—"

"Then you will have no difficulty making a public *shahada* of faith," Ismail cut him off smoothly. "*La ilaha illa Allah wa-Muhammad rasul Allah.* 'There is no God but Allah, and Muhammad is his prophet.' Once you have shown yourself a true son of Afghanistan, Qaderi can rid himself of you without losing face. Then the foreigners with their protests will go away, and all will return as it was before. My colleague who is administrator here will make the arrangements."

Ismail raised an arm in gesture, and the brown-bearded official drifted back through the metal grate, his escort at his heels. "When it is time, I will return. Meanwhile, thanks to your accomplices who have made sure the world knows you are here, I am informed you have visitors arriving. May I advise you to watch your tongue in answering their questions if you truly wish to escape this place."

The prison administrator stepped close to the bars, his nostrils flaring as he surveyed Jamil up and down. "Faah! You are as filthy and foul-smelling as a rotting corpse! You will cleanse yourself and dress properly before you are escorted to meet your guests."

Only then did Jamil notice that one member of the brown-bearded official's escort was shouldering Jamil's missing pack. Another carried a pail of water. More welcome was an enamel dish in another guard's hands, a slab of naan balanced across the top.

Unlocking the cell door so his men could carry their loads inside, the prison administrator added with derisive contempt, "Scrub well. We would not give cause for your family to bleat to the cameras of mistreatment."

Jamil's eager reach dropped away from the bread slab. "My—family?"

"But, yes. The orders for your visitors included a family member to make a sure identification."

A sudden narrowing of Ismail's eyes mirrored Jamil's own shock as the official added, "Your sister, I believe."

17

The prisoner's sister? Amy's heart jumped as the German doctor read off a list to a checkpoint sentry. To Kareem at her side, she whispered incredulously, "You found Jamil's sister?"

"Shh!" the journalist hissed close to Amy's ear. "No, I do not even know if Jamil has a sister. But this is the only way to get you inside. You are Ameera, Jamil's sister, come to offer identification of the prisoner. Only do not speak."

But Amy had already recognized her error, lapsing back into the silent black heap she'd been the entire trip. This had been longer than she'd expected. Sometimes paved, sometimes dirt, the road zigzagged out of the mountain basin in which Kabul lay to emerge onto a plateau as desolate and featureless as a moonscape. A colossal structure growing up ahead blended so completely into browns and tans and beiges of its surroundings that only its angular lines revealed it was not a natural rock outcropping.

This was Pul-e-Charki? Amy had braced herself for a duplicate of the sprawling, dilapidated Welayat complex in downtown Kabul that contained the women's prison. This was more like some vast medieval walled city.

A qualm that had been squeezing at Amy's stomach suddenly reached the point of nausea. Was she making the right decision to be passing through these gates with a bunch of strangers, all of them men? What if they found out she was not who she pretended? Not that the German doctor or his companions showed any signs of guessing Amy was not the Afghan woman she appeared. Perhaps because as appropriate, they hadn't so much as glanced toward their female passenger since she'd crawled after Kareem into the backseat.

In a worst-case scenario, Amy could always appeal to the single other expatriate in the group. Or would the German doctor consider a common status as foreigners motivation to intercede with local justice? What was the penalty for sneaking into an Afghan prison?

Maybe she'd have been wise to tell Steve her plans when he'd called. But, no! Even if there'd been time, Steve had been caustic enough about relatively innocuous prior outings. Amy could only imagine what he'd have to say about this venture.

At least Amy now knew why she'd never heard back from Steve, and she could wish she'd been less curt. Private security contractor Steve Wilson had his own life to live. And he owed nothing to Amy Mallory, much less to Jamil. *It's just he said he'd find out. And I've never known him not to keep a promise. I'd rather Steve was out of the country than think I was wrong about him.*

Sentries were now patting down Amy's male companions while others inspected the SUV's underbelly with a mirror on the end of a pole. Kareem's camera bag was emptied for a thorough scrutiny. Then the sentry checking paperwork nodded to Amy. "And the woman? She is not on the list we were given."

"She is a family member here to confirm identification of the prisoner," Kareem spoke up quickly.

With no female personnel to do a body search, Amy could see debate on the sentry's face. She held her breath until he shrugged, handing the authorization papers back to the doctor. "The minister of justice himself has sent orders that you are to be extended all cooperation. You may pass. But you will film only in the room with the prisoner. If you are seen taking any pictures of the prison, your camera will be confiscated."

A sentry climbed into the SUV as the gates opened for the vehicle to enter the prison grounds. At his directions, the Red Cross vehicle turned left to follow a graveled track that ran between exterior and interior perimeter walls. The driver slowed to inch around a troop transport. A column of prisoners, handcuffed and roped together, were being herded from the transport through an interior gate into a massive octagonal structure beyond. Among the soldiers unloading prisoners, Amy spotted two in body armor and Kevlar helmets who didn't look Afghan at all: one a tawny-skinned black man, the other freckled and sunburned. ISAF troops? Maybe even American ones?

Their narrow-eyed scrutiny of the Red Cross vehicle and a relaxed alertness in their stance brought Steve Wilson forcibly back to Amy's mind. If he wouldn't approve of Amy's current mission, she hoped Steve would understand her reasons. The security contractor had accused Amy more than once of being overly reckless. But it wasn't recklessness that had Amy fighting down continued queasiness. On the contrary, she'd give much to be elsewhere.

No, the fear and defeat she'd glimpsed on those prisoners' faces were reminder enough why Amy had jumped at Kareem's offer. If this place was terrifying to her, sitting unbound and free under her cloak of anonymity, what must it be like for Jamil in some cold, dank cell in that concrete fortress? And no matter how she rationalized it, her former assistant was back behind prison walls at least in part because he'd met Amy and taken seriously Amy's assurances of a love that could transform his life and nation. The love of her Savior, Isa Masih, Jesus Christ. So how could Amy now permit her own apprehension to keep her away if there was even the smallest help or encouragement she could offer Jamil?

Though when guards sprang to open another gate, the panorama beyond was not forbidding. Buildings were institutional rectangles, but freshly painted. Rose and grape trellises, cobblestone paths, a neat lawn were definitely not prisoner accommodations. As the Red Cross delegation climbed down from the SUV, a green police pickup roared out of the parking area, its speed churning up billows of dust so that Amy found herself grateful for the protection of chador and face veil. Her companions were choking and swearing as the sentry led them into the first building.

A uniformed official, a white streak splitting his full, brown beard, offered no argument when the German doctor insisted his delegation meet the prisoner alone. He led the way to an empty room. A moment later, a guard detail ushered a single prisoner into the room. Incredulous joy flaming into dark eyes told Amy she'd been recognized under the black chador. "Ameer—"

Kareem's warning cough cut off Jamil's exclamation. The young Afghan journalist already had a news camera perched on his shoulder. Retreating to the nearest wall, Amy watched quietly as the Red Cross party approached the prisoner. Jamil was thinner than Amy remembered, and he moved stiffly, a nasty bruise purpling his face. But he was free of bonds, freshly bathed, his clothing clean. He answered the German doctor's questions calmly even as his glance kept flickering toward Amy.

Yes, he'd been given food and water. No, he did not need medical attention. Yes, there were other bruises. No, he did not want photos to be taken. Nor did he wish to be examined. The doctor showed displeasure at this. But when Jamil kept shaking his head, he finally shrugged and handed his medical bag to an associate.

The remaining questions were quickly disposed of. Had Jamil been coerced in any way to make a confession? Did he understand the Red Cross had no influence to bring about his release but was here only to document his condition?

No one paid any attention to the lone and silent black chador. There were advantages to being little more than an animate object. Only when he was finished did the doctor turn to Amy, asking in brusque Dari, "You recognize this man, then? You can confirm his identification?"

He checked a clipboard in his hand. "One Jamil Yusof ul Haq Shahrani, birthplace Kabul, of Pashtun and Tajik mixed heritage?"

The full name was the one Jamil had given Amy for his package. She nodded mutely. Jerking his head toward Jamil, the doctor walked away, still scribbling on his clipboard. Only at Kareem's urgent whisper did Amy grasp she'd been granted permission to speak to her "brother." Silently Amy drifted across the room. How could she say what she wanted in front of all these watching eyes?

But Jamil made it simple by hunkering down in a corner, his gesture signaling Amy to join him. Kareem had turned his camera off. Now he strolled over to stand between the two crouched figures and the Red Cross party, a discreet nod making clear his action was deliberate. Jamil leaned forward, his English so soft it was barely a movement of his lips.

"When they told me my sister was coming to visit, I thought at first a miracle had happened and they had found her alive."

"I only wish it was." Amy could not quite manage that soft murmur, so whispered instead.

"No, I am glad it is you. I did not think to see you again, not after you left my country and not after they arrested me. How did you arrange this?"

"Your friend Kareem. He's been wonderful. He made sure all the media knows about your arrest. That's what pressured the authorities to let the Red Cross come. And he arranged for me to come as your sister."

Jamil let out a tiny sigh. "Then he is indeed the friend he claimed and a believer in freedom. I had hoped he would call to let you know. But to see you? This I did not believe possible."

Though the intensity of dark eyes made evident Jamil's joy in seeing Amy, she sensed an underlying fatigue and bleakness that ripped at her heart. "Have they really been treating you well? They . . . they didn't threaten you to make you say those things?"

Jamil spread his hands slightly, and this time his sigh was deeper. "They gave me food and water and permitted me to cleanse myself when it was found you were coming. But if you had not come . . ." Shrugging his shoulders, he added simply, "I believe I would have died in here without anyone ever knowing."

Jamil fell silent for a moment before he added reflectively, "It is truly strange. Not so long ago, I wanted only to die. To become a martyr. To be done with it all. This brought no thoughts of fear but relief. But now? I find that I wish to live as greatly as I once wished to die."

"Oh, Jamil!" Amy could not keep tears from welling in her eyes. "We'll get you out of here. I don't know how yet, but Kareem has the media on board. There has to be a way to put pressure on this Qaderi. After all, they eventually let that other man accused of apostasy go. Just—don't give up hope!"

"Ameera-jan, please, you must not weep." Jamil raised a hand toward Amy. When his motion drew glances from the Red Cross party, he dropped it again. Amy raised a corner of her face veil to wipe her eyes as he went on earnestly. "Ismail tells me they will certainly let me go once they see it is all a mistake."

Ismail. It took a moment for Amy to place the name. Her landlord's deputy minister. He'd been there when Jamil was arrested after the New Hope bombing. And when Khalid had forgiven Jamil and let him go. What did he have to do with all this?

"The mullahs are saying I am apostate. So Ismail says I must assure them I truly believe the almighty Creator is one god. And that Isa Masih was a holy man and prophet, not one of three gods with his mother Maryam. If the mullahs believe I am sincere, that proclaiming Isa's teachings does not mean I am faithless, they will let me go."

Amy's eyes above the face veil were all of her expression Jamil could see. But something in them must have reflected her dismay because he broke off to say quickly, "What is it, Ameera? You do not think this is what I should say?"

Amy's hands were twisting under the chador even as she shook her head. "Jamil, I couldn't begin to tell you what to say. Especially when you're in here, and I—I am free! You must say what you believe in your heart. But I can tell you what I know in my own heart to be true. What you've read for yourself in the injils of Isa Masih.

"Yes, there is only one God, the almighty Creator, as you say. I believe that too. But Isa is more than a holy man or a prophet. Isa is God come to earth. The injils say this clearly. Not *a* god, nor one of many gods, but one with God. Complete human and completely God. After all, Isa himself claimed to be Son of God. So if he isn't, if he's only a man, then he's neither a prophet nor holy, but a liar. Don't you remember what you said when you left? that only Isa's teachings, his way of love and forgiveness, could bring freedom to your people? But it's not just Isa's teaching that changes people's hearts and lives. It is Isa himself."

"Yes, I said that. And I believed it."

Jamil's pleasure at seeing Amy had drained from his face, so that now weariness and anguish were uppermost as he gritted out between clenched teeth, "But perhaps I was wrong. Because I have failed! I carried Isa's words to my people. I was so sure they had only to hear the truth to find freedom. That they would rejoice in Isa's ways and his love. But it did not happen. Some listened. But more were angry. They drove me away. And those who openly followed Isa, their own neighbors killed them. Just as they did to Isa himself. Perhaps Muhammad was right that men will only change at the point of a sword. And Isa—he was a great prophet and a good man. But he died. The miracles he did, they are beautiful stories. But there are no more such miracles today."

Though Amy and Jamil were speaking barely above a whisper, the urgency of their speech had been noticed or else it had gone on too long because the Red Cross team was crossing the room toward them. Kareem bent down to say hurriedly, "You must finish. It is time to go."

As the journalist stepped forward to intercept the others, Amy leaned forward to whisper urgently, "We're going to get you out of here. I won't stop working until you are free. But about Isa, do you remember the question you asked that day we spoke in the infirmary? and what I answered? I will pray that Isa himself gives you the right words to say. But about miracles, there I can testify personally that you are wrong. Don't you see, Jamil? You yourself are the greatest proof that Isa Masih lives and that he is still doing miracles."

A door slammed open, and uniforms crowded into the room. As Jamil sprang to his feet, Amy reluctantly followed suit. She had time for only one more phrase before the guards pushed past Kareem to collect their prisoner.

"He changed you, didn't he?"

Jamil's sister.

No one knew better than Ismail how impossible was such a statement. Despite impatience, the deputy minister had lingered at Pul-e-Charki to drink a courteous three cups of tea with the prison administrator. He'd need this man's favor again.

Now Ismail pushed the ANP pickup he'd commandeered to hazardous speed along the perimeter track back to the front gate. He hadn't missed the white SUV marked with crisscrossed red lines that was unloading as he sped out of the prison administrative sector. Within Pul-e-Charki walls lived thousands of inmates in conditions Ismail would not offer a dog or a pig, unclean animals though these were. But let a prisoner be noteworthy enough to find his face on a television screen, and infidel organizations such as the Red Cross came like termites swarming from a kicked nest.

So he'd taken pleasure in the dirt storm his exit tossed among dismounted passengers. Including a single enveloping black chador. The "sister," undoubtedly. Posing as a family member was a common ploy—and an accepted one so long as the bribe was sufficient—for getting inside to visit a prisoner.

But after his own long years in prison, who did Jamil know well enough to go to so much trouble? Even bent coughing from the dust, the black-draped figure was tall for a woman. A man in disguise? Prisoners had escaped from Pul-e-Charki in smuggled women's dress, but Ismail had never heard of one trying to get in as such.

Then the wind of his passing tightened black material, tore loose a hank of flaxen hair. The shape was definitely female, and Ismail now had a good idea who it must be. His lip curled further. Against Amy Mallory he did have reason to hold a grudge. Had she not filled his employer's property with female criminals? And that she'd rushed here today suggested it was her influence that had deflected Jamil from his original mission.

Still, Ismail could think of no threat the American woman's visit offered that was worth turning back. And so long as Jamil followed through on the groundwork Ismail had laid, he'd be quickly released. This time if the younger man possessed any wisdom, Jamil would gratefully accept Ismail's offer of exile. If he proved stubborn—well, perhaps once Jamil had sunk again into anonymity, it would be time to permanently dispose of a potential hazard.

Unfortunately Ismail's former protégé had already shown himself unpredictable. Only the dangled promise of finding Jamil's mother and sister had allowed Ismail to control him before. Once Jamil discovered that pledge to be false, Ismail had lost all ascendancy. How to recover it was the challenge.

Reaching the twin towers of the front entrance, Ismail honked his horn impatiently. Then his thoughts returned to the black chador. What Ismail needed was a "sister" of his own to persuade Jamil to be reasonable.

The gates were swinging open when Ismail reached suddenly for his cell phone. A few quick finger movements pulled up a saved image. Staring into unseeing lake blue eyes, Ismail wove strand after strand into a plan of action. If all went well, it would not be necessary.

Still, if a wise man always prepared a Plan B, a Plan C was even better.

18

If Jamil had any illusions that the past hour signaled a change of heart from his captors, these evaporated when the guards thrust him back into the same chill, dank cell. At least the foul-smelling bucket had been emptied, the filthy, tattered tushak replaced with one that looked relatively clean.

More significant was the return of Jamil's belongings. Though not all of them. The missing cell phone was to be expected. And his Dari and Pashto Scriptures had been confiscated. But to Jamil's surprise, the holy book that was Ameera's Eid gift had been left to him along with his health manual. Perhaps, unfamiliar with Western script, those sorting Jamil's belongings had assumed the English volume to be another medical text.

Pulling a second set of shalwar kameez over the first, Jamil wrapped his patu around his shoulders, then the blanket he'd been supplied. Almost he could fancy himself warm. How little it really took to satisfy a man's necessities.

The illusion of warmth enfolding his body was matched by a small, inner glow that burned away at Jamil's earlier despondency. After his first startled jolt, Jamil had assumed the prison administrator's bombshell must be some mistake. More so because of Ismail's evident astonishment. If a female family member had indeed turned up, Jamil's former mentor would be the first to know. And use that information to his own advantage.

Jamil was still dumbfounded that Ameera had placed herself at such risk infiltrating these impregnable walls. Was her action only the kindness and comfort he'd witnessed Ameera show to so many others? Or could he hope some at least was for Jamil alone?

And Kareem. Jamil was not so friendless as he'd felt.

Jamil picked Ameera's Eid gift from his diminished pile. She'd asked if he remembered the question he'd put to her that day in the infirmary. A day that now seemed so long ago when his mission had weighed heavily on his soul and hatred for Ameera's American soldier friend had twisted in his heart. But he remembered his question as he remembered every exchange he'd had with Ameera.

Why had Isa permitted himself to be martyred? With his power to stop storms and even raise the dead, why had he not prevented the soldiers from putting him on a cross?

That martyrdom was one part of the injils, the accounts of Isa's life, that still baffled Jamil. By their telling, Isa Masih could have called angels by the thousand to his rescue. A weak man might allow himself to be put to death out of sheer despair that the human beings he'd healed and fed and loved had turned against him, unwilling to listen to his words. Yet those accounts of Isa's martyrdom held no despair, but triumph. And despite his gentleness and kindness, Isa Masih was not weak.

The words from the John injil Ameera had quoted that day were now familiar to Jamil. In the scant light filtering through the boarded-over window, he read: *"For God so loved the world that he gave his one and only Son, that whoever believes in him shall not perish but have eternal life."*

Ameera had insisted that Isa Masih permitted himself to be martyred by his own choice, not out of despair, but out of love. The divine love of a Creator God for his lost creation. A shudder went through Jamil's body. It was one thing to endure agony because one had no choice. This Jamil knew from bitter experience. But could Jamil have ever forced his protesting body to remain acquiescent if he'd had the power to remove himself from his pain? It would take a strength of will Jamil knew was not in him.

But did that suggest Isa Masih was himself divine? These pages called the followers of Isa "sons of God," even as the Almighty was termed their heavenly Father. Jamil flipped back to the first page of the John injil.

"In the beginning was the Word, and the Word was with God, and the Word was God."

Lest any doubt the writer referred to Isa, this was clarified further on. *"The Word became flesh and made his dwelling among us. We have seen his glory, the glory of the one and only Son, who came from the Father, full of grace and truth."*

No, there was no mistaking John's claim that the prophet he followed was divine, one with the Creator of the universe. But perhaps this was only the writer's poetic license. Had Isa himself ever claimed unequivocally to be God? Jamil turned the pages examining every phrase Isa had uttered.

I am the bread of life.
I am the light of the world.
I am the gate for the sheep.
I am the good shepherd.
I am the resurrection.
I am the way and the truth and the life.

The truth. Jamil had turned his own life upside down in recognition that Isa Masih alone held truth.

Jamil read until the deepening shadows made it too dark to decipher the letters. When night passed and light crept back into his cell, Jamil continued his perusal, reading through the other injils as well. He'd once again reached the John gospel when he saw it. The tenth chapter where the mullahs of Isa's day had demanded that he declare whether or not he was the Christ, the Messiah, Son of God, Son of Man.

Isa's reply was so simple Jamil had missed it on earlier readings. *"I and the Father are one."*

But it hadn't slipped past the mullahs. They'd picked up stones to execute Isa. *"Because you, a mere man, claim to be God."* Those religious leaders understood well that if Isa claimed to be one with the Creator God of the universe, then he was also claiming divinity. *"The Word was with God, and the Word was God . . . The Word became flesh and dwelt among us."*

By his own admission Isa could not be just a prophet and miracle worker. Either he was truly, as Ameera had said, the Almighty Creator become flesh to walk with man. Or he was a liar and blasphemer and unworthy of Jamil's devotion.

That last image was so terrible, Jamil recoiled as though stepping back from a precipice. No, the Isa he'd come to know in these pages, whose touch caressed the leper and blind and widow and orphan, whose wrath thundered against evil and self-righteousness alike, who commanded storms and walked on water, whose words had been a gentle spring rain on Jamil's own parched heart—this man could not be a liar.

Which left one other choice. Isa was truly what he'd said. God himself, who'd laid down his life like an Eid sacrifice to take on the sins of the world. Jamil's sins. Risen in power, he was still working to bring about his Kingdom of Heaven, not through the sword but through the changing of human hearts.

"But it's not just Isa's teaching that changes people's hearts and lives," Ameera had said. *"It is Isa himself."*

Oh, how well Jamil knew that! He who'd hated enough to kill now loved deeply enough to weep and yearn over his own lost land. Even for those who'd lifted stones to drive him from their village. Who'd repaid Jamil's compassion with betrayal. Who'd killed his fellow Isa followers. The tears ran now down his face. *Father, forgive them, for they do not know what they do.*

How could Jamil be angry with others when he knew so well what it was to be locked as they were in a world of darkness and pain and rage? In his frustration that his efforts were bearing so little fruit, he'd let himself forget the miracle of his own new life. Perhaps this was how Afghanistan would see change, slow and arduous though it seemed, just one heart at a time.

Another day passed. Another night. A day. Jamil had again lost track, time marked only by the creeping of the sunbeam across the corridor and by meals each dawn and nightfall. While there was light, he read. In the dark, he pondered.

How God could be one and yet have a Son still mystified Jamil. Was it possible this signified something far different from the mullahs' portrayal of multiple gods jostling each other for power? Had God the one imbued part of his substance with human DNA, entered his creation to live a life bound by human limitations and experience, and in so doing fashioned as well the Father-Son relationship the mullahs found so objectionable?

Just as Jamil had studied in medical school how a human father took of his own essence, the DNA code that made each person unique, merging it with a woman's seed to produce a living person, separate from either. Yet here the union was immeasurably greater. *"I and the Father are one,"* Isa had said. Isa Masih had walked the dusty roads of this planet. He'd experienced hunger and thirst and pain and grief. Yes, and temptation too. He'd known and loved individual humans intimately as his personal friends. He'd lived contained within the same limited universe where Jamil spent his own days. And yet somehow at the same time he'd still been one with the Creator who held the very stars in their orbits and kept the atoms of Jamil's body from flying apart.

Which meant that Isa had never truly known what it was like to be alone in the universe. A speck separated from his Creator with all the despair and grief that entailed.

Or was that true?

"My God, my God, why have you forsaken me?" Isa had screamed out in agony during his dying.

It would seem that at the very point of his martyrdom when Isa had taken humanity's sin upon himself, offering his own sinless life as substitute, it had been necessary for a pure and holy Creator God to withdraw from any contact with that sin. Leaving Isa for that moment in time at least completely alone, carrying upon himself all the vast, incalculable burden of mankind's capacity for evil and hate.

Which made Isa Masih's martyrdom so much greater a sacrifice. The physical agony Isa endured had been great. But other men had endured equal agony. Even to achieve causes in which they believed.

But that Isa would separate himself from oneness with the Creator of the universe to take on the agony and pain and filth of humanity's sin? of Jamil's sin? That the Creator of the universe would be willing to separate himself from the Son who was also himself? What motivation could possibly be powerful enough in itself boggled human comprehension.

"Greater love has no one than this: to lay down one's life for one's friends."

"For God so loved the world that he gave his only Son."

Isa's disciple John had recorded those words of his master and friend. And later when Isa had returned to his Father in paradise, and the disciple John was an old man, he'd written to Isa's followers: *This is love: not that we loved God, but that he loved us and sent his Son as an atoning sacrifice for our sins."*

Such a love was greater than Jamil could wrap his mind around. Any more than he truly understood how Isa could be both man and God. How the Creator of the universe could hold that universe together and yet walk the very dust he'd created as a man. Some things were a mystery too big for the human mind, Ameera had also said that day in the infirmary.

But one thing Jamil could no longer question. Ameera was right. Isa was more than a human prophet as the mullahs had taught. And it was not only Isa's teachings that were worthy of his allegiance. That could transform Jamil's world, his own heart.

It was Isa Masih himself, Son of Man and Son of God.

Which should have been cause for rejoicing. But it was not. Because Jamil could admit that he was afraid. Not just afraid. Starkly, unrelentingly, overwhelmingly terrified.

Jamil had told Ameera that he, who'd once longed for the release of death, now desired intensely to live. How much that desire had to do with Ameera herself, he had not even allowed his own heart to pursue. But he would prefer a death sentence than return to the living hell that was prison. Especially since he couldn't count on the continued protection of solitary confinement. Jamil could endure scarcity of food and water, filthy living accommodations and token personal hygiene, cramped, airless quarters that were an indoor sauna in summer and freezing cold in winter. It was what else he could expect that brought sweat to his body despite the chill of his cell.

If technically "un-Islamic," *bacha bazi* or "boy play" had a long and accepted history in Afghanistan, the mujahedeen commanders with their "dancing boys" as much a stereotype as the burqa. A well-known Afghan saying—"boys for pleasure, women for babies"—was only the mildest of far more graphic humor. Perhaps an inevitable side effect of a culture that kept women so inaccessible. For poorer Afghan families, preadolescent boys were as much a sales commodity as their sisters.

Jamil was not ignorant of such matters, but they'd had minimal relevance for a petted son of an aristocrat family. Until the dark years. The worst had not been the days he'd wanted to die, but the days he'd been willing to submit just to draw another hour's breath. Until at last he'd been as afraid of death as of living because the hell promised those so ruined and sullied as he'd become was even worse than the torment in which Jamil spent his days.

Then came Ismail with his promise of freedom and martyrdom and paradise. *I would rather die than go back. But I long so greatly now to live free rather than die.*

The deputy minister had laid it out so nicely. Jamil had only to swear he was a good Muslim. That the Almighty was one. That Isa was a prophet, a miracle worker, a doer of good. And Jamil could walk out the door.

It would mean leaving Afghanistan, but he would be alive and free. As Ismail had suggested, were there not villages in Pakistan, even many Afghan refugees, who needed the healing gifts Jamil could offer? Was it an inconceivable dream Ameera might even wish to join such an endeavor?

You set me free, Isa. You took away the burden of sin and hate that made me long for martyrdom just so that I could be clean again. Would it be wrong to tell the judges what they wish to hear only until I am free and gone? Can I not serve you best if I am out of this place? You who know my heart will know my faith is truly in you.

Was it prudence or cowardice to know Isa for what he was and yet keep that knowledge to oneself? Omed had opted for the first to protect his family. Those other three Isa followers—well, they were dead, were they not?

If it is cowardice, then I am a coward. Because I cannot risk returning to such a life. I do not think I could keep from returning as well to the hate and rage.

As day continued to fade to night and back to day without further word or visitor, Jamil did not again open Ameera's Eid gift. Food and drink were thrust at intervals through the cell bars, but Jamil barely touched either. A horror of soul had gripped him so that he could not think or pray, sitting motionless for hours at a time, his unseeing gaze on the shifting shadows that were the far cell corner. *I do not know what to do. I cannot think what to say!*

"Be strong and courageous. Do not be terrified; do not be discouraged, for the Lord your God will be with you wherever you go."

Wherever I go? even into the depths of hell?

The creak of the metal grating down the corridor did not rouse Jamil. But the slamming of the cell door itself against the bars, a thud of boots entering, raised Jamil's head. Not one guard, but a full unit.

The leader snapped his fingers. "On your feet. The minister of justice requires your presence. And bring your belongings. You will not be returning to this place."

19

Jamil, where are you in that place?

The balcony where Amy stood overlooked a compound several times the area of New Hope's Wazir rental. Grape arbors and vegetable gardens were currently dried stubble, a fruit orchard leafless and in need of pruning. A water pump had once provided irrigation for the grounds. But the pump handle was broken off, water available only through the arduous process of hoisting a bucket from a well. The perimeter wall was of mud brick and in poor repair.

Still, this compound must have once been a country estate of some wealthy aristocrat because the residence at Amy's back was not adobe but plastered concrete. Two stories high, this wasn't built around an interior courtyard like the Wazir villa, but a solid rectangle perhaps half New Hope's floor space. Its paint had long since faded, plaster peeling from walls and ceiling. But the rooms were now swept and cleaned, walls freshly whitewashed.

The new AWR sanctuary.

The panorama Amy could see now beyond the perimeter wall held less human habitation than she'd have expected this close to the Afghan capital. On the far horizon to Amy's right, she could just catch a glimpse of adobe cubes that were Kabul's outermost suburbs. Scattered closer around a brown, treeless landscape were a few other compounds like the one Amy was now visiting. But what held Amy's gaze was a single massive construction set in a vast, empty no-man's-land directly ahead.

Pul-e-Charki.

Until the hired SUV had emerged from Kabul's mountain valley onto this plateau, Amy hadn't realized the new AWR sanctuary was in the vicinity of the high-security prison where Jamil was being held. Even from this safe distance, its wire-topped walls and high towers cast an oppressive pall. Perhaps the reason land-hungry Kabul residents hadn't encroached farther in this direction, since terraced crop beds bordering the no-man's-land indicated there was water enough for wells and irrigation canals.

A week had passed since Amy had set foot behind those high walls. It was two days since she'd last heard mention of Jamil's imprisonment on the news. And though Kareem called daily, this was only to communicate he had no new information.

"So what do you think?" Elsa inquired at Amy's side.

Amy dropped her gaze hastily to the compound yard. Despite its barrenness, she could already see in her mind's eye the greenness spring rains would bring to orchard and arbors, children racing ecstatically around, women bustling around the tandoor oven and digging in those garden beds.

"It's perfect," Amy answered sincerely.

"Then why do you look so distressed, Miss Amy?" Dr. Amrita asked quietly. "I see you are not unfamiliar with Pul-e-Charki. If you are worried we are so close, you need not be. On the contrary, if fear of the place keeps land cheap, it keeps evildoers away as well. An advantage for women and children living without a male wali. Or is it that someone you've known has been caught behind those walls?"

Something the elderly AWR activist undoubtedly knew more about than Amy. Had Dr. Amrita known prison herself during Soviet or Taliban years? The black eyes searching Amy's face were so shrewd that Amy turned hastily away.

"I was just . . . Do you happen to know who lives in that compound over there? It would make a beautiful sanctuary."

At least one wealthy Afghan was not troubled by proximity to Pul-e-Charki because the compound off to Amy's left and much closer to the prison walls was by far the largest on the plateau. Verdant foliage rising above high, white walls must be pine or juniper to be green at this season.

The villa inside was large, at least three stories high with red tiled roof and ornate wrought-iron balconies. An armed guard, not in uniform but mujahid dress, was visible on an upper balcony.

"Ah, yes, an impressive property. Our seller said it belongs to the deputy minister of interior. His ministry oversaw the aid your government sent to refurbish Afghanistan's prisons."

So that property belonged to Ismail, second-in-command to Amy's landlord. At least it showed better taste than Khalid's Candy Land monstrosity.

"What is your decision, Amy?" Elsa's impatient expression showed no interest in the white-walled mansion. "I'm returning to Germany in a few days. If you can transfer your group by then, I can take video and photos back to make my report."

A reasonable consideration. Amy hadn't yet approached Duane about the AWR proposal, partly because she'd held on to a hope of juggling budget funds for such a move on her own accord. But the New Hope country manager had flown in from Mazar-i-Sharif yesterday for the demonstration Amy had set up of vertical carpet looms. Ibrahim and his cousin had been wildly approving, more for the improved production potential than the weavers' comfort. The sizable order Duane placed on the spot had eliminated any hope of budget surplus.

Nor could Amy herself vacillate any longer. What she saw spread out below her was indisputably better for the Welayat women and children than their current overcrowded quarters. *All that matters is what's best for them!*

"My boss is in town. I'll talk to him and let you know by this afternoon."

As though she could read Amy's mind or perhaps her despondent tone, Dr. Amrita put in gently, "Just remember you are always welcome to visit. It does not have to be good-bye."

"Oh, I will definitely be visiting. At least while I'm still in Afghanistan." Amy broke off abruptly. Where had that come from? Why did it suddenly feel as though handing over the baton of the Welayat project had put a period on Amy's tenure with New Hope?

Another thought came to Amy's mind as the three women left the balcony. That city map Soraya had marked for Amy was still in her knapsack, along with the Pashto directions she'd photocopied from Ibrahim's files. One locally married Welayat bride Amy hadn't yet managed to visit was Roya, who had two young daughters, Loma and Shahla. But if Amy remembered correctly, those hillside outskirts she'd seen from the balcony must be in the general vicinity of Roya's new home.

Amy dug out her photocopies. "Dr. Amrita, would you be able to show me on my map this address here?"

It took only a few moments for Dr. Amrita to mark an X. "I know these streets well from our search for properties in this area. But you will have to ask for this man by name when you come to the street since the houses are not marked."

If the AWR leader knew the area well, Soraya clearly did not because her X was nowhere near Dr. Amrita's. *Next time I'm in the area, I'll stop in and see how Loma and Shahla are handling their mother's new marriage.*

Amy back arrived at the New Hope compound just as the children were swarming into the front yard to play. "Ameera-jan, Ameera-jan. Why do you no longer come to see us? When are you going to tell us a story?"

Amy could feel guilty at the eager, pleading faces. Still working her way through Duane's project list, she'd not returned home before nightfall all week, and then she'd been exhausted and preoccupied enough with Jamil's fate, she'd hardly thought of the children. "I know; I'm sorry I've been so busy. But you should have asked Farah to tell you a story."

Their faces fell, and one girl muttered, "Farah says she will not tell stories anymore. I think she is angry with us."

"Oh, I'm sure that isn't true," Amy consoled quickly. Whatever else, Farah had always seemed to enjoy the children as much as her storytelling and the acclaim she received for it. But then Amy had seen as little of the teenager this past week as the children. On chance encounters, Farah had offered no repeat of her earlier outburst. Still, Amy had now glimpsed a cauldron of seething anger and hurt tamped down behind the girl's docile, accommodating demeanor.

She has every reason to be angry about her life. And maybe it's better to stuff that anger down than let it explode, whatever the psychologists say. At least when there's nothing she can do about it.

"I'll talk with Farah. And see if I can come home earlier this evening."

Of average height with receding sandy hairline and pale blue eyes in narrow, tanned features, Duane Gibson was easy to pick out of the buzz of male activity that had taken over the downstairs salons. When Amy asked for a private word, he walked outdoors with her.

Amy laid out the AWR project. "We need to make a decision because the women's prison has called asking if we're ready to accept a new bunch of prisoners. An option would be to move the Welayat residents to a new property ourselves. The project is still our best human face for New Hope donors, and there's certainly need for more than one such sanctuary in Kabul."

But Duane was already shaking his head. "You know the budget's tight right now. This takes care of your Welayat bunch and does it on Germany's nickel. It's perfect! Especially since Ibrahim and I were just discussing turning this whole property into a vocational training center. Carpentry. Tailoring. Of course we'd keep female employment opportunities like carpet weaving. In fact, there's a project for you, Amy. We'll need a survey on cottage industries we could offer women. Maybe even explore export opportunities. There's a huge sympathy market for handicrafts from Third World widows, orphans, war victims, etc."

Amy tried to rouse enthusiasm. Finding ways Afghan women could make a living was not an uninteresting challenge. "Then I'll notify Dr. Amrita it's a go. Oh, and just one other thing. I'd like to keep one resident on as my personal assistant now that Soraya's so busy with Ibrahim's projects."

Duane shrugged. "That's up to you."

As Amy called Dr. Amrita, she headed upstairs. Soraya and Ibrahim were both sifting through government forms in the New Hope office. Since Ibrahim spoke no English, Amy switched to Dari as she explained the new developments. "The women will have to pack everything up first thing tomorrow morning. And we'll need a truck since we'll be sending along the tushaks, kitchen equipment, and other living supplies they've been using."

Amy hadn't discussed the latter with Duane, nor did she intend to. If New Hope could donate supplies all over Afghanistan, then Amy's

Welayat charges could at least leave with the possessions they'd acquired over the last months.

And of course, Gorg.

Next on Amy's list was to find Farah. The girl had pleaded to be Amy's assistant. Would she be excited at Amy's offer? Or with the attitude Farah had been displaying lately, maybe the girl herself would choose to walk away. Maybe she'd prefer to go with Dr. Amrita and her colleagues who'd fought for the freedoms and education Farah so desperately wanted.

Either way for once in her life, it would be Farah's choice!

But Amy didn't need to look for Farah. Emerging from the New Hope office, she found the girl standing in the archway leading to the carpet workshop. The expression on her face made it clear she'd overheard Amy's conversation.

And misunderstood it.

"I . . . I came to tell the weavers their meal is ready. And then I heard—" Farah opened her mouth, snapped it shut, opened it again. "Is it true? You are abandoning us as you swore you would not? To think I believed that you were not like all others! That you at least would not break your word."

"Farah, it's not like that," Amy tried to break in.

But Farah swept on. "Are you sending us away from here? And you are not coming with us?"

"Well, yes, but—"

Farah broke in again, her expression as stony as her lake blue eyes were stormy. "Then it is clear. You have broken your promise. You are as faithless as . . . as a Welayat guard."

"Farah, let me explain." The jangle of Amy's phone interrupted her. Kareem's daily bulletin from the caller ID. Amy let it go to voice mail to step toward the angry girl. "I'm just trying to do what is best for all of you."

Amy's phone rang again, then as Amy impatiently cut it off, a third time. Still Kareem, and at the insistence of these repeated calls, Amy flipped open the phone. "Yes?"

Spinning on her heels, Farah stormed back through the archway to join the weavers heading wearily down the courtyard stairs toward their noon meal. *I have to go after her! I have to explain!*

"Miss Ameera!" The tension in Kareem's voice drove all thoughts of following Farah from Amy's mind. This was more than a report of no news. "I am at the German embassy. The Red Cross doctor has just informed me Jamil's hearing will be today."

Amy's heart chilled. "Is this good news or bad?"

"It could be very good," Kareem answered cautiously. "Jamil is not foolish. And Minister Qaderi, I think he is now seeing that Jamil's arrest may cause him great trouble for the campaign. If there is a way out that will save face, I think he will take it. All Jamil has to do is continue as he did when he was arrested. Insist that this is a mistake. That he is a good Muslim. That he follows the prophet Isa, but that he does not believe the Christian heresy that Isa is a god. Even better would be to swear he will speak no further of Isa. But Jamil is stubborn, and I think he will not swear an oath he would not keep. If all goes well, perhaps even today he will walk out of Pul-e-Charki."

Amy was silent a moment, her emotions conflicted. What was she to respond? She wanted Jamil freed as much as Kareem did. Maybe far more. But at the cost of denying that the Isa Masih Jamil had pledged himself to follow was indeed God come to earth, Emmanuel? Every atom in her body cried out against it.

But then how did Amy know what Jamil believed? Was she assuming wrongly that Jamil had come to share her faith? In their last conversation, he'd sounded as conflicted as convinced about his current mission. Or the efficacy of Isa's words to change his country. Maybe he could in all honesty tell the judges just what Kareem had suggested.

"What matters is that Jamil be truthful about what he believes," Amy said steadily now. "So when will we learn the outcome?"

"But this is why I am calling. Such proceedings are usually restricted. But Qaderi is not unconscious of public interest in this affair. So he is permitting the Red Cross team to observe so that none can complain of injustice. And to film."

"You mean—?" Amy said hopefully.

"Yes, I will be going. And since you were there before, I do not think anyone will question your presence. Unfortunately the Ministry of Justice has given us little notice. We are leaving immediately."

"What if I met you at Pul-e-Charki?"

"Well, perhaps, if you were at the gate when we arrived."

Straightening out Farah's misconceptions would have to wait until this evening. "I'll be there."

20

How quickly a news story burned out without fresh fuel to fan its flame.

Steve aimed a remote to silence a CNN anchor spouting from the Condor Security command suite wall but continued browsing headlines on his computer screen. Since returning from Jordan, he'd been checking daily for media coverage mentioning Jamil's detention. There'd been a fresh spate after a Red Cross inquiry into Jamil's prison conditions. Their findings negated worries that Amy's former assistant would be maltreated in Pul-e-Charki.

Qaderi himself had played well to the cameras, touting the Red Cross report as validation of Jamil's arrest, followed by an angry denouncement of foreign media attempts to interfere in Afghanistan's legal system. The Afghan press had jumped on this angle, which had helped push the minister of justice up in the polls so that he was currently running neck and neck with Khalid.

Steve's Internet search had yielded only a few persecution watch posts urging prayer for an Isa follower arrested for his faith. He was closing his browser when a sheet of paper fluttered down onto his keyboard.

"You requested the minister's public appearances for this coming week?"

Ismail's glance took in without expression the subject of Steve's Internet search before the screen went blank. This was the first time since Steve's return from Jordan that he'd run into Khalid's deputy. Understandable as Ismail had spent recent days flying around Afghanistan in Khalid's Mi-8 helicopter, meeting with tribal leaders to drum up support for his employer's campaign since security concerns made it too dangerous for Khalid to do so personally.

Steve glanced over the movement schedule. "Back in town awhile?"

"The helicopter has been malfunctioning. Your subordinate, Bones, says we cannot fly again until he takes the engine apart." Ismail tapped the schedule. "Khalid will be at the police academy this morning. This was not planned, but the foreign police commissioner who supervises training of poll security will be giving an address. It will be on the news."

And Khalid wasn't about to pass up a photo op! Ismail's comment was a reminder that if the deputy minister had pursued his own investigation of Jamil's arrest, he hadn't seen fit to pass that intel on to Steve.

Looking up from Khalid's schedule, Steve asked abruptly, "By the way, the data I inquired about on our Wazir bomber Jamil who was arrested last week—were you ever able to turn anything up on his whereabouts?"

Ismail's eyebrows shot up. "But of course. He is at Pul-e-Charki. You were not aware?"

"Actually, yes, I'm aware he's at Pul-e-Charki," Steve responded evenly. "But since I never heard back, I wasn't sure whether you'd received this information."

The deputy minister's shoulders rose and fell under his fine silk chapan. "Do the police not answer to me? I had only to inquire. Since you did not ask again, I presumed you had already acquired the information. Especially when I saw the American woman at Pul-e-Charki."

"The American woman?" Steve repeated carefully.

"The aid worker at Khalid's Wazir rental in whose security you have taken such an interest. She was at Pul-e-Charki with the Red Cross delegation. What should I suppose but that she was in communication with you?"

Steve did not care for Ismail's knowing glance. Deliberately he adjusted his face muscles to match the deputy minister's own bland expression. "Condor Security is no longer involved in any way with security at that location. But Ms. Mallory, you say she was at Pul-e-Charki as a member of the Red Cross delegation?"

"No, I think they said she was there as his sister." Ismail was already walking away, tossing the statement over his shoulder. Steve was glad he didn't have to respond. Amy at Pul-e-Charki? And posing as Jamil's sister?

What are you up to, Miss Amy Mallory?

Steve's thoughtful gaze followed Ismail's billowing silk robes out the door. So Ismail too had been at Pul-e-Charki when the Red Cross visited? Was he less disinterested in the man who'd tried to blow up his boss than he projected? Or did his visit to Pul-e-Charki have nothing to do with Jamil?

Steve had known Ismail as long as he'd known Afghanistan. And yet if the deputy minister was more than a mouthpiece for Khalid, if he'd any thoughts and dreams and ambitions of his own rather than his master's, Steve had never seen them evidenced. Perhaps there really was nothing else behind that bland expression and smooth speech. But ignorance always made Steve uneasy.

Lighten up! Ismail's ridden on Khalid's coattails the whole way. His welfare and future depend on Khalid's own well-being. Reason enough to trust his loyalty.

An electronic beep alerted Steve to a Skype call. A moment later, Phil Myers was gazing at him from the computer screen. The Special Forces medic looked tired but serene.

"How's Jamie?" Steve asked.

"Better than expected. The bone marrow transplant took well. The doctors are being cautious, but they anticipate full remission. Which is why I'm calling. Just wanted to give you a heads-up I'll be on tomorrow night's flight into Kabul. You can reschedule that vacation."

"Phil, you know that's not necessary!" Steve said forcibly. "I have no problem finishing out this contract."

"But I do." Phil's single good eye and narrow, bony features were adamant. "It's one thing to grab a lifeline when you've got no other options. It's another to take advantage of a friend when it's no longer necessary. I've only got another month till the clock runs out anyway. Then I'll be looking for work stateside. Maybe permanently if this training upgrade works out."

Steve didn't try to argue further. Mainly because he'd have done the same in Phil's place. Which meant that Steve would again be free to pursue his own future.

Somehow that Jamaica beach no longer seemed so appealing.

Amy pushed the Toyota Corolla as fast as she dared through crowded Kabul traffic. She was turning off the main highway when she spotted in her rearview mirror a white SUV marked with crisscrossed red lines well back in traffic. Relaxing, Amy turned the hatchback into an open lot that was visitor parking. She was trudging down the road toward the front gate's twin towers when the Red Cross vehicle pulled up beside her.

Whatever explanation Kareem had given, Amy's reappearance roused no curiosity. Once through the gates, their assigned guide directed the Red Cross vehicle to the same administrative sector. But this time they were escorted to a much larger room, dim and wood-paneled. At the front of the room, a prayer rug with Arabic calligraphy woven into the pattern was mounted on the wall like a tapestry. A sword and a whip flanked the rug. The emblems of sharia punishment.

Below the rug, a middle-aged man in white robes and turban, his long black beard streaked with gray, sat behind an ornately carved hardwood desk. If this was Minister of Justice Qaderi, he looked nothing like the man Amy had seen on the news. In front of him were a small stack of books and an open file. Chairs on either side held a dozen men of varying ages, all bearded.

Beyond the judge panel, a two-sided barricade of the same richly carved hardwood as the desk turned the farthest corner into a square enclosure. A witness box, perhaps. The rest of the courtroom was empty except a dozen more chairs lined up against the rear wall. The Red Cross delegation was taking seats there when a guard unit crowded through the doorway, escorting a single flexicuffed prisoner.

Two other men entered behind the guards. The official in uniform with a white-streaked brown beard had overseen the Red Cross interview. His companion, a tall, lean man in expensive silk chapan, looked vaguely familiar. Then Amy placed him. Khalid's deputy Ismail. Jamil had mentioned Ismail coming to his aid. Had some lingering guilt on Khalid's part prompted the intervention? Or did Ismail have his own reasons?

But Amy was too focused on the prisoner to dwell on the matter. The bruise on one cheek had faded to mottled green, and from an ease of walk, there'd been no further injuries. Clothing was again fresh, dark curls and beard washed and neatly trimmed. Jamil's captors were avoiding any censure from the Red Cross delegation or the world's cameras.

As Jamil crossed the room, his glance swept the Red Cross party, lingered briefly on the black chador. He'd recognized her, Amy knew. But his expression didn't lose its bleak resignation, and he turned away immediately to face the judges.

"You are Jamil Yusof ul Haq Shahrani, birthplace Kabul."

As the turbaned judge at the table read dispassionately from the file in front of him, Kareem hurriedly raised his camera to one shoulder. This time his feed was going live to the news services, he'd whispered to Amy. The guards fanned out against the walls, leaving the prisoner standing alone in front of the tribunal. If distressingly reminiscent of the last occasion she'd witnessed Jamil face a panel of accusers, the proceedings as they unfolded were nothing like Amy's idea of a trial. There were no lawyers. No witnesses. Not even a presentation of criminal charges. The chief justice simply shuffled through his file, then looked up at Jamil.

"We have reviewed the evidence submitted against you, and it is clear enough. But since the charges are serious, and we would not have anyone accuse this court of lacking mercy or being unjust—" a hooded glance went to the Red Cross team—"it has been granted that you may speak in your own defense."

Sitting next to Amy, the German doctor leaned over to ask an Afghan colleague, "Where's Qaderi? I thought the minister of justice was overseeing this."

"The minister of justice is shrewd," his companion answered gravely. "This man's arrest was useful in bringing attention to his election campaign, but it has proved more controversial than anticipated. So Qaderi stays away and lets a local court deal with the man. If the prisoner is found blameless and released, he can say the arrest was a mistake of underlings. Thus he shows himself merciful even as he demonstrates his commitment to the purity of Islam. Both will do him good in the polls."

So Jamil and Kareem were right to hope these ridiculous charges would be dismissed, this trial just a formality for the world's cameras. Amy's spirits rose slightly.

"You are accused of abandoning the faith to become one of these Christian infidels who bring their alcohol and dirty movies and prostitutes into our country. What is your plea?"

Kareem had moved to one side of the room so his camera could catch Jamil's face as well as the judges. Amy wished she could follow suit because right now all she could see was Jamil's back, tight with tension under the thin material of his shalwar kameez. But his answer was even and clear.

"I have not abandoned faith in the Almighty, and if by infidel, you mean that I have chosen to follow evil ways such as is shown on foreign television, then no, I am a true son of Afghanistan. I believe in the one true God who created heaven and earth. I pray. I fast. I do not break the law with alcohol and immoral women."

"But you are a follower of Isa. We have you on video admitting such. And you read from infidel holy books." The judge spread out that small stack of books, and Amy realized they were the Dari New Testament and Pashto Bible she'd given Jamil. "Do these not show you are apostate?"

Despite the pointed questions, the judge's tone was mild, as though simply following a preset script. The tautness of Jamil's shoulders did not ease, but his voice grew in confidence.

"Did not Muhammad himself say there is much good in these books? Yes, I follow the teachings of Isa. Blessed are the peacemakers for of such is the kingdom of heaven. Do to others what you would have them do to you. Be kind to one another, forgiving each other. Love one another, even your enemies. Are these not good words? If all men followed such teachings, the foreign nations that are called Christian as well as the followers of Islam, would we not truly see paradise on this earth?"

A sudden murmuring swept the panel of judges. The chief justice at the table looked thoughtfully at Jamil before he responded, "You are right that the prophet spoke highly of Isa Masih and even commended his teachings of righteousness. If these are the teachings you have been spreading, perhaps we should encourage more such Isa followers in Afghanistan. We would not wish other nations to accuse us of intolerance and a rush to judgment."

Again his response sounded rehearsed, as though designed for the camera. Amy's hands twisted together under her chador. *He's doing it! They're going to let him go free.*

And then what? With his face so well-known, Jamil could hardly return to his itinerant evangelism. He'd have to go into exile. Perhaps asylum in the U.S. Maybe even back to medical school. Have a real future. *Oh, Father God, have you allowed this for Jamil's benefit, not harm?*

Then the chief justice spoke again. "But if you are to be commended as a good Muslim, there is one more question you must answer truthfully. The Christian infidels believe Isa Masih to be more than man and prophet, but divine himself, Son of the Almighty. It is this heresy the Quran condemns. If you will assure your accusers and the world that you do not share this heresy, that you are indeed not an apostate to Islam, then it will be the pleasure of this court to release you."

Amy couldn't breathe. This was the question she'd been afraid the judge would ask. And Amy now knew with certainty the reason for that bleak expression she'd seen earlier on Jamil's face. *He doesn't want to go back to prison. And how can I blame him?*

The whole room seemed to be holding its breath with her. The panel of judges leaned forward expectantly. The Red Cross team on either side of Amy did the same. Jamil himself did not answer, his immobility that of a statue—or a corpse. Amy's heart thudded hard in her breast once, twice, a third time. Then the chief justice cleared his throat.

Amy caught the moment tautness precipitously left Jamil's slender frame. She saw him straighten his shoulders before taking a slight step forward. She watched him turn his head so that it was to the camera as well as to his prosecutors. When he spoke, there was not only confidence but, unexpectedly, joy in his voice.

"In that case, though I did not consider myself to be an apostate, I must confess that I am. Because I do believe Isa Masih to be divine and Son of the Almighty. More, I believe that he is the Creator of All himself come to earth, born as a man, to show humanity his love. Like the Eid sacrifice, Isa Masih, though guiltless of sin, permitted himself to be martyred on a cross to pay the penalty for my sin and yours. By the power of his divinity, he rose from the dead. He is alive and with me here today. And it is his power that permits me, a sinner, to stand before you cleansed of my guilt and to know with all certainty that one day I will be with Isa in paradise."

The room exploded with noise. The other judges were shouting, and Amy had no difficulty picking out one phrase. "Death to the apostate."

The guards surged forward, weapons coming up. As they closed in around Jamil, the chief justice raised his voice to drown out the others. "Are there any further words with which you would like to condemn yourself?"

"Only this." Jamil had turned so that Amy could now see his face. His dark eyes met hers, and though his voice rose to ring out around the room, Amy knew his words were for her.

"I came here today afraid. Not afraid of the questions that would be asked or the judgment I would face. Afraid I would not have the courage to speak the truth of Isa. But it did not prove so hard. Isa himself gave me the words. And the courage."

21

"Hi, John, I'll be over as soon as I can shake loose." Steve tugged at the Velcro straps of his upper body armor as he wound up his cell phone conversation with John Atkins. He'd spent the morning pulling security duty for Khalid's police academy appearance.

Now Khalid was back in his Sherpur nest, schmoozing local bigwigs for the rest of today. Leaving Steve to return to what was supposed to be an off-duty shift. He'd spent numerous hours at the Afghan Relief Mission compound working out perimeter defenses. Finding ways to improve security on a shoestring was a challenge he was actually enjoying. If he'd be departing Kabul shortly, Steve wanted to leave the project finished. But first some food before the team house chef cleared away the midday buffet.

Steve filled a plate and carried it into the living area, where Bones, the team mechanic, was poring over schematics of a helicopter engine with logistics manager Cougar.

"Steve, I was hoping I'd catch you!" Cougar looked up from the blueprints. "You happen to know any American-passport operatives available on short notice? Hamilton just called to ask if we'd subcontract a small job. All their available personnel are tied up in election-related projects."

"What's the job?"

"DEA's got a team flying in to interrogate some high-level counter-narcotics detainees at Pul-e-Charki. They'll be staying at the embassy, so we're talking personal security while up at the prison. A few days, one week tops. But with sensitive intel involved, the operative's got to have top-level State Department clearance. Unfortunately, we're as short on those as Dyncorp."

"Hey, Wilson, are you seeing this?"

The interruption came from Bones, who'd abandoned the helicopter schematics to stare at the flat screen. The police academy coverage had given way to some gathering of local mullahs. Then the camera angle shifted, and Steve saw the armed guards, the bound figure standing with quiet composure in the center of the courtroom.

"Isn't that your repentant suicide bomber who got himself arrested a while back?" Bones demanded. "Looks like they decided to put him on trial after all. What do you think the perp's up to now? Or do you think any of that conversion stuff is legit? If so, the guy's just tucked his neck into a noose!"

Steve turned up the sound. His mouth twisted cynically as he listened to the Afghan judge's questions and Jamil's answers. Both were clearly planned in advance to offer the prisoner an easy out while allowing the religious establishment to save face.

The guy's a survivor, whatever else he is! At least Bolton will be pleased. The freedom of worship issue will be one less headache to deal with in this election.

A twinge of disappointment surprised Steve. Despite his response when he'd uncovered Jamil's plot to assassinate Khalid—and his reasons for it—Steve had felt grudging respect for the younger man's commitment to his mission. His willingness to give his own life for what he believed. And to abandon that mission when his convictions no longer supported it.

So though he could applaud the prudence of the answers Jamil was giving the judge, he found himself wishing for—what? The guy to march himself into a firing squad?

No, to do what I haven't, Steve admitted silently. *To go after what he believes to the very end, at whatever cost. Because if nothing else, that's the kind of man Amy deserves in her life.*

Then in the next moment, Steve stiffened. Behind him, Bones drawled, "Hey, did I get the Dari wrong? Or did that guy confess on international news to being an apostate? Doesn't he know the penalty here? Is he crazy?"

"No, just a true believer." Steve could no longer doubt that was the truth. The sincerity in Jamil's tone had been unmistakable. This was no act. The man had laid his life on the line for what he believed. *And when was the last time I did that?*

On the TV, the chief justice was still speaking. "You will be returned to confinement until your fate is determined."

As the guards closed in on Jamil, the news camera that had been filming that confession rotated to show the rest of the courtroom. Crossed red lines on a medical bag identified the Red Cross delegation. Next to a uniformed official was a face Steve recognized. Ismail. So this was why Khalid's deputy minister hadn't been at the police academy event.

Then the camera brushed over a black chador, and Steve stiffened again. Even without Ismail's mention of Amy's earlier visit to Pul-e-Charki, Steve would have recognized that motionless, seated shape, the tilt of the head, the long-lashed hazel eyes that were the only visible feature.

Steve was already grabbing for his cell phone, though he wasn't quite sure what he intended, when it rang. Jason Hamilton sounded more agitated than Steve had ever known the tough Dyncorp manager.

"Have you seen your boy Jamil on the news? We've got trouble bigtime. State Department's going ape. Bolton has already contacted your principal for an immediate powwow. As per standard op, he expects his security head and Khalid's to stand in as agent-in-charge, no subordinates. That's you and me. Meaning he's planning a few choice words for your client. We're on our way over now."

So much for a day off! Better let John Atkins know to start without me.

The courtroom had disappeared from the screen, replaced by a new face. Qaderi. His tone was not hard but sorrowful, even kindly. Though Allah detested the apostate, the Creator of All welcomed a contrite heart and any wayward who returned to the truth. Which was why, despite serious accusations leveled against this Isa follower Jamil, Qaderi had ordered that the detainee be given opportunity to proclaim his allegiance to Islam, the only faith permitted by law to be propagated on Afghan soil.

Regrettably the criminal had chosen to spurn that kindness, proclaiming his guilt for all the world to hear. And for the unrepentant apostate, sharia law offered only one penalty. As minister of justice, Qaderi must uphold that law as he had sworn to uphold all law and put an end to the current climate of corruption and impunity across Afghanistan.

The news camera pulled back to reveal the twin minarets and turquoise dome of Kabul's largest mosque. Its courtyard was packed, a roar of approval greeting Qaderi's words. This was no law enforcement report, but a campaign rally, and Jamil had just become Qaderi's key platform.

May you have mercy on him, Father God, Steve found himself unexpectedly praying, *because Qaderi sure won't!*

Amy was grateful now for the silence and anonymity the chador imposed as the Red Cross delegation made its way back to their vehicle. She knew the occasional pitying glance assumed Jamil's female relative was weeping over the verdict. Or for shame. How to explain that tears could hold grief and fear, yet joy and pride as well?

The Red Cross team seemed totally confused. The German doctor was demanding, "What happened? I thought they were going to release the man to our custody?"

Once through the main gate, the SUV pulled over to let Amy off where she'd been picked up. Kareem followed a few steps away to speak privately. "Do not cry, Miss Ameera. There are still means by which Jamil may be freed."

But neither his expression nor tone held belief in his words, and it was with an unhappy sigh that he added, "Though it will not be easy. I told you Jamil was stubborn. And courageous too. But great effort was invested to offer him this opportunity to walk free. Not just by myself, but others too. Could he not have held his tongue until he was released?"

"Kareem, I know you put a lot of work into all this," Amy answered quietly. "And I'm sorry it all went for nothing. But no matter what happens, I for one am proud Jamil had courage to speak up for what he believes. Isn't that what you said you were fighting for?"

"Yes, but perhaps I did not mean it sincerely. Because I am willing to admit I am afraid. For Jamil. For myself, should any learn I have worked on his behalf. It is one thing to support a Muslim's right to speak of Isa. It is another to whisper a good word of a confessed apostate. I do not think after today you will hear any Afghan journalist speak favorably on Jamil's behalf."

His message was not hard to comprehend. Whatever oblique support Kareem had offered to date, Jamil was now on his own. As was Amy. Kareem hurried back to the SUV. Amy waited for the Red Cross vehicle to disappear toward Kabul before heading to the Toyota Corolla. Jamil's "sister" would not be driving a car. Her own impulse was to race home to do something, anything. But she could think of nothing useful at this moment.

As she climbed into the hatchback, her eye fell on the map Dr. Amrita had marked earlier, thrusting out of a side pocket of Amy's knapsack. A reminder that Jamil was not her only concern. Amy had promised herself to check in on Roya and her daughters her next trip out this way. Now here she was with no real reason not to seize the opportunity. The visit would require only a short detour, and maybe by then some fresh brainstorm would have occurred to Amy.

Roya's new neighborhood was carved literally from the mountainside as it climbed toward the plateau where Pul-e-Charki sat. Each home involved digging a terrace big enough to enclose with mud brick and add a few rooms inside, so that from a distance the entire zone looked more like a termite hill than any human habitation should.

Forced to a jolting crawl to negotiate deeply rutted switchbacks, the Toyota Corolla was collecting an unwelcome entourage. Mostly children, but teenage boys and men too. Keeping easy pace with Amy's vehicle, they peered inquisitively in the windows, pulled themselves up on the bumper, perched on the hood.

Masquerading as an Afghan woman no longer offered any advantage. Amy tugged loose the face veil and pushed back the head covering to reveal some flaxen strands. A sudden inspiration had her digging in her knapsack for her first aid kit. Rolling down the window, she displayed the small, white box with its red cross. "Salaam aleykum, could you please help me? I am looking for—"

Amy read off the family name. "They live on a corner two streets beyond the chaikhana. There is a woman and children I need to see."

It could have gone either way. But these were no arrogant and bigoted madrassa students such as Amy and Farah had encountered, just curious neighbors. They nodded knowingly over the Red Cross symbol. If Afghan women didn't drive, there was no accounting for the strange practices of countless foreigners flooding their city. To Amy's relief, her entourage chose to find her intrusion entertaining rather than offensive. As the children chattered excitedly, a man pushed through to the window.

"You are a *dokter* then for women? Will you attend my wife? I live right over there."

"I would be happy to," Amy answered. "But first I need to find these people."

"I will show you. You, get off! Where are your manners? Leave the *dokter* in peace!"

The man directed her to a cinder-block wall where a jinga truck's colorful panels thrust up above a metal gate. Roya's new family would seem to be relatively prosperous. Amy's guide knocked on the gate. "I will stay here to guard your car."

A powerfully built man in his thirties opened the door. His suspicious stare held none of his neighbors' cheerful curiosity. Yes, Roya and her daughters lived here. Yes, they were at home. Where else would decent women be? Yes, a brief visit would be permissible. Emphasis on *brief*.

The man was so unsmiling, his answers so curt, that Amy found herself reluctant to step inside. But a woman squatted over a basin in the dirt courtyard had already surged to her feet. "Miss Ameera, it is you! You are back in Kabul."

Roya had been the senior of New Hope's Welayat residents, her stooped frame and careworn features looking much older than her actual forty-plus. Beaming, she left the clothes she'd been scrubbing to hurry forward. But before she reached Amy, a missile thudded into Amy's midriff, a cinching grip wrapping her waist. Amy gently lifted the small face pressed against her ribs. Nine-year-old Shahla.

Tears brimmed brown eyes. "Ameera-jan, I thought I would never see you again."

"Well, now you have," Amy said soothingly. "And I am so happy to see you too, Shahla-jan. Where is Loma?"

Amy glanced around to take in whitewashed rooms, water pump, neatly laid-out garden. The nearest door stood open, revealing colorful rugs and cushions, a hardwood sideboard, even a glass-fronted cabinet. The man who'd let Amy in disappeared inside, slamming the door. He seemed much too young to be Roya's new husband, while this whole place displayed too much affluence to be in the market for a cheap, ex-convict bride.

Roya had wiped wet hands to offer her own embrace before Amy spotted Shahla's older sister emerging from a room. With their flawless oval features framed by dark curls, Shahla and Loma gave a glimpse of what Roya herself had been before a hard life left its marks. At nine and eleven, they were at an age when Afghan girls donned headscarves and began hiding themselves from male eyes. At New Hope they'd reveled in racing around with male playmates. Both had soaked in Fatima's teaching like thirsty sponges and were among Amy's biggest story fans. Lively, vivacious, they'd seemed as yet unscarred by life, and though Amy did her best to be impartial, she could admit to a special soft spot for the pair.

Now instead of bareheaded curls, Loma was wrapped decorously in a head shawl. Kohl lined her eyes, her soft mouth bright with lip gloss. In these past few months of good nutrition, the eleven-year-old had shot up several inches, and seeing her now after several weeks, Amy noted that Loma's frame, once thin and straight, was taking on curves. With added maturity, the pretty little girl would soon be a beautiful young woman. But a frozen look in the huge, brown eyes watching so silently from across the courtyard disturbed Amy. Why hadn't Loma rushed forward to embrace her? Was Loma, like Mina's daughter, Tamana, resentful of her mother's new marriage? Did she blame Amy?

Amy turned to Roya. "I have missed you and Loma and Shahla. Are you well? Are you happy here?"

"Well enough." Roya shrugged. "Please, you must stay for tea. Come, come."

As Roya urged her guest to cross the courtyard, Amy hesitated. "I don't think I'd better. Your . . . uh, husband? . . . says you are very busy. I don't want to cause you trouble with him."

"Tariq?" Roya tittered, a hand covering her mouth as the laughter exposed missing front teeth. "Oh, Miss Ameera, do you truly think any man would marry such a worn-out creature as myself? Can I still bear sons? No, Tariq is Loma's husband, not mine."

"Loma's husband!" Amy felt as though she'd been hit in the chest. "But . . . she's only eleven years old—"

Amy broke off. Roya had undoubtedly been married by Loma's age as were a good portion of Afghan women. *But not my New Hope children! And not to that man! He . . . he's old and angry-looking! No wonder Loma looks so different!*

"I don't understand. I thought you wanted your daughters to study, to get an education. That you didn't want them to marry so young as you did. Did you think you couldn't stay on at New Hope? Is that why you let this man take Loma? Because you thought you would have no home?"

Amy broke off again. What was done was done. Reproaching Roya would not undo the situation. But the very thought of the lively little girl who'd snuggled up to hear Amy's stories in the embrace of that stern, unsmiling stranger made Amy feel physically nauseous.

Roya had lost her welcoming smile. "Do you think I wished my Loma to marry?"

Casting a scared look toward the slammed door, she lowered her voice to a bitter hiss. "I wished to stay as you promised at New Hope. Or if we had to leave, to find work to support myself and my daughters. To let Loma and Shahla grow into women before finding them husbands. Then Tariq came to the mechanics yard with his truck. When he saw my beautiful Loma playing and desired her for himself, what could I do? I am not her wali. The arrangements were made. I was given no say."

"What do you mean, Loma's wali?" Roya's daughters had no wali to make such decisions for them. Amy was beginning to feel some déjà vu. Hadn't she had this same conversation with Farah when she'd assured the sixteen-year-old that no one could marry her off against her will?

"Are you saying the girls' father came for Loma?" Roya's former husband had dumped her for a teenage bride when she'd been arrested for tilling his opium crop. "That he arranged Loma's marriage with Tariq?"

"No, not their father. He does not even know where we now live. Did he not throw us from his life? Does he not now have a son instead of daughters to capture his love? No, it was Soraya's husband who arranged the marriage."

"Ibrahim." Amy was suddenly furious. "But he had no right to do that. Roya, why didn't you just say no? You are their mother. It's up to you to make that decision, not anyone else."

"But that is not true. I am a woman. A woman has no rights to make such decisions for her daughters. Yes, I could refuse to marry, and I would have, though I were beaten to change my mind. Other Welayat women like Aryana and Mina married of their own choosing. But they are widows or divorced, not virgins. But my daughters—by law their wali may make arrangements whether their mother agrees or not. You placed Soraya in charge of the women when you left. Ibrahim is her wali. So by law he is also wali to every girl child in his household."

Another twist that had never occurred to Amy when she'd invited Soraya's family to move in to New Hope. "I wish you'd come to me. Even if it is the law, I wouldn't have let it happen, even if I had to fire Ibrahim and Soraya and kick them out."

"But you were not here," Roya answered simply. "And we did not know you would ever come back."

No, Amy hadn't been here. But Duane had been. Why hadn't he prevented this? And Soraya. She'd graduated with a master's degree, allowed her own daughter to earn a teacher's degree. That she couldn't have spoken up, Amy simply didn't accept.

"It is not so bad. Tariq is not a cruel man." Roya gestured to Loma, and at last the young girl crossed the courtyard. Passively, she allowed Amy to hug her, but a blank remoteness in her eyes, the complete absence of the vivacious child who'd laughed and played in that beautiful, lithe body just weeks ago, left a painful ache in Amy's chest.

As Loma rested her head against her mother's shoulder, Roya went on, "At least he permitted Shahla and myself to come with Loma and did not separate us. Though this was not so much kindness than that he has a brother who lives here too and is unmarried. Now he will have Shahla without such a high bride-price as Tariq paid for Loma. Since Tariq's brother is many years younger, they are permitting Shahla to remain unmarried until she reaches her womanhood."

In other words, until the nine-year-old began menstruation. Which could be as early as a year or two from now. But something else Roya had said disturbed Amy more. "Roya, what did you mean by a bride-price for Loma? Soraya told me the reason for men coming to New Hope was so they could find a wife without paying a bride-price they can't afford. I know from Aryana and Mina themselves their new husbands were never charged anything for them."

"Yes, because they have been in prison and are not unspoiled property. But for a young virgin, the bride-price has grown very high. That is why Tariq and his brother have remained unmarried though they are hardworking and own three jinga trucks. Do you think any wali would surrender one as beautiful as my Loma without a high price? Have you not seen Ibrahim's new vehicle? Though Tariq offered all his savings for Loma, Ibrahim would not accept it until Tariq added his personal vehicle to the bride-price."

22

The minister of interior's florid features held a thunderstorm of fury as Steve shepherded Deputy Chief of Mission Carl Bolton and Dyncorp country manager Jason Hamilton into Khalid's reception suite. Steve wasn't surprised to find Khalid's own deputy absent. But servants were still pouring tea when Ismail strode into the suite, silk chapan dusty from what must have been a record-setting race back from Pul-e-Charki.

"Forgive my tardiness, Minister. I was at some distance when you called."

Steve was not the only one who'd paid attention to the courtroom drama's backdrop. Carl Bolton immediately spoke up. "Yes, I see you were up at Pul-e-Charki for today's hearing, Deputy Minister."

Ismail's shrug was noncommittal. "The young man's arrest and publicity surrounding it are an unfortunate development at this season. So it seemed prudent to monitor the situation closely. I had hoped the matter could be settled discreetly so as not to distract from the election campaign. Unfortunately this is no longer possible."

Bolton wasted no time in coming to the point. "Precisely why I'm here. My embassy is deeply concerned with today's developments. This man's trial and Qaderi's talk of the death penalty are already hitting airwaves and the Internet. I'm sure you remember the global uproar last time the Ministry of Justice ordered an apostasy trial. Especially since your new constitution had already been ratified, guaranteeing the international bill of human rights."

"Except where this bill contradicts sharia law," Khalid pointed out. "No law can be above Allah's law. So says the constitution too. Which your government also ratified. So why are you so disturbed now? As you say, this has happened before. And though your religious idealists and media screamed, my people know you did not halt your aid and weapons and soldiers whether this infidel was tried according to our law or yours."

"Unfortunately, times have changed," Bolton countered patiently. "In that former case, the American people were still convinced they needed only patience to see Afghanistan becoming a peaceful and prosperous democracy. Which allowed my government to give yours a pass, especially since your courts did eventually declare the man mentally incompetent so he could leave the country in peace. Any hope of this happening here?"

To Steve's surprise, it was Ismail who spoke up, shaking his head decisively. "Too many have heard this Jamil speak on these YouTube videos. They can see he is not insane, but an educated man, a healer. The mullahs will never consent to free him for reasons of mental defect."

"And there's our problem." DCM Bolton suddenly leaned forward. "And if I may speak bluntly, Minister Khalid, your problem too, should you become Afghanistan's next president. My government remains committed to your country. But it's been a decade now since the Taliban were run out of town. The American taxpayer has poured considerable funds into rebuilding this country. And frankly, they're beginning to feel they aren't getting much for their investment. The insurgency's as bad as ever. Afghan opium is flooding the global market. Corruption in your government is getting a lot of bad press. I can assure you it won't just be religious leaders and media demanding we pull the plug if Afghanistan commemorates its next presidential inauguration by sentencing a man to death for his personal beliefs in God."

Khalid's shoulders hunched irritably under his Italian suit coat. "So what do you want of me?"

Bolton's eyebrows shot up. "You're the minister of interior. The police are under your authority. You think we don't know you could force this man's release, should you choose?"

Khalid was shaking his head emphatically. "Then you would have me hand the election to Qaderi. You may understand your own people. But you do not understand Afghanistan. My countrymen may not know how to read and write. But they have all learned their Quran, and they are devout. The mullahs hold power and make law in the villages. To publicly defend this apostate is to denounce Islam. Who will vote for me then? No, I cannot intervene on this man's behalf. It is bad enough that it gives my opponent ammunition to contend he is more devout than I and so more deserving of votes."

The DCM's tone was equally emphatic. "And if you don't intervene, it's going to be evident to the American people and the world there isn't an ounce of difference between Afghan presidential candidates. They'll be screaming for a halt to funding the farce democracy has become over here. And believe me, our democracy does listen to the will of its citizens."

Bolton shook his own head with bemusement. "Surely Qaderi's aware that if he becomes president, he'll have to deal with Western nations funding his administration. Is there any hope he'll listen to reason? at least bury this issue until the elections are over?"

Khalid waved a hand. "For that you had best ask Ismail. He once worked for Qaderi and knows his thoughts as I do not."

A surprise to Steve. As far as he'd known, Ismail had been attached to Khalid since long before his mujahedeen days. Ismail shrugged indifferently. "It is true I once studied under Qaderi, so I came to know him well. The minister is a pious man, but he believes technology and medicine are essential to a modern Islamic state. The Taliban are illiterates whose idea of medicine is drinking camel urine. So when they gained control, Qaderi went into exile in Syria. That is when I joined Khalid to fight the Taliban.

"You ask if Qaderi will free this Jamil in order to retain the aid of foreigners. Never! He is known as a just man, but an unyielding one. He lives for the law and purity of Islam. Nor does he care what others think of him, foreigners and infidels least of all. He will condemn this man because sharia decrees it. What the consequences are for Afghanistan he will consider of no account."

Did that impersonal narration hold respect for Ismail's one-time employer and current boss's chief rival? But then Steve knew what it meant to have respect for an adversary, even if you hated everything he stood for. Like Jamil, Qaderi would seem to be true to what he believed, mistaken though that might be.

Unlike Khalid, who was true only to his own skin and personal well-being. And so was for sale as Qaderi was not. Therefore a valued ally to Steve's country as Qaderi would never be. But then corrupt, greedy dictators had always been easier to control than true ideologues. Talk about a mixed-up world!

Bolton looked genuinely distressed. "Then we're at a stalemate. Neither Qaderi nor you, Khalid, will release this man. And the American people will not consent to continue paying Afghanistan's bills if you flout international opinion with another highly publicized apostasy trial. And that would destroy everything we've worked for as well."

The DCM rubbed a hand over his face. "It's really too bad this had to happen now. If the man had just kept his mouth shut. At least till after the elections. Or if he hadn't put himself all over the Internet. Then maybe he could have been discreetly shipped out-of-country to India or Sri Lanka or somewhere else his conversion wouldn't be such an issue."

Left unaddressed, Steve thought with disgust, was the core issue here: Jamil's right—the right of all Afghans, Muslims, and every other human being on the planet—to follow any belief system or worship any way they jolly well chose. *You're not upset because they're trying Jamil for apostasy. You're upset because Jamil's conversion has inconvenienced your foreign affairs policy!*

"That is not such a bad idea." Khalid stroked his beard thoughtfully. "If the young man disappeared, so would this problem, would it not? India. Sri Lanka. As long as he is gone, why should it matter?"

To Bolton's credit, he actually looked alarmed. "That will not do! If the man disappears, it will be as damaging as an apostasy trial. The media and religious freedom watchdogs will insist he has been quietly put to death."

Once again it was Ismail who unexpectedly spoke up, quietly, thoughtfully. "Perhaps there is another way. After all, it is this man's claim to follow Isa Masih which causes Isa's followers in your own country to scream in his defense. But what if the world sees that this man is not truly an Isa follower at all, but a terrorist and criminal who has deliberately chosen this path to provoke just such trouble as we now see? Would not outrage at this man's deception shut all mouths?"

"Sure, if you could do it. But I can't see how—no, never mind. Plausible deniability and all that. If this . . . uh, difficulty could be handled discreetly, my government would be as grateful as your own. Just tell me, do you really think you can pull it off?"

"I know I can." A secret amusement in Ismail's confident statement narrowed Steve's gaze.

Jason Hamilton met Steve's questioning glance. But the shake of the Dyncorp manager's head said he'd no more idea what Ismail had up his expensive silk sleeve than Steve.

23

Ismail set aside rage during the short drive from Sherpur to Wazir Akbar Khan to consider his options coldly. He'd prepared for Plan C as soon as the scheme came to mind. But he'd no longer expected to use it. Not after his discreet conferences with assorted mullahs, prison officials, and Qaderi himself.

Qaderi had remonstrated, but Ismail had painstakingly laid out the disadvantages of turning Jamil into a martyr for the foreign media. Qaderi's aspirations for a modernized Islamic utopia were as much at risk as the mansions of Khalid's allies, should their foreign benefactors withdraw funding. How much better a platform speech from the mosque courtyard, to be timed with the prisoner's release, lauding Islam's mercy as well as justice? Not to mention Qaderi's.

For Ismail's wasted efforts alone, Jamil deserved to die. But not until he'd undone the damage he'd caused.

At Khalid's Wazir property, Ismail's sharp command sent the guard scurrying to summon the chowkidar. Rasheed was the reason Ismail was acquainted with this property's latest business venture. It was one he approved heartily. The sooner these delinquent females were back where they belonged under male authority, the better. In fact, he'd sent Rasheed several less prosperous mujahedeen comrades to make their choice of brides.

"So now you come to choose your own," the chowkidar suggested slyly, leading his guest up the cobblestone path.

Ismail passed over a photo. "Only if this woman remains available."

Rasheed's eyebrows shot into his turban. "I know her. She is young and beautiful with a fire in her eyes that bodes well for the man who tames her. But I am told she is also unmarried and a virgin. And the infidel woman cherishes her like a sister. I do not think she will consent to her marriage."

"We shall see. Is the American woman here?"

Rasheed shrugged. "I was not requested to drive her, but her vehicle is gone, and I have not seen her since early morning."

The black chador had still been at Pul-e-Charki when Ismail sped away. He'd hoped she wouldn't be back yet. Not that he couldn't deal with Ms. Mallory if necessary. But this would make things easier.

"Then take me to the wali of these women."

The villa's entrance hall had been blackened and shattered on Ismail's last visit. It now looked restored to its original splendor. Among a maze of desks and file cabinets filling the left-hand salon, a yellow-haired foreigner was going over ledgers with several male clerks. At Rasheed's summons, one of them hurried out.

Ismail recognized Ibrahim easily enough from the day of the explosion. Ibrahim in turn paled when he spotted one of the officials who'd commanded his arrest. He was fervent with relief when Ismail explained curtly why he'd come, and he immediately led the deputy minister upstairs to an office. There behind a computer sat the woman who'd identified herself that day as Ibrahim's wife.

Pulling forward a chair for Ismail, Ibrahim seated himself behind a desk. His demeanor as he arranged a stack of files combined the arrogance of a born aristocrat with an obsequiousness that acknowledged the deputy minister's current superior position. Both of which Ismail detested.

"Yes, the girl is still here. But she has made clear she will not entertain the arranging of her marriage. Unfortunately, the American female who brought these women here insists they must give free consent, and she has taken a personal interest in this girl. If only you had come before Ms. Mallory returned to Afghanistan. But the infidel male who is now her superior has agreed to Ms. Mallory's decrees. So unless the girl herself should change her mind, there is nothing I can do."

If Ibrahim sounded genuinely regretful, Ismail had no doubt this was prompted more by lost profits than any desire to please. He spread out the stack of files. "Perhaps you wish to examine other candidates?"

With one sweep of his arm, Ismail sent the files fluttering to the floor. "I am not interested in other candidates, only this woman. Nor is it a bride I search for. The girl has relatives who have been seeking her a long time. She was believed to be dead. Now that she is confirmed to be living, urgent family matters require she present herself immediately. An issue of inheritance, you will understand. Must I remind you a snap of my fingers can return this woman to prison? Perhaps you would do well to acquaint her—and your foreign employers—with this fact."

"You are welcome to do so." The spread of Ibrahim's hands was placating. "Then you can make whatever arrangements you wish. It would resolve both our difficulties."

"No, it would not," Ismail denied impatiently. "I have no such time to waste, and the girl's willing cooperation is essential."

"Then offer her money." Ibrahim's wife, a stately woman older than her husband, spoke up quietly from her keyboard. But her detached statement held an icy edge that hinted at some personal impetus to her proposal.

As both men turned to stare at her, she shrugged. "The girl wants to control her own life. She is intelligent and open to persuasion. Offer her what she desires, and I believe she will agree to go with you freely. What you do then with her will be up to you."

The girl's expression held the same sullen defiance as her photo when Ibrahim led her into an upstairs salon. At Ismail's curt request, Ibrahim left the room, shutting the door behind him. The girl snatched her scarf over her face as she found herself alone. But long-lashed blue eyes above the scarf held both fear and recognition.

Ismail fixed her with a stern gaze. "You know who I am, do you not?"

Her voice was a whisper. "You are Deputy Minister Ismail. I have seen you on the news. And here with the police the day of the bombing."

"Then you know the power I hold. Come over here. And uncover your face so that I may see it."

Dropping the shield of her scarf with clear reluctance, the girl sidled over to the table he indicated. On it were two prison files and several photos. Ismail tapped one. "The face is right. You are Farah?"

The photo was one of two that had been in the girl's prison file, not the scrawny, boyish waif in the mug shot taken upon her arrest, but the more recent one currently stored in Ismail's cell phone. Neither its purpose nor the Welayat wardens' trafficking in female flesh was any revelation to Ismail.

The girl recoiled visibly from the photo, but the defiance in her expression now strengthened her voice. "And if I am? I do not know what Mr. Ibrahim has told you. But I am not interested in marriage now as I was not then. And you cannot force me to go with you."

A sudden waver in her voice revealed the girl's own doubt of her claim. But Ismail just tapped the second folder. "I have no interest in your marriage. I am looking for the sister of this man. You know him?"

A still from a shaheed video Ismail had once shot in an abandoned building, this image was both dark and somewhat blurred. But the girl's eyes widened with instant recognition. "That is Jamil! He used to work here."

"Yes, Jamil Yusof ul Haq Shahrani. And you—" Ismail tapped Farah's prison file—"are his sister."

The girl leaned forward over the folder. "'Farah ul Haq Shahrani.' That was not the name written there before. What is this? My family is all dead. I have no brother."

So the girl could read. "You have one now, should you wish to help save this man's life."

"Yes, I heard he was arrested. Is it true—?" Farah's voice faltered again. "Surely you do not mean they will execute him?"

"He is in great trouble. Unless you help him. Would you care, should they execute him?" Ismail suggested slyly. "This young man you have seen working here? perhaps have even come to hold in some regard? He is a handsome man, after all."

The girl was silent, studying the photo. When she raised her eyes, they held no expression. "To care is to allow one's heart to be taken hostage. Why should I care to help a man who means nothing to me?"

Approval twitched at Ismail's mouth. "I was told you are an intelligent girl. Let me make this simple then. I need your assistance, and in return I will assist you."

Reaching into his chapan, the deputy minister drew out a small, rectangular bundle and spread its contents across the scattered files. Dozens of one-hundred-afghani notes. A gasp escaped Farah. She reached automatically toward the money before snatching her hand back. Ibrahim's wife was right. This girl could be bought.

"I had thought to give this to your guardian as reward for your delivery. But it will be yours instead and ten times more if you do what I require."

The girl stared at the money, desire and suspicion warring in her eyes. "What is it you require? You say you wish me to be Jamil's sister. But why? To pay so much money for a pretense—"

"I wish to save this man's life. It does not suit my own plans for him to die. That is all you need to know. But this Jamil is stubborn. He has been deceived with the teachings of the Isa followers, and though he has only to deny them and swear his allegiance to Islam, he has refused to do so. It is because of a woman, of course. Ms. Amy Mallory, for whom he worked here and with whom it would appear by his stubbornness he has fallen in love. This Ms. Amy Mallory—she is an Isa follower, is she not, like so many of these foreigners?"

Under his severe gaze, Farah's eyes fell. "I—yes, I believe so. Do you truly believe Jamil loves Miss Ameera?"

"And would you care?" Ismail said shrewdly. "Perhaps I am not the only one with cause to hold a grudge against this foreigner. Or have you too been influenced by this woman's heresies? Has she persuaded you to follow Isa instead of Muhammad?"

The girl straightened up hastily. "No, of course not! I am no apostate. Nor do I wish to hear more of Miss Ameera. She claims to care for the Afghan people. But she is faithless and a liar like all others. If Jamil believes otherwise, he has been foolishly deceived."

Ismail studied the sullen droop of the girl's full mouth before nodding satisfaction. "Then help me return Jamil to the proper path. For many years now he has been searching for his sister and mother. There is nothing he will not do to be reunited with them. So you see why I come to you. Jamil's love for his family, his blood, is a bond more powerful than this heresy he has embraced or desire for a beautiful foreign woman. If his own sister begs him to renounce this Isa foolishness so that he may be restored to her, how can he not consent?"

The girl did not look convinced. "But why should Jamil believe I am this sister? Would he not know it is a lie as soon as he began to question me?"

"I have read your files as I have read his. Your name is Farah. Such was the name of his sister. You are much of an age. Your own father and brothers were killed in the fighting when the valiant mujahedeen and their foreign allies drove out the Taliban. So was Jamil's family. His sister was just a small girl child when he last saw her. And does not the trauma of war cloud memories? Other details I will teach you. For anything else, you need only say you remember little of those days."

"That would be easy because it is truth." The girl had abandoned fear, if not her suspicion and sullenness. "And his real sister and mother? Do you know what happened to them?"

The deputy minister shrugged. "Who can know? I believe myself they are dead, or they would have resurfaced by now."

"But will he not be suspicious? Why should he not believe this to be what it is, a trick to make him do as you wish? He has seen me before, after all. Why should he believe I am his sister, only because I say so? Yes, a girl child changes much, but not the color of hair or eyes or skin."

"You think I have not thought of that?" Ismail answered sharply. "Why do you think you were chosen? You have the eyes of Jamil's sister and the hair and skin. Eyes the blue of a mountain lake are rare enough for an Afghan. But there is more. Look closely."

The deputy minister pushed forward the two photos he'd displayed so that Farah could examine them side by side. One was male, the other female, their coloring very different. But the two faces bore strong similarities in bone structure, in the wide-spaced, long-lashed gaze, high-bridged nose, and wide, full shape of the mouth.

Ismail placed a third photo next to the other two. The man in this photo was an older version of Jamil, but his coloring was Farah's. The same dark blue eyes and fair skin. The same riotous brown curls tamed by a neatly trimmed beard and haircut.

"Jamil's father was a well-respected surgeon here in Kabul before the fighting. It was not hard to find a photo of him. You see why Jamil will not ask questions when he is told the sister he sought was unknowingly close by all these months."

The deputy minister laid a final, larger photo on top of the others. "This sister."

Farah's hand shook as she reached for the portrait so that she had to drop her arm back to her side to hide the tremor. Her shock she hid more easily, the mask of sullen defiance and suspicion that had served her so well over the years hardening on her face as she stared at the dog-eared, faded photo. Trauma of war had indeed clouded her memories. But not all.

"Do not cry, little one. I will be back soon, I promise."

"That is what you said before. You said the days would pass like the wind, but they did not. It was so long before you came home!"

"It only seemed long because you were small, Farah-jan. Now you are grow-ing bigger, so the time will pass more quickly. This time when I come, I will bring you a gift worthy of the princess you are."

"I do not want a gift. I only want you. Please, why can you not stay here with me?"

"Because I am a man now, and men must go forth to do what they are called to in this world. I will come back to you, little one, if you will only be patient. And one day when I am a doctor like Father, perhaps you may come and live with me. At least until we find you a prince for a husband. But for now I must go. And you must be brave. A princess does not cry."

A princess. Farah knew she was indeed a princess, if a princess in exile, because the adults of her family spoke often of the kingdom they'd lost. A kingdom of surpassing beauty where they'd possessed great power and wealth and a gracious palace with lush gardens and bountiful orchards. Nothing like these crowded salons and courtyards into which they were so unpleasantly crammed with other refugees.

Since she'd known no other quarters, Farah didn't find them so inade-quate. She had food, shelter, other children with whom to play, and the immediate family members who were the center of her small world.

Above all, her brother.

He wasn't her only brother. There were two others, already grown men, as preoccupied and absent as her busy, distant father. Farah's youngest brother was only a decade older than herself, and if she as an only daughter was the family's reigning princess, her nearest sibling was a prince from the Persian and Arabic tales her mother told at bedtime. Tall, at least to the perspective of a small girl child. Handsome, with tumbling black curls, smiling dark eyes, and beardless, olive-toned features. Though just what those features looked like had faded from Farah's memories.

But she hadn't forgotten that he'd been her first and best playmate, despite the vast difference in age. He'd permitted her to curl up nearby while he studied even when she'd grown too old to be escaping from the women's quarters into male territory. He'd taught her to hold her first pen and how to decipher the graceful Arabic script so that she could read tales of princes and princesses for herself.

Then, just after her sixth birthday, he'd gone away. To study medicine like her father, she'd been told. It was a great honor to be chosen among thousands vying for the opportunity, she'd also been told. All Farah cared was that he was gone, returning only rarely for holiday feasts. It was before leaving again to begin his second year of studies that he'd promised to bring Farah a gift worthy of a princess.

And she'd promised not to cry.

She'd kept her promise, no matter how many times the tears threatened to spill over. It was her brother who had not kept his promise. He had not come home for the Eid al-Adha feast. Important exams, she'd been told. He hadn't come home either for the summer holidays. She'd no idea what an internship was, only that no matter how long she stood on her balcony, gazing down the cobbled street, her beloved brother did not come.

Instead had come a package. The delicate glass bangles inside, red and gold and blue and orange, were indeed worthy of a princess. But she'd stuffed them at the bottom of her storage chest. Not till her brother slipped them himself on her small wrists would she wear them.

And then it had seemed all promises, all wishes, were to be fulfilled. The evil usurpers who'd stolen her family's kingdom had been overthrown.

Their exile was over. Her youngest brother would meet the family at their reclaimed palace.

Beyond the cab window of her uncle's jinga truck, the scenery looked nothing like the stories Farah had heard, a bomb-cratered highway littered with burned-out trucks and buses, buildings shattered and fire-gutted. But the street onto which the jinga truck turned was as wide and tree-lined as described. The palace behind high walls was spacious with well-tended lawns and gardens and fruit trees. Perhaps the stories had not all been fairy tales. Only the absence of her youngest brother marred the excitement of homecoming. He would arrive soon, her mother assured. She had only to be patient.

Exploring the orchard, Farah had thought it was celebratory fireworks beyond the walls until an explosion turned the jinga truck into a column of smoke and fire. She saw the chowkidar sprinting across the lawn with a weapon in his hands. Then a glimpse of a slim, lithe figure racing through the fruit trees. Her youngest brother had arrived at last!

But before she could run to him, her mother had snatched her up and was running to take shelter with the chowkidar's female family members. Barred shutters and door blocked out light and noise and smoke, but not the screams and sobbing of the other women.

"*Don't cry*, madar!" Farah had urged. "*The war is over, remember? Baba and my brothers will not permit anything to hurt us.*"

Time and trauma had indeed buried deep the remainder of that day which had ended her world and begun a nightmare. But there were images Farah had never quite banished. Swarms of men in mismatched camouflage. A terrible pile of limp, scarlet human shapes.

Farah's mother had never spoken again of husband and sons, Farah's father and brothers. And though she'd no reason now to hold back her tears, Farah had not cried as her mother led her away. Neither tears nor bravery would restore her brother, her lost world.

"*I will come back to you, little one.*"

Except that the dead didn't keep promises.

Or so she'd always thought.

Farah did not raise her long lashes until she was sure she'd banished all expression from her face. Coolly she demanded, "If I do this, how do

I know you will truly pay me this money? And what will become of me when this is done?"

The deputy minister's harsh features showed sudden amusement. "So you do not trust me. Have I not said you are intelligent? But once this is finished, I will have no further use for you. So long as you hold your tongue, you will be free to go where you will. As to the money, what is there is yours now. For the rest, if all goes well, believe me that I will be pleased to reward you richly. But I have no more time. Come or do not come. Which will it be?"

Farah didn't hesitate any longer. Scooping up the one-hundred-afghani notes from the table, she tucked them into her tunic. "I will come."

24

Amy couldn't race away because her earlier guide was still loitering by the Toyota Corolla. Detouring to a tiny mud-brick enclosure, Amy found to her relief that the medical emergency was well within her training. A thumb sliced during food preparation had become seriously infected. After cleaning the injury, Amy left antibiotic ointment and bandages. "If it is not better in a few days, bring your wife to the free clinic near the city market."

Now she was free to indulge her fury. It took a near miss with a speeding bus for Amy to thrust aside all other thoughts and concentrate on her driving. Pulling unscathed into the mechanics yard, she spotted two New Hope boys scrubbing down Ibrahim's red Mitsubishi Montero. The sight enflamed Amy to white-hot rage. She hurried upstairs but found only Soraya in the New Hope office. Amy pushed the chador's head covering back onto her shoulders, shaking out damp, flattened hair.

"Soraya, I just found out where Ibrahim got his new SUV. It was a bride-price for Roya's daughter Loma. Did you know about this?"

Soraya raised a cool gaze from her computer monitor. "Of course I did. Do you think my husband brings home a vehicle, and I do not know from where it comes?"

Amy was left speechless. Finally she got words out. "And you think that's okay? So what other bride-prices has Ibrahim been collecting?"

Amy's mind was now racing. "And the carpet factory and shop downstairs, the boys working over in the mechanics shop and whatever else

Ibrahim has started around here. Can I guess he's been collecting profits on those too, along with his New Hope salary?"

Soraya didn't answer, but the smug twist of her mouth gave her away. Amy paced the length of the office and back again before she burst out, "I cannot believe you and Ibrahim would use New Hope Foundation for your own profit. After inviting you all to live here and giving you jobs and everything else I've—"

"—you've done for us?" Soraya completed smoothly. "You think we haven't earned all we receive here? Do you not earn far more for coming to my country? Or like all foreigners, you feel we should be grateful for whatever crumbs you drop into our laps."

Amy stared at Soraya incredulously. From the beginning of their working relationship, Amy had felt a wall separating her from the beautiful Afghan aristocrat. Though she'd regretted it, she'd never blamed Soraya. A member of Afghanistan's historic ruling class, intelligent, highly educated, and now as she'd insinuated, reduced to picking up crumbs from her country's latest foreign occupiers to support her family, Soraya had understandable cause for resentment.

But she'd never openly voiced that resentment, and once Amy had invited Soraya's family to move into New Hope, availing them once again of a decent living standard, Soraya had abandoned her earlier coldness. For Amy's own part, she'd thought they'd even developed some degree of friendship.

But there was no friendship in Soraya's unyielding gaze now. Nor any hint of penitence or shame at being caught out. Amy was still trying to find words when Soraya spoke again, and there was no mistaking the arrogance in her tone.

"You believe I should feel guilt for what Ibrahim and I have done? You are a child and naive. All that we have done has been for our family, to survive. You think that I should weep because a gutter child now possesses a husband and a roof over her head? that we should think first of the poorest beggar and not of ourselves? Yes, we have a place to live here. You pay us salaries. For now. But who knows how long it will last? Tomorrow your government may decide it is time to leave Afghanistan. Or your New Hope Foundation. Tomorrow there may be no more foreign aid. So we take what we can to build a future for our family. Does not everyone do the same?"

Amy found voice. "But isn't that the problem, Soraya? If everyone takes as much as they can for their own pockets instead of working together to help the whole country, how will Afghanistan ever get back on its feet?"

"That is not my problem," Soraya answered dismissively. "And when you speak of taking for one's own pocket, can you tell me your own people are not doing the same?"

A sharp response rose to Amy's lips, but honesty kept her from speaking. For every Becky Frazer or John and Ruth Atkins who came here as volunteers, raising their own funds, how many high-priced private contractors and expat corporate hires filled this city? While their companies profited billions in government contracts, they collected their exorbitant hazard pay from the safe distance of refurbished Wazir mansions, shopped in high-security malls, sipped forbidden alcohol in exclusive restaurants. And all before the first dollar of whatever taxpayer budget provided their living expenses ever reached Afghan streets. Even Amy's relatively modest stipend would seem a fortune compared to Soraya's own salary.

But that didn't justify what Soraya and Ibrahim had done. And whatever wrongs happened elsewhere, New Hope was Amy's own responsibility.

"This isn't over, Soraya. I'll be taking all this up immediately with Duane. To begin with, I certainly won't be employing you any longer as my assistant. Or keep you living here, so I hope your profits were enough to find you a new place to stay."

"Yes, of course you must take this up with your superior," Soraya agreed cordially even as her kohl-lined gaze shifted to a point over Amy's shoulder. "Mr. Duane, Miss Ameera wishes to discuss certain matters with you, so I will leave to give instructions as to the packing for tomorrow."

Startled, Amy whirled around to see the New Hope country manager standing in the office door. Soraya gracefully rose and headed for the door. But she paused in the doorway to add smoothly, "You may wish to discuss as well your former driver Jamil's confession of apostasy on today's news. Mr. Duane will be interested how Jamil became a convert to a forbidden religion while working here."

As an offensive, the volley Soraya had delivered was a stunning retaliatory blow. Squaring her shoulders, Amy faced the New Hope country manager. "I'm glad you're still in town, Duane, because like Soraya said, I need to speak to you urgently."

"You certainly do! You've got some major explaining!" The country manager's expression was tight with annoyance as he strode into the office. "I just saw the news Soraya mentioned. Okay, so this Jamil character who's been all over the airwaves this last week now openly admits he's converted to Christianity. Whatever! That's a matter of their law, not our business. But what's this about him working as your driver? Any reason you didn't fill me in on this little tidbit?"

"I didn't consider it was relevant," Amy began. *And I was concerned you might react like this!* "But that's not what I need to—"

"Relevant!" Duane cut her off with a sharp gesture. "How is it not relevant? You think the authorities won't be checking this man's employment history? All we need is for local authorities to accuse New Hope of using a humanitarian cover for proselytizing."

"But that's not true! I've never encouraged Jamil or any Afghan to change his religion. Nor spoken of my own faith except in response to a question." Amy drew in a deep breath to calm herself before she went on. "In any case, that's not why I needed to talk to you. Soraya just threw that in as a distraction. Have you any idea what she and Ibrahim have been up to?"

Swiftly, Amy outlined what she'd learned that afternoon. "We're practically back where I started here after our last Afghan manager and his relatives ran off with all the New Hope funds. At minimum, we'll have to dismiss Ibrahim and Soraya, even if we're not likely to recover the money they've been raking in. Which leaves us without staff again."

"On the contrary, this is nothing like that prior case," Duane responded coolly. "I've been monitoring the books. Whatever income Ibrahim and Soraya may have earned from private ventures, they haven't received a penny from New Hope funds outside their own salaries. Nor is what you've described illegal. If you know anything about Muslim custom, then you must realize that as this property's highest-ranking male, Ibrahim is also wali to its residents. He has not only a right but a duty to arrange marriages to ensure his wards' long-term security."

"Even eleven-year-old girls?" Amy demanded. "And putting the proceeds into his own pocket when Ibrahim hasn't spent a penny supporting his 'wards'? Maybe it's not illegal, but it's certainly unethical. I'm not suggesting arresting the guy! But we have every right to put our foot down over what code of behavior we expect from our staff. At least when New Hope is footing the bills. I didn't pour months of my life into this project just to refill Ibrahim and Soraya's family bank account."

"Yes, well, that's just it," Duane said agreeably. "It's not your project. Not anymore. And with everyone from warlords to expats getting stinking rich off the aid boom, why would I fire valuable local staff for looking after their own interests while they're also looking after ours? Ibrahim and Soraya happen to have family ties to half the bigwigs in this city. Which makes them indispensable to this venture."

More indispensable than a problematic female aid worker hung unspoken in the air.

"I've made clear from the outset that I don't get involved in trying to change local morality or customs. And if you can't deal with that—hey, you can always quit!" The New Hope manager leaned slightly forward. "I'll even make it easy on you. A bonus month's salary for all your hard work. I think it's become clear this isn't working for either of us."

It would be easier if Amy could tell herself Duane was a horrible person. But he wasn't; he was simply an undeniably competent professional who happened to have a very different vision than Amy's for New Hope and Afghanistan. Nor, though Amy hated to admit it, could she see any other solution than the one Duane had suggested. After today's events, Amy could hardly continue working at New Hope as though none of this had happened.

"You're right; this isn't working," Amy said quietly. "Please accept my resignation, effective today."

"A wise choice." Now that he'd won, Duane looked amiable enough. "I trust we can part on good terms. I do appreciate your hard work. You're good at what you do, and it's not your fault this part of the world isn't geared for women. Nor, despite Nestor's optimism, does it ever work for a former boss to stay on looking over their successor's shoulder. It should have been handled this way from the beginning. Your severance pay will be deposited as usual in your bank account. I'm guessing you'll want to fly out as soon as possible. Do you need help booking your ticket?"

"I don't know my plans yet. But you can be sure I'll be out of here as soon as I'm packed, even if I have to book into the nearest guesthouse. I'll make arrangements for moving the Welayat families to their new shelter."

Amy turned toward the door, only to swing back around. "Oh, and I'd like to take Farah with me if she wants to come. I'll still need an assistant as long as I'm in Kabul."

Even if Farah chose not to come, at least the offer would make clear Amy was neither abandoning the girl nor breaking any promises she'd made. But Duane's raised eyebrows conveyed incomprehension. "You mean, you don't know? Farah isn't here anymore. She left not an hour ago. In fact right before you stormed in."

"Left?" Amy repeated blankly. "How could she leave? And with who? She sure wouldn't have gone out by herself."

"I assumed to be married like the others. I was a little surprised when Ibrahim mentioned it because I remembered you talking yesterday about taking her on as your assistant. Maybe a husband and home sounded more attractive than being a career girl."

"I don't believe it!" Amy denied flatly. Could this afternoon get any worse? How terrified Farah must be right now! And if she'd so quickly misunderstood Amy's earlier discussion with Soraya, she must be convinced Amy was a liar and fraud to permit this to happen!

"Farah was scared stiff of being forcibly married off to some stranger. She'd have never consented willingly. Which means Ibrahim must have coerced her somehow. I've said I'll leave quietly. Whatever you do with New Hope or Ibrahim and Soraya's little financial empire, that's up to you now. But selling off Farah to the highest bidder like Ibrahim did with Loma is where I draw the line. I want Farah back. Ibrahim had better get her back. Because if I have to call Nestor Korallis and raise a stink, believe me, I will!"

Duane was shaking his head. "Look, I was here when that girl drove off. I saw no indication of coercion. But here's Soraya. Why don't you talk to her?"

Soraya was stepping into the office. Amy's frustration burst from her. "Soraya, you know as well as I do that Farah would never consent to an arranged marriage. How many times has she said that to both of us? So whatever you and Ibrahim have done with her—"

Soraya looked at Amy composedly. "It was nothing of Ibrahim's arranging. A man came who said he represented Farah's family. It seems she has surviving relatives who have been seeking her since the war."

"And I'm supposed to believe you just took the word of some total stranger and sent her off with him?" Amy demanded. "How would these so-called relatives even know Farah was here?"

"He had papers. And he was no stranger, but Ismail who serves your landlord, Khalid, the minister of interior. He was here with the police the day of the explosion. He told us an investigation into these criminal women you brought onto his superior's property had revealed Farah to be this missing girl."

Ismail. Why was her landlord's deputy popping up all over? Some lingering remorse on Khalid's part might explain why Ismail had inserted himself into Jamil's defense. But now Farah?

"The minister showed Farah these papers and pictures too, and she insisted on going with him," Soraya went on. "There was an inheritance involved, so perhaps she was persuaded by the money. Since you gave orders these women are free to leave if they choose, how could we prevent it?"

The criminal investigation was more convincing to Amy than anything else. It was a logical step for any landlord after the explosion and earlier break-in. As Khalid's deputy, Ismail had access to prison files. Farah had thought all her immediate family were dead. But if a survivor had traced Farah as far as the Welayat—yes, that was possible.

"Farah left this for you." Soraya handed Amy a folded piece of notepaper. If Amy couldn't read all the swirls and dots, she'd seen Farah practicing her signature enough to recognize it. "She writes that she is going to her family. Her real family, not those who once sold her. She says you will understand."

Some relative from her father's side then? Farah's early memories indicated a family with some wealth. If this was all true, Amy could be happy for Farah. As Soraya had said, Farah craved security and money. Now it would seem she'd have both.

If these relatives cared enough to search for Farah all these years, that's a good sign they'll be kind. I just wish I could have said good-bye in person. She was so angry with me. Will I ever have a chance now to explain? I can't bear to think her last memories will be that I am a liar who never really cared about her.

Folding the notepaper, Amy said quietly, "Soraya, if I've misjudged you, I apologize. Our customs are very different. But I have appreciated the opportunity to work with you these past months. I have learned so much about your country. Thank you for your patience. Now if you'll excuse me, I have some packing to do. Salaam."

Now that Soraya had won, she was all smiles again. Walking over, her former assistant hugged and kissed Amy with unfeigned cordiality. "I too have appreciated working with you and all you have done for my family. As you say, customs differ."

And yours is to fight for the survival of your own family above all other considerations. Amy's head was aching as badly as her heart as she hurried to her room and began throwing her belongings into two suitcases. She couldn't even muster up fury anymore. *Soraya really thinks she's doing right. In a culture where resources are scarce, you provide for your own before you concern yourself for other people.*

And yet there's basic right and wrong. Except that so much of what I regard as right and wrong are "Isa teachings," as Jamil would say. And Ibrahim and Soraya don't follow those.

The flannelgraph set had its own carrying case. Amy's other possessions fit easily into her two suitcases. She'd told Duane she hadn't decided on her plans. But by the time she snapped the second case shut, that was no longer true.

Becky had said Amy was welcome to come work with her organization. This Jamil thing might change her mind about that. If it could cause trouble for New Hope, maybe it would for them too. But Amy had no doubt the nurse-practitioner would be kind enough to let Amy crash there for the time being.

Amy's notebook laptop slid into her knapsack. She dropped after it a small, flat square wrapped in plastic and bound with duct tape. Taped to it was a note written in Jamil's careful English printing. *"This holds my life. Please keep it safe. I will call when I am gone from Kabul. If you do not hear or something happens to me, please open it and read what is within."*

Amy had, of course, not opened it since Jamil had in the end called. What it held, she'd wasted little time speculating. From its shape, her guess would be the recordable DVDs Jamil had used to cut PR videos for New Hope. He'd asked once to copy for a memento his footage of New Hope activities and children. Not to mention, she suspected, Amy herself. With his wanderings, it made sense he'd leave such a keepsake for safekeeping where dust and rough handling couldn't hurt it.

If something happens to me. Did Jamil's current predicament count? But, no. An arrest for apostasy could hardly have been in Jamil's thoughts when he'd left Amy that souvenir. It would be something to ask next time Amy saw Jamil.

If there was a next time.

No, you won't even think that way!

The Toyota Corolla was technically property of New Hope, but since Duane had not brought it up, Amy felt no compunction about requisitioning the vehicle until she finally did leave Kabul.

As she drove out the gate, Amy let her tears flow freely.

I started here with such high hopes, so sure of what I was doing. But everything I've built these last months has dissolved away—as completely as a sand castle on a Miami beach under incoming tide. Did I misread you, Father God, when I thought you were telling me to come here? when I stayed on after finding out it was going to be a bigger challenge than I'd ever handled before? Was I just being arrogant to think I could handle this?

Amy had always prided herself on not giving up. Never throwing in the towel. With enough dedication and hard work, a way through could always be found. But this time Amy could admit she was in way over her head and had been since arriving in Kabul. As Duane had suggested, maybe the best thing Amy could offer was to get on a plane and leave this place to those who knew what they were doing. She didn't even have the excuse of those student loans anymore. Duane's severance bonus would be enough almost to the dollar to pay her last loan.

Except for Jamil, Amy would be calling a travel agency right now. But she'd pledged to Jamil that she wouldn't rest until he was freed from prison. And suddenly as Amy turned onto the dirt lane leading to Becky's compound, her confusion and self-doubt hardened to stubborn resolve. Ibrahim and Soraya and Duane too could force Amy from New Hope, but they couldn't make her leave Kabul. Amy would stay here until her promise was kept and Jamil was free.

What exactly she could do to keep that promise, Amy had no idea. But if she succeeded, maybe her months here wouldn't be a total loss!

25

By the time Steve tore himself away, the afternoon was advanced enough that John Atkins would have given up expecting him. But if too late for the project they'd planned, right now all Steve wanted was to escape the cesspool of intrigue and calculation that constituted his client's personal ecosystem for something decent and worthwhile enough he wouldn't feel a need afterward to scrub himself off in carbolic acid.

Steve's route to the Afghan Relief Mission took him by the city's main mosque, its tall, needle-thin minarets and massive tiled dome silhouetted against a rapidly fading twilight like some Arabian Nights fantasy. Less benign was a rhythmic chanting amplified by a powerful PA system. "Death to the apostate. Qaderi for president."

Just one more day and I won't have to pretend to care anymore. Whoever wins this expensive exercise in democracy, Afghanistan is going to limp along, drowning in its own corruption and meanness, expecting everyone else to bail them out of their problems.

Steve took in the progress approvingly when he reached the compound. Blast barriers created on Steve's last visit by pouring concrete into fifty-gallon oil drums now turned the street into an obstacle course. Glass shards and triple strands of barbed wire adorned much of the perimeter wall. But a mob of poorly dressed women with wailing babies being shooed out the pedestrian gate indicated something had gone amiss. What had canceled the afternoon clinic? Nor should the vehicle gate be standing open and unattended. Then as Steve inched the Pajero unchallenged through the gate, he spotted one of Kabul's rare ambulances pulled up to the clinic door.

By the time Steve stepped out of his vehicle, paramedics were carrying a stretcher from the clinic, accompanied by John Atkins and Amy's American nurse friend Becky Frazer. Becky hurried over to Steve. "I'm glad you made it. As you can see, we've encountered a bit of an emergency. John's wife, Ruth, has gone into labor a month premature. They'd planned a home delivery with my services as midwife. But things aren't looking good. We're taking Ruth to the international clinic. Can I hope you'll take over here?"

"Of course. Let John know I'll wrap things up with the workmen. And if there's anything else I can do—"

"You can pray," the older woman said as she hurried away.

That at least Steve could manage. As the American nurse rejoined the ambulance crew, John Atkins swung around to offer Steve a slight smile and a thumbs-up. Becky had evidently passed on Steve's message. But the aid worker's smile faded immediately as he climbed into the ambulance after the stretcher. Empathy tightened Steve's throat. Loving brought with it the high risk of losing. As Phil had experienced. And Steve's mother. This was why Steve found it easier to walk alone. Losing friends was bad enough. Or a parent. But a wife and children offered the ultimate hostages to life.

And yet Phil and John both seemed to find what they'd gained worth every risk of loss. Even Steve's mother had opened her heart to new happiness. Could it be they had it right—and Steve was wrong?

Steve's excuses for wrapping his heart in body armor had always seemed reasonable. Watching one parent, then the other, take turns flying away until finally one never came back. Those growing-up years after his father's death when he'd needed to be tough and self-sufficient, his remaining parent burying her own grief in overseas duty, elderly grandparents bewildered at the rebellious teen they'd inherited. And there was the anguish of seeing close comrades die in combat that had come to seem senseless.

To shrink away from pain was human. To protect at-risk body parts was just plain smart. Yet in armoring his most vulnerable organ so tightly against pain, had Steve also sealed out its counterparts?

Joy.

Companionship.

Family.

Love.

It wasn't that Steve had shunned female company over the years. But none of the women he'd dated had ever tempted him to pursue a long-term relationship nor even lingered in Steve's mind so that he could easily pull up face or name. Though that story might have a different ending if a woman as exceptional as Phil's Denise or John's Ruth had ever crossed Steve's path.

Amy's nurse friend Becky was now climbing into the ambulance. As the paramedics began shutting the doors, she called across the yard, "Oh, Steve, one other thing. If you talk to Amy, could you let her know Ruth's going to the hospital?"

First Ismail, now Becky! Why does everyone assume I'm in communication with the girl? Steve demanded of himself even while he waved a hand in assent.

As though in mocking response, an image thrust itself unbidden into his mind. A tall, slim frame whose lithe grace not even its voluminous Afghan draping could disguise. A cascade of silken sunshine that, released from its covering, could impel a man to bury fingers and face in it. Maybe Islam's constraints held some reason. Wide, hazel eyes above a mouth curved to tenderness that would seem reserved only for children.

And convicts.

Steve ruthlessly shoved the image away. Amy Mallory was undoubtedly an exceptional young woman. As Ian Grant had once remarked, the kind of person you'd want at your back when the chips were down in a combat zone. Maybe at your side too in life's highs and lows, should Steve ever choose to peel that body armor from his heart.

But there was no point dwelling on such an image. Amy's heart certainly carried no body armor. Parents, siblings, disaster victims, stray orphans, and every hard-luck story found ample room in its all-inclusive embrace. But if any piece of Amy Mallory's heart was reserved for a particular man, that slot was now filled by a certain former assistant and reformed suicide bomber.

Steve was on a ladder, checking the sturdiness of metal rebar supporting the barbed wire when he noted headlights zigzagging through the oil drum obstacle course below. His gaze sharpened to alertness as the vehicle drew close enough for Steve to identify a Toyota Corolla hatchback. Brought in secondhand by the thousands from neighboring countries, the ubiquitous cheap Asian imports made up a significant portion of Kabul's vehicles. Steve had driven one himself for anonymity during his prior contract.

But for the same reason, too many car bombs going off around Kabul involved this model. So Steve kept an eye on the vehicle as it pulled up in the street below, and a black chador climbed out. A visitor then for the apartments.

But the black chador hadn't taken a step when Steve vaulted from the ladder. He reached the pedestrian door just as an electronic buzzer sounded.

"Get the gate, please," he addressed to the guard on duty. Steve yanked open the door as the black chador was turning back toward the Toyota Corolla. "If you're looking for Becky Frazer, she isn't here. John and Ruth are having their baby. Becky went to the hospital with them."

A soft cry of dismay escaped the black chador. Security spotlights were one defense the compound already had in place, and with nightfall now complete, these had just blinked on. One of them was mounted above the pedestrian door, and as the black chador whirled around so that the light shone on her face, it was Steve who had to restrain an exclamation of dismay.

Steve had seen those heart-shaped features alive with eager anticipation. The long-lashed hazel eyes ablaze with indignation, twinkling with mischief, softened to tenderness and sympathy. That small, pointed chin set with determination. The generous mouth curved to laughter and taut with anger. He'd seen alarm too, though less than would be appropriate for some of her exploits.

But not even after the New Hope bombing or the shock of Jamil's arrest had Steve witnessed nor come to anticipate from Amy Mallory's exasperatingly intrepid spirit such abject brokenness and despair as now turned blindly to him. While the only tears he'd ever glimpsed in those hazel eyes were for—

"I know about Jamil," Steve said abruptly. "I'm truly sorry."

26

Amy accepted without surprise the security contractor's sudden appearance. It even seemed inevitable. Striding over to the Toyota Corolla, Steve glanced inside. "What's happened? Why are you here alone like this without a driver? and with your luggage? No, never mind. Let's get you inside first."

The vehicle gate was now swinging open. Amy drove the hatchback straight through to draw up at the motel-like row of doors that was staff housing. She was pulling out a loose brick at ground level to recover the spare key Becky Frazer kept there when Steve arrived on foot. Without a word, he lifted Amy's luggage from the vehicle as she unlocked Becky's apartment door. Once inside, Amy flipped on a light switch while Steve set down her luggage to shut the door.

"Okay, what's going on? I saw you at Jamil's hearing this afternoon, so I thought I knew why you're here. But from your luggage, it's more than that."

"Why am I here?" Sinking down onto an armchair, Amy tugged the chador off her head, impatiently using a sleeve to mop at her face. In other circumstances, she'd care what a mess she must look right now. But her appearance seemed supremely unimportant as she stared at the tall contractor. "Why are *you* here? And—and what did you mean about John and Ruth and the baby? Ruth isn't due for another month. And Becky was going to deliver Ruth here. If they've gone to the hospital, something must be terribly wrong. And the hearing. How could you possibly know

I was there? Does that mean it's already all over the news? I didn't know the camera had caught me. And I was sure this—" Amy lifted the black material of the chador—"was one disguise no one would look past. But if you recognized me, how many others did too? Oh, I hope I haven't made things even worse for Jamil than they already are!"

"Hey, there's no reason to get so worked up." Steve crossed Becky's living room to settle himself into the armchair most distant from Amy. "Yes, the trial made the news, and the coverage did show a chador at the back of the courtroom, but not so anyone would recognize you. I only guessed it was you because someone told me you'd been at Pul-e-Charki with that Red Cross team pretending to be Jamil's sister."

Amy stiffened in consternation. "Someone told you! You mean, Kareem? He was the only one who knew it was me."

"Kareem? Is that the reporter who got Jamil into all this trouble?" Steve shook his head. "Amy, you've got some major explaining to do. But no, it was actually Ismail who told me about you."

"Ismail?" Amy's head shake echoed Steve's own. "You mean Khalid's deputy, the one who was there when you arrested Jamil? Yes, I saw him at Pul-e-Charki, but he showed no sign of recognizing me. Why wouldn't he stop me, arrest me, something, if he knew I was an imposter?"

"I wouldn't worry about it. From his comments, I'd say Ismail assumes you've got a personal interest in your former assistant. After all, he was there when you championed Jamil before. Bribing one's way into prison to visit a family member or lover is hardly unusual around here. That he told me, knowing I'm in contact with you, is Ismail's way of saying he knows but couldn't care less. As to why I'm here, I don't know why you're so surprised. You were there when I told your friend John Atkins I'd be happy to lend a hand on his security."

Steve's curtness caught Amy by surprise. Almost, one might think she'd wounded his feelings. "I didn't realize—"

The security contractor cut into Amy's halfhearted apology. "About Ruth, when I arrived this afternoon, she'd gone into labor. I stayed on with the workers so John could go with his wife. As for going into Pul-e-Charki with some reporter you barely know, you're lucky all that happened was Ismail recognizing you. When are you going to start thinking through the consequences of jumping feetfirst into every dangerous situation that crosses your path?"

This sounded more like the Steve Wilson Amy knew. His derision stiffened her spine enough to tilt her chin defiantly as she met the contractor's ironic gaze. "I *did* think through the consequences. But I had to go. Jamil deserved someone there on his side. Especially since Kareem—well, I thought he at least was Jamil's friend. But he seems as angry as everyone else about Jamil saying he believes Isa Masih is the Son of God."

Amy broke off to blink furiously. Across the room, Steve's deep drawl admitted quietly, "That took courage."

"Then you do believe him now? that he's really changed? that he's become a genuine follower of Isa Masih, and that's why he's doing what he's doing?"

"Sure, I believe him—now. I can't see any other explanation for the guy to deliberately slide his neck into a noose."

Horror snatched Amy's breath at the image. "Then you think they'll really try to execute him for being an Isa follower? You said the trial had already hit the news. Won't that kind of force them to let Jamil go like they finally did that other convert? What about our own government? Is there any hope the embassy will put pressure on the Afghans to respect international human rights? Or even . . ."

Amy straightened up. "Our government's mounted rescue operations for kidnapped hostages before. You were Special Forces, so you know a lot more about that than I do. If we approach them, do you think they might—?"

"Stop!" The harshness of Steve's command snatched from Amy voice and hope.

He went on forcefully. "Don't even go there! Sure our government's mounted such rescue operations. With as many boots as we've got on the ground here, even up at Pul-e-Charki, it would be doable enough. But those other hostages were American citizens, not an Afghan national. I can tell you right now—and don't ask me how because I can't say—that there'll be no interference from our State Department to free your friend, much less any rescue attempt. Oh, they'll continue to express concern just like they did last time around. But they won't raise a finger to interfere with Afghan sovereignty, especially during this election season. If Jamil is to be set free, it'll be the Afghans who have to make that call. And believe me, that's even less likely than a rescue bid from our side. Don't ask me how I know that either."

Bitterness in Steve's tone carried more conviction than his words. Amy dropped her eyes to hands clasped in her lap. "Yes, I heard that crowd out there. I guess I was hoping with all that's been on the news, there'd be Afghans who'd stand up against putting a man to death for his faith. But they were all applauding it. Even cheering for this Qaderi to be their next president."

"Not all Afghans feel the same, I'm sure," Steve answered quietly. "That mob you heard would be Qaderi's core supporters. But there's no denying you won't find a lot of support around here to free Jamil. Don't forget they've been told their whole life there's only one penalty for apostasy. And the mullahs, including Qaderi, know exactly what's at stake. Their entire control depends on their followers living in abject fear of leaving the fold. If Jamil had remained an anonymous do-gooder, or even taken the way out he was offered, the Ministry of Justice could afford to make everyone happy by showing mercy. Now the very future of the mullahs' political and spiritual stranglehold on the Afghan people requires sticking to their guns so no one else dares follow Jamil's example. And in public at least, the Afghan people will echo the party line, whether it's their personal conviction or not."

The ring of Steve's cell phone disrupted any response.

"It's your friend Becky," he said shortly as he took the call. Amy's eyes didn't move from his face as she followed his side of the conversation.

"Dubai? Yes, I'll let Amy know. She's here right now, lock, stock, and barrel with her luggage. . . . No she hasn't told me why yet. . . . Sure, I'll be happy to keep an eye on things till John makes arrangements. . . . No, it's no trouble, at least while I'm still in Afghanistan. My replacement actually arrives tomorrow, so I'll be free as a bird."

Steve answered Amy's questioning look. "They took the baby C-section. A boy. But he's having problems breathing. They're doing a medevac to Dubai. Your nurse friend said to make yourself at home. She'll call from Dubai when there's news."

"You're leaving Afghanistan again?" It made no sense that the security contractor's casually dropped info should hit Amy as forcibly as Becky's bad news.

"I only came back to stand in for Phil Myers, as you're aware," Steve responded. "His son's marrow transplant was successful, so Phil's free now to finish his own contract. After tomorrow, I'll be done with Condor Security."

"I'm glad to hear about Phil's little boy. But poor Ruth and John! They wouldn't call for a medevac unless the baby's life is in danger. Or Ruth's. Oh no, this is so terrible!" Swallowing hard, Amy wiped the chador sleeve again across her face. "I'm sorry. I'm being such a crybaby. There's no excuse for this. It's just—I keep thinking this day can't get any worse. And then it does."

The taut planes of Steve's face showed no expression, and Amy wished she could read whether a hard glint in the gray eyes was for the situation in general or finding himself saddled with a hysterical female. "Your friend Becky seems pretty optimistic," he said gruffly. "As for Jamil, hey, don't listen to me! I'm the eternal pessimist. If enough international pressure comes to bear, there's always hope Qaderi will back down."

Under those hard eyes trained on her face, Amy swallowed again, but the tears would not slow. "It . . . it isn't only that. It's everything. The children. The Welayat women. Soraya and Ibrahim. And now Farah too. I know I'm being selfish when John and Ruth and the baby are in so much trouble. I guess I hadn't realized how much I was counting on getting over here to talk to Becky. To ask her advice even if there's nothing much she could do."

Steve didn't move, but Amy could imagine a fractional softening of that hard glint as he said quietly, "I'm not Becky, but I'd appreciate knowing what's happened since I talked to you last. And not just your little side trip to Pul-e-Charki. What's going on with the children and Farah and the others? I do have an interest in New Hope, if you've forgotten."

Amy did not answer immediately. But when neither the gray eyes nor Steve's expression showed any sign of yielding, she began to talk, at first reluctantly, barely above a whisper. Then, caught up in the horror of her narration, it spilled out of her faster and faster, even as the tears poured unchecked down her cheeks.

"I thought I could save them. I thought I had saved them. And now they're lost, so many of them. Loma and Shahra—I'll never forgive Ibrahim for that. The others Soraya insisted were fine and left of their own will. Who knows what really happened? And Farah. Maybe I should just be happy for her, but I can't help feeling something's terribly wrong with her leaving like that. And now Jamil too. Everything I came here to do is gone. Everything good I thought I'd done is destroyed."

It was as well Amy had come to the end of that painful narration because her sobs were now too great for her to continue talking. Nor could she bear to witness anymore the unmistakable anger blazing in gray eyes despite the controlled mask that was Steve's expression, the compressed line of self-restraint that was his mouth. Sliding from the armchair where she was sitting, she buried her face against her arms on a coffee table, her efforts to stifle her sobs shaking her slim body.

From a distance, Amy heard Steve get to his feet. His firm footsteps crossed the room. She felt him sink down onto a sofa inches away from her bowed head. A knee brushed Amy's chador as he settled his long legs into place. When he finally spoke, his rough drawl held the anger that had been in his eyes. But his words did not.

"This isn't your fault, Amy, none of it. Surely you can see that. If you'd never come here, it would have been even worse for these people. If you couldn't save them, that's Afghanistan's fault, these people's own choices, not yours! Just let it go. Don't let them hurt you like this."

Amy raised her head, and though she had to bite her lip to keep it from quivering, it was with quiet conviction that she shook her head. "I know it's not all my fault. At least when I'm being objective. I couldn't have kept Ibrahim and Soraya—no, nor Duane either—from making their choices. And I wouldn't have wanted Jamil to make a different choice, no matter what happens. I know I can't make everything better for an entire country. Nor even for my Welayat families. I'm not that foolish. It's just—"

It seemed suddenly imperative for Amy to make Steve understand. She groped for the right words. "I guess the reason it hurts so much is because I've come to love these people so. Not only the Farahs and Royas and the other women and children who've been hurt so much. Even the Ibrahims and Sorayas who will lie and cheat and sell little girls like stock animals because they too have been hurt and never learned any better way. I'd give anything, even my own life, to make things right for every one of them. Only I can't because like you said, for good or for bad, they've got to choose their own future and the course of their country."

Meditatively now, Amy went on. "It just makes me wonder, if their choices can hurt me so much because I love them and want the best for them, how God must feel when he looks at everything we've done as a human race to this beautiful world he created and to its people. If I can grieve for these people, how deeply must God's heart grieve because he loves all of humanity so much more than I can possibly love the Afghan people.

"You said I need to let go. Becky Frazer said the same. That I couldn't stay here and love the Afghan people unless I was ready to let go. And I can see now how right you both are. I don't have to stop loving. But I do have to let go of these people. This place. To release them both to God's love and care and protection, not mine."

27

The fury of Steve's thoughts seethed behind the tight control he'd placed over his expression. If a certain Duane Gibson or any of his cohorts were in front of him, he'd be hard-pressed not to rearrange a few features.

Amy was still looking at Steve, but he wasn't sure she really saw him as she reflected aloud. Something in that faraway expression twisted sharply in Steve's chest, as though a wound finally healing over had just been painfully exposed again to the air. Hers was a face that had always held more character than classical beauty, and right now there was nothing pretty in it, the hazel eyes swollen and red from weeping, her fair skin blotchy and streaked with tears. A bit lip hadn't quite banished the quiver from her mouth.

That the absence of physical appeal did nothing to curb an overpowering impulse to pull the girl into his arms and kiss away those tears proved only too painfully how inadequate were the defenses Steve had worked so hard to build.

A sudden restless twisting of Steve's body had broken into Amy's meditative words. But she couldn't have seen his mental surrender as he sprang up to make a swift turn around the small living area.

It's not Amy who needs to let go. It's me! I can't fight this anymore, God. I can't fight you anymore! I've believed in you since I was a kid in Sunday school. And once I too thought I could change the world. But when I found I couldn't even save Afghanistan, I guess I threw in the towel. I didn't want to believe again in a mission and find it wasn't worth shedding blood over or losing a friend. I didn't want to open up my heart to people who might die or be taken away or prove less honorable than I'd believed.

Just do your job, but don't get involved. That's been my philosophy. You can't salvage people who don't want—or deserve—salvaging. As to loving them, what's the point? You're only opening yourself up to get hurt.

And then I run into Amy and others who pour such love into places like Afghanistan even when they know that they may—no, that they will!—get hurt. That they'll be betrayed. That so much of their work will go down the drain. Oh, maybe the occasional changed heart like Jamil's—and look where he's ended up. Yet they keep doing it.

But Amy's right. It's exactly what you did. You looked down on this messed-up world. On me—and like it or not, I'm no better prize than Khalid or this Ibrahim. And somehow you saw something worth coming down here to live and die for. As Amy and her friends seem to find in Afghanistan. If I've never found a mission since I first left Afghanistan to which I'd give my life, I've come to believe in Amy and her friends. In their love. In the mission they've chosen. A mission as worth believing in as the God they serve.

So now what, God?

Catching Amy's puzzled stare, Steve returned to his seat. Not the sofa, too close to Amy for self-control, but his original armchair across the room. By now Amy had pushed herself from her slumped position back to her own seat. As she watched Steve sink into the armchair, he saw thoughtful deliberation dawn in those hazel depths, along with—was that hope? trust?

Steve stirred restively. Why did she look at him like that? What did she expect of him?

He quickly found out. Eyes never leaving his face, Amy said pensively, "Maybe there is something I can do to help Jamil. Or rather something you could do, if you'd be willing. You did say it would be a cinch to break Jamil out of Pul-e-Charki. And isn't that what you do for a living? I mean, people hire you to do missions, right? You mentioned you'd be finished tomorrow at Condor Security. So if you're really sure our embassy won't help Jamil . . . I don't know what your usual fee is, but I haven't spent any of the salary I've earned over here."

Where she was going was so unreal, Steve bolted upright to interrupt with stunned disbelief. "You're suggesting hiring me to bust Jamil out of Pul-e-Charki? You're joking, right? Sure, I said it was doable. For the State Department with all the resources of our military and government on the ground here. Not for a private citizen in hostile territory. Or can I hope you weren't serious? that if I say no, you won't go searching for some other dumb schmuck at the end of his contract and bat those pretty lashes to talk him into a suicide mission?"

"Of course I'm serious. Jamil was willing to risk his life to take a stand on his faith. Do you think I'm going to run and hide from possible risk if there's anything I can do to save his life? But no, I'm not stupid enough to try hiring some random security contractor who might turn around and warn the embassy or even Qaderi. Or blow the job if he did take it. I guess I thought that you at least would be willing . . ."

The intensity of hurt and anger that squeezed at Steve's chest was unexpected.

Leaning forward, Steve demanded harshly, "And just why would I be willing? Because it's my fault Jamil is in there to start with? Because if I'd made different choices all those years ago, been less gullible in believing Khalid, your friend wouldn't have spent years in a hellhole? and maybe wouldn't find himself now in a position for this to happen? I assume by now you've let him know who he can blame!"

But Amy was shaking her head even as she met his narrowed gaze steadily. "No, of course not. How could you think I would blame you for what happened to Jamil, any more than I should keep blaming myself for everything that's happened at New Hope? As for Jamil, if anyone ever tells him about your past connection, it will be you. No, I just thought of you—"

Now it was Amy who leaned forward, her hands twisting tightly in her lap. "I thought of you because I know the kind of person you are. The best soldier he'd ever known, your chaplain friend Rev Garwood called you. I figured if anyone could help Jamil, you could. And I . . . I trust you. You're the only one I could think of who'd understand saving Jamil is a mission worth doing. You know he doesn't deserve to be in Pul-e-Charki. You know he really is what he's professed to be, a follower of Isa Masih, Jesus Christ, the Son of God. And you know he'll never back down just to save his own life. If you won't help and you're right that no one else will, then Jamil will let them kill him before he denies Isa Masih, just as he was once willing to die to revenge himself on Khalid."

Steve's fury left him as fast as it had arisen. His own self-reproach had made him misread Amy's plea. And though her hurried explanations might have been intended to stroke his ego, change his mind, sincerity breathed in her tone, blazed in her eyes. How to let her down easily, make Amy understand the impossibility of what she'd suggested?

"Look, believe me that I wish I could be more helpful. But you've seen Pul-e-Charki. It would take an army to breach those walls."

Or was that strictly true? Hadn't Steve himself been this very day offered the means and opportunity to breach Pul-e-Charki's walls? At least if Cougar hadn't yet found someone to babysit that visiting interrogation unit. *If nothing else, I could do some recon, see if I can find out exactly where they've stashed their "apostate."*

Steve found himself for the first time thinking through Amy's suggestion as though he'd been handed a legit mission target. Steve didn't bother letting Amy in on the multimillion-dollar budget of an operation like Khalid's security detail. Or how fast her recent months' salary would disappear covering even a small security contract's daily expenses.

Still, he'd been furious at Bolton's cavalier dismissal of Jamil's God-given right to worship as he chose. Something the American Constitution and people and government purported to hold as a nonnegotiable tenet. Whether such a rescue was prudent or even any business of the United States was another matter. But Bolton's reasoning dealt only with his embassy's political advantage, and maybe his own. And that infuriated Steve!

A covert extraction rather than overt? Even the best-case scenario that came to mind demanded manpower, resources, time Steve didn't have— and the kind of blind luck to which he'd never entrust a mission. *There's no point in speculating until I've eyeballed the place. Question is, would this be a mission worth committing to, even with every chance of something going wrong?*

Steve suddenly realized there was no hesitation in his answer. *Yes! You wanted a mission worth believing in. You just got it!*

Amy had fallen mute, her brows knit together as though she was confused by his sudden silence, but she spoke again, softly. "You're right; it was a crazy idea. When you mentioned you'd be free tomorrow to accept another contract, it seemed some kind of sign. But—I've been wrong about so many other things. I guess I was wrong about that too."

"I'll see what I can do."

"You owe nothing to Jamil. Or—or me. And I guess no amount I could pay you would compensate the risk it would put you in." Amy broke off as Steve's quiet statement sank in. She stared at him. "You will? You'll take the contract, mission, whatever you call it?"

"Hey, I said I'd look into it. Don't get your hopes up. I can't guarantee there's anything I can do. As to your savings, keep them to pay your student loans. Bottom line, you couldn't begin to pay enough to hire me for a job like this. But . . . let's just say it's a mission I believe in."

Amy might as well not have heard his warning caveat. As her face lit up to an incredulous joy and relief that did much to banish the ravages of her tears, Steve's mouth tipped into an ironic twist that should have held bitterness but, to his own surprise, did not. There was no more denying the truth, at least to himself.

Steve was deeply and irrevocably in love with Amy Mallory. He'd not only fight at her back any day but would willingly lay down his life for her.

And now in a final quirk of fate along a life journey full of them, Steve had just committed himself to risking his life—for no matter how he downplayed it, risk was inevitable—to restore to the woman he loved the man who held the heart Steve so achingly longed to possess.

Ameera was right. Isa did give me the words to speak when the time came. I was not even afraid.

Jamil paced the holding cage, adrenaline from those last electrifying moments in front of the judges still pumping through his veins. Had Ameera grasped Jamil's message at the end that was to her alone? He'd seen the tears spilling from hazel eyes. But shining through her fear for Jamil, he'd also glimpsed pride in his courage, joy for his faith.

So what now? Jamil's bundle and tushak had been tossed into the holding cage, so it would seem he was not returning to his former cell. But despite the judge's somber proclamation, Jamil had no expectation of imminent death. Not after seeing the Red Cross delegation and Kareem with his camera. The very prudence that had motivated Minister of Justice Qaderi to offer Jamil a way out would now send him scrambling for a face-saving resolution. At least while the eyes of the world were still turned his direction.

To continue in this cage would not be so bad. They have left me Ameera's holy book. They are no longer withholding food and water. So long as I am left alone, I can endure anything.

But Jamil had only just consoled himself when a tramping of boots approached. One of the guards clanged his baton against the bars. "Retrieve your belongings. You are being moved."

A high wall divided the prison's administrative sector from general prisoner accommodations. Night had fallen during Jamil's pacing, but floodlights revealed his destination as his escort shepherded him through a gate in the wall. The octagonal concrete fortress where he'd been held till now. But this time the corridor into which weapon butts prodded Jamil was neither in disrepair nor unpopulated.

No resources had been wasted on illumination. As the clanging of a steel door shut floodlights outside, one of Jamil's escorts produced a flashlight. But the smell alone would have told Jamil where he was. The stench of unwashed bodies and urine. Rotting food and mildew. Above all, that peculiar acrid musk that in its collective perspiration told of fear and anger and hate and despair.

As a key clinked in a lock, the light touched a surge of bodies stumbling to their feet. A wave of the flashlight signaled for Jamil to enter the cell. Jamil raised his head high, steps lengthening to a firm stride as he walked past the guard. Now he needed the courage that had come to him when facing the judges.

Wherever I go.
To the end of all time and space.
I am not alone.

The cell was not large, but in the flashlight's bobbing beam, Jamil estimated at least a dozen other prisoners sinking back to their disturbed slumber with angry mutters. Spotting an opening in a far corner, he reached it just as the retreating light plunged the cell into blackness. He'd crouched down to spread his tushak when a hand grabbed his wrist. The grip was too powerful to shake free, untrimmed fingernails digging into Jamil's flesh painfully enough to break skin.

Jamil couldn't breathe. This was what he'd braced himself for, what he'd feared. *Isa, you are real. You are here. You have changed me. I will never doubt this again. Now as you taught your followers to pray, I beg you to deliver me from evil!*

But even as the prayer rose from his mind, Jamil realized the hand clutching at him was burning to the touch, its pincer grip that of desperation, not ill intent. A moan came out of the darkness beside him. "Please, water. In the name of Allah, do you have water?"

Using his free hand to probe along his assailant's arm and shoulder, Jamil came in contact with a bearded face. Damp flesh under his fingers was even hotter than the hand gripping his wrist. Now Jamil understood the opening left in this back corner. No other prisoner wanted to sleep too close to their sick cellmate.

As Jamil fumbled in the dark to open his pack, he remembered he'd drained his water bottle during the long hours in the holding cage. He called softly into the darkness. "Does anyone have water for this man?"

The only response was a chorus of irate curses. Jamil's neighbor was now tossing feverishly on his own sleeping mat. His moans gathered strength in the dark. "Please, water! Have mercy, water!"

Jamil could stand it no longer. He stood and groped his way in the darkness. A limb jerked under his sandal, and a hard blow knocked him forward to sprawl across other prone bodies. Now furious shouts were drowning out the sick man's moans. The uproar had drawn the guards, so by the time Jamil rolled to his feet, a flashlight was shining through the cell bars. "What is going on in here? Do you all want the whip?"

Jamil stepped up to the bars. "There is a sick man here. Can you call a doctor?"

"A doctor!" the guard sneered. "Do you think this is a hospital? The prison medic will be making rounds in two days. If a prisoner has complaints, he will see them then. Meanwhile if I hear any more noise, I will order ten lashes for each of you."

"Then can you at least bring clean water and fever tablets?"

The guard looked more astonished than angry at Jamil's persistence. "Did you hear me? Shall I make it twenty lashes?"

"The man may die before morning without attention," Jamil answered quietly. "Will this not cause you even more trouble?"

"Are you a doctor to say whether a man will live or die?"

"I am not a doctor, but I am a healer. I will attend this man if you will bring me clean water and medicine. You do have an infirmary, do you not?"

"If there is an infirmary, its services are not free. Nor are mine. What do you have to offer?" The guard leered. "Yourself perhaps?"

It was a barter system Jamil knew only too well. Prison guards were little better situated than the prisoners themselves, their meager salaries augmented only by what they could squeeze out of their charges. Prisoners with money or well-off family members could bargain for better food, luxury items, even freedom if their crime was small enough or the bribe was right. Without money—well, Jamil had suffered the consequences of being a prisoner with neither resources nor family for protection.

Jamil had to step over prone bodies to reach his bundle, where he pulled out the sky blue shalwar kameez and embroidered vest he'd purchased with his first paycheck from Ameera. This left him with a single change of clothing, but Jamil didn't hesitate to carry the outfit back to the bars. "I will trade you these for water and fever capsules. A light too so I may attend the man."

The flashlight played over fine cotton material before the guard said brusquely, "It is enough. But only because I do not care to deal with a dead man in my sector."

Reaching through the bars, the guard snatched the clothing. As his flashlight receded, Jamil didn't dare shift his feet lest he tread on someone. But the guard was soon back to thrust a liter of bottled water and a dozen ibuprofen tablets through the bars along with a small, disposable flashlight. Its beam permitted Jamil to retreat safely to the far corner.

The other prisoners were no longer making any attempt at slumber. Jamil could make out the glint of eyes watching him all around as he examined the sick man. A heavyset shadow nearby spoke up. "I know now who you are. You are the apostate healer of whom all Pul-e-Charki has been speaking."

"I am a follower of Isa, the greatest healer of all," Jamil admitted. Under the flashlight beam, he could see that his patient was skeletally thin, eyes sunk deeply into their sockets, skin loose with the wrinkled-paper quality of extreme dehydration. The man was also shaking with chills despite his burning temperature.

Spotting the sick man's blanket tossed aside nearby, Jamil tucked it around him, then added his own patu. He lifted the man slightly before holding the bottled water to cracked lips and coaxing in two tablets. The sick man swallowed, then drank thirstily again as Jamil added, "One of Isa's teachings is to treat others as you would have them treat you. If I found myself ill like this man, I would wish someone to help me."

"Then you are a fool!" The sullen voice was the same that had spoken up earlier. "This man has not been able to care for himself in days. We are waiting only for him to die or be taken away lest we all become ill as well. And now that you have so foolishly contaminated yourself, you will keep your distance, or I swear I will slit your throat as well as his."

"Be silent and let us sleep!" someone else snapped.

The sick man had subsided into a comatose state. Though he still burned with fever, there was nothing more Jamil could do for him, so he extinguished his light even as he agreed gravely, "That is a wise thought. I will be sure to keep my distance."

Stretching out on his own tushak, Jamil pulled his spare set of clothing around his shoulders. Now he could be thankful for the cell's overcrowding, the body heat of a dozen men alleviating the chilly temperature somewhat. With the cessation of his activity, the stench pressed in on him again, and a chorus of snores promised a sleepless night. But a glimmer of amusement was replacing the apprehension with which Jamil had walked into this cell.

I prayed for your protection against evil men, Isa Masih. I could not have guessed you would give me as shield and protection a sick man and fear of contagion.

28

So this is how a princess lives.

Farah turned a full circle in the middle of the room. Only faded recollections of that family palace, so briefly restored and lost again, held comparable luxury.

Farah hadn't arrived last night until long after dark. Her new employer had been in such a hurry, she'd barely been granted time to scribble a note and bundle up her scant possessions before climbing into the cab of a green police pickup.

But there had been several stops, including a compound swarming with police uniforms whose sign identified it as the Ministry of Interior. At some point Farah fell asleep against her bundle, her next recollection tall metal gates opening ahead of the pickup's headlights. The men who closed the gates behind the pickup were hardened-looking, bearded individuals whose civilian shalwar kameez belied their easy handling of the weapons they all carried.

Farah hadn't liked their avaricious eyes on her and was relieved when Ismail led her up several flights of stairs into a room where he indicated Farah was to sleep. The rumble of a generator explained sparse lighting along the way.

But now sunshine streamed through slatted shutters, illuminating a room larger than many poorer Afghan homes. As large in fact as the salon Farah had shared with numerous other women and children at the New Hope compound. Most astounding were its sleeping accommodations.

Not a tushak such as Farah had slept on her entire life but a shiny brass frame topped with a thick, yielding mattress, in turn piled high with soft blankets and silk-covered pillows. Storage chests of richly hued hardwood matched a dresser with a mirror attached. Handwoven rugs such as she'd labored over in the carpet-weaving shop offered warmth under Farah's bare feet.

Farah had already discovered a second door leading to a bathroom as ornate as those at the New Hope compound must once have been. Water emerging from its gilt fixtures wasn't heated, she'd also discovered when she'd scrubbed herself before putting on fresh clothing from her bundle. Still, what kind of people were wealthy enough to have a private bathroom in their sleeping quarters?

The dresser's contents—brightly colored tunics and pantaloons, intricately embroidered chapans and scarves—gave evidence Farah's sleeping quarters had been occupied by another woman before her. Lifting out a turquoise blue silk scarf embroidered with tiny sapphire and emerald glass beads, Farah draped it around head and shoulders. Its color intensified the deep blue of Farah's own eyes as she studied herself in the dresser mirror.

I am beautiful! she recognized with astonishment. *I look like a princess!*

Then, rebelliously, *And why should I not? If there are others who live like this, why not I?*

The thought was a reminder of that bundle of afghani bills she'd now tucked into her clean tunic.

And Jamil.

When Deputy Minister Ismail had made his astonishing proposal the day before, Farah's initial response was overwhelming relief that she hadn't been summoned from her weaving duties to an unwanted marriage. The afghanis he'd offered, more money than Farah had ever seen, were admittedly tempting. But Farah trusted neither strange men nor any scheme that could warrant such an extravagant incentive. Even while her mind had whirled with questions about Jamil, she'd been phrasing a cautious refusal that would permit her to escape the room and deputy minister.

Then he'd displayed that dog-eared photo. Farah's memories of her busy surgeon father were few, less because of trauma or time's passage than because he'd appeared so rarely in the women's quarters during her early childhood. She could summon up a kindly but stern voice. A brown beard that scratched her cheeks during rare embraces. Eyes a piercing blue no one but she shared in the household. If she'd instantly recognized the photo, it was because an enlarged, framed copy of that same portrait had hung in their home-in-exile's receiving room.

But if the brown-haired man in the photo was undoubtedly Farah's father, it did not follow that Jamil was truly his son. Certainly that blurred photo of Jamil bore little semblance to Farah's faded recollections of a slim, beardless teenager.

And yet from the moment she'd first glimpsed Ameera's male assistant upon arriving at the New Hope compound, something about Jamil had drawn Farah's eyes time and time again to somber, bearded features, strained her ears for the cadence of his voice. Had her heart recognized what her mind did not?

That final photo had removed doubts this was some cruel trick to make Farah think she still had a family member left alive. It was Jamil the deputy minister sought to deceive, not Farah.

And if Jamil was indeed the brother she'd believed dead—

Her brooding was cut abruptly short by authoritative footsteps approaching her sleeping quarters. Stuffing the turquoise silk back into the dresser, Farah snatched her own scarf over her face as the door slammed open and Deputy Minister Ismail stepped into the room. Behind him, a guard carried a tray holding teapot, cup, and plate of fresh naan, all of which he set on the nearest storage chest, then disappeared.

Surveying the room indifferently, her new employer did not bother with a polite salaam of greeting. "I trust you find your accommodations adequate? You are now ready to begin your task?"

Farah's stomach grumbled just then audibly, but she answered without expression, "Yes, of course, immediately. And the accommodations are beyond any I could ever expect—*tashakor*. Though I fear I have dislodged another woman from her quarters. Please convey my gratitude and apologies. And I would be pleased to move to quarters more suitable to such as I so that she might return to her own."

But the deputy minister only looked mildly amused. "You have dislodged no one. My wives and children pass the winter school break at our family estate in the Panjsheer Valley. As to accommodations, I'm afraid my home offers none more suitable to such as you. Not unless you wish to lodge with my chowkidar. Or the guards."

His implied insult was made worse by a complete lack of animosity or emotion of any sort. Any lingering compunction about lying to this man or taking his money left Farah. Swiftly lowered lashes hid her rage as she responded with deceptive meekness, "Then I thank you again for your hospitality, Deputy Minister. And if you will take me now to Jamil, I will trespass on it no longer."

The eyebrows in front of Farah rose sharply. "Are you so stupid, woman? Did you think to do this without preparation? Jamil will not simply accept your word that you are his sister. You must be prepared to convince him. It is fortunate he has not seen his sister since early childhood, but there are details, memories, family history you will need to give him. And you cannot afford a single mistake. He is already suspicious of such claims."

Without elaborating, Ismail reached into his robe to pull out a sheaf of papers. "I have written down here everything you need to know. Can you read?"

That her skill was rudimentary, Farah would not admit, so she simply nodded sullenly.

"Then you will take these papers and study them. When I return, I will test you until I am satisfied you are capable of doing what I ask without error. You will have time. A few days, even a week. Jamil too must be— shall we say, prepared for this assignment? Meanwhile, you will not leave these quarters. This is for your own safety." A smile that touched bearded lips was slight but unpleasant. "Though you need not fret yourself. I have given strict orders to my men that you are not to be molested. At least not without my consent."

The threat was so repugnant, Farah's defiance drained immediately away. This man was no friend to her. But it had been a mistake to regard him as an ally either, or even a business partner. Farah raised her lashes to ask in a low voice, "Even if I convince Jamil I am his sister, do you truly think he will care? Why should he if he has not seen this sister for many, many years? What is a sister after all?"

"That he will care is the only thing I am sure of," the deputy minister replied. "Jamil came to Kabul with only two thoughts in mind. To revenge himself upon those who destroyed his family during the war. And to find out what had become of his mother and sister who were torn away from him then and make provision for their safety and future. However foolish he has shown himself, he will not allow stupid questions of theology to separate him from the family he has sought all these years. *If you play your part correctly.*"

The deputy minister was already striding out of the room. Farah waited until his authoritative tread receded before rushing to the door he'd closed behind him. It wasn't locked, but when she peered outside, she saw one of Ismail's mujahedeen patrolling the corridor.

Retreating, Farah surveyed her luxurious quarters with less favor. Gilded though it might be, this room was no less a cage than her Welayat prison cell. Farah turned to her breakfast tray, hungrily finishing both tea and naan before picking up her assignment.

The deputy minister's handwritten script was neither neat nor easy to read. Farah had worked her way through only half a page before growing weary of it. Dropping the papers onto the bed, she wandered restlessly toward the slatted shutters. These reached the floor like folding doors rather than a window. Farah opened them and stepped out onto a wrought-iron balcony.

Now she could see that her new quarters were on the top floor of a three-story cubic building as large as any mansion Farah had passed with Ameera when they visited the neighborhood literacy project. But here were no gaudy colors or wildly juxtaposed towers and domes, just white walls, wrought-iron trim, and fired-clay tile roofing. Though fruit trees, grape arbors, and rosebushes were currently only dried limbs, cedars and mountain pine made expansive grounds a pleasant oasis even in late winter. All this was Deputy Minister Ismail's personal residence? And only one of two, from his earlier statements. Meanwhile, children starved in Kabul streets!

The world is not fair. But when has it ever been? One must think of one's own survival. Seize what one can for oneself.

But Ameera had not so done when she'd left her homeland to come to Afghanistan.

No, Farah did not want to think of the foreign woman she'd believed her friend. From this third-floor vantage, she could also see that she was no longer in Kabul. Beyond the perimeter wall, a featureless, barren plain stretched to the accordion folds of rising mountain ridges. Dominating the horizon was a single massive structure that might have been a stone outcropping were it not for its regular edges.

A military installation? Or perhaps a prison? Even the one that held Jamil? Farah had leaned over the balcony's wrought-iron railing for a better view when two men strolled into sight below. Though they were talking and laughing, weapons slung casually over shoulders, their appearance was a stark reminder that if Farah was no prisoner in that fortress across the plain, neither was she free to come and go as she chose. Something in her startled withdrawal from the railing drew the guards' attention upward. Automatically Farah snatched her headscarf across her face.

But even as she did so, mutiny rose inside her. Why should she not be able to stand on her own balcony barefaced? to breathe in deeply the spicy sweet fragrances of cedar and pine instead of cotton cloth? to survey her surroundings unobstructed? Would Ameera hide her face for such as these?

I will not be invisible!

Dropping the scarf, Farah defiantly stared out over the landscape. But it was not so easy to ignore the bold stares, unpleasant smiles, and pointed gestures from below. When laughing shouts drew more guards to stare upward, Farah admitted defeat, pulling her scarf high and retreating into her room. Her new quarters no longer seemed sumptuous, but echoingly empty. In all her short life, Farah had neither known nor expected privacy. Except for her long-ago escape from that mountain fortress, there'd always been other women around to talk to, fight with. Other children when she'd lived on the streets.

I did not think I would miss the others so. And Ameera. I was so angry with her. I did not even permit her opportunity to explain.

Yet what was there to explain? Ameera had admitted her abandonment of Farah and the others. And if Farah's new employer was right that

Jamil's current difficulties were also Ameera's doing, her transgressions were greater than any broken promise. Had Farah's brother been miraculously restored to her from the dead, only to be snatched away again due to the foreign woman's influence?

Farah felt something inside her turn to stone as she pulled the wad of afghanis from her tunic. Though she'd handled money too rarely to know their buying power, surely so many bills were enough for two people to start a new life, even if Deputy Minister Ismail didn't keep his own promise of further payment.

I am no longer alone, even if Ameera has betrayed me. Nor am I penniless either. And once Jamil is freed, I will need no one else, for we will be together as he once promised.

Tucking the money away, Farah picked up the handwritten notes scattered across the bed. That she could convince Jamil she was his sister, Farah no longer had any doubts with what she'd read so far. Of greater urgency would be letting slip no detail beyond those contained in these pages.

But misgivings stubbornly lingered as Farah bent to her studies. Even if Jamil believed her to be his sister, was Ismail right that he'd care enough to change his course of action?

Or would a brother's love prove as much an illusion as all other love Farah had known in her life?

29

Like Kabul, Pul-e-Charki had changed since Steve had seen it last—and it hadn't.

When he'd last driven onto this dusty, featureless plateau overlooking Kabul, it had been with a convoy of victorious Northern Alliance mujahedeen and Special Forces troops. The Taliban guards had already abandoned their posts, front gates swinging broken on their hinges, prisoners largely fled. Smashing locks to release a few remaining detainees screaming behind cell bars for food and water had felt to a younger Master Sergeant Steve "Willie" Wilson rather like liberating concentration camps at the tail end of WWII.

It had been a good feeling.

New steel gates hung now between two square guard towers, machine-gun nests topping their turreted parapets. Plaster and paint had done much to cover over ravages of rocket fire and disrepair. And the four-story concrete "wheel" that housed prisoners was crowded instead of empty.

"About three thousand and growing," Dyncorp country manager Jason Hamilton elucidated as the two contractors stepped through an interior gate into the closest wheel "spoke."

Phil had arrived on the morning flight, limping more than usual from the aftereffects of the bone marrow transplant, but quietly euphoric over his small son's good prognosis. Much of Steve's day had been spent clearing up paperwork to turn the detail back over to his friend. By the time Jason Hamilton met up with Steve outside Pul-e-Charki gates to hand him a security clearance badge, it was late afternoon, and Steve hadn't yet found time to review his new mission, much less Jamil's situation. Well, here was his opportunity to kill two birds with one stone, if such a bloodthirsty adage was appropriate to a rescue mission.

The corridor down which the two contractors walked made Alcatraz look like the Ritz Carlton. Walls crumbling and unpainted. Lighting fixtures empty of fluorescent tubing. A dozen or more prisoners crammed into each cell. Clothes were rags, hygiene arrangements negligible from the smell. Sullen, apathetic faces pressed up against cell bars to watch the two foreigners transit their territory.

Steve stepped hurriedly after his companion into an octagonal court- yard formed where the concrete wheel's eight spokes came together. "Wow, that place looks like a mutiny begging to happen."

Jason's shoulders hunched dismissively. "You're not so far-off. Riots are becoming downright routine around here. Protesting living conditions but also detainment. It doesn't take more than an accusation or even a bribe to get someone thrown in here. And it's not unusual for a prisoner to spend years without even finding out what he's been accused of."

Jason led the way across the courtyard. "In any case, I'd apologize for dragging you through that, but it's the quickest route on foot. Good news, your clients won't need to venture into that cesspool. Our people do their thing over here."

The wing to which Jason steered Steve boasted fresh paint and roofing, a contrast even more marked because the spokes on either side were still a dilapidated ruin. Inside, the layout was identical to the corridor they'd just traversed. But here was more fresh paint, functioning lights, shiny- new steel bars on both windows and cells. Each cell contained a porcelain sink, flush toilet, and no more than one or two prisoners.

"Dyncorp carried the reconstruction bid on this as well as its current security contract. Our condition for refurbishing this wing was full access to certain high-level prisoners."

Presumably, the *our* referred to was the American military and State Department rather than Dyncorp personally, though Steve wasn't con- vinced his companion saw any particular difference.

These prisoners at least looked well-fed, even portly. Many had open

Qurans. Others were praying. Nor would it seem the prisoners were always locked up. Opposite the cells, narrow window slits overlooked a triangular courtyard that was the space between spokes. It held a volleyball net as well as portable soccer goals. At the moment a lively volleyball game was under way.

In fact, except for the bars, their accommodations were superior to most of their countrymen. Steve felt no impulse to sympathy, especially when he caught a murderous glare from eyes outlined in black with kohl. The signature of a Taliban fanatic. These men at least, Steve had no doubt, were in here because they were both dangerous and ruthless, willing to kill their own countrymen's as well as foreign troops and the entire Western world if they had their way.

Jason nodded toward a rear exit door. "That leads to the administrative sector and an Afghan National Army outpost. The embassy convoy will park over there so you can bring our clients straight in without going through the prison."

Wandering the corridors were soldiers with ISAF and USA insignia, as well as several civilians. DEA? CIA? A metal detector arch divided the main spoke from the T-junction with the outer rim of the concrete wheel. The muscled types in safari-style clothing and Dyncorp ID badges gave neither Steve nor their own boss a pass on stepping through the arch while their badges were fed into an ultraviolet reader.

All of which from a professional standpoint Steve approved heartily. With this level of security, watching the backs of a few counternarcotics interrogators was going to be a snooze. Jason showed him around a command center. "That locker's yours. Your ID badge works as a magnetic key."

But he'd lost Steve's attention. The command center sported the inevitable flat-screen TV flickering local news images. Stepping over to turn up the sound, Steve listened incredulously as the news headline ran its course. "Did I just hear right? I thought you said prisoners could be in here for years before they came up for trial."

Jason had paused beside Steve to listen. "Unless you're an apostate, I guess."

On the screen, Khalid's florid features had followed the news headline.

Steve's former employer was walking a skillful line, not going so far as to suggest an apostate be forgiven his transgression, but making the case for a public and speedy trial. Unambiguous was the insinuation that Qaderi had used Jamil for his political advantage and was deliberately dragging the apostasy case out through the elections to give himself a platform.

A brilliant offensive that made Khalid appear to any international audience a champion of civil rights while avoiding the more dangerous issue of Jamil's apostasy. Had it come from Bolton's brain?

But now the press conference had shifted to Qaderi's wire-rimmed glasses and white turban, his soft-spoken discourse coming across as composed and intellectual as Khalid had appeared forceful and passionate.

An Islamic tribunal was no stage play for onlookers such as the West made it, but a private matter between a sinner, his judges, and his Supreme Arbitrator. However, so none might accuse Afghanistan's own supreme arbitrator of ignoble motives, this apostate whose self-confessed crimes were wasting so much national dialogue would be bound over to immediate public trial at Qaderi's own first calendar opening ten days ahead, a full two weeks before the elections. Moreover, in rebuke to gross interference from the imperialistic and infidel West into an Afghan internal affair, the Ministry of Justice invited—no, demanded—the attendance of his fellow presidential candidates to demonstrate their own devotion to the faith and solidarity in defending national sovereignty of the *Islamic* Republic of Afghanistan.

Qaderi's single emphasis in his calm speech reminded foreign as well as native audiences that Afghanistan was—by ratification of these same Western nations now raising objections—a religious state under the banner of Islam.

Steve's mind was racing as the minister finished speaking. He now had a deadline for this mission, and a short one. Maybe a guilty sentence wouldn't result in immediate execution. But Steve couldn't count on that. Nor that Jamil would remain accessible—if one could call it that—once the trial was over.

Even finding out where in this madhouse Jamil had been stowed was going to be a challenge. With three thousand inmates, Steve could hardly wander the corridors until he stumbled over his target. Not without drawing more attention to Steve's own person than was prudent. Ditto using more official channels to inquire.

At Steve's side, Jason was shaking his head disbelievingly. "I'd say Qaderi won that round. Bolton is not going to be happy. Our best hope now is that Ismail really can deliver in discrediting this kook before he manages to derail the election process, not to mention our entire mission here in Afghanistan."

Steve managed to keep his tone mild. "And if the man isn't a kook, but a true believer?"

Jason raised an ironic eyebrow. "Hey, I've got no problem with religion, but on this matter I'm with Bolton and Ismail both. Back home every politician's a Bible-thumper come election time, no matter how many secret mistresses or offshore bank accounts he's got in private. It's no different here. Locals I know pay enough public compliance to satisfy the mullahs while privately they live as they choose. That's how you survive in these parts. This Jamil could have kept his mouth shut, head down, his personal religious beliefs private. At least till after the elections. But he chose to break the rules of the game. And here Islam *is* the game. Which makes this guy either nuts or suicidal."

Steve reminded himself that the Dyncorp manager didn't have his personal link with Jamil. That he needed this man's goodwill. Still, irritation boiled over. "So little things like freedom of speech and faith are just optional items we're lucky to enjoy back home? You talk about our mission here. You want to explain just what that's supposed to be? I mean, say ten years from now we've managed to impose enough stability the Afghans can police their own streets and our troops can all go home. Then what? Saddam Hussein enforced peace on his streets. So did Hitler. Afghanistan will still be a totalitarian Islamic regime where a man can be sentenced to death for voicing his belief in a different God. Where a woman can be sold off to pay her male relatives' debts. Where to live publicly what you believe privately is a capital offense. So what are we fighting for here?"

Steve moderated his tone, but the words gritted through his teeth. "The way I see it, we can't walk the fence forever. Sooner or later the nations that call themselves free are going to face one of two choices. Either they'll have to face head-on an oppressive, corrupt ideology that dictates to a billion people how they can or cannot pray, think, act, believe. Which will be a problem since in the meantime they've been arming regimes practicing that ideology to their collective teeth. Or they're going to wake up one day and discover that their own freedoms are gone. What *won't* happen is that the 'free West' can keep enjoying forever their own freedoms while tacitly conceding those are now considered optional for the rest of this planet."

To Jason's credit, he looked less exasperated than amused. "You're an idealist, Steve. To be blunt, it's your one big flaw in this industry. Me, I'm not interested in making the world what it should be. Only in surviving as it is. And making sure my country survives on top.

"On the other hand, it makes you an honest man, and we need honest. Glad to have you on this job." The Dyncorp manager clapped Steve on the back. "I'll meet you at the embassy bright and early tomorrow to introduce our clients."

Steve grinned at the other contractor. Even if they'd never agree, Jason Hamilton was a good man as well as a decorated warrior.

Rather than walk through that sullen mass of prisoners again, Steve chose a longer detour through the unrepaired spoke that lay between his new duty post and the wing by which he'd entered. Much of the four-story rectangle was sealed off by rusting security grates that had once partitioned corridors and locked off stairwells, perhaps why he spotted no guards wasted on these corridors. Chunks of fallen concrete and plaster littered vacant cells. Entire collapsed ceilings explained why this sector was still in disuse.

As he walked back toward the main prison entrance, his mind was already sifting through one idea after another. Steve knew his own preferred option. Grab a helo on the next dark night. Rappel down with an assault team. Blow open a few chained grilles. Grab the target and cinch back up to the helo. Then speed over those barren mountain ridges on the horizon before the ANA outpost next door could roll off their sleeping mats to interfere. Enough of Steve's Condor Security buddies were as disgusted as he was with this place and their own humdrum employment, he could probably round up a posse to handle such an op for sheer recreation. *What would it take to "borrow" Khalid's helo?*

Unfortunately any mission well-executed enough for success would inevitably point accusing fingers at the elite forces to which Steve had once belonged and even his own government. *I'm willing to stick out my own neck, but I can't put anyone else in harm's way over this.*

Besides, it wasn't enough to spring Jamil from Pul-e-Charki. Jamil had to be gotten out of Afghanistan—and in such a way he could live out his future in peace and anonymity. There was no point in rescuing the man from execution only to make him a target for every Muslim fanatic wanting to curry favor with Allah by eliminating an apostate.

No, if in little else, Khalid was right in suggesting the best solution was for Jamil to simply disappear off the face of the planet.

Steve was delayed at the main entrance for a swirling mass of gray-blue uniforms. These gradually separated into a guard contingent leaving the prison and another entering. The evening shift change. Guard badges weren't the hi-tech magnetic card necessary to get Steve into the restricted wing, but credentials were carefully examined while those entering received a pat-down and scan with a metal detector rod.

Taking photos at any Afghan government facility was a direct route to one of those overcrowded cells behind Steve. But a pen in his breast pocket, once available only to fictional spies but now sold in any surveillance-tech catalog, discreetly snapped one digital image after another. By the time Steve cleared the checkpoint and was striding toward the visitor parking area, his deadpan expression masked a satisfied smile. He had it, just how he'd do this thing.

Sliding behind the Pajero's steering wheel, Steve suspended his strategy planning long enough to assess his own emotions. What he had in mind was a crime against this country's laws. Possibly even those of his own country. Certainly if caught, Steve could count on being treated as a criminal. Did he feel any guilt about going forward? Was Steve stepping over a line he'd no business crossing?

But his mental examination uncovered neither compunction nor hesitation. It was the Afghans who were breaking international law here, not Steve or Jamil. And if this wasn't a mission his own embassy would sanction, it should be!

Steve's cell phone was to his ear before the key turned in the ignition.

Ismail had every intention of delivering on his vow to discredit a certain madman who was turning Afghanistan—and the deputy minister's own schemes—upside down. But for Jamil to fade quietly into the night was no longer part of Ismail's plan. He'd found another use for his former protégé.

And the girl.

In fact, if all went well, Jamil's role in this mission, willing or no, would in one move bring about everything Ismail had spent his adult life working toward. What had the Soviets called it in the game their soldiers so loved to play back when Ismail was taking up arms against them?

Ah, yes!

Checkmate.

30

"I should be back in a couple more days, as soon as Ruth and the baby are discharged here in Dubai. Meanwhile, make yourself at home."

Becky Frazer's cheerful update rang from the cell phone as Amy exited through the pedestrian gate of the AWR compound. Last night the nurse-practitioner had called Amy on the heels of Steve's surprising agreement. During Becky's prolonged chronicle, Steve had slipped out with a murmur that he needed to get back to the workers but would be in touch. A restless night in Becky's guest room included unhappy dreams where Amy too was a prisoner at Pul-e-Charki and Jamil was being led away to a firing squad, so she'd been thankful for the distraction when Elsa's call woke her with the news she'd arranged videographer and truck to move the Welayat group that morning.

The rest of the day had been a whirlwind of unpacking, dividing women and children among empty rooms, setting up a kitchen. Amy had resisted calling Steve, well aware the security contractor would need time to arrange whatever plans he had in mind. But she'd shown less resolution about redialing Kareem's sat-phone number every time she had a breathing space.

Even if Steve comes up with a plan, who knows how long it might be before he could actually mount a rescue operation. There's got to be a way to let Jamil know he hasn't been abandoned. If Kareem isn't willing to risk helping anymore, maybe he's got some contact who would.

But every call had been cut off so abruptly Amy hadn't even been able to leave a voice message. By the fifth or sixth time, Amy recognized this was no problem with the phone but the Afghan journalist deliberately cutting her off, so she'd quit trying. Now as Becky rang off, she fingered her cell phone. Should she try Kareem again or Steve?

She was unlocking Becky's apartment door when her phone rang. She fumbled for it eagerly as she pushed the door open with a foot. But the caller ID displayed no number she recognized. And though the voice on the other end proved to be Kareem's, it sounded far from happy.

"You must not continue to call my phone! Do you not know the authorities can trace such calls? Do you wish them to ask why a foreign infidel woman should be calling me? the same woman who once employed the apostate they hold in prison? Or would you see me too in Pul-e-Charki?"

"I'm so sorry, Kareem. We'd talked before on the phone, so it didn't occur to me it might cause trouble for you."

"That was before Jamil confessed himself to be an apostate. It was a foolish risk even so, but I did not then fear trouble. Now, should the police choose to investigate Jamil's past associations . . ."

Amy didn't need Kareem to spell out the picture. "I'll get off the phone. And I won't contact you anymore, I promise. I was just—well, I'd hoped you'd know someone who could negotiate a visit for me with Jamil. I'm willing to pay generously." *Interpret that as a bribe, if necessary!*

"You do not need to get off this phone." Kareem sounded mollified as he went on. "I purchased it when I left work so I could answer your calls. It is not registered to my name, so the police will not know to trace it. You see, I too wish to speak to you again. I have been thinking much about your friend and mine."

"Your friend," Amy repeated. "Then you aren't angry with Jamil anymore?"

"If I was angry, it is because I counted Jamil a friend. I wished him to be free. I even risked my own life and future on his behalf. When after the efforts of so many, he refused to take his freedom, to comply with what seemed such a small thing, it seemed at first he had spit on our friendship. And though I have never been very religious, to publicly acknowledge himself as apostate . . ." Kareem's thickened tone held a lifetime of programmed revulsion. "But then last night I began reading Jamil's holy book, the one you gave him. I had read its words once long ago. 'Do to others what you would have them do to you.' 'Love your enemies.' If these are foolish expectations for human behavior, I see no evil in them. Especially when such teachings encourage Afghans to be kind and peaceful and good."

The Afghan journalist sounded troubled. "More so, if a man like Jamil, who is no troublemaker, but a healer and teacher, cannot speak freely what his heart dictates, then how will journalists like myself ever know freedom to speak openly what they know to be truth? Already in the TV station where I work, I have learned how many stories are not covered for fear of the mullahs or government officials. And how many journalists have been arrested or disappeared or been killed and their killing blamed on the Taliban. Which is why I am no longer angry at Jamil but at Qaderi and his mullahs and a government—mine and yours—who tell the world Afghanistan has *dee-mo-cra-see* because there are elections but offer my people no true freedom."

"Then you're willing to help?" Amy asked eagerly. "I wouldn't want you to do anything that could put you in danger. But—well, you got me in to see Jamil before."

Kareem's rejection was immediate and emphatic. "It is not a question of danger. I was able to get you in before only because the Red Cross requested a cameraman to document their investigation, and my story on Jamil gave me Qaderi's ear. But journalists are not otherwise permitted access to Pul-e-Charki. Not unless they have much greater authority than I and a story that will make prison officials look good. The foreign media have already been clamoring to speak to Jamil, and Qaderi has refused."

"I understand." Amy struggled to hold back her disappointment. "Then I'm sorry to have taken your time for nothing."

"No, no, I wished to explain in person, so you would understand I am not still angry. And to assure you Jamil is my friend. If there was any way I could help him, please believe I would do so without considering my own risk."

Kareem broke off suddenly, then after a meditative pause, went on more slowly. "Perhaps there is a way. There is one person they cannot prohibit from visiting Jamil. But that would require identification papers and much money for government offices."

"Whatever it is, I'll do it."

By the time Kareem explained, a beeping warned Amy another caller was on her line. Seeing Steve's ID, she said hastily, "Let me make the arrangements, and I'll get back to you," then switched to the incoming call.

"Hi, Amy, just calling to let you know we're in. Pul-e-Charki, that is."

"You got into Pul-e-Charki already?" Amy responded incredulously. "Did you see Jamil?"

"Not yet, but I'm beginning to think we can do this." Though Steve's tone was cool and matter-of-fact, Amy could almost hear a grin of elation as he outlined his recent activities. "Except that I'll need Jamil's cooperation to get him out, and making face-to-face contact isn't proving so easy."

"I think I've got an answer to that. If I can come up with ID documents."

Amy had braced herself for Steve to balk at Kareem's continued involvement. But as she explained, he only responded mildly, "And if I object? If I decide this proposal is too big a risk?"

Amy's own response was immediate and sharp. "That's not your decision. Steve, I'm grateful for all you're doing. But please don't insult me by suggesting that because I'm not Special Forces or I'm a woman or whatever, that I shouldn't do my part or risk my own safety for Jamil. Especially since it's hardly the level of risk you'll be taking. I mean, if I do get caught, what are they likely to do except kick me out? You've said Ismail already knows I was up there and did nothing. As for Kareem, if you're worried I'll spill anything about your plans in all this or why I want back in, I'm not stupid!"

"Hey, hey, cool down a notch! You're right; I apologize for even suggesting you stay behind the front lines." Amy could hear the grin again in Steve's voice. "I'll admit if I could keep you out of this, I would. But I should know you better than that by now. So if you're going to insist on doing this anyway, then I think you've filled in my last puzzle piece for this mission. As to the ID documents, I can handle that."

"I appreciate that. And of course, any way I can be of assistance to your plans, you've only to ask," Amy conceded graciously. "Speaking of which, what other puzzle pieces are you referring to? How exactly do you plan to get Jamil out?"

"Sorry, but those details will be on a need-to-know basis." Steve's terse response left no latitude for negotiation. "Nothing personal, it's just the fewer who know the plan—"

"—the fewer to screw it up," Amy finished resignedly. "I get it. My brother the Marine was always quoting that need-to-know stuff."

"I'll call as soon as I have something for you. Just be aware that if you don't hear from me much these next days, I'll be on the job. And as soon as it's feasible, I *will* get Jamil out."

"I know you will."

Amy's words held conviction, but she'd been less successful at keeping renewed distress from her tone because Steve demanded sharply, "What is it, Amy? Is there something you still haven't told me? Because if you've some indication Jamil is facing imminent threat, that changes the equation of how fast I need to move."

"No, no, there's nothing you don't know. And I certainly wouldn't want you to risk yourself or Jamil by rushing in without careful planning. It's just—all this is going to take so long! And I know what terrible things happened to Jamil before in prison. I'm so horribly afraid they're hurting him again." Amy's voice shook slightly before she steadied it. "Especially because I know how afraid *he* was of it! I can't bear to think of him in there alone, maybe wondering if anyone's even out here doing something to help him."

Steve was silent a moment. "Tell me, Amy, do you think Jamil did the right thing when he declared himself publicly as a follower of Isa Masih, Jesus Christ?"

"Yes, of course I do."

"Then don't you think the Son of God to whom Jamil swore allegiance on international news is capable of protecting him even in Pul-e-Charki? that God's love can reach him there where yours can't?"

The private security contractor's quiet rejoinder held such conviction that Amy blinked in surprise. It was, in fact, such a statement of faith as she'd have expected from her own mouth, not his. Had Steve, like Jamil, undergone some profound change of heart since their past arguments when he'd always seemed to scoff at Amy's beliefs? Or did Amy simply know the contractor even less well than she'd thought?

"You're right; Jamil isn't really alone," Amy said slowly. "Thank you for reminding me. I was always telling my New Hope kids their Creator is with them wherever they go. I believe it fully for myself. And yet I've been allowing myself to forget that for Jamil."

"Then you'll be okay there?" There was only the slightest note of impatience in his query. "I hate to cut this short, but my Pul-e-Charki contract arrives in the morning, and I've still got arrangements to make."

No, I'm not okay! These last forty-eight hours had been horrible ones, and now that Amy had shut herself inside, Becky's small apartment seemed echoingly empty and silent. Suddenly, desperately, Amy wanted nothing more than to prolong the comfort of that quiet, confident drawl on the line. Was it spineless to cling so to another human voice to keep her worries and uncertainty at bay?

Aloud, she answered composedly, "Of course I'll be okay. And I'm not really alone, remember?"

"Good girl!" The warm approval in his praise was as heartening as any hug.

Then silence settled again over the apartment.

31

Did he trust this Kareem?

Steve considered the matter as he stepped cautiously into a narrow alley. Trust wasn't something that came easily to Steve, but the man's actions to date seemed to corroborate basic good intentions. Amy's young journalist friend sounded, in fact, like just the kind of new generation this country needed if Afghanistan was ever to crawl off the top-ten-places-you'd-never-want-to-be-born list.

Amy Mallory, Steve did trust. But there were unintentional slips, accidental disclosures. Bottom line, the aid worker was a rotten liar, every worry and care and indignation that crossed her thoughts broadcasting itself from heart-shaped features, flashing from hazel eyes. An attractive attribute to any man tired of hard-boiled, devious females, but an undercover operative Amy would not make. If she ever faced an interrogator, however unlikely that eventuality, Steve intended to ensure Amy could state truthfully she'd no idea what Steve had in mind.

This was as simple as it was audacious. No helo. No assault team. No heroics. Steve and Jamil were just going to walk out Pul-e-Charki's front door. With three thousand inmates, the personnel employed at the prison easily topped several hundred. The guards could not all know each other. As Steve had tested, the entry checkpoint did a reasonable job of checking bags and packages as well as bodies. No bomb would be smuggled into Pul-e-Charki.

But a pair of guards leaving the prison among dozens of others at the end of a long night's shift? If all went well, there'd be no reason to ever associate Jamil's disappearance with a foreign contractor's brief stint at Pul-e-Charki. Qaderi's campaign showpiece would have seemingly vanished into thin air, in itself common enough at Pul-e-Charki to rouse fury, irritation, but hardly a surprised eyebrow.

Ensuring all went well was what brought Steve to the back alley of a neighborhood insalubrious even by Kabul standards. Piles of decaying vegetable peels, a slick of cooking oil too rancid for reuse might have been designed to discourage trespassers. The alley dead-ended in a heavy wooden door, where a fluorescent lantern hanging overhead illuminated two men in shabby local dress, turban ends drawn across their faces giving the impression of masked bandits. The guns they raised as Steve approached were fully automatic Uzis. A certain South African mercenary had steered Steve to the right place.

Spreading his palms in the time-old gesture of meek compliance, Steve stood still for a quick pat-down. He'd returned to the CS team house long enough to change into Afghan dress, and the lack of body armor under his tunic or automatic weapon over his shoulder made him feel uncomfortably naked. But unlike Ms. Amy Mallory, Steve was amply experienced in hiding what he thought and felt and planned behind his current bland expression. Neither sentry evidenced suspicion Steve was anything but what he appeared: a well-fed, well-muscled warrior type, of northern Afghan ethnicity by the gray eyes, representing a master who could be a local warlord, politician, government official, or just a rich merchant shopping for home security.

The sentry patting Steve down withdrew a Glock 21 from a pocket. Steve offered no apology. To come completely unarmed would have been more suspicious than a hidden pistol. Removing the ammo clip, the sentry handed the gun back, then tapped on the door. As it opened, Steve stepped through into a dirt courtyard where more fluorescent lanterns revealed a ring of canopied stalls.

Pakistan possessed the planet's finest black-market arms bazaar, where rocket-propelled grenade launchers could be purchased as easily as an Uzi or hunting rifle. But with Afghanistan currently awash in weaponry,

Kabul's own black market was offering Islamabad some stiff competition. Steve strolled the stalls with the cynical disinterest of an experienced bargainer. Israeli Uzis. Chinese and Czech AK-47s. Enough American M4s and M16s to take out a small city. Not to mention body armor and other combat gear. Some of it perhaps legitimately stolen, but far more, Steve was well aware, sold off by the very Afghan police and army recruits Steve's country paid to train and equip.

Then they come back claiming the stuff was stolen and ask for more! That's the problem here. For every Kareem, there's a dozen creeps like these!

Said "creeps" encompassed the vendors behind laid-out samples, hawkeyed, hard-faced men who looked amply proficient in the use of their merchandise. Steve didn't linger over the weapons. If his plan succeeded, there would not be a shot fired. If it didn't, none of this would do him much good.

Beyond the weapons were uniforms. Police. Afghan National Army. Private security companies. Steve gritted his teeth over a selection of USA and NATO camouflage fatigues. But he didn't let his distaste show as he dickered over two gray-blue police uniforms. The vendor showed zero interest in what his client planned to do with a uniform to which he'd no right. How many bombings or just plain criminal actions had this man's shady business transactions facilitated? Steve's final stop was an actual shopfront at the rear of the courtyard.

"Best document counterfeiter in town," the South African mercenary had bragged. "Arms permits. Customs. IDs. If you're in too big a hurry for city hall, or just don't want to mess with their shenanigans, he can do it for you."

The shop was a mere hole in a mud-brick wall, metal shutter rolled up, its customer counter a rickety wooden table. But electric lights came from a small generator, and a state-of-the-art copier, laminator, and other equipment would have rivaled Kinko's.

"I need identification cards for a woman and three men. These names, ages, addresses." Steve handed a scribbled paper to the short, plump clerk bent over a selection of ID cards, badges, and government documents. Examining Steve's neat Dari script, the clerk quoted a price. This was higher than Steve had expected, but he nodded.

"And I need this duplicated for two of the men." Steve laid his iPhone on the table. Its screen showed a close-up of a Pul-e-Charki guard's security badge. A tap advanced the image to one of the back side. He'd downloaded both images from footage his pen camera had captured while a guard exiting in front of him was showing his ID at the gate checkpoint. "Can you do it?"

"But of course. Though the price is high for such a task." To Steve's disbelief, Mr. Kinko immediately shuffled through his wares to push forward a facsimile of the badge on the screen. The price he quoted was many times that of the ID cards. "Such an item must be marketed discreetly and sparingly, lest its use be detected and so lose all value."

Steve picked up the laminated card. If this wasn't a legitimate Pul-e-Charki badge, he sure couldn't tell the difference. Settling with Mr. Kinko would clean out Steve's supply of afghanis. Still, maybe he should be thankful the price for circumventing Afghanistan's meager security safeguards was so high. It was ironic that the greed of Mr. Kinko and his fellow vendors might just be the best protection available to Kabul's more law-abiding citizens.

Mr. Kinko was now pushing forward a box filled with ID photos. Mostly male. Some female. All ages. Dark-haired, olive-skinned Pashtuns. Light-skinned, Slavic-featured Tajiks and Uzbeks. Black, green, gray, brown, even occasionally blue eyes.

Steve quickly selected three male photos. Thankfully in Afghanistan as elsewhere, no one ever looked exactly like their ID photo. Choosing a female photo was both easier and harder. Afghan women did not typically possess IDs nor even birth certificates. As appendages and possessions of their male relatives, they were rarely outside the home enough to necessitate documenting their existence. But city-dwelling females who dealt with any government bureaucracy, especially those of a class to attend higher education or hold any official position, were now required to show proper documentation. And despite social mores, that required photo ID. Headscarves made female faces agreeably difficult to tell apart. But none of the likely candidates Steve chose from the box displayed a hairline of flaxen gold.

Steve made a choice. *Sorry, Amy, but you're about to get a color job.*

Jamil didn't need dawn's pale rays to confirm his patient was unmistakably worse, breath rattling loudly in his chest, fever even higher than the night before. When breakfast rations of tea and naan were handed out, Jamil managed to coax hot liquid and more ibuprofen into the sick man, then helped him to the cell's malodorous hygiene facilities, a squat toilet around which a blanket hung as screen.

As the hours passed, the fever tablets no longer stemmed a tossing delirium. Which at least kept the other prisoners at bay, though sporadically Jamil heard last night's troublemaker, revealed by daylight to be a heavyset Pashtun with overgrown beard and broken front teeth, muttering the epithets "apostate" and "infidel."

The prison doctor arrived midmorning the third day. Younger than Jamil, undoubtedly an intern assigned to this unpleasant duty, he did not enter the cell but brusquely ordered Jamil to prop the sick man up for examination.

"The fever comes and goes with medication," Jamil volunteered. "But the breathing has grown much worse. If it is not influenza, I fear it is pneumonia."

The doctor turned a sharp glance directly on Jamil. "You have studied medicine?"

"Yes, though I never finished my studies."

"Then you may remain to tend this man. As for the others—" The doctor snapped his fingers impatiently for the guards. "We cannot afford more sickness. You will remove these men to another cell."

Jamil's cellmates showed no reluctance to gather up their possessions. Guards were already redistributing inmates as the doctor issued instructions. "Whether influenza or pneumonia is impossible to tell without testing. Antibiotics might help, but I have none available. I will leave more ibuprofen and give orders to bring water and bleach so that you may scrub this cell to destroy infection."

The obvious health dangers to Jamil himself were not mentioned. Jamil didn't care. To be alone, albeit with an unconscious companion, was worth any risk of contagion. Once the doctor had moved on, the guards brought buckets of water, bleach, and a broom. Jamil had no means to clean the sick man's soiled bedding and clothing. But by the time he'd scrubbed down cell and patient, rummaging in the man's own abandoned bundle for a change of shalwar kameez, the guards appeared with two tushaks and a pair of blankets, well-used, but reasonably clean. They would not touch the contaminated material but were happy to escort Jamil to carry it outdoors to an incinerator.

That their sudden cooperation signaled less compassion than fear of contagion, Jamil was certain. But so long as it produced results, he couldn't care less about their motives. Ibuprofen and the cold bath had brought down the sick man's fever, and his breathing was now ragged but steady. It was with a certain tired satisfaction that Jamil settled himself on his own tushak and pulled Ameera's holy book from his bundle.

He'd now worked his way through its pages to a section called Daniel. Jamil had once translated for Ameera the story of angels rescuing the captive refugee from a lions' den. But the next pages held a story Ameera had not told. Daniel's three friends, Shadrach, Meshach, and Abednego, had refused to bow to a huge idol of gold, even at threat of death. But it was their challenge, thrown defiantly at their powerful captor Nebuchadnezzar, king of the mighty Babylonian empire, that gripped Jamil.

"If we are thrown into the blazing furnace, the God we serve is able to save us from it, and he will rescue us from your hand, O king. But even if he does not, we want you to know, O king, that we will not serve your gods or worship the image of gold you have set up."

It was as though the story was a message sent directly to Jamil. *Yes, Almighty Creator, heavenly Father, you are able to save me. Have you not shown your power? I am clean. I am safe. I am fed. And you will rescue me from this prison, I have no more doubt. Ameera is working to secure my release. She will succeed. Or you will provide some other escape.*

And then?

I want to live as much as I wanted to die.

I want to love as much as I wanted to hate.

To show your love, Isa Masih, to those still blinded with hate and despair who do not know your hand is outstretched to them.

And to love also a wife and children as other men. There are places where I can live free and still tell my people of Isa's love. Like those Isa followers on Omed's radio. Perhaps as Ameera once said, I can at last finish my medical training.

And Ameera? Now that she'd returned to his life and world, could it be his love for her was no longer such an impossible dream?

But as his silent queries became a pleasant reverie, Jamil found himself tracing again the words he'd read. *"The God we serve is able to save us . . . But even if he does not, we want you to know, O king, that we will not serve your gods."*

A chill shook Jamil despite the warm blanket wrapping him tight. Daniel's three friends had not walked into a fiery furnace with certainty that they would be rescued. The Almighty was powerful, but he was also sovereign, not a servant to do a man's bidding. And clearly his choice was not always to rescue, for Isa Masih himself had died a martyr's death. And though an angel had rescued Isa's disciple Peter from prison, another disciple Stephen had been first to be martyred for proclaiming Isa as Son of God.

Jamil slapped the holy book shut. Why did the Almighty sometimes rescue so spectacularly, while at other times he refrained from intervening even when his followers were laying down their lives for his sake? Jamil himself had renounced martyrdom, either to destroy his enemies or to gain paradise. But was there something about martyrdom—Isa's own martyrdom, the willing martyrdom of so many of Isa's followers—that Jamil still was missing? Why should the Creator of All, who stopped lions' mouths and quenched fiery furnaces, ever choose to permit the martyrdom of his followers?

And would Jamil ever have such courage as those three men, torn like himself by war and evil men from family and home, to walk unflinching into a furnace far hotter than that incinerator where he'd burned his patient's soiled clothing, as willing to die as to live to affirm their devotion to the Almighty?

Jamil was relieved when a hoarse whisper interrupted his reading. "Are you a doctor?"

For the first time since Jamil's arrival, his patient seemed aware of his surroundings, the sunken eyes clear and intelligent. Turning his head, the sick man took in the emptied and cleaned cell. "Is this a hospital?"

Jamil hurried over to the other tushak. "No, this is not a hospital. And I am not a doctor, only a prisoner like yourself."

"Then I am still in Pul-e-Charki. I was dreaming—a beautiful dream. I thought I saw my wife, my children." The sick man's breathing was more labored now that he was conscious, and despite the man's responsiveness, Jamil was under no illusion this signaled improvement. He'd encountered before the preternatural alertness that so often heralded an impending end to human suffering.

"Has it been long since you've seen your family?" he asked quietly.

"Five years." The man managed to spit out a weak curse. "Since my brother-in-law accused me of stealing his sheep and had me thrown in here, though it left his own sister and my five children without a man to care for them."

The eyes blinked at Jamil. "I remember your voice. You gave me water in the night. Am I going to die?"

"Only the Almighty knows the number of a man's days," Jamil deflected gently.

The man turned his head away, but tears were leaking down the side of his face. "If they have taken away the other prisoners, they must believe I am going to die. And I am afraid. Afraid to face the judgment of Allah."

Sunken eyes found their way again to Jamil's face. "I know it is true I am dying, so I will tell you. I did steal those sheep. There was no work, and my children and wife grew thinner every day. My brother-in-law had food in plenty, but he would not help us. So I took two sheep and sold them for food. I am a thief. And now I must face Allah, and though I have prayed and fasted and begged Allah for forgiveness these last five years, I am afraid it is not enough. I will not wake up in paradise, but in the burning fires of hell."

Jamil's patient was becoming agitated, flushed cheeks and wild brightness of eye signaling his fever was again rising. Pouring water, Jamil coaxed another dose of ibuprofen into the man. "Shh, do not strain yourself. What is your name?"

"Yousef." The man's hoarse words were but a thread now, but when a wasted hand clutched Jamil's wrist, its grip was surprisingly strong. "Yousef, son of Rafi, from the town of Bulkhak not far from here. If . . . if you survive this place, will you find my family and tell them I died thinking of them?"

"I will do my best," Jamil promised, carefully freeing his wrist from the man's grip. "And I will not lie. You are very ill. You need a hospital and proper medical care."

Another weak curse gave Yousef's opinion of that likelihood.

"But you must not despair. It is true you can do nothing to earn forgiveness for your sins. But let me tell you of another thief who found his way to paradise, though he was dying for his crimes, hanging on a cross with a fellow criminal. Even as he hung there, he met the only one who can take away the burden of a man's sins. The one who has forgiven my sins, though they are worse than anything you have done."

The sick man was silent for a moment, his thin chest rising and falling rapidly under the blanket. Then he got out, "I know who you are now. You are the apostate healer who was brought here last week. All of Pul-e-Charki has been speaking of you."

"I am no apostate, only a follower of Isa Masih, the great healer who martyred himself upon a cross so that a thief might find paradise. Will you hear his story?"

The guards were bringing the evening meal now. Jamil lifted the man's head so he could swallow tea and rice gruel before settling himself cross-legged beside the tushak. "This story cannot be told without speaking first of how man was driven from paradise. At time's beginning, the Almighty created a beautiful garden, and in it he placed the first man and woman. He gave them only one command. But there was a serpent . . ."

After a time, Yousef's eyes closed, his breathing shallow again as though asleep or lapsed back into a coma. But when Jamil broke off his narration, the sick man's eyes opened abruptly. "No, please go on."

"But the Almighty so loved these human beings he'd created that he sent his only Son, Isa Masih, God born into human flesh, to walk among us and lead us back to God." Jamil's own voice grew hoarse as the hours passed. The night was now well-advanced, disturbed only by snores and the occasional cry of nightmares or abuse from other cells. And still Yousef's hot fingers grasping Jamil's wrist urged him to continue.

"So you see, if Isa could forgive that thief on the cross and promise him a place in his kingdom, his hands are open to you as well. Those who place their faith in Isa Masih will join him in paradise."

"Paradise." The thread of a whisper was the last word Yousef uttered. Jamil waited until the sick man's grip fell away from his wrist before retreating to his own tushak. Falling into an uneasy doze, he didn't know at what hour Yousef gave up breathing. When dawn entered the cell to prod Jamil awake, the bundled shape on the other tushak was silent and still, but the gaunt features bore a smile. Now Jamil's face was wet with tears as he clanged on the bars for a guard. *Let Yousef have found peace with you, Isa!*

The guards cleared out the dead body with a speedy dispatch that spoke of regular practice. When Jamil's prior cellmates were herded back inside, a savage grin from the first night's troublemaker made plain his gratification at encountering Jamil without his human shield. Dropping his bundle and tushak, he strode across the cell. "You, apostate, you are now mine!"

Bile churned in Jamil's stomach as an unkempt beard and broken teeth thrust themselves close to his face. *Isa, give me courage. Do not let me betray you with fear and hate.*

Words rose unbidden to Jamil's lips. "If you become ill with what killed Yousef, who of these men do you think would care for you?"

The heavyset Pashtun drew back fractionally. From across the cell, another inmate called, "He is right. The man is a healer, and how many are there in this hell? Leave him in peace. You do not know when any of us might have need of him."

With a grunt, the man retreated. Jamil sank down on his own tushak to hide a slight tremble in his limbs. Why had he not thought to attempt such negotiation when he'd been in prison before? Had he not possessed the same medical training then as now?

Because then you were a victim, filled with hate and rage and fear. Now you are truly a healer, filled with the love of Isa, Healer of Healers.

"Jamil Yusof ul Haq Shahrani?" A guard appeared at the cell bars. "You have been granted a visitor."

Jamil sprang to his feet. "My sister?"

But the guard was shaking his head. "Not your sister. Your lawyer."

32

"There are so many people! Where are they all coming from?"

A line stretched from the squat twin towers of Pul-e-Charki's entrance all the way to visitor parking, where a city bus was dumping dozens more people. Only now was Amy realizing how privileged she'd been on earlier visits to be whisked through security in a Red Cross vehicle.

"It is a rest day when family members are permitted to bring food and supplies to the prisoners. And in your case, legal counsel."

Amy didn't need Kareem's tactful reminder of the roles they were currently playing. She tucked a strand of hair more tightly under her chador. This was no longer shining gold but the dark brown of her ID photo. Her escort wore a cheap Western suit and carried a briefcase. Black-framed glasses he didn't need added five years to youthful, round features.

Amy's lawyer.

"If few prisoners have a lawyer, this is a matter of money," Kareem had explained when he'd outlined his alternative for getting into Pul-e-Charki. "I have a friend whose cousin was in Pul-e-Charki for some months before the family was able to negotiate his freedom. It is not enough to hire a lawyer. One must pay certain fees for permission to meet with the prisoner, others for speedy processing. If the fee paid is high enough . . ."

The hunch of Kareem's shoulders needed no explanation. "My friend's cousin was in for only a minor offense. A matter of transporting opium. So purchasing his release was not too costly. For Jamil that will not be possible. But for his sister who identified him to contract a lawyer will be expected. If you can display the necessary documents, the rest is only a matter of money."

Not even such a large sum of money by standards of any Western economy. When Steve had dropped by the morning after his Pul-e-Charki reconnaissance to deliver identification documents along with a packet of hair coloring, he'd ignored Amy's attempt to reimburse him. But she'd been more successful in covering subsequent bribes, as Kareem's "fees" were in fact, if only because Amy was the one who'd accompanied Kareem from one Ministry of Justice office to another. While neither Kareem's fake legal credentials nor Amy's photo ID raised any eyebrows, it had still taken three full days to fast-track the necessary permits for Kareem to visit his client.

Which was going to take all day in this line. If their expressions ranged from sullen despair to anger, the waiting visitors were standing stoically and silently. So they couldn't be responsible for an angry rumble that grew as Amy plodded at Kareem's heels toward the gate. Then, as the maze of parked cars no longer blocked her view, Amy saw the crowd milling outside high stone walls. Amid a furious babble, Amy could pick out shouted slogans.

"Justice for Pul-e-Charki."

"Trial or release."

Along the perimeter wall and tower parapets, guards shifted nervously, automatic weapons clutched tightly in their hands. But they made no move to interfere, perhaps because of several vans pulled up among the protesters. Near each was a cluster of caterpillar microphones and cameras. News crews.

Amy held her face veil slightly away from her mouth to whisper anxiously, "What's going on? This can't be about Jamil, can it?"

"Not just about Jamil, but politics." Behind black-rimmed glasses, Kareem's round features showed unease. "At the TV station where I work, I have heard candidates speaking angrily against such a speedy trial for the apostate when so many prisoners have waited for years. They claim Qaderi is perverting Afghan justice for his own election campaign. It is not surprising the prisoners' families have gathered to protest, but such a response as this with so many news crews reveals the hand of Qaderi's opposition. And not only the opposition. Look there!"

As the city bus pulled away, a new van drew into its place. But this was no news crew. A side panel boasted a blown-up photo of Qaderi. Amy found the multiple bullhorns of a loudspeaker system hard to follow, but Kareem was murmuring a synopsis in her ear.

"It is Qaderi's campaign. They are telling the protesters that the minister has heard their demands. If he is elected president, all prisoners held more than one year without charges will be tried immediately or released. Of course a good journalist will ask why Qaderi did not do this before, since he has been minister of justice for many years. Or those men will!"

The sudden worried note in Kareem's tone swung Amy around to follow his line of sight. Two pickups had pulled up behind the campaign van, their beds jam-packed with passengers, all male. Jumping down, they raised placards stamped with the same enlarged photo as the van's side panel. Only here Qaderi's features were ringed by a red circle with a diagonal line running through it. The universal symbol of repudiation.

Heading toward the crowd, the pickup passengers raised their own chant. "A vote for Qaderi is a vote against justice."

"There is going to be trouble." Kareem lengthened his stride toward the prison entrance, waving frantically for Amy to keep up. "We must hurry to leave this place."

"But—the line!"

"We will not have to wait in that line. I have paid for a fixer." The Afghan journalist indicated a cheap suit similar to Kareem's own now hurrying forward from the checkpoint. The "fixer," that reprieve for anyone with funds to bypass an inefficient and corrupt bureaucracy. As always, Amy felt guilty following the fixer past earlier arrivals, but not enough to refuse the privilege. *Jamil's what's important now, not an unfairness I can't fix anyway.*

But with the protest gaining force outside Pul-e-Charki walls, this was hardly a prudent moment to remind those waiting that a speedier justice was already available to anyone with funds. Behind Amy, a grumbling voice rose, then another. Those farther back in line began jostling forward so that those in front were pressed against the checkpoint barrier. A burqa cried out in pain. A hand came down on Amy's shoulder. Others were plucking at her chador. Guards spread out behind the barrier, weapons raised. *We're going to be ripped apart or shot!*

Then the sharp crack of a single shot exploded so close, Amy could smell the acridity of gunpowder. The jostling queue froze, and even the protesters stilled their chants momentarily.

A guard lowered the weapon he'd fired in the air. "Get back, offspring of camels, or no one will be visiting your criminal relatives today."

The fixer had now led Amy and Kareem through the barrier. Even for the privileged, there was a security check, and today with its mixed crowd, two female guards motioned Amy behind a screen. Now Amy could appreciate Steve's insistence on coloring her hair because she was made to remove the chador. While one female guard ran her hands over Amy, the other examined her ID photo.

Satisfied, they rummaged through Amy's shoulder bag. This was not her usual foreign-made knapsack but a locally woven carrying bag from which rose the fragrance of fresh-baked naan. The bag contained as well a small thermos, Styrofoam cups, and a selection of packaged cookies, hard candies, and other goodies.

Steve's additional instructions were the reason Amy's hands had gone clammy and damp as the two female guards dug deeper into the bag. Surreptitiously she fingered a speed-dial number on her cell phone, then cut it off immediately so that it would register as a missed call.

A guard was now returning Amy's bag, minus a slab of naan. Tearing this, she handed half to her partner as she warned, "Do not attempt to leave your cell phone in the prison. The guards check carefully for such things. Your relative will be in great trouble if they discover it on him."

A warning Amy appreciated since the thought had crossed her mind. Forewarned, she silently handed each woman a small box of tea and package of gum before rejoining Kareem. Even during the short interval of the security check, pandemonium had spread through the crowd, a garble of competing chants drowning out Qaderi's campaign loudspeaker.

Nor did the turmoil lessen once their fixer led Amy and Kareem through the main gate and across the perimeter track. The prisoners within that concrete fortress rising above the interior wall could not possibly see what was happening outside Pul-e-Charki. But they could surely hear the roar of an angry mob, and they were joining in, shouting and banging enamel plates or other objects against their bars until it seemed the entire prison must be in uproar.

Leading the way through an interior gate, the fixer deposited Kareem and Amy inside a large, crowded reception hall before hurrying away. Here standing in line couldn't be avoided, but Kareem was soon opening his briefcase to hand papers across a desk. Would the clerk in police uniform even now reject their hard-purchased documents? or worse, take one good look at their personal IDs and call for a guard?

But to Amy's relief, the clerk barely glanced through the papers. "Ah, yes, the roster indicates this prisoner's lawyer and a female family member are scheduled for this hour. Though the woman's first name is different on the list. A mistake, undoubtedly, since the Ministry of Justice papers match your ID and not my list."

Stamping a form, he handed it to Kareem. "You are scheduled for a private interview chamber. Proceed down the hall to number twelve."

As Amy followed Kareem into the specified corridor, a relieved sigh left the Afghan journalist. "A private chamber! I did not even request such a privilege. In fact, to this very moment, I feared Qaderi had perhaps issued special orders prohibiting Jamil from seeing a lawyer, and that his clerks were simply pocketing our fees. It must be true what they told me. Despite the controversial nature of this case, Qaderi has refused to interfere in the normal judicial process."

Amy looked at Kareem sharply. "You sound almost as though you approve of him."

Kareem hunched his shoulders under the unaccustomed constraint of his suit. "Qaderi is known to be incorruptible, unlike so many ministers and government officials. He will not contravene his own laws. That is a quality we need more of in our country."

"He's also sending Jamil to execution because he chooses to worship God differently, remember?"

"That too," Kareem admitted soberly. "Which is why I am here helping you today. But if we could only have integrity and freedom both, what a country this would be."

"That could be said of any country," Amy answered with equal sobriety.

Though they'd been speaking in Dari and hardly above a whisper, the closest guard was staring at them. At Amy's warning glance in that direction, Kareem straightened, hefted his briefcase, and said more loudly, "Come! My client is waiting, and my time is valuable."

Farther down the hall, guards stood outside doorways on either side. The doors themselves had been removed. Through each open rectangle Amy could see scattered tables where manacled prisoners faced family members and legal counsel. Only the room marked with a number twelve held just one table.

The guard looked over the stamped form, glanced into Amy's bag, then moved aside to wave Kareem and Amy through the doorway. His shift offered Amy her first clear view of a prisoner who sat with bound wrists resting on the table, a chain around his waist anchoring him to his seat.

Jamil.

33

"Ameera." Though Jamil spoke quietly, joyous flames blazed in his dark eyes. "When they said my lawyer had come, I could not think of whom they spoke. But I knew you would come in due time. And you, Kareem, I was not wrong to have faith in you, my friend."

Though the Afghan journalist beamed gratification, he shook his head warningly. "Today I am Kamaal, the lawyer your sister is so generously paying to work for your release."

Amy was already setting out the tea fixings she'd brought, piling naan on a cloth, unscrewing the top of the thermos. The packaged goodies would go back with Jamil to his cell. As she poured out hot, sweet tea, Kareem carried a Styrofoam cup and slab of naan to the guard who watched inquisitively from the doorway. Sliding into one of the chairs supplied opposite the prisoner, Amy leaned forward under the guise of pushing a cup of tea within reach of his manacled hands to whisper urgently, "Jamil, I've been so worried! Are you well? Have they treated you as—as badly as you feared? I've been praying that Isa would protect you."

"I am well," Jamil answered simply. "The others were angry at first to have an apostate among them. But now that it is known I am a healer, they leave me in peace."

There was far more to that matter-of-fact narration, Amy had no doubt. A "more" that had to do with Jamil's bearing of serene victory, where not so long ago she'd witnessed fear and despair. Kareem had now returned. As he took a seat, Jamil turned his head to look directly at him.

"Isa has protected me as I never dreamed possible. If I ever doubted he is all the holy book claims, I would do so no longer."

The journalist shifted uncomfortably, and Jamil didn't wait for a response. "But though my heart is glad to see you both, you have not come to hear my tale. Nor, I fear, to bear good news that Minister Qaderi has undergone a change of heart and wishes to set me free. So whatever news you bring, whether good or ill, tell me quickly that you may be on your way back to safety."

"A trial date has been set for one week from today. But you must not despair." Kareem glanced toward Amy. "You have friends who have not forgotten you."

The unabated prisoner uproar outside the walls was enough to cloak their low-voiced Dari, nor had anything been said that couldn't have been known elsewhere. But now Amy needed to communicate Steve's instructions. Her surreptitious speed dial rang Kareem's phone. As arranged, the Afghan journalist pushed to his feet to stride around as he exclaimed loudly, "No, it cannot wait until tomorrow. The client is a powerful and wealthy family. You will complete the documents today."

As Kareem continued haranguing his sham associate, Amy switched to swift, low English. "Qaderi is determined to make a public show of your trial for his presidential campaign. And it doesn't look like there's much hope our embassy or any Western governments will put pressure on your government to honor international accords on religious freedom. But we've got a plan to get you out of here before the trial. Do you remember Steve Wilson? the American contractor who put in the security at New Hope?"

"The foreign warrior who protects Khalid, the man who butchered my family? who wished himself to throw me into Pul-e-Charki and let me go only at Khalid's orders? Yes, I remember him well. But what could this Steve Wilson have to do with helping me? It cannot be on behalf of his government, since you have already said they will not interfere. Nor would Khalid, who is his employer, raise a finger on my behalf."

"Steve isn't working for Khalid anymore; he's working for me!" Amy had been concerned that her former assistant might be angry when he found out his one-time adversary was involved in his rescue, but Jamil seemed more stunned than angry. "I mean, well, actually, he's working right here in Pul-e-Charki. But he's working *with* me. Which is what I need to explain to you."

"Ah, now I understand," Jamil interjected even more flatly. "I had forgotten he is a mercenary and will do whatever task for which he is hired. But you should not have spent your money so. Not on my behalf. Nor can a hireling be trusted. How do you know he is not even now whispering into Qaderi's ear?"

"I'm *not* paying Steve to help you. He's not taking any money at all for this; just the opposite!" Amy was beginning to feel panicked. How did she explain in the fleeting minutes they had all that had changed since Jamil had last seen either Amy or Steve?

"I know what's been between you two in the past." *More than you do, in fact!* "But Steve believes in justice. And he believes it's wrong for you or anyone else to be imprisoned for your faith in God. When he thought you wanted to kill Khalid, he did feel you belonged here in Pul-e-Charki. And even after that day, I don't think he believed you'd really changed. Not until he saw you refuse to renounce Isa to walk free from that courtroom. Like I said, Steve believes in justice. Enough that he's willing to do whatever's necessary to free you from here."

Jamil still looked stunned. "Then this American warrior, he too is a follower of Isa?"

Amy no longer had any hesitation in answering that. "Yes, he is. But what matters is that he is a friend to you as well as me. A friend we both need. Right now there are people all over the world who are angry that you are in prison only for being a follower of Isa Masih. There are people praying for you. Even people I'm sure would risk their own lives to break you out of this prison if they could. But none of them are here. And Steve is. He's got skills and connections neither Kareem nor I have to help you. And don't you think it's possible Isa Masih himself sent Steve here to help you? Problem is, we don't have time for discussion! So I have to just ask that you trust him. At least enough to do what he asks."

Jamil shook his head slowly. "I don't need to trust him. I trust you. With my life. With my heart. And I do not doubt you are right that Isa Masih sent him. It is like the story in your holy book of the fiery furnace. You know it?"

"Yes, of course, Daniel's three friends."

"I read the story while here in Pul-e-Charki. I knew this was a message from Isa Masih himself that he would rescue me as well. I did not imagine Isa would send a man I once considered my enemy to take part in my rescue. But if Isa could so change my heart, I do not know why I should be so surprised. If you say this Steve Wilson is trustworthy and a friend, that is enough. So now tell me swiftly what it is I must know."

Amy was already lifting the thermos, pouring it over Jamil's cup as though offering him the last of its contents. The last inch of fluid held tea bags, and as they spilled into Jamil's cup, one made the slightest thunk. Amy said softly, urgently, "The tea bag holds a device that will permit Steve to find you anywhere in the prison. You must hide it where it cannot be found. He says you'll understand. When he comes for you, you must be ready to do whatever he asks. I don't know when that will be, but for sure before the trial."

Steve had been right that Jamil would understand. Without changing his expression, Jamil lifted the cup with its spilled tea bags to his mouth and drained it. When he set it down, one tea bag was gone. He wiped a wrist across his mouth, then dropped both hands to his lap. When, a moment later, Jamil lifted his hands again to reach for the last piece of naan, they were empty. "Tell your friend I will be ready."

Amy let out a breath she'd been holding. "Then that's settled. Steve will have papers and funds to get you across the border. I have friends in Peshawar, Isa followers who I know will gladly give you sanctuary."

"And what of you?"

"I'll be leaving Kabul just as soon as I hear you're safe."

"Then you will be joining me?" Fresh joy flared in the dark eyes. "I had dreamed, I had prayed, but I had not dared let myself hope—"

Before Amy could correct his assumption, the crack of a gunshot rang out somewhere above the continued uproar outside. Shouts and a drumbeat of heavy boots erupted into the corridor beyond the interview room. Behind her, Amy heard a low, warning cough as Kareem hurried back to the table.

Jumping to her feet, Amy began restoring dirty cups and thermos to her bag, scooping foodstuffs into a plastic bag she'd brought for the purpose. "I'd hoped we'd have more time, but we'd better go. I'll see you very soon again if Isa wills. Meanwhile I'll be praying night and day for your protection."

Jamil's manacles clinked as he reached across the table. But instead of taking the foodstuffs Amy pushed his way, he suddenly enfolded Amy's fingers between his own two chained hands. He'd never deliberately touched Amy before, and its sheer unexpectedness made the warmth of his fingers on hers a far more intimate gesture than its reality.

"Yes, you should leave quickly. But there is one more thing I must say first. I would not have dared speak when I thought I would die in here. But now that I am confident Isa's power will bring me safely from this place, I can say what is most truly on my heart. I love you, Ameera-jan. You showed me once long ago where the holy book commands men to love their wives as Isa Masih gave himself up for his followers. I did not know then how any man could care for a woman to give his own life for her. But I understand now because such is the love in my heart for you, Ameera-jan. A woman of such beauty and virtue and wisdom I never dreamed this world contained, in whose heart the love of Isa himself overflows."

His declaration should not have taken Amy by surprise, Jamil's feelings for her no secret. But in this place at this time when she'd braced herself for a carefully casual farewell, it did, and Amy found sudden dampness blurring her eyes as she shook her head helplessly against that passionate flow of words.

Oh, Jamil, I don't deserve your opinion of me. You're the one who was willing to give up his life for what he believed. And to give it up again for love of your Savior, for faith in Isa Masih. Who has shown strength and courage and sacrifice, so that even Steve has come to admire and respect you.

But me? I'm just an ordinary girl who loves Jesus, sure, and wants to share that love. But nothing I've ever done has really been a sacrifice. Even coming to Afghanistan wasn't deliberate, just a sort of accident. And look how that's turned out!

The commotion down the corridor was now approaching their own interview chamber. Amy got out shakily, "Jamil, I wish I was that woman you describe, strong and brave and wise. But I'm not! If you only knew how far I fall short, you wouldn't say such kind things. Or even want someone like me in your life. You're not seeing me as I really am."

"Perhaps you do not see yourself as you really are. Or as Isa sees you. As I see you through his love. And now that I am to be free from here, we can share Isa's love and teachings together. I know it will be necessary to go into exile for a time. I may even see your country. But I have seen you love my people as I do. In time surely Isa will open the way to share his love here in Afghanistan again, this time together. At least . . . I had thought . . . Is there a family member, your father perhaps, to whom I should be speaking of these things first? I am not familiar with the ways of your country. Or . . ."

Jamil's rapid speech faltered for the first time. Slowly he released Amy's fingers and drew his manacles back across the table. "Perhaps I am wrong in believing that the love Isa placed in my heart he has given as well to you for me. Do you love me, Ameera-jan?"

Amy's quick brush of fingers across her eyes brought back into focus the slim figure, the thin, bearded features still marred by fading bruises, that confidently pleading dark gaze. Any woman would be privileged to be loved by this man, to spend the rest of her life loving him in return.

It wasn't just that Jamil was attractive, young, intelligent, all that any culture's females looked for in a mate despite his current shackles. It was the integrity he radiated. A strength of character and will forged through suffering. A compassion that emanated from him so that even Amy, who'd been there, had a hard time believing this man could ever hate enough to take another's life. It was as though Jamil had indeed passed through that fiery furnace he'd talked about, emerging as precious metal refined and purified.

As perhaps in some fashion he had.

So why were words hesitating on Amy's lips?

"Jamil, you must know that I do love you, but—"

There was no time to say more. A thud of running boots burst into the room, hands yanking Jamil to his feet, a metal key clanking against padlocked chains. As the knot of uniforms swept the prisoner and his visitors apart, the bellow of a PA system briefly drowned out the pandemonium outside. "Visiting hours are hereby suspended. Prisoners must be returned to their cells. All visitors will leave the prison immediately."

34

The Klaxon blare of a siren added to the bedlam as Steve hurried at a quick trot toward the prison's main entrance. He'd been conscious of Amy's presence within Pul-e-Charki walls since a missed call had alerted Steve the insertion was under way. Unless Amy speed-dialed a panic alert, wisdom dictated staying as far as possible from her and Kareem's masquerade. But Steve hadn't liked the look of that mob when his convoy had driven through it this morning, and from his duty post outside an interrogation chamber door, it had been impossible to ignore the escalating tumult from the inmates themselves. The PA announcement suspending visitor privileges only heightened growing disquiet.

Slipping away proved simple because DEA station chief Ramon Placido had accompanied the guest interrogators to get in on today's interview target, a certain Jabbaar, who just happened to be the same Uzbek opium merchant whose escape at Khalid's arranging had so infuriated Steve. With Placido's own security detail congesting the hallway, Steve's presence was superfluous enough to excuse himself briefly.

Outside the main entrance, the visiting day checkpoint had been closed down, its security personnel retreating through the gates even as ejected visitors poured down the steps. But while the multitude held any number of female shapes, Steve couldn't make out which of them might be Amy. She was either safely away with Kareem, or she wasn't. She'd completed her assignment here, or she hadn't. And dashing through those gates into a seething mob to search for her wasn't going to improve the situation.

Steve had turned reluctantly back when a trio jostling ahead of him upstream against the exiting crowd caught his eye. The brown-bearded prison official and a pale blue burqa were of minimal interest to Steve, but the same could not be said of their companion.

Deputy Minister Ismail.

Steve lagged behind deliberately until the newcomers disappeared through the steel interior gate. By then the gates were slamming shut. A rattle of stones against the bars signaled the fury of visitors who weren't going to see their incarcerated loved ones today. As Steve headed for the interior gate, a cloud of dust barreled down the perimeter track from the administrative sector, where the Afghan National Army had its outpost. Screeching to a halt, it metamorphosed into two troop transports. Someone had called for reinforcements.

Inside the concrete fortress, police and army uniforms were now racing through courtyards and swarming up onto catwalks. Steve ducked from the commotion into the derelict cellblock through which he'd detoured on his first reconnaissance visit. If crumbling walls and collapsed ceilings made the place a safety gamble, at least it was private. He'd threaded most of the corridor when his breast pocket vibrated. A text message this time. *All clear. Package delivered. See you at home.*

Then Amy and Kareem had made it away safely. Relaxing fractionally, Steve called up a screen on his iPhone. A blinking dot was moving across the screen as would be the case if Jamil were headed back to his cell. Not that security couldn't be faking the same movement. But no guard here was likely to recognize the device Steve had slipped into that tea bag. And if Jamil couldn't keep an item smaller than two inches hidden from scrutiny, he'd wasted almost a decade behind bars.

Ismail, on the other hand, would recognize such a device immediately. If it didn't surprise Steve to see Khalid's deputy minister here, it did worry him. He hadn't forgotten Ismail's pledge to make the problem that was Jamil go away. And the deputy minister faced Steve's same deadline of Qaderi's well-publicized upcoming tribunal.

Steve could only hope Ismail's appearance wasn't going to put a kink in his own plans. The tracker's battery was good for a full week. Steve hadn't planned to make a move until the interrogation team left. But thanks to

Jabbaar's current loud cooperation, this had been put off several more days. And Steve hadn't anticipated the scope of protest now agitating outside Pul-e-Charki walls, nor the ferocity of the prisoners' own contribution. Moderate pandemonium was no drawback to his plans. In fact, it might even offer a useful distraction. But a full-scale riot could make it more difficult, not less, for Steve to move freely. Maybe even trigger a facility lockdown.

Which was why Steve had decided to make his move tonight. The presence of Placido's sizable security detail offered a perfect excuse to ditch the return embassy run. His Dyncorp colleagues would not know Steve hadn't in fact left Pul-e-Charki at all. If Steve could move Jamil undetected from his cell and through dawn's shift change, Jamil's ID and police uniform would allow him to hitch a bus or truck ride across the border to Peshawar, only a few hours' travel away, where Amy had assured Steve she'd have no difficulty arranging sanctuary. Leaving Steve to hoof it into Kabul in time for his regular embassy run. If all went well, Jamil would be calling Amy from a safe house in Peshawar before a dumbfounded Pul-e-Charki security ever admitted he'd gone missing.

A thought that roused less anticipation than it merited. Steve stopped abruptly in the middle of fallen rubble. *God, I can't do this! Not the mission. I think I've got that pretty well covered now. But what kind of man am I that I can't even be glad it's all working out? that I can't just be happy for Amy and Jamil?*

A selfish one! This was not about Steve Wilson. Not about his hopes and wishes and dreams. Once long ago Rev Garwood had preached a sermon on offering one's life as a living sacrifice. Something that hadn't particularly resonated because Steve's profession was all about dying sacrifices. Throwing oneself into imminent danger—even knowing it only too possible one might not come home, like Private First Class Devon Archer—was part and parcel of being a soldier, a sacrifice Steve was both accustomed to and willing to make.

But now Steve was catching a glimpse of what Rev had been talking about. To live daily as Amy's mission ally and nothing more. To finish this job, then walk away and start over, alone as he'd always been. To accept—no, rejoice—in Amy's getting a good and decent man out of all this. In Jamil's finding at last a life and love and future. These were harder sacrifices than rushing into a Taliban firefight.

Yet if he could accept the ultimate sacrifice God himself had offered on Steve's behalf, how could Steve balk at such negligible sacrifices requested of him now and still see in the mirror a man of courage or honor?

You offered your life as well as your death for humanity, Isa Masih, Steve prayed silently, using the local pronunciation of Jesus Christ impulsively as he'd heard Jamil do in that courtroom. *For me, Steve Wilson. You stayed on that cross when your call could have summoned ten thousand celestial Special Ops troops. So if I have to spend the remaining decades of my life alone, let me make them count for something. Let me offer the years ahead in that daily living sacrifice Rev spoke of. Meantime, whatever it takes, let me finish this mission—for Amy and Jamil both.*

There was a certain peace in total surrender. Which was well because Steve stepped out of the abandoned corridor into chaos. Army uniforms were setting up barricades in the octagonal courtyard. Rooftops now sported machine-gun nests and snipers. If there'd been pandemonium earlier from the prisoner accommodations, now a unified chanting floated down through barred windows.

"Death to the apostate."

"Death to Qaderi."

"Justice now, not later."

Punctuating each demand was a cry Steve had heard too often on the crest of an attacking wave of enemy combatants. "Allahu Akbar. God is great."

The war cry of Islamic jihad. Somewhere in one of those tricornered courtyards dividing the spokes, gunfire rang out. Worse, it drew an immediate rat-tat-tat response that came from automatic weapons. This was no simple prisoner rebellion or facility lockdown.

Steve had to hammer on the steel door to get a guard to let him back into the high-security wing. Inside, every prisoner was on his feet chanting, the Afghan security personnel nervously fingering their weapons. But Steve reached the interrogation side corridor to find all calm, his Dyncorp colleagues in a huddle.

"Where have you been?" Placido's detail chief demanded. "We're making the call whether we should shut down shop."

"I've been taking a visual of the riot," Steve responded vaguely. "It's a madhouse out there! Anyone know just what's going down?"

"What's going on is the prisoners got wind of Qaderi's promises for immediate trials and prisoner release if he's elected. They know if Qaderi can do it later, he can do it now. They're demanding immediate redress, and to make their point, they've seized several cellblocks and taken some guards hostage. So what's your pleasure, Wilson? Do we shut down for the duration?"

Steve considered only briefly. "I don't see any point. This sector's sealed off from general population. Police and army units have control of the perimeter. With that mob outside, we're actually safer in here. I say ride it out, but let's call up some reinforcement vehicles for this evening's convoy."

Steve settled himself outside the interview room, but not without another surreptitious check of his iPhone. Jamil's tracking signal was still moving freely. Was the cellblock in question under guard or prisoner control? Jamil was a healer. Perhaps those movements signaled he'd been roped in to deal with casualties.

One thing was for sure. Steve wouldn't be completing this mission tonight after all. Not without a miracle.

35

"These journalists are a plague!" Ismail grumbled, shouldering through the throng streaming across the perimeter track. "If such disorder is the fruit of democracy, it will destroy our country. And if you order your guns to disperse this rabble, the media of the world will no doubt call us savages."

The deputy minister had spied the news vans and riot from his own compound when he'd stopped to collect the burqa following silently at his heels. By the time they'd arrived at the prison, a loudspeaker was announcing suspension of visitor privileges. Only an armed police detail had permitted them to push through the tumult to the front towers, where the prison administrator himself joined them to usher Ismail's party through the gates. They were now tardy for the arranged interview between Jamil and his "sister."

"The world has changed since we killed Soviets and Taliban to the cheers of those same news cameras." Ismail's companion shrugged philosophically. Appointed by Khalid himself before Afghanistan's prison system was shifted to Ministry of Justice oversight, the prison administrator was like many such appointees a former mujahedeen comrade. "I can tell you in confidence, my employer is wishing he had not started this."

"And mine is wishing he did not have to support yours in order to prove his faithfulness to Islam," Ismail returned. "It looks like both your employer and mine have the same need—to draw the fangs of this particular serpent. So we find ourselves again allies, though we now serve different masters."

"And if a taste of bullets is no longer permitted in our new Afghanistan, I will not risk the lives of my subordinates any further to that mob." Raising a hand radio to his mouth, the prison administrator barked out, "As soon as our last guest is out, bar the gates and begin firing tear gas until the crowd disperses."

A command decision hardly designed to avoid exacerbating the situation. But Ismail offered no objections. Just ahead now, a steel door was vomiting out the prison's ejected guests, who stepped hastily to either side of his own party like water parting around a boulder.

"Ameera!"

At the faint exclamation, Ismail swung around. The burqa at his heels had turned to stare after the departing visitors. "What did you say? Whom did you see?"

The burqa shrank visibly under his harsh tone. "Nothing, no one! I was only wishing . . . I am afraid to go alone in there without another woman."

"You will do as ordered," Ismail answered brusquely. "Do not think you will now regret your choice. Come!"

But as the burqa scooted forward through the interior gate, Ismail lingered to glance back. While he spotted nothing in that congestion to merit the burqa's notice, there was one tall, powerful frame he recognized, hurrying out a gate farther up the perimeter track. Steve Wilson. He'd been informed that Khalid's former head of security was now protecting the foreign interrogators visiting Pul-e-Charki.

Ismail permitted himself a sour smile as he followed the burqa through the steel door. His informant had not left out that it was the Uzbek opium merchant Jabbaar who so interested the visitors. Ismail himself had delivered this particular bone to the Americans when Jabbaar was foolish enough to break his deal with Khalid by creeping back into Afghanistan. But if the foreigners thought to find any meat on this bone, they'd be disappointed. He was too fond of his own skin and comforts for his more devout business partners to trust him with any information the foreigners would find useful. Still, it kept their infidel allies busy and satisfied with Afghan cooperation in their doings.

Precisely the intent.

Inside, a uniformed clerk did not glance up from a ledger as Ismail's party approached his desk. "All interviews are canceled for today. You will have to reschedule."

A hand slapped down hard on the desk. "Do you know whom you address? You will expedite this party immediately."

The clerk's head shot up. He jumped to his feet as he recognized the prison administrator. "Please forgive me, sir. I did not realize—"

Ismail stepped forward to drop paperwork onto the desk. "The prisoner Jamil ul Haq Shahrani is scheduled to meet at this hour with his lawyer and a female family member, Farah ul Haq Shahrani. You will take us to him immediately."

Listing a nonexistent lawyer as Farah's companion rather than Ismail himself was a subterfuge to avoid speculation by low-level bureaucrats who handled documents. But at Ismail's demand, the clerk's eyes widened with dismay.

"Yes, this prisoner was brought to chamber twelve for an interview. But his lawyer and sister already arrived at the scheduled time. Though the female's name was not the same as my roster. I noted the discrepancy, but they had the proper documents, so I assumed there was an error."

The clerk shuffled frantically through papers. "Here it is. Not Farah, but Ameera. Ameera ul Haq Shahrani. They met with this Jamil before the order came to return all prisoners to their cells."

"Ameera?"

The clerk quailed visibly under the cold menace in Ismail's softly hissed echo. "If there has been an error, I take full responsibility. The criminal is perhaps still in this sector, since the guards are only now removing the prisoners. Shall I give orders to have him returned to the interview room?"

But Ismail had already broken into a run. The last family members and legal counsel had cleared the corridor beyond, so Ismail faced no delay in reaching the security grille. This didn't open directly into one of the cellblocks, but a wedge-shaped courtyard which now heaved with the gray-blue of guards and mismatched rags of the prisoners they escorted. The detainees in the courtyard had taken up chants floating down from window bars above. "Death to Qaderi! Justice now! Allahu Akbar."

Above the chants sounded a sharp metallic thud of fists pounding on a metal door at the far side of the courtyard. Where were the guards who should have been funneling prisoners back to their separate cellblocks? Then Ismail spotted the particular rags and unkempt dark curls for which he searched. "You there! Your prisoner, Jamil ul Haq Shahrani, bring him back immediately!"

If Jamil's escort had heard, they gave no indication. But among the crowd, a slim figure stiffened, a head turned. Ismail rounded on the guard manning the security grille. "Open this immediately!"

The guard was fumbling at the lock when the door across the court-yard burst open under pounding fists. As gray-blue uniforms stepped into view, a shot rang out. A prisoner escort dropped in an explosion of scarlet. Then another. The prisoners surged forward as it became clear the uniforms shooting from inside were not prison security. Their escorts, low-level guards who did not carry weapons, scrambled back toward the security grille. Jamil had disappeared into the melee.

The prison administrator appeared beside Ismail, the burqa hovering timidly at his heels. "Deputy Minister, I regret I must request your departure. It appears the prisoners have taken over Pul-e-Charki!"

Guards were pouring back through the security grille, the prisoners they'd escorted now disappearing into the cellblock. Only a single bloody shape remained splayed on the concrete. Ismail swung instead on the burqa, the cold menace of his tone chilling to pure ice. "You will now tell me of this Ameera whom you did not see."

Jamil was supremely conscious of the alien object pressing against his groin, so that it took alertness to walk with a normalcy that drew no guard's eye. And to mask the euphoria that buoyed Jamil's steps despite the steel grate clanging shut behind him. To think so few days past, he'd despaired of life itself. Resigned himself to prison walls at best, degradation and torment at worst. And now?

Though Ameera's response had been cut off, to know her heart held love for him was enough to make Jamil's own heart sing. A wind whistling through the courtyard was chill and musty. But Jamil could almost believe he caught on it the gentle scent of impending spring with its warmth and new life and joy such as he'd known only in memory for countless long years now.

You are truly my protector, Isa. You are my liberator. And now do you also restore to me all the dreams I once thought forever lost?

The uniform responsible for ensuring family members introduced no contraband into the prison—that was the guards' prerogative—offered only the most casual pat-down before rummaging through Ameera's bag for his own share. In any case, such searches looked for weapons or cell phones, not an item smaller than Jamil's little finger tucked within folds of flesh. The tea bag itself now lay shredded and trampled underfoot in the interview room. It would seem Ameera's foreign warrior friend knew well the ways of prisons. Could such a tiny mechanism truly tell this Steve Wilson where Jamil walked and sat and slept within Pul-e-Charki walls?

Steve Wilson. The name rolled strangely off an Afghan tongue. A friend only, Ameera had insisted, and there'd been nothing but truth in her eyes and voice. Though Jamil did not believe for a heartbeat that the American felt only friendship toward his countrywoman. He'd witnessed the look in steel gray eyes when they rested on Ameera, such a look as a mirror might reveal in Jamil's own gaze.

Still, just why this Steve Wilson should choose to aid Ameera and Jamil himself mattered less than that he had. Even while Jamil had counted the man an enemy, he'd recognized Steve Wilson to be a warrior of both courage and honor. Nor had Jamil forgotten his automatic instinct to summon the foreign warrior to Ameera's aid when intruders penetrated the New Hope compound.

For his part, Jamil could be glad Ameera had such a powerful protector. He could even muster compassion for his former adversary. Did he not know what it was to yearn for a heart and love beyond reach?

Jamil had time for such musing because his progress across the courtyard had been halted by a press of bodies ahead. Security personnel manning a door through which the prisoners should have been funneling were not responding to furious knocking. The seething restlessness of other prisoners, the sudden tension of their escorts, a firecracker staccato of gunfire in the distance all surged adrenaline through Jamil's veins. He knew the signs of impending trouble.

"You there! . . . Jamil ul Haq Shahrani!"

Jamil had recognized the authoritative tones even before he swung around to spy a tall, robed frame through the bars of the security grille. Ismail. What did his former conspirator want of him now?

But there was no more time for questions. As the blocked door slammed open, gunshots rang out that were not distant. At Jamil's side, the guard who'd taken possession of Ameera's bag threw his arms up. The bag went flying as the man slowly toppled forward. Jamil dropped beside him, arching his body over the fallen man as the courtyard erupted into a stampede. The other guards were already scrambling to safety. Under Jamil, a scarlet stain was rapidly spreading across the gray-blue uniform. Groping for something to stem the tide, Jamil's manacled hands found only the bag that had contained Ameera's gifts, its contents trampled and scattered under running feet. Shaking it free of crumbs, Jamil pressed the plastic down hard over the spouting wound. Nearby, another fallen guard was clearly beyond need of emergency attention.

A rough hand grabbed at Jamil's arm. "Leave him. There are other casualties for you to attend."

The speaker wore a gray-blue uniform, but Jamil recognized instantly the troublemaker from his own cell. A pistol in his right hand smelled of hot, burnt gunpowder. Jamil did not release the pressure under his hands. "I can't leave him. He will die."

"Let him!"

Again, the right words rose to Jamil's lips. "He is more valuable as a hostage than dead."

"Then bring him."

Jamil kept pressure on the bag while two other prisoners helped drag the fallen guard inside the cellblock. He was already snapping orders as the metal door slammed shut on a scene straight out of hell's corridors.

36

Farah had known boredom, anxiety, eagerness during the days she'd been shut away inside her luxurious cage. But not, until now, fear.

With nothing to do but pace and eat meals, Farah had studied well the lessons she'd been assigned. What was missing as much as what was included. Her employer had seemed pleased enough when he'd tested her before the drive over to that fortress on the horizon.

Fear had begun to rise up at the shouting multitude, high, stone-faced walls and swarming guards terrifyingly reminiscent of the prison from which Ameera had rescued her, so that she'd spoken truthfully that she was afraid to go forward into its depths. Then had come that unexpected glimpse of Ameera, her own outburst such an involuntary response she hadn't realized what she'd done until she'd caught Ismail's coldly incredulous glance.

Despite his icy demand, the deputy minister had given Farah no opportunity to respond, hurrying her out as quickly as he could collect his armed escort at the front gate and force passage back to their vehicle. Only once they'd covered the short distance back to the compound and Farah was marched upstairs had Ismail repeated his demand.

"But I did not see Ameera!" Farah cried out. "I saw only—"

What had she seen? A black chador taller than others in the multitude. A walk that seemed subtly un-Afghan. Had the woman she'd once considered her savior truly usurped Farah's meeting with Jamil? And by pretending to be *her*, Jamil's sister? The hot surge of jealousy and anger that rose in Farah was startling.

She raised her head proudly and rebelliously, her face a cold, indifferent mask. "If I had seen the infidel woman, I would have warned you. There was a chador among the crowd, a tall one, who brought Miss Ameera to my mind, that is all. But I did not believe it truly to be her, for how would she have obtained passage into the prison?"

"Yes, how? That I intend to ascertain."

Farah's fear ebbed, for if her new employer still looked furious, it was no longer directed at her.

"Meanwhile, do not forget your studies, for we will return to carry out your assignment as soon as I make new arrangements."

"How soon will that be?" Farah took a step after him. "I . . . I do not think I can bear to stay here much longer alone."

Ismail's irritation abruptly returned. "It will be when it will be. Still, it will not do to have you hysterical before you fulfill your usefulness."

He'd departed, but not without leaving instructions, for with Farah's next meal had been delivered as well a portable DVD player and box overflowing with DVDs. An electrical cord powered the player when the compound's generator was turned on at night, charging the unit as well for a few hours' use during the day.

The DVDs all proved to be mind-numbingly dull cartoons targeted to very young children. But at least they whiled away hours that turned to days until Farah lost count of how many had passed since Ismail's last appearance. When she stepped outside onto her balcony, she could see that while protesters no longer rioted outside Pul-e-Charki walls, in their place were army tanks and personnel carriers. Whatever crisis had prompted the abandonment of Farah's own assignment was still clearly unresolved.

Along with a lookout post, the balcony offered the beauty of greenery below and snowcapped mountains on the horizon, a perfume of fresh air, sunshine warm on Farah's face, sometimes even the music of birds among pine boughs. But Farah did not often avail herself of that distraction. If fear of her new employer had been quickly allayed, Farah had come to both loathe and fear the mujahedeen sentries who guarded Ismail's compound. They lingered in the doorway while one of their company carried in Farah's meals or retrieved the tray. They loitered below her balcony, and if Farah stepped to the railing, a shrill whistle immediately drew a gang to stare.

Allah formed men to be lusty as a fine stallion, her wali's senior wife had reminded Farah repeatedly during early years when she'd forgotten to snatch headscarf across her face every time a male wandered into view. It was a woman's duty to safeguard a man's virtue and purity by proffering him no temptation. Any woman who failed to do so could not blame a man for acting upon the urges with which Allah so generously endowed him. Rebelliously, Farah had wondered why men shared no responsibility to learn restraint even as the quick tug of cloth across mouth and nose became automatic.

Here the mujahedeen roaming corridors and balconies and grounds were held in restraint by their employer's orders more than her own modesty. But they didn't bother restraining their eyes, and those greedy, avid stares were as unpleasant as hands on her body. Conscious that she'd no means to lock her door, Farah slept uneasily, and when she did, her dreams were so unpleasant, she postponed retiring to her silken pillows as late as possible.

The dreams were all similar, a repeat at first of the one she'd suffered after listening to stories on Ameera's tiny machine. A multitude. A white-robed figure cradling a child whose place she wept to take. Only this time Farah never saw his eyes, only the back of that dazzling white robe, because the one in her dream was walking away though she stretched out her arms and begged him to turn around.

Nor did the one walk alone. To either side, his strong hands grasping theirs tightly, which should have been impossible since in her dream Farah knew he still carried the child, walked Ameera and Jamil. Their voices floating back to Farah were filled with joy and delight.

And so much love.

But though Farah called and called, beseeching them to let her come too, they either did not hear or chose not to turn around. Farah always woke with sobs shaking her body, the pillow wet under her cheeks.

Reason explained the dream easily enough when Farah was awake.

She'd seen that black chador walking away from her, then Jamil in turn. Worry and anger and bitterness had allowed those images to creep into her dreams.

But reason could not dispel a growing conviction. *If this universe holds love that is no illusion, it is not for such as I!*

No, Ameera's turned back might be real enough. But Jamil's walking away was only figment of a bad dream. *Ismail has promised to help free Jamil. I will again have a brother, a family.*

Then came a morning when the dream dissolved into distant explosions and gunfire. Forcing herself out onto the balcony, Farah spotted smoke drifting up from the stone-walled fortress across the plateau, swallowed down a familiar acrid taste of spent gunpowder in her throat. Creeping back inside, she did not touch her breakfast tray nor turn on the DVD player but sat unmoving on the floor until long after all grew quiet again. When her door slammed open without a knock, she raised her head with listless apathy, assuming her visitor to be the sentry on duty returning for Farah's untouched tray.

"On your feet, girl." Ismail snapped his fingers impatiently. "It is time."

Waiting was harder work than all the planning and preparation. For six days now Steve had continued to ferry his embassy charges to Pul-e-Charki as though nothing had happened. The prisoners retained control of their cellblocks, holding an indeterminate number of hostages and an even more indeterminate amount of weapons and ammo. But the court-yards in between were eerily quiet, the prisoners firing on any security personnel who showed themselves, while several attempted breakouts of prisoners had been picked off by rooftop snipers, their bodies left splayed on the concrete as warning to fellow mutineers.

Pul-e-Charki's army outpost had given Qaderi and Khalid's closest competition in the presidential race, Minister of Defense General Abdur Rahmon, pretext to join this dogfight. Along with police vehicles, at least a dozen tanks were now drawn up outside the main gates while hundreds of Afghan National Army troops had joined prison security and police reinforcements. Water and electrical lines along with regular food delivery had been cut off to the besieged wings, offering the prisoners no way out beyond unconditional surrender. But either they'd squirreled away more food supplies than calculated, and water too before the lines were shut off, or they simply were willing to endure hunger and thirst and darkness.

Steve's own clients had twice now extended their stay, Jabbaar like most bullies having proved happy to spill anything he knew under the first threat of unpleasantness. So he was taken aback when he arrived at the embassy to find his clients lingering over breakfast with DEA chief Ramon Placido instead of heading for their convoy.

"We've pulled the plug," one interrogator commented bluntly. "Jabbaar's just jerking our chain now. And since we can't get back to Pul-e-Charki till who knows when, that little toad isn't worth missing our flight again."

He broke off at a sharp glance from Ramon Placido. Steve's mental antenna shot up. "What do you mean, we can't get back there?"

The DEA chief intervened smoothly, "We've just been advised this might be a good day for some sightseeing. You won't be needed anymore, but I've authorized Hamilton to have Dyncorp cover your contract through the end of the week. Sorry for the inconvenience."

Meaning the embassy had received a tip-off they'd no intention of passing on to a civilian contractor. Steve's eyes narrowed speculatively. "If the rest of the contract's canceled, I've got some gear I'll need to clear out of a locker at Pul-e-Charki."

For one brief hesitation, Steve thought Placido was going to break protocol and tell him what he'd learned. Instead the DEA chief shrugged. "No problem, but I'd wait a day or two."

So something was going down at Pul-e-Charki. And it was no peace rally if the Afghans were warning their American allies to stay out of harm's way. Best bet, precautionary arrangements were being made for a prisoner surrender. Which would be a relief. Steve had assumed Jamil's continued well-being largely because his tracking signal was still moving around. But the battery would be dead within another twenty-four hours. Meaning Steve needed to get Jamil out of Pul-e-Charki by then or another battery into place. Neither of which would be so easy once Steve no longer had VIP access to the prison.

This evening was the scheduled date for Jamil's televised tribunal. With the mutiny making its defendant inaccessible, a postponement seemed a safe assumption. But once the standoff ended, Qaderi wouldn't waste time rescheduling. *If the siege is really being lifted, my best bet is to get Jamil out tonight.*

All of which required Steve getting back into the high security wing before someone got around to canceling his magnetic pass. And contacting Amy Mallory to make other necessary arrangements. Steve was hitting speed dial before he'd cleared embassy security. But Amy didn't answer her phone, though Steve continued to try as he threaded through traffic out of town toward Pul-e-Charki. He'd cleared Kabul's smog and could see Pul-e-Charki's walls and towers on the horizon when he finally tried Becky Frazer instead.

"Amy? She left early this morning. Something about visiting those women and children she housed." A wail of small children in the background indicated he'd caught the nurse-practitioner at the clinic. "Try calling her cell. You have the number?"

No curse actually slipped past Steve's lips, but the sentiments were there. He was now approaching the Pul-e-Charki perimeter. It took one glance to see that neither negotiations nor a peaceful surrender were under way. Not when rooftops and walls had been cleared of personnel and sniper nests. To the tanks outside the walls had been added armored personnel carriers and army transports, while the Afghan National Army uniforms spread out along the perimeter had doubled since yesterday. Among them Steve spotted rocket-propelled grenade launchers.

Steve slammed on his brakes for an army checkpoint. The uniforms waving him back showed no interest in seeing ID. Steve was reversing when his phone rang.

"Hi, Steve, you've been calling?"

Steve spun around in a U-turn that enveloped his vehicle in dust. "Amy, where are you?"

"Actually, I'm looking right at you." The aid worker's tone held an impish note. "At least if that's your Pajero leaving Pul-e-Charki right now. Your voice messages said you were heading that way."

Steve swerved to the shoulder of the dirt track. Climbing out of the SUV, he shielded his eyes with a hand to search the horizon. Within eyesight were only a few scattered compounds.

"Okay, it's definitely you." Steve could now hear a distinct smile in her voice. "As to where am I? Take a look off to your right. Mud-brick wall. Two-story house, run-down. I'm standing on a balcony. There's a really fancy compound nearby, lots of trees, high, white walls."

Steve had already identified the white-walled compound. "You mean, Ismail's place."

"Yes, that's right. We're the next compound off to my left, your right."

Steve followed the horizon about a half kilometer to the right. "Got it! I'll be there in ten. You be out at the gate waiting."

"Yes, sir, at your service, sir."

Amy's amused sarcasm broke off at the same explosion that whirled Steve around. A mortar shell had slammed over Pul-e-Charki's interior perimeter wall into a cellblock, sending chunks of concrete flying. As a second armored personnel carrier fired, another missile exploded onto a roof. Then a tank gun belched, its round smashing through window bars.

Steve climbed back into the car as a rain of mortar shells and high explosive rounds was joined by a rat-tat-tat of the huge stationary machine guns topping the square entrance towers. Black smoke billowed from shattered windows. So much for negotiations.

37

He'd made it in under five.

Amy stepped through the compound gate just as an approaching whirlwind collapsed behind her own Toyota Corolla's bumper, revealing a Pajero SUV. By now Amy was too worried and relieved to see the tall contractor unfold himself from the driver's seat for annoyance at his brusque officiousness. "Steve, what's happening out there?"

From the gate, a watchman had been uneasily fingering an antique AK-47 until Amy's greeting made clear this new arrival was no stranger. Husband to Dr. Amrita's younger associate Masooda, Arif had worked as security guard for a foreign company until the couple had moved to provide the new AWR compound with chowkidar and schoolteacher. Much older than Masooda, Arif was a kindly man who displayed pride in his wife's controversial activities and their two small daughters. At Amy's reassuring nod, he disappeared inside.

"Someone got tired of waiting to starve out the prisoners." Steve was frowning as he glanced around. "What is this place? And why are you here alone and not answering your phone?"

Amy hadn't seen Steve since he'd passed her the tracking device. He'd called each evening after returning his clients to the embassy, but only to report tersely the continued stalemate. With Becky's return, she'd been grateful to plunge into the nurse-practitioner's own busy routine, lending a hand in the clinic, cleaning the small apartment, and cooking meals. But Amy couldn't speak openly with Becky. Whether the older woman would be horrified or approving, Amy didn't dare involve her friend in Amy and Steve's covert activities. In fact, Amy's biggest concern beyond Jamil himself was ensuring that nothing in this mess negatively impacted the Afghan Relief Mission or any other aid organization.

Working at Becky's side, Amy had remained on constant alert for a heads-up from Steve that their arrangements could move forward. But as day after day passed with the siege unchanged, she'd finally decided her conscientious hovering was ridiculous. She'd driven over to visit Roya and her two daughters, above all to let them know that sanctuary existed only a reasonable hike away. Loma had seemed both more alive and resigned, all three joining in animated plans to visit the other Welayat women next time their menfolk were on the road.

The hillside neighborhood offered no cell phone reception, and when Amy reached the AWR compound and checked her phone messages, she found a dozen missed calls from Steve. She'd called back as soon as she could pull herself away from welcoming embraces.

"Didn't I ever tell you? This is the Welayat families' new home." Amy flinched at another loud explosion. "Steve, I can't bear to even think what could be happening to Jamil in there!"

Rapid fingers on Steve's iPhone screen drew up a map of Pul-e-Charki, its tiny schematics astonishingly detailed. A red dot blinked partway along one spoke. "So far, so good. And no, you didn't tell me. Nor that you were going out this morning."

Steve's rejoinder held so much restrained wrath that Amy was startled. "Why are you angry with me? What did I do this time?"

Steve ran a frustrated hand through his hair. "I'm not angry. Okay, maybe I am, a little. You weren't answering your phone. Not even your nurse friend knew where you were. If a member of my unit took off without backup or so much as checking in with his mission leader, I'd yank him back to latrine patrol so quick, his head would be spinning. You are now my mission team. My only team. I need to be able to count on you. More than that, I need to be free to carry out my mission without the distraction of worrying about what might be happening to you or where you are."

So Amy's well-being was a distraction? Even as hot and painful pressure built up in her chest, Amy knew she wasn't being fair. She wasn't ignorant of Steve's world. When a soldier was focused on carrying out a dangerous mission, her brother in the Marines had once lectured her, he couldn't be distracted looking over his shoulder to check on his teammates. That mentality could get a whole unit killed.

An ally, Amy had called Steve. And whatever his opinions of Amy, or even of Jamil, Steve had made amply evident he was an ally she could depend on completely. She'd never need to look over her shoulder to wonder if he was at her back. Nor doubt whether he was doing what he'd promised.

But she'd never thought of herself as Steve's own backup. His mission team, he'd called her. And he'd every right to expect from Amy the same reliable, steadfast ally she'd come to expect from him.

"You're right; I should have let you know where I was going," Amy said quietly. "I'm not used to having a . . . partner to figure into my activities. So what was it you needed from me?"

The easing of a taut jawline indicated he tacitly accepted her apology. "Just your vehicle. As you may remember, I had a Corolla like yours when I was here before. No one looks twice at a secondhand taxi." Steve nodded toward the Pajero. "That, on the other hand, is a little conspicuous. I was hoping you'd be willing to trade wheels."

In the distance, the explosions were tapering off. Amy caught her breath as the implications of Steve's request sank in. "You think the standoff is over? You can go forward now?"

"What it means is I'll be heading in just as soon as that wasp's nest over there calms down. As to our friend, that depends on what I find. This chaos may even work to our favor. Though it's going to take time to restore order."

Amy trailed behind as Steve walked along the compound wall to the corner. Beyond it, an open field offered a panoramic vista of Pul-e-Charki. "This is actually as good a lookout as any to wait."

Settling himself on the dusty ground, back against the mud-brick wall, Steve stretched long legs out, one ankle over the other. Amy spread out her cloak before sinking down gingerly beside him. "So did you know it was coming? Is this why your team didn't go to Pul-e-Charki today?"

"Actually, they won't be going back. Another reason I'm concerned to move forward immediately." Steve didn't turn his narrowed gaze from the prison walls as he gave a brief explanation. Ending, he queried, "Are your friends inside going to be wondering what happened to you?"

"I think they already know." A giggle overhead punctuated Amy's wry response.

Steve's mouth curved sardonically as his upward glance took in several small heads thrust over the wall. "Somehow, this wasn't where I'd pictured your Welayat bunch ending up. Can't say much for the view, but at least the air's cleaner. So how have the women and kids taken the move? More importantly, how do you feel?"

Amy waved toward their giggling audience. "The kids are happy so long as they've got food, shelter, and room to run around. And their moms are content because their kids are. How do I feel?" Amy paused to consider it. "I feel . . . finished. Like I've handed them off to someone who really can take care of them. Better care, to be honest, than I could give them. Dr. Amrita has so many plans for schooling and occupational opportunities, even growing their own food. I'll miss them all, but I don't feel anymore like I'm abandoning them."

The bombardment had at last fallen silent, wind beginning to blow away the black cloud of smoke above Pul-e-Charki. Beside Amy, Steve was now absorbed in his iPhone screen, his shuttered expression giving no indication he'd even heard her response. Amy felt herself swallowing a lump in her throat. What had ever happened to the easy friendliness that had sprung so naturally between Amy and the private security contractor that Thanksgiving not so many weeks ago?

Even when sparks had flown, starting with their first encounter on a Kabul street, there'd been an—an *awareness* between Steve and Amy, so that she'd somehow always known when the tall contractor entered a room, his eyes automatically finding hers in the same way. He'd rushed without hesitation through a riot to her side. Interfered, sometimes unmercifully, for what he considered her best interests. On that they'd more often than not disagreed.

But always Steve had *seen* Amy.

Now he'd reverted to an impersonal matter-of-factness as though Amy were indeed just some subordinate under his command. Or a task he was in a hurry to complete. Not that she could blame him. Since the beginning, Amy and Jamil both had been nothing but trouble and nuisance for this man.

With difficulty, Amy got out evenly, "Excuse me for boring you with all that. I have a tendency to chatter when—well, when I'm trying not to think of other things. And right now you're the only person I don't have to watch my tongue around, which puts you on the receiving end. But I'll try to keep quiet. Unless . . . would you rather I went inside and left you alone?"

A rocket screaming into a nearby wall had crumbled plaster like an eruption of ash and hail over prone human shapes. Jamil brushed flakes from his eyes with one hand as the other maintained pressure on a spouting neck wound. He'd spent the last hour as he had the last week, tending the wounded. Most were injuries easily enough tended with first aid supplies scavenged from guard stations. But the guard for whom he'd intervened was barely clinging to life, a collapsed lung, Jamil suspected. And two inmates had arrived so severely beaten, they were mercifully still unconscious.

Jamil didn't ask how his patients acquired their injuries. As hoarded food and water grew scarce over the days of siege, Pul-e-Charki corridors had deteriorated into the bestial survival mentality of a jungle. Or *Lord of the Flies*, a Western novel that was tolerated school reading since it depicted the degeneracy of infidels and swift decline of society unrestrained by Allah's strict laws. Fortunately for Jamil, his services had been deemed sufficiently indispensable that the mutineer leaders had assigned him a protective detail and even minuscule food allotment.

Now so many wounded were being carried in, their injuries so serious, Jamil was becoming increasingly desperate and overwhelmed. He released pressure on the neck wound as he saw that the man was no longer breathing. Swiftly he turned to a new arrival bleeding from multiple shrapnel gashes. How many more would die this day?

But no more explosions followed. After a week of defiant standoff, it hadn't taken the mutineer leaders long to concede they were beaten because prisoners were now shifting the barricade that blocked a steel door at the end of the corridor. As it swung open, a flood of armed uniforms poured in.

"Hands behind your head. All prisoners outside."

Those of Jamil's patients who could push themselves to their feet were already scrambling to obey. Jamil continued to twist a tourniquet until a machine gun barrel prodded him in the chest.

"Are you deaf? Get on your feet." A forefinger tightening on the firing mechanism begged for an excuse to complete the action.

Jamil coolly finished tying off the tourniquet. "I am a healer. I cannot leave this man or he will bleed to death."

The uniform glanced around as though taking in for the first time neat lines of tushaks, scant medical supplies, patients too injured to rise. Then his eye fell on bloodstained gray-blue material, and he shouted down the corridor to a superior. The prison doctor who arrived with a team of paramedics ordered the injured guard carried out first. But the paramedics quickly returned with more stretchers.

Steve hadn't missed the hurt note in Amy's stiff offer. His hands tightened on the iPhone. Didn't she know how difficult this was for him? Maintaining aloofness from the safe distance of a phone call was hard enough. But sitting close enough to breathe the perfume of her hair and skin? Watching that faraway look? Offering disinterested sympathy, impersonal professionalism, when all he wanted was to snatch her close—or get away as far and quick as possible? All necessitating more self-control and endurance than the Q course that had been the brutal finale of his Special Forces training.

No, of course she didn't know.

Steve's peripheral vision caught rapidly blinking eyelashes, an unhappy droop to the full mouth. This was far worse for his companion. A man she deeply cared for was over there in harm's way, and despite that optimistically blinking red dot, Amy's mind had to be following every possible scenario of what could be going wrong. If a little friendly conversation would help Amy keep unpleasant thoughts at bay, then maybe that living sacrifice Rev talked about involved more than simply being willing to let go and walk away. Steve cleared his throat. "Actually, I'd appreciate your company. And I sure didn't mean to give the impression I wanted you to keep quiet. As you've noticed, I'm not the world's greatest at small talk. I was just . . . working some things out. And checking on this."

On the iPhone screen as Steve tilted it toward Amy, a pulsating red dot was now emerging visibly into a courtyard. "You understand what this means?"

Amy's breath left her with a force that indicated she'd been running through just such mental scenarios as he'd envisioned. "Jamil's alive and able to walk at least."

"Not only that, but if I'm reading the quiet over there right, the prisoners must have surrendered."

"Then—you're going in now?"

"Not yet. I can't make a move until after dark. Now that I've got transport lined up—I'm assuming that was a 'yes' on the Corolla—I've got some time on my hands." Steve slanted a faint smile Amy's direction. "So if you're still wanting to talk, I'm all yours for the next hour or two."

"Just like that?" Amy eyed him dubiously. "Well, of course what I'd like to ask is what you're planning to do over you know where! Since that subject's out—let's see, how's Phil's little boy Jamie?"

"Doing good last I heard. John, Ruth, and the baby?"

Amy actually laughed aloud. "Nothing new since you last asked. Okay, maybe we need a list of conversation topics like they do for talk shows and such."

"You mean, like favorite color or flavor of ice cream?" Steve suggested wryly. "There's a conversation topic I can handle."

"And one I've always hated. God created this planet with such incredible variety of colors and tastes and smells and sounds. I love my mom's

Cuban cooking, Thai curries, Greek, Mexican, Chinese, and everything in between. I've got friends from every continent, and I love their differences in culture and music and even friendship. So why should I be expected to tie myself down to a single favorite when there's a world of fabulous choices to enjoy?"

Amy broke off with a wrinkling of her nose. "Okay, that's my pet rant for the day. Of course that doesn't apply to people's spouses or kids. I guess you'd better have a favorite there."

"I'm sure John and Ruth would appreciate that." Steve hid a smile as he responded gravely. "And I'll admit I do have favorites. Ice cream? That's easy. Chocolate. Movies? Lord of the Rings. I've always fancied myself Aragorn, the misunderstood wanderer who of course in the end gets both the girl and kingdom."

Steve's strategy was working. Under their easy conversation, Amy relaxed visibly, even when ambulances and Red Cross SUVs began racing down the dirt road toward Pul-e-Charki, crossing paths with tanks and personnel carriers lumbering back toward Kabul. Under Steve's judicious probing, Amy spilled more perhaps than she'd realized of her own happy childhood and family in Miami. In turn, Steve dug up tales of Army and contractor days that ranged from funny to hair-raising. As though by mutual decision, neither spoke of Jamil, though Amy's eyes followed Steve's fingers as they pulled up headlines for news on the riot or checked the tracking signal.

"I guess there's no point asking which country has been your favorite duty station," Steve asked idly when there was at last a lull in conversation. "But how about your *least* favorite?"

"That's easy," Amy said promptly. "Afghanistan. Not just physical things like dust and smog, freezing in winter and the electricity always cutting out. Or even the lack of so many freedoms I took for granted. Always having to keep my head covered. Watching everything I say. All the security precautions because you never know when someone might want to shoot you or kidnap you or blow you up.

"No, I think it's the meanness I've come to hate more than any place I've ever lived. The constant humiliation and oppression in every aspect of a woman's life. The corruption that lets rich people buy their way to the front of every line while ordinary Afghans spend their lives wading through a system so unfair it's hard to blame them for turning to violence. The warlords and politicians building mansions while the police chase starving beggars off the streets because they're an eyesore."

When Steve made no response, Amy turned her head toward him. "You don't want to say, 'I told you so'? that you aren't surprised?"

Steve was watching a green police pickup barreling along one of the plateau's crisscrossing dirt tracks toward Pul-e-Charki. From where he sat, only the rear wall of Ismail's luxurious compound was visible across the plain, but the pickup's trajectory was such that it could have originated there. A reminder that whatever Ismail's plans had been, they too must have been obstructed by the prison uprising.

When he did answer, Steve was surprised at the intensity of regret he had to excise from his tone. "Actually, I was thinking of that card you sent me all those years ago. I never told you how much that meant to the troops out here. To me personally. Oh yeah, we kicked and screamed about headquarters making us take time to answer letters. But it meant a lot that folks back home hadn't forgotten us out here, seeing the things we saw, doing the things we did. I'll never forget you writing how proud you were of us for bringing freedom and democracy to this place. How when you were old enough, you wanted to come to Afghanistan to make a difference too."

A stifled voice came from beside him. "I remember."

"I know you never figured freedom and democracy would still be a joke here all these years later. And I'm truly sorry things didn't work out for you as you hoped. I guess my question is, where do you see yourself going from here? Away from Afghanistan of course, but frankly I can't picture you—or Jamil either—settling down to Miami suburbia. Like you said, once you've traveled the planet, it's hard to settle down to one flavor of ice cream. Is there anything or anyplace where you can see yourself five, ten years from now that wouldn't have you bored out of your skull in a month?"

"In other words, is there anything I'm passionate about enough to give it the rest of my life?" This time it was Amy who fell silent, and when she spoke, she sounded surprised at herself. "Afghanistan. Oh, I know that sounds crazy. But truth is, I've come to love this place as much as . . . well, as much as I hate it. Or love its people at least. Okay, so maybe that sounds schizophrenic. Especially when I'm on my way out of this country. Or maybe, as John and Ruth and Becky like to say, Afghanistan gets into your blood, and you just can't walk away. Right now I've no idea what I'll be doing with the rest of my life. But you're right that I can't imagine just settling down to house, two cars, white picket fence, and all the rest of the American dream when so much of our planet has no access to that dream."

Amy looked at Steve. "What about you? You told me once that there was nothing wrong with being passionate. That passion was the only way to get great things done. So what are you passionate about enough to give it the rest of your life?"

Steve tamped down the first thought that sprang to mind as he looked her direction. "I also said, if I remember correctly, that caring enough to be passionate was a great way to get hurt. I learned a long time ago—the hard way—to keep my mind on doing the job and to keep emotions out of it. As for what you're passionate about—"

Despite his best efforts, Steve couldn't keep a rough edge from his tone. "Funny, but I'd have thought Jamil would be at the top of your list."

He'd put an effective and immediate end to the easy give-and-take of their conversation. Amy turned her head to give Steve a long, considering look, and perhaps it was as well he couldn't read the expression behind lowered lashes. Then she said flatly, "Jamil is Afghanistan."

38

There seemed nothing more to be said. Amy hadn't expected to find herself almost enjoying these last two hours. Knowing Jamil was alive, still mobile, and might even be free within the next twenty-four hours was in itself a weight lifted. And as she'd discovered on that Thanksgiving Day outing, when Steve Wilson wasn't being deliberately obdurate and provoking, the security contractor could be a stimulating and agreeable companion.

But now Steve was on his feet again, his expression retreating to its earlier shuttered remoteness. Amy hadn't missed that he'd neatly avoided her question about his future plans, but she didn't press it. Rising to her own feet, she brushed dust from her clothing as Steve held up his iPhone. The screen displayed a gesturing Afghan official in a much-beribboned army uniform.

"Minister of Defense Rahmon is announcing full control restored at Pul-e-Charki with virtually no casualties. I've got some preparations to make before heading inside, so if you've got those car keys handy, let's make that switch. And speaking of preparations, do you have those friends in Peshawar lined up?"

Amy was already digging her keys from her knapsack. "They know there's an Isa follower who might need a place to stay at a moment's notice. When the time comes, it's just a matter of giving them a call."

"Good! Then what I want of you now is to get back to Becky's. Stay there visible and doing nothing until you hear from me. And don't call or leave voice messages. Even on vibrate, that can give away a location, and you can't know where I'll be or who might be listening. I'll contact you once safely away from Pul-e-Charki, either both of us or myself, depending on what I find inside. But if all goes well, this will be over tonight."

"If all goes well," Amy repeated hollowly. Now that the time had arrived, every qualm she'd ever had was rising up inside her. What if instead of rescuing Jamil, she was just sending Steve into imminent danger—or worse? "And if I don't hear?"

Steve hesitated before adding bluntly, "If you haven't heard from me by tomorrow evening, assume there's been a serious glitch, and make your own plans to get immediately out of Afghanistan."

As a backup plan, it was both logical and necessary, but supremely unwelcome. A chill went through Amy that raised hair on her arms. "Am I crazy—are we both crazy—to think we could pull off something like this? What if this fails? What if something happens to you? Either of you. Both of you. I wouldn't even know! At least if this were a real contract, you'd have real backup, not . . . not just me!"

"We're not going to fail." Steve's hands reached out to grip Amy's shoulders hard. "Are you regretting you started this? Are you wanting to back out? Because for my part, I've already given my word to you; I've given my word before almighty God himself, that I will not stop this thing now until the mission is finished, Jamil is out of Pul-e-Charki, and he and you both are safe and free to live your lives in peace."

There was a steel conviction in the soft words. A grim resoluteness in the tightness of his jaw. A determination of purpose in the tensed muscles and forward tilt of his body line. Steve had told Amy bleakly that he no longer believed in passion, and between the well-edited lines of his reminiscences, Amy had glimpsed just what heartaches and disillusionment might have led to such a cynical avowal.

But it isn't true. He'd never have been so disappointed and bitter if he hadn't cared so much to start with. And whether or not he still believes in passion, it burns in him. He's passionate about whatever mission he's committed himself to. He's passionate about keeping his word. About justice and doing what's right. About keeping bad guys from hurting the helpless. And about his faith, though I'd never fully realized it before.

The passions of a good and honorable man.

Amy stepped back from his grip. "Then let's do this."

The walk to the vehicles was a silent one, Steve's expression when Amy glanced upward so tight with concentration, she didn't venture to disturb his thoughts. Would she ever see the tall, lanky security contractor again once this night's doings were complete?

The sigh in her throat offered no sound as it emerged, but a deep drawl above her head said quietly, "It's going to be all right; it really is. Don't think of the next few hours. Think of this time next week, when you and Jamil will both be safe far beyond Afghanistan's borders and free to choose whatever you want to do with the rest of your lives."

"As will you," Amy reminded as quietly.

The only item Amy had to remove from the hatchback was her flannel-graph box she'd tucked in for today's excursion. Steve in turn grabbed a small duffel bag from his backseat. "I brought some gear for Jamil, since he'll have to leave everything behind."

As Steve headed around the Corolla to slide into the driver's seat, she called softly after him, "Just watch your back, okay? I'll be praying."

The tall security contractor stopped abruptly, swinging around on his heel to face Amy, and though his gaze was hooded, she saw the jaw-line relax into a faint smile. "That's one thing I've never doubted for an instant."

If Jamil had any expectation his dedicated labors might qualify him for preferential treatment, the last hours standing in a courtyard with fingers laced at the back of his neck would have banished it. Sorting hundreds of prisoners into their original cellblocks was no easy task, and the sun was past zenith by the time Jamil's group was ordered forward. His stomach chilled as he saw that each prisoner was being stripped naked. Though he'd bound the tracking device more securely under deliberately dirtied, bloodstained bandages, those would not thwart a serious body search.

But Jamil was still waiting his turn when a guard detail trotted up. "That's the man. Bring him."

Marched into an undamaged interview room, Jamil recognized the prison doctor eyeing his watch impatiently. And the official with white-streaked brown beard beside him. The doctor glanced at Jamil briefly. "Yes, this is the healer who was caring for your injured guard when I arrived."

"The apostate," the prison administrator corrected coldly. "Can you certify he is in adequate health to stand trial tonight with no further delays?"

Trial? Jamil stiffened. He'd lost all track of days since the prison uprising had begun. Had so many truly passed?

"Why not ask the man himself? He is capable of judging his own condition." The doctor turned to Jamil. "Are you in need of medical attention?"

Jamil's clothing was blood-spattered enough for such a question, but little of it was his own. "I am in good health. A few minor cuts from the rockets. And the guard? Will he live?"

"Thanks to you, he will."

"Enough!" the prison administrator interrupted. "I will inform Minister Qaderi all may move forward on schedule. Prepare the prisoner for his visitors."

Doctor and prison administrator strode from the room as the guards shackled Jamil into a chair. He was less surprised than irritated when Ismail strolled in, a curt gesture ordering the guards out of the room. But he was not expecting the pale blue burqa who sidled in on Ismail's heels. For an instant Jamil's heart leaped. But that horrified gasp was not Ameera's voice.

Ismail's eyebrows rose as he looked over Jamil's seated figure. "They said you were uninjured."

"The blood is not mine. I have been tending the wounded. Why are you here?" Jamil demanded as icily as if he, not Ismail, were the one free of shackles.

"To bring you a last chance." The deputy minister slapped a paper in front of him, neatly lettered in the Dari of Afghan officialdom. "I have drawn up for you a petition that pleads mental illness during the last court hearing. You did not know what you were saying and rescind your statements of apostasy. It requests you be allowed to seek exile in another country where you may receive treatment for your mental disease."

Jamil did not look down at the paper. "That this comes from your crooked hand is reason enough to refuse it."

"Then I will let you speak to someone who may change your stubborn mind," Ismail answered coldly.

"You do not know me if you believe there is anyone at your command who can do that."

"Even your lost sister for whom you once offered me your life? Farah ul Haq Shahrani?"

At Ismail's gesture, the burqa moved forward to take a seat across from Jamil, tossing blue veil back over light brown hair to reveal pale, young features.

"Did I not promise I would find her, though you called me a liar?"

Jamil's initial stunned astonishment was already giving way to burning fury. "What trick is this? I know this woman from the foreign compound where you sent me to work. You think you can fool me simply because she shares my sister's name?"

Raising manacled hands to indicate Ismail, Jamil addressed the girl directly. "Farah, why have you left Miss Ameera to be with this man? And why are you pretending to be my sister?"

"It is no trick. I am your sister. Though I did not know it myself until the deputy minister found me and showed me pictures to prove it. I had thought all my family was dead." Even as she spoke, Farah was drawing photos from inside her tunic. "I was a small child when my family was taken from me. But I recognized this man. My father. You look like him, though your coloring is different. As you say, it could be a trick."

Farah laid each photo down facing Jamil. Then she drew out another photo, this one larger. "But if I still doubted, I did no longer once I was shown this."

39

Ms. Amy Mallory never completely left Steve's mind these days. But as the adobe compound walls receded behind the Toyota Corolla, he pushed all thoughts of her to his subconscious. From this point, his focus must be on the mission alone.

Since he'd still had time to kill, Steve had detoured to a nearby open-air market, where he filled a backpack with bottled water and food staples— provisions for Jamil's travel. Tanks and personnel carriers were gone when Steve turned in to Pul-e-Charki's visitor parking lot, but prison walls still swarmed with both army and police uniforms. Gate security was too busy waving back media vans that had invaded on the heels of the departing army convoy to offer a foreign-dressed contractor's Dyncorp credentials more than a glance.

The assault had concentrated solely on the mutinied cellblocks, and once through the gates, residual indicators of a prison siege and its brutal ending were surprisingly few. Fresh gouges in already pitted and crumbling concrete walls. Shattered window openings and broken-down doors. Limp human shapes under a tarp in one courtyard belied General Rahmon's claims that the siege had ended with minimal casualties.

Steve headed toward the high security cellblock. Here at least all looked normal, though the interrogation wing was empty except for two Dyncorp operatives manning the command center. A lanky, blond Australian glanced up from a computer screen. "Hey, mate, you're back.

Quite the show out there, eh? Hamilton just flagged us your contract wound up early. While you're here then, you can turn in your pass."

It was the kind of tight security Steve would normally applaud. Now it simply added urgency to finishing his mission. "Yeah, they called it quits. Just came by to clear out my stuff."

Opening his locker, Steve lifted out a small sports bag before handing over his magnetic pass. "I didn't figure anyone was working today."

The other operative, a Denzel Washington look-alike from New Orleans, set aside an Uzi automatic he was cleaning. "Neither did we. Dyncorp's handling security for AP and Reuters at this trial shindig. With all the chaos, we were figuring on the night off. But now that their defendant's back in hand, Qaderi's announced all is on as scheduled. A smart move on his part, if inconvenient. General Rahmon may be trigger-happy, but there's no overlooking he ended this Pul-e-Charki fiasco while Justice and Interior sat around wringing their hands. Focusing voter attention back to this trial is the best shot Qaderi's got left in the presidential race. And since the other candidates won't want to see Qaderi hog all the limelight, we're figuring on a full turnout, short notice or not. Want to lend a hand?"

This was a wrinkle Steve might have foreseen. With the siege ended, there was no particular reason for Jamil's trial not to go forward, since this wouldn't be held in prisoner territory but in the comfortable surroundings of Pul-e-Charki's administrative sector, untouched by the recent assault. But like his Dyncorp colleagues, Steve had counted on Qaderi taking some time to get reorganized.

"Sorry; I've got evening plans." Steve shouldered his sports bag. *The one thing you'll be missing tonight is a defendant if I have anything to do with it!*

Jamil's anger dissolved again to stunned astonishment as Farah laid the final photo on top of the others. It hadn't been taken in Kabul under Taliban rule because the woman standing to one side of four males wore neither burqa nor chador. Dark curls escaping a headscarf, olive complexion, high-bridged nose all denoted Pashtun blood.

Not so a small girl smiling mischievously in the arms of the oldest male, her brown curls, light-toned features, and laughing blue eyes a feminine version of the bearded face above hers. Two other males, both grown, shared the older man's coloring. The fourth, a beardless adolescent, had the same darker coloring as the adult woman, but his features were startlingly like the oldest man. "I remember when this photo was taken. The day I left for medical school in Islamabad. I was sixteen, my sister six. How did it fall into your possession?"

This time Jamil's demand was addressed to the girl's companion. Ismail strolled forward. "When he never returned, your father's personal effects were placed in storage at the hospital where he worked. I recently negotiated their recovery. It would seem Dr. Shahrani was fond of his family, for this was among them."

Dr. Shahrani had in fact spent far more time with that framed portrait than its subjects. Jamil remembered well his father's impatience to leave the farewell party that had been occasion for the family portrait. But his sister?

Jamil's mind was still reeling at Farah's words. He'd relinquished hope of ever finding out what had become of his surviving family. Certainly not without a miracle from Isa himself. If this teenage female he'd glimpsed for months among the New Hope residents were truly the small sister he hadn't seen since her seventh year, would he not have known?

But then he'd paid little mind to the Welayat prisoners nor been so discourteous to allow his eyes to linger on unveiled features. Now Jamil leaned forward to search the beautiful, young face across the table. Yes, the resemblance was undeniably there. But more than one young woman could be found to resemble a small girl child, as Ismail had proved before. Or to give the right answers if well coached.

"You could be the girl child in my father's arms," Jamil admitted. "If so, what can you tell me of the last day our family was together?"

Farah did not ask which day, answering unhesitatingly. "When my father heard the Taliban were leaving Kabul, he had our belongings loaded into a jinga truck. We drove all day and night to our family's property. You were to meet us there. But after we arrived, the mujahedeen believed us to be Taliban and attacked. They killed my father and brothers and any other men inside, though they permitted the women and children to go.

But how is it you were not among the dead? I saw you return that day. Even my mother believed you had died."

"I arrived in time to be taken captive but not killed. And the mujahedeen did not believe we were Taliban, whatever lies they told afterward. They only coveted our home. The same home that is now the New Hope compound."

The blue eyes held only baffled incomprehension. Jamil's glance toward Ismail was unfriendly. "Then he did not tell you the compound where you have been living was taken from our family? You have said nothing that could not come from Ismail himself. He was there that day, after all. It is possible my sister would not recognize our home today. She was there only briefly, nor does it hold now any of the beauty of my childhood. But this man has played such tricks on me before. And he does not know I myself helped Miss Ameera transcribe the Welayat files. Yours does not bear my family's name."

If Jamil had expected startled guilt in the blue eyes, he saw only continued bafflement, and he added more gently, "Or perhaps this man has led you to truly believe you are the child in this picture. My sister was after all very small when the war swept us apart. As were you. Small enough to confuse your own memories with those this man has taught to you."

Ismail stepped forward as though to intervene, but it was Farah who spoke up fiercely. "This man may lie to you, but I do not! If Ameera's files do not hold my true name, it is because the name given to the police was of my wali, the relative who sheltered my mother and me, then condemned me to prison as a runaway bride. In truth so many years have passed, I had forgotten I ever bore another name until I saw it on papers and photos this man showed me. And yes, I was very small. But I remember what it was to have a family, father, brothers."

Farah closed her eyes, her expression receding to a distance. "I remember my father holding me for that picture, the tickle of his beard against my skin. And if my older brothers were grown men and, like my father, always gone, I remember my youngest brother well, though he too was many years older. He was kind to me. He let me ride upon his shoulders. He read to me from his books. He taught me to hold a pen and read my letters. I wept bitterly when he went away to study. And after that—"

Farah's eyes flew open, but now they held a sheen of tears, a horror of memory. "Of the years that came after, I do not wish to remember, so do not ask it of me."

Jamil raised a shackled hand to cut her off. "You need say nothing else, Farah-jan. I have seen the files Miss Ameera holds of you. I know what terrible things your life has held since the war, and it grieves my heart bitterly. Someday if life permits, you will tell me of them yourself. But for now I have only one other question. My *madar*—our *madar*—does she still live?"

"No, she died the first winter after the war." Farah stared at Jamil. "Then—you believe me?"

"Yes, I believe you." The pain and longing in Farah's narration had convinced Jamil as much as the images she evoked. In his own memories, his younger sister had been a rather-spoiled only daughter, accustomed to being the reigning princess of her small empire. But that she'd adored the brother nearest her in age, Jamil remembered vividly.

A desolation in Farah's face, the drooping of her shoulders squeezed at Jamil's heart. He leaned forward far enough to be able to ignore Ismail's watchful gaze. "Don't look so sad, little princess. Do you remember that is what we called you? You looked just so unhappy the last time I left to university. And I promised to bring you a gift if only you did not cry. A gift fit for the princess you were. When I had to stay in Islamabad over the Eid holidays, I sent the gift instead. Had I known it would be years before I saw you again, I would have left my exams to bring it myself. Do you remember what the gift contained?"

The desolation left Farah's face so suddenly, it went blank. "I . . . I . . . How am I to remember one gift among all I received that Eid? It was so long ago. I was but a small child."

Something in that stammered response narrowed Jamil's gaze with renewed suspicion. Then lake blue eyes flickered to the man hovering above her. At what he glimpsed in them, Jamil demanded incredulously, "What is it, Farah? Why do you fear?"

Farah stiffened immediately. "I am not afraid. But I have said I do not wish to keep speaking of the past. As to gifts, I never wanted gifts from my brother, but only his return to me. So why did you not return? Where were you that you never came to find me—us? If you had come before *Madar* died, perhaps she would not have despaired of life!"

Farah had shifted the attack to Jamil himself, but he was already nodding acceptance. "Yes, that is what you said to me. You wanted no gift, but only my return. As to why I did not come, this man here can testify I was long years in captivity myself. As soon as I was released, I began a search for you. But the trail was cold, and when I returned to my family home, it was to find an enterprise of foreigners. How could I have dreamed that among those Miss Ameera sheltered was the sister I had looked for so long?"

"Enough! There will be time for such family reminiscences elsewhere." This time Ismail leaned over the table so he could not be ignored. "Jamil, are you satisfied this woman is your sister? that I have kept my word?"

Jamil looked directly at Ismail. "You have kept your word. But you do nothing without benefit to yourself. Why have you brought her here? What is it you want of her?"

Ismail nodded at Farah. "Tell him."

Farah's hands clasped beseechingly on the table. "I have come to beg you to do what this man asks. Sign his papers. Please, Jamil, my brother, are matters of dead prophets and religious arguments of more value than your family, your sister? I have money now to begin a new life. For both of us. Only come home to me."

He should have braced himself for this the moment he'd discovered just who the burqa concealed. Had not Ismail always used Jamil's family to impel cooperation? Jamil let out a soft sigh. "Farah-jan, my heart rejoices to know my sister lives. But you do not know what you are asking. You do not know what I became after I was taken captive. I was so filled with hate and anger. Then Isa changed me, gave me new life. He is not dead but alive, the almighty Creator come to call men back to his ways and his love. Once I did not believe I had courage to declare this truth. Isa gave me the courage. And now—I cannot go back to what I was. I would give my life for you, Farah-jan. But I cannot again deny Isa."

Farah's pleading expression had turned into a stony mask. "Then it is as I have thought. The love of a brother is as much an illusion as any other love. All these years I believed you were dead, and I grieved for you. I believed that you did not keep your promise to return because you could not. But now you choose death above your sister, and that I cannot understand. I wish I had never discovered that you still live."

Farah pushed back her chair with a violent scrape. "I am finished here. I would like to go."

Prudence dictated letting her leave. Once Jamil was freed, there'd be a lifetime to clarify misunderstandings. But Jamil knew the corrosive acid of anger and hurt and bitterness too well to send his sister away with those feelings burning inside.

"You must believe how much I care! Nor is it death I have chosen, but life. You will understand one day. And we will be together again, you will see. You must have faith."

"Faith! Faith in what?" Farah scoffed. At Ismail's sharp gesture, she rose, tugging her burqa over her head.

The deputy minister leaned in close, hands on the table, to demand coldly, "A better question would be, why do you not fear, Jamil? You seem overly untroubled for a man who faces a death sentence this very night on apostasy charges."

To Jamil's uneasy mind, it seemed the black eyes were boring right through clothing and bandage to the object taped against his inner thigh. He'd striven so desperately for courage these last weeks, it hadn't occurred to Jamil there might be profit in dissembling fear and defeat.

"I have faith Isa will protect me," Jamil answered steadfastly. "And you have already learned I will not do what you wish, so I do not know why you continue to return here."

"You *will* do what I wish! You simply do not know yet what that is." Ismail studied Jamil thoughtfully. "But just in case your foolish faith includes false hopes of liberation, it is time to return you to more secure accommodations."

Ismail left without looking back, pale blue burqa at his heels. As the guard detail came into the room, the prison administrator was with them. "Bring the prisoner this way."

This time as chains were removed, Jamil no longer had to feign panicked dismay.

40

As though bracing herself for punishment, the girl shrank into a corner of the pickup cab. Ismail would not have bothered with praise if he didn't need her continued cooperation. For a little while at least. "Ibrahim was right. You are an intelligent girl and worth the afghanis I have spent on you. The tears and anger were a fine touch. A performance worthy of a Bollywood actress."

"But I failed! He would not sign your papers. If he is condemned to death now, it will be my fault!"

"If he dies, it will be Qaderi's will—and his own stubbornness." Despite her denials, Ismail had no further doubt this woman coveted her false brother's affections as much as the money he'd offered. The emotion that had invested her tale with credibility made that only too evident. But if this woman had truly believed Jamil would meekly capitulate to her pleading, she was as foolish as Jamil. Ismail's protégé had been a true believer during his first mission. He was clearly a true believer now, mistaken though his convictions might be.

Fortunately, signing that petition had never been part of Ismail's plan.

Ismail's cell phone rang as he drove the police pickup through his compound gates. As the girl sidled past lounging household guards, Ismail strode out to the orchard for privacy.

"Have you seen the latest news coverage? Our success rests now on the cutting edge of a knife blade. One more misstep, and all we have worked for since the sugar factory bombing—no, for long years before—will be swept away."

The voice on the phone ranted for interminable minutes longer before inquiring more calmly, "Is your new plan ready to be put into commission? Is your weapon sure this time? You failed me once. For your own sake, I trust you do not bring news you have failed again."

It was well the unseen speaker could not see fury tightening Ismail's face muscles. "I have done all possible. He appears to have no doubts this girl is his sister. And it seems he still possesses a taste for martyrdom. Even so, I cannot say with certainty this will be enough to compel cooperation."

"Will you excuse failure before it even comes to be? If avenging the deaths and honor of his family no longer sets fire burning in his entrails, then find out what does. And this time you will ensure he succeeds, or I will set you to take his place."

Amy didn't hurry herself to leave the AWR compound. Since Steve wouldn't be making his move until after dark, there was no reason not to carry out her purpose in this visit, especially since she didn't know if she'd have another opportunity before leaving Kabul. With no electricity, the Welayat families could no longer use the television they'd enjoyed at New Hope. But Amy had brought as her farewell gift a solar-powered radio with AM/FM and shortwave capacities. The compound residents crowded around eagerly as Amy set up the radio in a downstairs salon.

The women didn't ask about Amy's recent visitor. While female, Amy was also a foreigner, placing her in that ambiguous "third sex" permitted to mix freely with men. But the children were less reticent. "Is he not the foreign warrior who came to the other compound and gave us the baby wolf and Eid gifts? Is he your wali, Ameera-jan?"

Her wali, that authoritative male guardian who dictated a Muslim woman's life? *He'd like to think so sometimes!*

"Yes, he is the one who gave you Gorg," Amy acknowledged. But she was no longer paying attention to their continued queries. She listened with dismay to a news bulletin on the FM station she'd just tuned in.

"Do they speak of Jamil, who was your helper, Miss Ameera?" Najeeda, whose beauty was marred by missing teeth and misshaped nose, results of beatings from her husband and mother-in-law, inquired anxiously. "Will they really try him as an apostate?"

Amy quickly shifted to another station. Perhaps bringing the outside world back into this compound hadn't been so well-timed. She was able to avoid an answer because Najeeda's small son was tugging on Amy's tunic. "Ameera-jan, will you not tell us a story before you go?"

Amy had brought her flannelgraph for this very purpose. While she retrieved it from the Pajero, the women made tea and set out naan and fried cakes so that by the time they'd all settled down amid rugs and cushions, the promised story time had become a celebration. But as Amy laid out the felt figures, her mind was racing wildly.

Steve said not to call, but he needs to be warned the trial is going forward after all. Though I guess he'll find out for himself since he's in there. Either way, I can't imagine how Steve will possibly get Jamil out tonight.

Amy had chosen as appropriate to their move the story of Joshua leading his people into the Promised Land. As cheers greeted the tumbling of Jericho's walls, Amy finished, "And like Joshua, remember that no matter where you go, the almighty Creator, who loves you so much, will always be with you. When you're afraid or sad, you can pray—"

"Mees Ma-lo-ree?" An unobtrusive cough gave no indication how long Masooda had been standing in the doorway. Amy shed Gorg and two toddlers as she scrambled hastily to her feet.

"May I speak with you?" A glance shifted to Amy's audience. "Alone?"

Masooda was not smiling, and Amy's heart sank as she followed the other woman. Was the AWR leader upset over Amy's drop-in visit? or her impromptu storytelling? How had Amy let herself forget this was no longer her project? that she could no longer do whatever she chose with these women and children?

"Please forgive me if I was inappropriate," Amy began in her halting Dari as soon as they were alone in a hallway. "The children became accustomed to my stories at the other compound. But I should have asked your permission here first. And before dropping in unannounced. I didn't mean to distract them from chores and activities you had planned."

Masooda's eyebrows only rose in gentle surprise. "But you are always welcome here. Have you not loved and cared for these women and children far longer than we have? And your story was a beautiful one. To teach the children that their Creator loves them, that they must pray faithfully, how can there be any harm in that?"

Dr. Amrita's associate was a petite, dark-haired woman not much older than Amy despite two school-age daughters. Her expression softened as she looked up into the taller girl's face. "Mees Ma-lo-ree—may I call you Ameera as the children do?—I know who you are. I know the story you were telling comes from your holy book. But I am not of those who name the followers of Isa as infidels or would banish them from my country. Does not the Quran itself teach that Christians too are people of the book and worshipers of one God? What I see before me is a woman of deep faith, even if the faith you follow differs from mine. And I have seen the wealth and comfort your country holds. You have sacrificed much to come to my country and serve these women and children."

Not you too! Aloud, Amy answered, "Please believe me that what little I have done here is no sacrifice. Not compared to what you and your colleagues have gone through, standing up against the Taliban, fighting for women's rights and education."

Masooda shook her head. "But we are fighting for our own country, our own families, our own sisters and daughters. In any case, that is not why I wished to speak away from the others. You know these women. I wondered if you might name one or two with skills to help in organizing and managing the group's needs."

Yes, Farah, Amy wanted to say. If only the teenager could have seen this place. Seen for herself how far afield were her fears and accusations that Amy was abandoning her Welayat charges. *She could have been happy here. She could have found opportunity here, even further education.*

Instead Amy suggested, "Najeeda is excellent for running the kitchen. And Yalda was a farm laborer and knows gardening."

Amy ran through other possibilities before bringing up a question on her own mind. "Masooda, I've been wanting to ask. These women and children, they'll be able to stay as long as they want? I don't know if Dr. Amrita told you what's happened at New Hope—"

"You are concerned these women or their daughters may still be married off against their will?" Masooda finished gently. "You do not need to worry, Ameera. I give you my own word no one will be sent from here unless it is of their own choosing. But you must understand that life does not stay the same. These children will grow up. They will need to have proper marriages and livelihoods arranged. And there will be women who prefer to marry again and have a home of their own than to stay here with so many others. It is the way of our country, after all. Nor is it all evil. My own marriage was arranged, but I am happy enough with Arif. He is a good man who has never condemned me for bearing no sons but works with me to give his daughters a better future. So, yes, there may be more marriages here. Even arranged marriage. But not against any woman's will."

With that Amy had to be satisfied. It was in any case past time to be taking her leave. Though winter was now giving way to spring, evening still came early. Becky would be worried if Amy wasn't home before nightfall added to the perils of Kabul's rush-hour traffic. But even when Arif closed the gates behind her, Amy didn't immediately start the Pajero.

Amy's decision to leave Afghanistan had been carefully considered and sensible. She would not be here now except for Jamil's continued captivity. Certainly she could do as much or more good elsewhere on the planet. And now the one matter that held her in Afghanistan was about to be resolved. If Steve could pull off whatever he had in mind, twenty-four hours from now she'd be introducing Jamil to a whole new and free world.

So why should the thought of sliding behind that steering wheel, driving into Kabul to buy a ticket out of Afghan airspace, bring such an ache to her throat?

I know I have to leave. And for Jamil, it's his only hope of a future. But now that it's time, I can admit I don't want to walk away. Not like this, slinking off into the night. Even if—when—Jamil is safely over the border, it will still seem a defeat because they'll have won. Qaderi and all the others like him. They'll have silenced Jamil even as they'll have silenced any further talk of religious freedom in Afghanistan. No matter who wins this election, the Afghan people can forget any hope for real freedom and democracy.

Leaving knapsack and flannelgraph case inside the Pajero, Amy walked along the mud-brick wall to the corner where she'd looked out over the plateau earlier with Steve. To the west, Kabul's smog blanket was tinged with glorious streamers of red and orange flame. But to the east, the first stars had emerged above a distant mountain range. And straight ahead, where darkening twilight now laid long shadows across the parched barrenness of the plateau itself, a new constellation blinked into being.

Amy knew it was only Pul-e-Charki's security lighting turned on for the night. But at this distance against the growing dusk, those sparkling dots looked as though they'd spilled to earth from the vast expanse overhead. The fading sunset, the glimmer of stars, the triangular silhouettes of mountain peaks, even the sharp angles of Pul-e-Charki's walls and towers outlined in twinkling luminosity, interwove a stark beauty, as though nightfall were drawing a veil over dirt and pollution and human misery and despair.

What is it you are seeking to remind me of here, Father God? That you've created no place on this planet that does not hold your beauty? that whatever mess we humans have made of that beauty, your love and majesty and power are great enough to cover it? that Qaderi and the others really haven't won because in the end you will have the last word?

41

Was it possible to hate and love at the same time?

Or rather to long for the illusion of love while hating the perpetrators of its deception?

The sun had dropped below the mountains by the time Ismail's police pickup pulled out of Pul-e-Charki's front gate. Retreating past the compound sentries, then up three flights of stairs, Farah had just reached the refuge of her sleeping quarters when the compound's generator rumbled to life. Tossing aside her burqa, Farah discovered with as much fury as dismay that her hands were shaking as she fumbled with the single lamp she'd been supplied.

Farah had been sure she'd failed when Jamil asked that last unexpected question. If she answered truthfully, Ismail would immediately know of her deception. As it was, though she'd remained within the information Ismail had given her, Farah had feared the strength of her emotions had already betrayed her. But though Farah had seen renewed suspicion in Jamil's dark eyes, both men in the end had seemed to accept her dissembling.

Only for Farah to fail again when her brother did not even hesitate to reject her plea. *He does not love me. Though he believes me to be his sister, he does not care that he leaves me alone in this world.*

Would Ismail still pay Farah as he'd promised? Even if he did not, she was now eager to be gone from this place. The afghanis she'd received would be the start of a new life. There was nothing more she could do here. *I will leave with dawn's light. But where will I go?*

Farah had been relieved when Ismail proved calm, even magnanimous, at her failure. Once inside his own walls, he'd headed off to some other part of the compound. So Farah wasn't prepared for her door to slam open just as she'd managed to turn on the lamp. Her employer entered the room with angry strides.

"So now I am to be threatened for your failure? How does it feel that you cannot make a man care for you? Not as a woman, nor even as a sister. What good are you to me if you cannot fulfill the use for which you were brought here? What more can be done to move a man who cares neither for his family nor his faith nor his own life?"

If he was trying to wound Farah with his insults, she was past caring for such things. Instead Farah kept her eyes lowered as she answered carefully, "If Jamil does not love his sister, what is it to me? I have done what I was hired to do. If I am so useless, just pay me, and let me go."

Bitterness welling up inside her, Farah raised her head to add resentfully, "There is only one person I know who might persuade Jamil to do as you ask. And that is Miss Ameera, for whom Jamil cares as he does not his sister, nor even his own life, I think. Was it not to please her that Jamil embraced these teachings that now endanger his life? If she begged him, told Jamil her stories of Isa are no more than mere stories, perhaps he would change his statement to please her. But not for a sister's pleading nor any other."

Ismail stopped his irate pacing and looked at Farah contemplatively. "Perhaps you are not so useless. It is an excellent thought. I had forgotten you owe her a grudge as well as I. If this Ameera is the lever that can move Jamil, she must be brought here to do so."

Farah stared at him. "I did not mean that. She will not come at your asking. And if she did, she would not do as you ask. She believes in this Isa as sincerely as does Jamil."

Ismail sighed. "When will imbeciles stop questioning my capabilities? In any case, it is not I who will bring her here, but you."

"I?" Farah's eyes widened. "How am I to bring her here either? And if she came, what good would it do? I have already told you she will not help you change Jamil's mind."

"That is not your concern," Ismail answered coldly. "As to how, I possess her cell phone number. You will call her and ask her to come to you."

"No!" Now Farah's eyes were narrowed with suspicion, and she raised her chin defiantly. "I have done everything you asked of me. And yes, I have been angry with Miss Ameera. But if she, like all others, did not keep her promises, she was kind to me. I do not know what you wish with her, but I will not help you bring her here with a lie. Nor do I wish to stay here any longer myself. If you will not pay me my money, then I will go without it."

"You will go nowhere until I find no further use for your services," Ismail intoned. "And it would seem I have been too accommodating with you. Let me show you why you will take my phone and beg your Ms. Mallory to come to you."

Farah's employer was already striding to the door. It clicked shut behind him. Sitting rigidly on the edge of the bed, Farah listened to a murmur of male voices in the hall. Then the door opened again. But this time it was not Ismail who strolled into the room.

The last ribbon of red and orange had faded to paling green. A cold wind tugged at Amy's winter cloak, so she headed reluctantly at last to the Pajero.

She heard her phone ringing even before she opened the car door. This was far too soon for any call from Steve to be good news. Becky, perhaps, wondering why Amy wasn't back? Or even Kareem? Steve and Amy had told the Afghan journalist nothing of their plans, though Amy had every intention of letting Kareem know his friend was safe once Jamil was beyond reach of pursuit.

The voice was female, but not Becky's, its frantic speech in Dari and so distraught Amy didn't at first recognize it. "Miss Ameera, is this you? Please, I need you. You must come and help me."

"Who is this?" Amy demanded sharply.

"It is I—Farah. Have you forgotten me already?"

"Farah! Of course I have not forgotten you. Where are you? What's wrong?"

The only answer was quick breathing, stifled sobs.

Amy said urgently, "Farah-jan, Soraya told me you'd left New Hope to go to family members who'd been looking for you all these years. That Deputy Minister Ismail himself had come to escort you and that you had gone willingly. They gave me a note they said was from you. Are you not then with your family? Or—have they been unkind to you? Are they trying to force you into marriage? Is that it?"

More quick breathing. "I am not yet with family as I was promised. This Ismail who took me away brought me to a property of his own. But there are no women with me, only men. Many men."

"Have they—hurt you?" Amy demanded sharply.

"Not yet, but I am afraid of them. Please, Ameera-jan, Ismail has told me he will send a car to New Hope to bring you to me. I told him you would not come, that you do not care about me anymore. But I—I need you. Will you not come to me?"

That Farah's panic was genuine, Amy could hear in the terrified timbre of her plea, and with all Amy knew of Farah's past, she could understand why such a situation as she'd described would be cause for hysteria, even if Farah was unharmed.

"Farah, I hope you will believe me that I care for you very much. I'm not at New Hope anymore nor anywhere close. But if you can explain where you are, I will see what I can do to get help and come for you."

Whatever Steve's estimation of her foolhardiness, Amy wasn't so reckless as to venture unaccompanied into a household of Afghan men. Or get into a strange car either, even at the bidding of a deputy minister. *But I know Becky will come with me. Maybe some male coworkers too.*

Then an incredible thought rose to Amy's mind. She left the Pajero to walk back to where she could see across the plateau. Off to Amy's left, where high, white walls enclosed Deputy Minister Ismail's luxurious residence, a few dots of light along the perimeter indicated a generator. Above the wall, the compound's square, three-story villa looked dark, as though deserted. But for one top-floor balcony, where a yellow glow leaked through closed drapes or shutters.

"You said the property where you're staying belongs to Deputy Minister Ismail. You mean, in Kabul, where he works?"

"No, no, it is far outside the city. A big house with high walls and a garden and trees. He does not stay here, only his guards."

"Have you been able to see what is beyond the walls? a big fortress, perhaps, with stone walls and towers?"

"You mean, Pul-e-Charki." Farah was beginning to sound calmer now. "Yes, I can see it from the balcony of my sleeping quarters. How could you know?"

"Because if you're where I think you are, then I'm only a short distance away." Amy's own calmness belied a mounting excitement. "Farah-jan, I want you to do something. You said your room has a balcony. If you can, step out onto it."

Across the open plateau, that yellow seepage of light became a bright rectangle. A silhouette appeared briefly against it before the brightness winked out again. Farah's voice now held both hope and incredulity. "Did you see me? Are you truly nearby?"

"Yes, I did, and yes, I am. If you can believe it, the new home to which the New Hope women and children have moved is only across the fields from where you are staying. Close enough for you to walk to us, if you can get outside the gates. Can you do that?"

"No, the guards will never let me outside, not without Ismail's permission. And how would I ever find you? I don't know which direction to go."

The panic now back in Farah's voice was enough to push Amy into an abrupt decision. "Then I'll come to you. Look, Farah, you told me once how you went over a compound wall to escape. Do you think you could do that again, if you can't get out the gate?"

An oddly muffled silence followed, as though she'd perhaps put her hand over the receiver. Somewhere in the background, Amy detected an agitated murmuring. Then Farah's voice came back. "Ameera, are you there?"

"Yes. Are you not alone?" Amy asked sharply. "I heard voices. Is someone with you who might overhear?"

"No, no, it is the guards. They are watching television in the hallway. I can do as you ask. Below my balcony is another, then a fruit orchard. The branches reach the wall, and there is much clothing here from which

I can tie a rope. It is dark out now, and they will not be looking for it. They will not believe I possess the courage."

A tinge of defiance had ameliorated Farah's earlier hysteria. Amy answered encouragingly, "Good. I'll come over behind the compound where your balcony is closest to the wall. Wear something dark, and we'll simply walk back here. You'll be safe because the guards won't know you have a refuge to which you can escape."

"And if they do discover us?"

"We'll deal with that if it proves necessary. But you are not a prisoner or a possession, Farah-jan. Those guards have no right to keep you against your will if you want to leave. There are reasons why I would—well, prefer to do this quietly if we can. But if necessary, I'll call up Deputy Minister Ismail myself. I've dealt with him before regarding matters of the New Hope compound. I can also call Dr. Amrita, who is now in charge of the Welayat project. You have every right to rejoin the other women if you choose."

Questions still abounded in Amy's mind. What had precipitated Farah's very evident panic now after all these days she'd been gone? And why was Farah still in Ismail's custody instead of delivered to these family members?

But those questions could wait. Steve said to go nowhere without backup or letting him know. But he could never have anticipated this situation.

Amy debated taking the Pajero. But headlights would give away her approach, while finding the right dirt tracks in the dark would save little time over a walk across the fields. For such a short expedition, she left behind her knapsack, heavy with notebook computer, first aid kit, food and water, and other essentials. But she slid her cell phone into a pocket, though not before setting it to a quiet vibrate.

She hadn't added a flashlight, as revealing as headlights on this open plain. But before she'd covered a hundred meters, Amy was regretting its absence. Twilight had darkened to full night, the moon not yet risen, so only a jeweled splash across black velvet of star patterns offered faint illumination. The plateau proved less flat than it looked; irrigation canals and low embankments divided crop plots, catching Amy off guard, so that she tripped repeatedly, every thud or rattle of stones and dirt worryingly loud against the night's silence.

But Amy reached the rear compound wall without sound or light from inside indicating any alarm had been raised. The perimeter seemed poorly lit, a floodlight at each corner. Another high above on the parapet of the villa itself.

Nor did Amy see any sign of the mujahedeen types she'd glimpsed patrolling balconies during daylight hours. With their employer away, perhaps they'd all retreated to that television Farah had mentioned. Which boded well for finding the younger girl awaiting her.

Amy's winter cloak and headscarf were dark gray, rendering her invisible at any distance, and by the time she'd edged close to where tree branches thrust out above the wall, her racing heart had slowed to something approaching normal. Here were no floodlights, but the reflection of starlight on white paint gleamed palely. Enough for Amy to spot a human shape wrapped in dark cloak crouched at the base of the wall.

With relief, Amy stepped forward to call in a soft whisper, "Farah, I'm over here!"

When the shadow didn't rise, Amy took another step forward. "Farah-jan?"

The skittering of a displaced stone was her only warning. Amy whirled around as two shadows rose from where they'd lain hidden. She caught a glint of teeth, heard a low, satisfied chuckle, before a blanket or cloak enveloped her like a net. The material filled her mouth, bound her limbs tight so that she could neither scream nor move nor even breathe.

Amy was slipping into unconsciousness when the suffocating material was yanked away, and she could both breathe and see again. The cloaked shape was now rising, taller and broader than Amy would have expected.

"I am pleased you have chosen to join us, Ms. Mallory," Deputy Minister Ismail said smoothly, even amiably. "As you can see, we have been expecting you."

42

The abandoned cellblock that was Steve's usual detour had not been an object of today's assault. Steve ducked inside before consulting on his cell phone screen. This wasn't his regular iPhone, but a similar model with an unregistered local number. If anything went wrong, Steve wasn't about to have on his person a phone linked to Condor Security, even to Amy herself.

Since Steve's last check, the tracking signal had moved from the court-yard back into a cellblock, welcome confirmation Jamil was not one of that mound of bodies he'd spied. Losing his security pass on top of Qaderi's announcement had cut Steve's operational window to a minimum. But if all went well, he wouldn't need much time. Among other counterfeit documents the sports bag held was an order for prisoner transfer. Shift-ing Jamil for trial would offer an even better rationale than the story he'd originally cooked up. Another discreet detour into this ruined corridor would leave Jamil's prison rags along with Steve's own gear well-buried under the rubble. By which time security would be too busy with VIPs and media arriving for the trial to focus on two off-duty guards headed out the gate.

Wait a minute! Steve broke off strategy planning as he took a closer look at the cell phone screen. The spoke now registering Jamil's location wasn't as expected within regular prisoner accommodations, but the other derelict cellblock on the opposite side of the high security wing. Since the other abandoned wing was even more dilapidated than this one with nothing beyond it but a rear corner of the perimeter, Steve had noted one difference in the other abandoned wing. A functional steel door securing its entrance from the octagonal main courtyard.

Why would an inmate be shifted from general prisoner accommodations to a derelict shell? Unless . . .

The prisoners who rated special accommodations from Afghanistan's foreign allies were largely al-Qaeda and opium cartel types. But the Afghans must have their own occasional "special" detainee whose offenses held no interest to Steve's own embassy.

If I wanted to maintain a discreet "isolation wing" where I wouldn't have to worry about my infidel allies' squeamishness when it comes to interrogation techniques, what better than a supposedly vacant and sealed-off cellblock?

"Search her."

Rough hands probed Amy with an insolent thoroughness more terrifying than her struggle for air. The dye applied for her last Pul-e-Charki visit had been only a temporary wash, and as a sharp tug jerked her headscarf away, appreciative hisses greeted the silvery glint of flaxen hair in starlight. One captor tossed her cell phone to Ismail.

By the time they were finished, Amy was too shaken to offer rebellion as she followed Ismail through a narrow gate. Its camouflage of white paint explained why Amy hadn't noticed it earlier. A graveled path was succeeded by dark verandas and hallways, then a wide, marbled staircase lit sparsely by a dangling lightbulb at each landing. The two guards who'd seized Amy stayed so close on her heels that every time she slowed, their bodies as well as weapons jostled against her. Once a hand groped again so audaciously, Amy whirled on the stairs to slap it away. Only Ismail's sharp order inserted several steps between Amy and her assailants.

The top landing opened onto a hallway where a low table held remains of a meal and a hookah. Amy saw no sign of the TV Farah had mentioned. The deputy minister's quick strides led to a sumptuous living suite. Soft, yellow light from a lamp and slotted balcony shutters suggested this was the room from which Farah had signaled.

The room also held more armed men. But Amy had little time to take all this in before a female shape threw herself into Amy's arms. "Miss Ameera, I am so sorry! But he said he would give me to the guards if you did not come. I was so afraid! But now that you are here, he will let us both go if you will only do what is asked of you. Oh, Ameera-jan, I hope you can forgive me."

"He?" Wrapping her arms tight around the sobbing girl, Amy turned her head to stare at Ismail. Her assumption upon the deputy minister's materialization was simply that Farah had been discovered in her escape attempt. Still, Amy hadn't lost sight that Ismail knew of her original masquerade with the Red Cross delegation. And Jamil had told Amy it was Ismail who'd coached him on how to placate his own captors. As Khalid's deputy, Ismail certainly had a stake in defusing the problem Jamil had become.

If so, could Farah's departure with Ismail so immediately after Jamil's original trial be less happenstance than Amy had been led to believe? Though what possible benefit could the deputy minister gain by lying to Farah and bringing her here?

Me! Amy recognized with sudden dismayed clarity. *I'd never have come here on my own. But I didn't even hesitate when Farah said she needed me.*

As to why Ismail should wait all these days, that at least made sense. The deputy minister would have been deterred by the same turn of events that had delayed Steve and Amy's own plans. The prison uprising. But Jamil was no longer inaccessible, his trial back on for this evening. *Does Ismail think that by bringing me here, holding me hostage, he can somehow convince Jamil to change his position this time around?*

Picking through a minefield of possible reactions, she asked quietly, "Why have you brought me here? What is it you want? This girl is supposed to be under your protection! How can you let your men torment her like this? They have her terrified!" *And me too!*

By unforgiving lamplight, Amy's two captors and their companions were an unprepossessing lot. While ranging several decades in age, all showed marks of hard living. Embedded shrapnel bits pocked one face while a jagged scar slashing another had turned an eye milky with blindness. A hand gripping an AK-47 barrel lacked two fingers. Rotted and missing teeth were on full display because all were grinning widely, their greedy gaze on the two women both repellent and alarming.

But Ismail only looked bored. Strolling across the carpet, he yanked Farah away from Amy's embrace. "Do not let the tears fool you. This woman is an accomplished liar. As to what I wish, why not ask her? Is it not at her suggestion that you are here? Now we will see if Jamil's infidel lover will prove more effective than his sister in prompting cooperation."

As Amy stiffened incredulously, Ismail's sneer revealed his own perfect white teeth. "Oh yes, you are not the only 'sister' Jamil has had to visit him in Pul-e-Charki. Did you think this woman was brought here against her will? On the contrary, she is here because she has accepted my generous offer of employment. You see, your Farah bears a close resemblance to Jamil's own family. Enough to convince him she is the sister he has not seen since she was a small child. Unfortunately it appears Jamil cares little what should become of a mere female member of his family. But Farah assures me it will be otherwise with his infidel lover, Ms. Mallory."

Ismail's tone held contempt. So did his gesture toward Farah. "It would seem this girl bears you a great grudge, or simply wishes you gone to have this man herself, for she was quick to offer up your name."

So Amy had been right about Ismail's role in this. At least he'd shown no awareness of Amy's other activities. But Farah? Amy turned to the younger girl, hoping to find baffled incomprehension. But the expression she saw on Farah's face, half shame, half defiance, roiled her stomach. "Is any of this true, what he's saying, Farah?"

Farah clutched at Amy's arm to say pleadingly, "Ameera-jan, all he asks is that you too beg Jamil to deny he is an Isa follower or apostate. They do not even care if it is true, only that he confess before the cameras. I have pleaded with Jamil to give up this quest for martyrdom. But if he does not care enough for his own sister to do so small a thing, it is easy to see he cares for you more than all else, even his own life. If you assure him you do not wish his allegiance to your foreign religion at the price of his death, will he not listen? And once he does as they ask, we will both be free to leave this place and Jamil as well. If you care at all for Jamil in turn, you cannot refuse!"

Even with the evidence ringing in her ears, Amy was still struggling to assimilate the appalling fact that Farah had lied to her, had deliberately led her into this trap. But she shook her head decisively.

"Farah, I don't know what this man has told you. But you seem to believe Jamil became an Isa follower only to please me. That isn't so, though it is true that I too follow Isa. I could not ask Jamil to lie about his faith, not to please me or to save his own skin. And if Deputy Minister Ismail knows Jamil at all, he is well aware it would be no use. So if you really think this man has brought me here, or you either, just to talk to Jamil, then it is you who has been deceived."

Ismail looked more amused than angry. "The infidel woman speaks truth. It is not your words I require, only your bodies."

At Farah's sharp cry, the deputy minister let out a bark of harsh laughter. "Alive, of course. The matter is quite simple. My men have been in this place without women for a long time. Either Jamil does as I command, or his sister and infidel lover will be given to my men as bonus for their loyal service. I trust you are not so foolish as to believe I will not do as I say."

Farah was crying again, hysterically, her headscarf pulled across her face to muffle her sobs. Amy dredged up the only defense that came to mind.

"Do you really think you can just make me disappear, that people won't come looking for me here if I don't come home? This isn't Taliban days that a government official can kidnap an American citizen and not be held to account. Look, if you'll just let us walk away—"

Crack! The slap was hard enough to knock Amy off her feet, to fill her mouth with blood where her teeth had been driven into her lower lip. Ismail bent low so that Amy could feel saliva landing on her face as he spat out venomously, "I am *sick* of foreigners telling the Afghan people what we can or cannot do. You do not rule our country. You do not tell us which of Allah's sacred laws we shall or shall not require our citizens to obey."

Cruel fingers in Amy's hair dragged her to a sitting position, and she could hear Farah's frightened whimpering over Ismail's furious invective. "Above all, I am sick of their women who speak as though they are as good as men and encourage our own women to rebel against proper authority. You especially, Ms. Mallory. You have interfered enough in my business, in my country. And if you are right that your lover will not cooperate to save your pale, soft skin, it will be my pleasure to see your arrogance trampled into the dust. Or perhaps even if he does. Nor am I impressed by your lies that others know you are here. You would not have come alone and on foot in the dark if you wished others to know of your scheme to steal away this woman."

Amy stared into rage-engorged features only because those merciless fingers in her hair forced her head back. In the last half hour, she'd been kidnapped, fondled, punched. But only now was she completely terrified, more terrified than she'd ever been in her life, more terrified than she'd dreamed she was capable, her breath coming quick and shallow, her bitten lip stinging and salty from tears pouring down her cheeks.

Amy had felt she was beginning to comprehend what it was like to be an Afghan woman. The frustration of stumbling along in a burqa. Having to snatch up a scarf at every approach of men. Dealing through male counterparts to get anything done. The segregation and confinement.

While pitying, she'd even questioned why Afghan women didn't stand up more for themselves, join together and assert their rights. In their place, would she cower or retreat into invisibility just to survive? Or would she show the spunk Farah had once demonstrated in running away, useless though that had proved?

In reality, Amy had never doubted she'd be among those who fought back. A Dr. Amrita or Masooda, not the cowed, defeated victims too many of the Welayat women were by the time Amy met them.

Ismail's single blow had changed Amy's entire perspective. This was what it meant to be an Afghan woman! Not Dr. Amrita, raised in an enlightened home, attending medical school at a time when few Afghan males knew how to read and write. But a rank-and-file female who lived every moment knowing that her life and even her body were under absolute control of her household males. That she'd no say in either her present or her future. That the smallest rebellion could mean a beating or worse.

Above all, that as a woman there was no redress. Even when such control proved relatively benign like Masooda's husband and undoubtedly many such households across Afghanistan, it was still at the mercy and whim of men.

Yanking Amy painfully onto her feet, Ismail shoved her own cell phone into her face. "Your lover wishes to hear your voice. You will tell him where you are and what is to become of you if he does not follow my commands!"

"Ameera?"

Any hope Ismail was lying evaporated as Amy recognized the demand. Either Steve had not yet reached Jamil, or he too had failed. Amy took the cell phone with fingers that were icy and trembling.

I can't let Jamil know how much trouble I'm in. He has to be free to go with Steve if—no, when he comes! But I'm so afraid! Afraid that I'll break down and beg Jamil to cooperate just to get away from here! And that would be worse than anything these men can do to me!

Yet Jamil too had been terrified. In the end, he'd told Amy, Isa himself had given him courage and words. Amy closed her eyes for a brief instant against the hate-filled glare before her. *Father God, I've messed everything up, maybe even Jamil's chance to escape. But help me be strong now for Farah as well as myself. Give me the courage you gave Jamil in that courtroom.*

Straightening, she took a step away to say quietly into the phone, "Jamil, I'm fine. I'm here with Farah and Ismail. Ismail knows I came to see you with the Red Cross team."

Would Jamil understand her mention of the humanitarian delegation signified Ismail had shown no knowledge of her more recent visit? and therefore of neither the tracking device nor Steve Wilson's plans to rescue Jamil?

Amy switched to swift English. "Jamil, they want me to ask you to cooperate. But don't listen to them. Just . . . just stick to your own plans. Once everything's over and they have no more use for us, they'll let Farah and me go. I am sure of that!"

Another stinging blow. Ismail snatched the phone from Amy's hand. "You think I do not understand your language? No matter, the prisoner's 'sister' here will explain instead what you can both expect, should he be foolish enough to listen to you."

But Farah's eyes had been on Amy as she spoke, fear warring with disbelief and a dawning respect. Now, as though taking direction from Amy's own rebellion, she shook her head at the phone Ismail was holding out.

The deputy minister's show of teeth was savage. "It appears the girl needs another lesson in obedience. Hassan!"

The guard who stepped forward was one of those who'd searched Amy, but this time, hard, probing hands were making no security check, and Amy could comprehend fully Farah's terror and hysteria when she'd called. Defiance gave way to the desolate, grief-stricken sobbing of an abandoned child, and Amy saw the exact moment Farah's eyes rolled back whitely in their sockets. Fury burning away her own terror, Amy thrust herself between the Afghan girl and her assailant. "No, no, leave her alone! I . . . I'll speak to Jamil again. Only leave her alone!"

"That won't be necessary." Ismail held up the cell phone with a satisfied sneer. "I think he has heard enough."

But to Amy's surprise, Farah suddenly stepped away from Amy's arms. Tears still ran down her cheeks, and she was shaking uncontrollably. But she raised her head proudly. "No, I wish to speak to my brother."

Taking the phone from Ismail's unresisting grasp, she spoke as swiftly as Amy had earlier. "Jamil, you asked what gift you sent me that last Eid. It was bangles. Red and gold and blue and orange that sparkled like stars in the sky. Beautiful enough for the dowry of any princess."

43

Farah could hear in Ismail's sucked-in breath immediate comprehension. A slap rocked her head back in an explosion of pain as the deputy minister snatched away the cell phone.

"So you are more accomplished a liar than I believed! Be sure you will pay for this upon my return."

Into the phone he snapped, "I am on my way. While you wait, I suggest you meditate on the image of other men's hands enjoying the soft, unspoiled flesh of your women."

The deputy minister was already striding from the room. As a snap of his fingers drew the guards after him, Farah sank shakily onto the side of the large, brass bed. Her body still trembled with revulsion at the guard's assault. And her astonishment at Ameera's intervention.

Farah had seen the terrible disappointment in the foreign woman's eyes. Knew Ameera believed Farah to have betrayed her. Yet still she'd sprung to Farah's defense like a snow leopard defending its young.

And suddenly in turn it had seemed urgent for Farah to spill forth truth at last. To banish that final vestige of suspicion she'd seen in Jamil's eyes. But in so doing she'd now lost her one protection.

Ameera didn't rush to Farah's side when the door slammed shut, but into the bathroom. She emerged with a dampened washcloth pressed to the cut in her lip. Seating herself beside Farah, she used another to gently wipe Farah's tear-drenched face. Farah hadn't even realized Ismail's blow had split open her own cheek until the washcloth came away scarlet.

Only when she'd finished did Ameera say evenly, "Farah-jan, I don't know what happened just there with Ismail or . . . or any of this. But I'm trying to understand. I can see why you lied to me on the phone. Those men threatened you, and I don't blame you for being afraid to disobey. But how you could be working for this man, pretending to Jamil you are his sister, that I don't understand. If you only knew how much it means to Jamil to find his real sister, how hard he has searched for her. To let him believe he has found you—her—it's cruel! I . . . I believed you cared for Jamil. Never would I have considered you capable of doing this to him. Or—or to me!"

As the foreign woman dropped damp washcloths into her lap, deep pools of sorrow brimmed brown-green eyes. "Farah-jan, do you truly hate me so much?"

Farah cried out instantly, "No, no, Ameera-jan, you must not believe I hate you. It is true I was angry because you did not care about me anymore, because you were sending me away."

"But that isn't true. In fact, I'd asked Mr. Duane to allow you to stay on as my assistant. I was going to tell you about it the very day you left."

Farah waved away the interruption. "It does not matter now. And there is no reason why you should care for me, I have come to understand. I am not your sister nor your daughter. But Jamil truly is my brother. And now Ismail knows it is so."

Pulling out the photos still tucked into her tunic, Farah laid them out as she explained. By the time she'd finished, the sorrow and disappointment in Ameera's eyes had given way to amazed belief. "You never told Ismail when you realized Jamil was your brother? Why not?"

"I did not trust him. He thought holding Jamil's sister would give him power over my brother. Because he needed me to convince Jamil that I was this sister, he could not treat me unkindly. But if he knew Jamil truly was my brother, it would give him power over *me*. So I let him believe I did not care what became of Jamil, that I was following his commands only for the money."

Farah retrieved the pictures, scorn edging her voice. "Ismail is too arrogant to consider he was being fooled in turn. So when I forgot and spoke to Jamil as a sister truly would, Ismail simply believed he had taught me well. Then Jamil asked if I remembered the gift he had sent me for Eid, the last I ever received from him. I could not answer truthfully, or Ismail would know who I was. But I could see my answer had made Jamil suspicious again that I was not his sister."

"The bangles!"

"Yes, I could not bear any longer to let Jamil believe I had lied to him. Though it was a foolish risk since it does not matter if I have convinced Jamil or not." Farah had withdrawn deep enough onto the bed to sit with her legs drawn up, arms wrapped around them. She dropped her face against her knees to add with muffled voice, "I loved my brother. I was a child; I believed he loved me in turn. He called me his princess. He said he would always come back. When he became a doctor, and I was old enough, I was to live with him until he found me a prince for a husband. If he did not keep those promises, I believed it was because the dead cannot keep a promise. But now I know he did not truly love me."

Farah raised her head again, defiance and bitterness mixing with her shame as she admitted, "That is why I told Ismail of you. I was so angry that Jamil did not care what should become of me. And I knew Jamil cared for you as he did not for me. But I did not know Ismail would take you captive. When he told me to call you, I said no. Only he brought his mujahedeen into this room, and they—they touched me! They told me all the things they would do if Ismail gave me to them. And they laughed as they did so! Because I am a coward, I surrendered. I hoped you would not answer my call. That you had even gone back to your own country, where Ismail could not send a car for you. Who could have foreseen you were so close? Even then I could have warned you, but I was so afraid! I do not blame you if you never forgive me."

Farah dropped her face back onto her arms. She did not want the weakness of tears again. But though she fought it, the sobs were shaking her shoulders, dampness wetting the sleeve under her face so that she could taste salt on her lips. She would not speak. She could not ask of this foreign woman, in whom she'd once foolishly deposited the trust and affection—yes, and love—pent up inside since her mother's death, the question that had burned hot and unanswered in her breast for so long. But the words would not stay between her teeth.

"What is wrong with me that no one can love me? Even your Isa walked away. Is all love such an illusion? Or is it only I who am so stupid and ugly and useless and cowardly as to be unworthy of love?"

Amy settled herself on the brass bedstead, where she could wrap both arms around Farah's huddled frame. Such tragedy and pain this child had faced in her short life, and always with head held defiantly high. This current masquerade with Ismail had taken enterprise and brains as well as courage. The Afghan girl was in fact every bit as beautiful and intelligent and valiant as any heroine in the Arabian Nights tales that Afghan children grew up hearing.

And yet she could think herself unlovable!

Amy tenderly smoothed brown curls away from the buried face. "Farah-jan, of course I forgive you completely. I can't imagine what I'd do, how terrified I'd be in your place. There was no shame in doing what you had to do to keep from being raped. And you're no coward, that you've proven again and again. Coming here to help Jamil, for one. In any case, we're here together now and safe. Whatever happens at Pul-e-Charki, Ismail will have no use for us after tonight. He will let us go."

Amy wished her raging thoughts held as much conviction as her words. If only she knew what was happening over there at Pul-e-Charki. Steve was imminently resourceful, so even if he was delayed, he might now be carrying out some Plan B. But with each passing moment, the odds of getting Jamil out before prison personnel showed up to escort him to his trial were growing slim.

Firmly Amy said, "No, I'm glad you called me. I'd rather be here than know you were alone with those terrible men."

Farah raised her head from her arms. "I am glad too you are here with me, Ameera-jan. But you are wrong to say you do not know what you would do. For did you not refuse to beg Jamil? Did you not instead tell Jamil he must do what is right no matter what happens to you? Why could I not show such courage?"

The younger girl looked so woebegone that Amy tugged the tousled brown head against her shoulder as she assured tenderly, "But I was not alone as you were. I had you beside me. And Isa was with me too. I prayed he would give me courage as he did to Jamil when he stood before his judges, and Isa did. He is not an illusion, Farah, any more than love is an illusion. Speaking of which, what did you mean by Isa walking away from you?"

When Farah had described haltingly her dreams, Amy shook her head. "Oh, Farah, Jamil and Isa and I walking away—that was just a bad dream. I can see with all you've been through why such a nightmare might come to you. But what your dreams showed you of Isa's love is real. And yes, it's true human love can turn out to be an illusion when people are greedy and selfish and just plain evil. I'm afraid you've encountered more than your share of such people. But you are not only so lovable, you are loved! From what you've told me, I don't think you can question how much your mother loved you, enough to do everything she could to keep you safe. And I love you. It is why I didn't hesitate to come here tonight when I knew you needed me.

"But, Farah-jan, you must believe Jamil loves you too. He told me once how he'd never given up trying to find you and your mother. If you think he wouldn't give his life for you, then you are wrong. But to deny his faith in Isa, even to be with you again, that he cannot do. And I for one wouldn't wish him to, not for my own life. Let me try to explain to you why. It's time you knew exactly what happened that day the bomb went off at New Hope."

Someday when they were far from this place, it would be Jamil's prerogative to tell his sister the full story of all that had happened since they'd been separated. But Amy could share the horrors and pain, the actions and motivations, that Jamil had shared with her. As she did so, she could see that Farah had a far clearer visualization than Amy of the grimness Jamil's lost years held. She looked fiercely approving rather than dismayed at Jamil's suicide mission.

"I wish that he had succeeded! Though not that he should be dead, of course."

"But don't you see that if Jamil was willing to offer his own life out of hate, he could not be less willing to do so out of love? Love for Isa Masih, who changed his heart and life. Love for you. Love for the people of Afghanistan. That he isn't willing to do as Ismail wishes, as the mullahs demand, does not show how little he cares about you, but how much love is in his heart. Do you understand now?"

"Not really." Farah shrugged. "But if Jamil could give up killing Khalid, this Isa must truly have great power to change hearts."

"He is King of kings, the almighty Creator come to earth. He made you, Farah-jan, the wonderful, beautiful person you are. And that makes you a princess, just as your brother told you. Now let us not cry anymore over what is past. Do you know of any way we might get out of this room and house?"

Farah shook her head. "There are guards always below the balcony and in the halls even at night. At least six that I have counted."

"In that case, we might as well make ourselves comfortable." Amy heaped up cushions sofa-style against the headboard, then shook out the bed's soft down comforter.

As the two girls huddled together under the blanket, Farah looked at Amy wonderingly. "Are you not afraid, Ameera-jan? for Jamil's life if not your own and mine? Especially if, as you say, his faith and courage are too great to ever repudiate your Isa."

"I am, a little. But—" Amy stopped. She'd have liked to tell Farah why she was not afraid for Jamil. That a security contractor named Steve Wilson was on the job, so no matter what happened in the trial, Jamil would eventually be freed and safe. But this wasn't Amy's classified information to divulge.

There was another way to share her confidence. "Isa will protect Jamil and bring about his liberation. And us as well."

"That is what Jamil told me," Farah admitted, then added hesitantly, "I was thinking, if we must wait, I would like to hear again the story of Isa. Would you tell it to me?"

"I'll do my best, though I don't know the words well in Dari."

"Then we will tell it together." At Amy's surprised glance, Farah shrugged. "Have I not heard it before? I even told it once to the women. Where I forget, you can tell me."

Farah rested her head against Amy's shoulder as she began, "This is how the birth of Isa Masih took place. His mother, Maryam, was pledged to be married to Yousef, but before they came together, she was found to be with child."

Could the greatest story ever told sound more beautiful than from the lips of an Afghan orphan girl? Amy closed her eyes as the melodious cadence of Farah's Dari rose and fell against her ear.

Father God, thank you that at this moment we are unhurt, fed, and warm. Thank you those guards are on the far side of that door. And whatever is happening right now with Steve and Jamil, please watch over them. In the name of Isa Masih, Jesus Christ, Emmanuel, God with us.

44

When Steve exited the abandoned corridor, he was dressed in the gray-blue uniform of a Pul-e-Charki guard. The sports bag slung over a shoulder was one of the cheap Asian imports prison personnel routinely used. As he'd timed, night had fallen, the evening shift change due to get under way. Uniforms still swarmed thick, and the nighttime security lighting offered bright illumination. But neither floodlights nor guards had been lavished on the empty space between octagonal fortress and the interior wall dividing prisoner accommodations from the administrative sector. Steve kept to deep shadows when walking past the rear exit of the high-security wing, whose outside sentry at least might recognize his face under the billed cap.

But the derelict wing beyond lay in darkness with no guards in sight beyond roving patrols on rooftops and catwalks. From Steve's vantage, it was easy to see why this particular spoke was not restored to use. This segment of "wheel rim" had sustained a direct missile hit, its roof collapsed into upper floors. But as Steve had noted in the octagonal central courtyard, the rear entrance to this wing boasted a solid metal door of much later date than the bombardment it had suffered.

Steve carried a certain multipurpose tool no larger than a Swiss Army knife, which in many U.S. states could get him a burglary charge. But when he strolled casually close to the door, he saw that it stood slightly ajar. Steve winced at a grating creak as he eased the door farther open. But though he froze for several heartbeats, he heard no sound from inside to indicate he'd raised any alarm.

Stepping through, Steve eased the door quickly back to its ajar status. This left him in absolute darkness, but he'd come prepared. After rummaging in his sports bag, Steve settled into place a pair of night vision goggles. In ghostly green, he could now see a corridor ahead so choked with rubble and empty of life, Steve would have retreated if that steadily blinking signal on his cell phone didn't insist Jamil was in here somewhere.

Then Steve heard a hollow echo of footsteps, the distant murmur of voices. Not on this floor, or he'd see a light, unless NVGs were being issued to Pul-e-Charki personnel. But a path had been cleared ahead through the rubble as far as a stairwell blocked off by a security grille. The grille stood open, a chain and padlock dangling loose.

Easing forward in the dark, Steve made his way noiselessly up the first flight of stairs. Even before he emerged on the landing, he could see there was no point in climbing farther, the stairwell to the next floor fallen in and choked with debris so that overhead was a jagged, open hole. Down the corridor a white flame blazed in the NVG field of vision, and Steve pushed them up onto his forehead.

Now he could make out far down the corridor a light moving his direction. Just as he moved stealthily to retreat down the steps, he heard a recognizable creak, then footsteps entering as he had below. Hastily tugging NVGs down, Steve looked upward instead. Though the stairwell above was a hazardous mountain of rubble, enough broken remnants protruded from the wall to offer handholds. Steve had just reached the next floor when a flicker of light breached the stairwell below. He flattened himself at the edge of the broken-away floor and watched a lantern rise up the steps to meet two sets of footsteps approaching from down the corridor. The three owners of those footsteps merged on the landing directly below Steve. The conversation that ensued was brief. Then the newcomer headed down the corridor. The other two lingered on the landing, preventing Steve in turn from moving a muscle. He quieted his breathing to a hushed whisper of escaping air.

Steve had recognized a burly frame and brown beard split by a single white streak: the prison official he'd glimpsed with Ismail the day they'd smuggled Jamil the tracking device. By Skunkbeard's brusque orders, the other was a subordinate guard.

But it was the identity of their third companion whose footsteps were receding down the corridor that left Steve dumbfounded. What was Khalid's right-hand man and Steve's one-time mujahedeen driver and translator doing here? And more significantly from those authoritative gestures and commanding tone he'd just heard, giving the orders!

If Jamil had not forsworn hatred, he could have hated Ismail enough right now to strike down that sneer, leaving his body bloody and lifeless on the ground. "You are truly an evil man, Ismail."

A pistol trained on Jamil's midriff did not waver as the deputy minister shrugged indifferently. "I am not evil, but a warrior and patriot. Was I not fighting for my country while your father chose to flee to the comforts of exile? I trust you have reflected on the image of your infidel lover and young sister screaming under the caresses of my mujahedeen."

The cell to which Jamil had been led after his interview with Farah appeared to be in the same vacant, derelict corridor where he'd been thrown upon his first arrival at Pul-e-Charki. Daylight creeping through the boarded-over window had given way to nightfall before he'd heard footsteps, the metallic scrape of the security grate opening. Jamil's first wild hope was that Ameera's American warrior friend had come at last.

But the fluorescent lantern coming into view illuminated a white-streaked brown beard. The prison administrator had handed Jamil a cell phone, leaving again as soon as the call was over. But Jamil had little time before the deputy minister's own arrival to fight down images Ismail's threats and his sister Farah's broken sobbing had evoked.

Yes, Jamil's sister. Farah's last words had banished any lingering doubt. So she'd remembered the bangles Jamil had sent with the careless notion their colorful glitter would be ample consolation for his own continued absence. *You answered my prayers, Isa. You brought my sweet Farah-jan back to me. How can I now permit harm to her or Ameera? But how can I think again either of denying who you are? how you have changed me? that you are the only hope for Afghanistan?*

"What is it you want me to say?" Jamil asked dully aloud.

"It is not what I wish you to say. It is what I wish you to do. What you *will* do."

As Ismail strolled forward, the lantern in his other hand threw into sharp relief a hooded, black gaze and a cold, implacable expression that warred with the satisfied curve of his hard mouth. And at once, Jamil *knew*.

"You do not care what I say at my trial," he whispered incredulously. "You still wish me to carry out my mission. You want me to kill Khalid."

An eyebrow rose. "What brings you to that conclusion?"

"Because it is the same as before! How did I not see it? A gathering of powerful and corrupt leaders, many who were there last time. Above all, Khalid. I have wondered that you did not carry out the mission yourself once I was gone."

Studying those pitiless features above the fluorescent light, Jamil added more slowly, "What I have cared little to wonder is why you desire so strongly Khalid's death. It is not enough to say he is evil, therefore better dead. Are there not many such? But you have served Khalid since Taliban days. It is why I never guessed his deputy to be the veiled man who sought my services. Did Khalid harm your family as he did mine? But no, he would not then be foolish enough to keep you as his aide. A personal grudge, then?"

"My reasons are not your concern," Ismail responded sharply. "Only the task at hand. As to why Khalid still lives, that is easy. The foreign mercenaries have watched him too well. And I have no desire for martyrdom."

Ismail strolled forward another step. "But you still retain the thirst for martyrdom, or you would not show yourself so reckless and stubborn. I have never understood how a man can long for a paradise he cannot see above the pleasures of a world he can. Perhaps because I do not have your faith, misguided as you have shown it to be. Still, if you remain so determined to seek paradise, then I will help you attain it. And in so doing, achieve my own purposes as well."

Jamil's breathing came hard and fast. "I do long for paradise. And

368

when it is Isa's choosing, he will welcome me there. But not by killing. I have told you I no longer wish to kill. That I will not kill. Moreover, I no longer believe the almighty Creator ever intended men to kill others to guarantee paradise."

How he could possibly choose, if forced to weigh Farah's and Ameera's virtue, perhaps even their lives, against making some insincere statement of orthodoxy to the judges, had been heavy on Jamil's heart and mind while he'd awaited Ismail's arrival. But Ismail was making the choice an easy one. Because wrapping himself again in explosives and walking as a living bomb into a group of human beings was so little an option, Jamil did not have to hesitate. *Forgive me, Ameera, Farah.*

"I would give my life for my sister and the foreign woman as well. And in the name of all you hold holy, I plead with you to let them go. Hurting them will not change my mind, so why allow their blood on your conscience? But I will not kill. And you must know if you try to force me, I will simply warn their security."

Ismail's next step brought him so close, Jamil could feel the cold metal of the gun muzzle through his tunic. "You clearly do not understand. The question is not whether you will kill, but only how you will die. Do you think I need your cooperation to make you into the weapon I need? If you must be carried in chains with your mouth taped shut so that you appear an obstinate defendant, so be it!"

"Then they will know it is not of my doing. You cannot make it appear a shaheed martyrdom."

"On the contrary, for I still have this." Ismail drew out a small video camera. "Such passionate avowal of devotion to Allah and resolve to destroy Afghanistan's corrupt leadership, of whom you name Minister of Interior Khalid Sayef as foremost. It has been a pity to leave it unused. Your confession will be broadcast to the world as soon as the deed is done. Then all will know you were never truly a follower of Isa, but only another fanatic feigning apostasy in order to strike your blow of holy jihad. Inquiries will be made regarding the accomplices you paid to acquire this explosive device. All managed more easily if you are seen to have approached death under your own strength and will. Which is the only reason I offer you this alternative."

If his adversary's face held anger, persuasion, the smallest uncertainty, Jamil might have clung to doubt this man could do as he said. In stunned belief, he whispered, "Who are you that you can do such things? Who are you truly working for? Qaderi himself? Is that how you order your own will within the very walls of Pul-e-Charki? Does Qaderi hope to eliminate his competitors for the presidency by luring them to this mockery of a trial?"

"That is not your concern either. What matters is that you believe I will do as I say."

Though Ismail had once lied to him, cleverly and effectively, Jamil could discern no lie now in his gaze or words. Reluctantly, slowly, Jamil nodded.

"In one hour, men will come to conduct you to your tribunal. Do not fight them. If you arrive bound and gagged, if I receive report of resistance or trickery, then I will make a phone call, and my mujahedeen will have cause to celebrate. Walk of your own accord, do as you are told, speak not at all, and your women's virtue is guaranteed. You cannot change your own fate, but it is still in your hands to decide theirs."

As though in a game of chess, a pastime prohibited by the Taliban but one at which in his carefree youth he'd been skilled, Jamil examined each piece Ismail had presented, searching for any weakness in the other man's arguments. If there was one, his frantic mind could not perceive it. All left to consider now was the safety of the two women he loved. Though even if not for their sake, did not retaining his body under his own will and power offer more alternatives for fate to still intervene than submitting himself to be bound and gagged?

No, not fate.

Was Jamil forgetting how the Almighty himself had intervened to save three men cast into a fiery furnace? There was still an hour. And Steve Wilson, a chess piece Ismail had not calculated into his game plan.

"Enough! There is no more time," Ismail said shortly. "Which order do I leave? That you be bound or walk free?"

"What choice do I have?" Jamil spread his hands in surrender. "You were right when you said I had no idea what you wished. And that I would do it."

45

Though Steve could not move, his mind was speeding. That Ismail should give orders here was not such a mystery. Pul-e-Charki had not so long ago been under Khalid's jurisdiction and therefore Ismail's. The prison official below undoubtedly owed both men favors.

But if Ismail really thought anything he had to say at this late date could sway Jamil's words or actions, the deputy minister knew less about this prisoner than Steve had come to know.

Ismail was not gone long. His curt instructions carried up to Steve. "We will not return again tonight. But an escort will retrieve the prisoner in one hour to be washed and dressed for his trial. Ensure they are not kept waiting."

An hour. Not much time, but enough.

One fluorescent lantern retreated down the stairs with Ismail and Skunkbeard. The guard picked up the other and disappeared down the corridor. Steve waited until he heard the creak of the cellblock's rear door before working his way back to the second-floor landing. Through the NVGs' ghostly green glow, Steve could make out a security grate of untarnished steel halfway down the debris-strewn corridor.

So far he'd seen nothing to indicate additional security personnel. Easing noiselessly along the dark corridor, Steve saw there was indeed just one guard. The man clearly anticipated neither trouble nor visitors because he'd retreated with the lantern into an abandoned cell made comfortable with tushaks, cushions, and a gas brazier.

Thanks to Ismail's explicit instructions, Steve's counterfeit release document would no longer cut it. Steve thought swiftly. The preparations he'd stored in his sports bag didn't include weapons. Gate security was not so lax he could smuggle in a gun, while Dyncorp weapons were strictly accounted for at the end of each shift. Nor, despite Hollywood depictions, could even the best Special Ops team hope to shoot their way out of an armed camp like Pul-e-Charki. In any case, Afghan prison security were simply local hires working to support their own families. Not even if it meant aborting this mission would Steve consider using lethal force to get Jamil or himself out of here.

But Dyncorp's Pul-e-Charki outpost kept less lethal toys on hand. Steve noiselessly pulled a smoke grenade from his bag and lobbed it into the commandeered cell. Coughing and choking, the guard erupted into the corridor. Steve sprang, his left arm wrapping across the man's throat, the crook of his elbow squeezing against the trachea until the guard relaxed into unconsciousness.

Letting the limp shape slump to the floor, Steve dug a ziplock bag from his sports bag. Inside was a pungently damp facecloth. By the time Steve opened the Baggie enough to expose its contents, the guard was already recovering consciousness. Steve held his own breath as he pressed the Baggie firmly over the semiconscious guard's mouth and nose. *One thousand one. One thousand two. One thousand three.*

Chloroform was iffy stuff. The man might be out ten minutes or an hour. So as the guard again lapsed into unconsciousness, Steve took time to twist flexicuffs around wrists and ankles, slapping a strip of duct tape over his mouth. In the movies good guys simply piled unconscious perps behind them, who inevitably recovered consciousness to cause more mayhem. No real operative would neglect immobilizing his victims. *Sorry, man! Nothing personal, and no permanent damage!*

Having purloined the lantern and a set of keys, Steve set off at a run. Once he'd unlocked the security grate, Steve could see why the guard had preferred to keep his distance. The air here was rank with untreated sewage, the musk of unwashed humanity, dried blood, and vomit. A dozen cells had been cleared of rubble. The nearest had rusted shackles bolted to the rear wall, a hook and pulley contraption hanging from the ceiling. A torture chamber.

But whatever interrogations had been carried out here, Steve's probing with the light now revealed only emptiness. Had it been Qaderi's own orders that exiled Jamil to this hellhole? Or was this all part of Ismail's endeavor to force the "apostate" to cooperate?

Steve's activities had been carried out in near silence. Which might be why a kneeling figure prostrated on a tattered tushak in the final cell had ignored the approaching fluorescent lantern. As the light beam filtered through metal bars to touch a bowed head, it lifted. "They told me I had an hour."

Then dark eyes rose to the rugged face above a gray-blue uniform, and Jamil rose hastily to his feet. "You are no guard."

Unlocking the cell door, Steve stepped inside. "You remember me, then?"

"Of course. Ameera's warrior friend," Jamil answered simply. "I prayed you would come before it was too late."

"Well, we don't have much time." Steve shed sports bag and lantern to dig for the second police uniform. "You need to change quickly into this."

But Jamil made no move to take the clothing, and instead of excitement or relief, the lantern beam revealed both anguish and hope on thin, bearded features. "No, I cannot go with you. They have Ameera and Farah. It is to them you must bring help and quickly."

"Ameera?" Steve repeated blankly. "You mean, Ms. Mallory. And Farah?" Steve's memory banks dredged up a fair-skinned teenage girl he'd met at Amy's heels. "The girl from New Hope?"

"Farah is my sister. Ismail is holding them hostage for my cooperation."

None of this was making sense. Steve had left Amy headed safely home in the Pajero. As to this Farah, Steve was not even aware Jamil had a sister. But Ismail's mission in this abandoned wing suddenly clicked into place. The deputy minister wasn't so foolish after all to believe persuasive arguments or promises of freedom would sway Jamil. Instead he'd stooped to threats against those the man cared about.

There was no time to waste in debate. Steve shook his head urgently. "Ismail is lying to you. I couldn't say about this Farah girl, but I was with Amy . . . uh, Ameera, not two hours ago. She's safe with friends, believe me."

"No, he was not lying. The prison administrator himself brought me a phone. I spoke with Ameera and Farah both." Jamil closed his eyes briefly as though blocking out a disagreeable image as he went on thickly. "Both women spoke with courage. But I heard their cries and fear. If I do not do as he asks this night, Ismail has sworn to give Ameera and Farah to his mujahedeen. You must believe he will keep his word. I know this man well."

Steve had his cell phone out before Jamil finished speaking. When it didn't ring through, Steve tried again. On the third try, a male voice answered suspiciously, "Salaam? Who is this?"

Breaking immediately off, Steve felt his face harden into cold, hard stone. He'd killed before in combat. But it had never been personal. Nor had he ever felt the impulse to murder someone. Now Steve understood the deadly rage that could make someone like Jamil strap on a suicide vest to go after the man who'd slaughtered his family.

Jamil's eyes had opened again on Steve's face. What he saw must have satisfied him because he nodded abruptly. "You will go after them then and free them."

"Yes, I will free them," Steve said flatly. "Do you know where they are being held?"

"No, but it cannot be far because it did not take long for Ismail to come from them to see me here."

"Then I know where they must be. Ismail's compound is just a few minutes' drive. As soon as we're clear, we'll go after them. But if we're to be well away from Pul-e-Charki before Ismail's men come for you, we need to leave now."

"No, you need to leave." Jamil's own bearded jaw was set adamantly. "You must see I cannot go. What if Ismail discovers I am gone before you have freed Ameera and Farah from his power?"

"That is a risk," Steve admitted. "But I can hardly ask you to forfeit your own chance of freedom on that possibility. You don't understand. I'd planned to come back later after the trial if I couldn't get you out now. But once I go after the girls, Ismail's going to know you got word out somehow, even if that guard out there doesn't give it away. And after tonight I no longer have free rein at Pul-e-Charki. It's not going to be so easy again to come after you. I couldn't promise how or when it might be."

"I do understand," Jamil answered steadily. "But if this were your choice, would you walk out of here for the sake of your own skin if even the smallest risk existed of evil men harming the women of your heart?"

His words evoked such a sharp picture of Amy as Jamil had described her, frightened and hurt and trying to be brave, that Steve closed his own eyes against it. "No, I would not."

"Then do not insult me by suggesting I do less for my own sister and for Ameera. It is not my safety and freedom that matter now, but theirs. Only be careful. There is something else you should know. Ismail is not who you think. When I still desired to kill Khalid, it was Ismail who freed me from prison and brought me to Kabul to be a shaheed martyr."

Steve was already stuffing the uniform back into the sports bag. Now he straightened up, stunned. "You can't be serious! I thought Ismail's shenanigans here were all about getting Khalid elected. Now you're telling me he's the one behind those attempts to kill his boss? Why would he do that? He's been Khalid's right-hand man for years!"

"I do not know why. But I know who placed on me the bomb intended that day for Khalid. If you do not believe me, there is proof. I made a video recording. That is why Ismail let me walk free after the New Hope explosion, because he was afraid it would be made public. I gave the recording to Ameera to keep, though she does not know what it contains."

"I don't need to see it," Steve answered grimly. "If Ismail could do what he's done today, I can believe anything of him."

Picking up the lantern, Steve took a step to leave. He wasn't quite sure what impulse made him swing back. "There's something you should know too, Jamil. And I can only ask your forgiveness, though I understand if you can't give it. All of this—Khalid, your family, all those years in prison, Ismail and the bombings, even this mess today because it all started back there—I'm responsible."

Now it was Jamil's turn to stare with confused disbelief. "I don't understand. How can you say you are responsible?"

"I was there that day. The day Kabul was freed from the Taliban. The day you came home to Wazir Akbar Khan."

Jamil's sucked-in breath whistled sharply through his teeth. "You were one of the foreign mujahedeen who helped Khalid seize my family's home?"

"Yes, though we truly believed we were fighting Taliban. When you told me your side, I wrote you a note to give the interrogators up at Bagram. I checked on you there later, but they wouldn't give me any information. Until the day of the explosion, I'd always assumed they had released you. I couldn't even really blame you then once I learned what Khalid had done to your family."

"I remember," Jamil said slowly. "You wrote the note in a New Testament, though I did not know what it was. After you left, Khalid tore it up and told the Americans he knew me to be a Taliban. So it is true what Ameera says? You too are a follower of Isa?"

It was the last thing on which Steve had expected the younger man to fasten. "Yes, I am, though there have been times when I've wandered far from his ways and forgotten just who it was I was created to follow."

Jamil stepped forward. "Then we are brothers, are we not, if we are both followers of Isa? And you were not responsible that day, only Khalid. Nor have I forgotten that you alone showed me kindness, though for long years I believed you had forsaken your promise to return and speak on my behalf. It gladdens my heart to know you did not. But forgiveness? Isa has helped me forgive Khalid, who is my enemy. But for you, my brother, there is no reason to ever speak between us of forgiveness."

Steve met the younger, slighter man's resolute gaze for a long, silent moment. He had not come face-to-face with his former adversary since the day of the New Hope explosion. Funny how in planning this mission at Amy's request, planning it because it needed to be done, he'd never really allowed himself to consider the flesh-and-blood person who was Jamil Yusof ul Haq Shahrani, but only the objective to be accomplished.

Perhaps because it was easier that way.

But now despite the urgency for haste that Jamil's intel had roused, Steve found himself studying the other man with intense deliberation. Two or three inches shorter and several years younger than Steve, Jamil had been on that long-ago day of their first encounter the pampered scion of an aristocratic family, a good-looking youth with tumbled, dark curls and olive-toned coloring typical of the Pashtun tribes.

When they'd crossed paths again all those years later, it was no wonder Steve hadn't recognized the youthful aristocrat, for those well-fed good looks had been thoroughly erased by the malnourished gauntness of prison life. Deep grooves of bitterness and a sunken, hollow gaze had made Jamil look older than his years, while a wealth of hatred and defiance and fury had seethed behind a sullen expression, smoldered in the dark eyes, at least when Steve was present.

And now?

If life and time had admittedly matured the "pretty boy" into a prepossessing enough male by any female estimation, the younger, smaller man still had a wiry slightness that spoke of deprivation. *I could break him in two in physical combat!*

Though that was hardly the measure of a man. *Phil is twice the man I am with two body parts missing.*

More significant was the quiet composure, a lack of fear Steve had already noted in that courtroom video. A lift of head that was not arrogance, but a confidence won through fire. The serenity in that steady gaze meeting Steve's of a soldier who'd passed through deadly combat, emerging the victor, not just over the enemy but over his own doubts and fears.

This was hardly the defiant fugitive Steve himself had hauled before another tribunal not so many months ago, and Steve found himself envying the evolution. Jamil had found what he believed in and gone after it with all his heart. Did that change what he'd been? or just reveal what kind of person he really was? Or both? In either case—

This is a real man. As good a man as I could ever hope to know. As good a man as I could ever hope to be.

My brother.

"Yes, we are brothers." Putting a hand out, he clasped Jamil's in the hard grip with which he would take leave of a comrade-in-arms.

But Jamil instead reached up to embrace Steve Afghan-style with a kiss on each cheek. Quietly, urgently, he said, "Then as my brother, I can speak to you from my heart. You too love Ameera-jan, do you not?"

Steve did not have to find a response because Jamil went immediately on. "May I beseech you, as one brother who loves her to another, will you not keep watch over Ameera-jan for me? She will need you in the days ahead. And my sweet little Farah, I entrust her into your hands and Ameera's both."

Steve cleared his throat. "Jamil, you don't have to ask me to watch out for Amy and your sister until you're out of here. I would do that anyway. But believe me, you'll be watching over them yourself soon enough. Whatever happens tonight, however long it takes, I won't rest until you are freed. I hope you believe that."

"Yes, I believe you. And I know I will be freed soon. Of that Isa himself has given me assurance. Until we meet again, my brother, farewell."

Though Jamil's words were straightforward, some note in them troubled Steve. But he'd no more time to probe the matter. Steve left the cell at a dead run. The guard was still sleeping peacefully. Steve collected the flexicuffs and duct tape, then returned the guard's keys to his belt. He didn't bother retrieving the smoke canister. Its lingering fumes cloaked the smell of chloroform, and with any luck, the grenade would be assumed to be a stray lob from this morning's assault. Let the guard try to convince his superiors he'd been assaulted rather than carelessly tampering with a stray grenade. At least he was alive. In any case, Steve was feeling less generous since he'd seen that torture cell.

After retracing his steps, Steve changed back into his contractor clothing before heading to the prison gates. Media vans and dignitary convoys were already lined up for security check, and Steve's exit proved as unremarked as he'd hoped it to be with Jamil. He was accelerating dangerously away from Pul-e-Charki when he reached a hand into his parka. But groping fingers didn't find the cell phone it sought. He patted down all other pockets before admitting with chagrin what must have happened. Jamil must have lifted the cell phone during that last embrace. Why, Steve had no idea; perhaps with some hope of communicating with the outside world, even Amy herself, before his trial. Nor, remembering the look on Jamil's face, his last words, could Steve even be angry. Jamil knew the risks as well as Steve did. He'd just have to trust Jamil to keep the instrument undiscovered until Steve could return for him.

Without slowing, Steve rooted under his seat for his original iPhone. As he punched in a number, it was no longer Jamil that occupied Steve's mind, but murder.

Forgive me, brother. Jamil's fingers played swiftly over the cell phone's panel until he was sure he understood its functions. Pickpocketing had been one skill he'd learned from other inmates during those long prison years. He could only hope that when the American warrior discovered the purpose for Jamil's theft, he would understand.

So much had passed since Jamil sat in a high, cold aerie of broken walls, speaking into a camera, it had truly slipped his mind that he was not the only one possessing the weapon of a video document. Ismail's reminder had come as a shock, and with that reminder had evaporated the last hope that Ismail's plan could not succeed.

The American Steve Wilson, who had once been Jamil's enemy and was now his brother, even as Ismail had once been Jamil's ally and was now his enemy, believed he could rescue Ameera and Farah, then return for Jamil at a more propitious time. Jamil knew a more propitious time would not come. Not without an intervening miracle.

And if no miracle transpired, who would ever believe Jamil was not a jihadist assassin? or that his shaheed statement had been videotaped before Jamil's change of heart and life? Unless he could tell them otherwise.

When Jamil had made arrangements with the chaikhana to receive Ameera's package, it had been necessary to leave a phone number. Jamil's memory of the sat-phone number Kareem had dictated was hazy, and it took several tries before he hit the right combination. As soon as Kareem answered, Jamil hung up again. Reaching for his bundle, he dug out the small flashlight a guard had given him for tending the sick man, Yousef. He'd been saving its light for emergencies. But there was no reason to hoard it any longer.

His time was short, but one thing Jamil needed to see. Flipping through Ameera's holy book, he read again the words that had so grabbed his heart.

"If we are thrown into the blazing furnace, the God we serve is able to save us from it, and he will rescue us from your hand, O king. But even if he does not, we want you to know, O king, that we will not serve your gods or worship the image of gold you have set up."

379

Jamil had seized on that verse as Isa's promise of rescue from his own fiery furnace that was Pul-e-Charki and the looming threat of a death sentence. A rescue that would inevitably be followed by reunion with Ameera, a new life and future.

Now Jamil focused on the second part of that challenge. *"But even if he does not, we want you to know, O king . . ."*

Even if he does not.

Jamil had once asked himself what could make the man Isa, who was also the almighty Creator of the universe, remain mute and acquiescent through excruciating martyrdom when a single cry to his heavenly allies would set him free. Love, Ameera had told him. Which had not then made any sense to Jamil. Surely there were other, less painful ways to show love. Healing the sick. Comforting the grieving.

But he understood now because it was the same reason Jamil had not walked out of this cell when Steve Wilson offered the opportunity. Great though Jamil's desire had become to live, his love for the two women who held his heart—Ameera and his little sister, Farah—was far greater. Just as their safety far outweighed the consequences to himself for staying behind.

In how much greater a fashion had Isa's love for humanity, his knowledge of the consequences should he decline to sacrifice himself on men's behalf, infinitely outweighed his physical suffering, the agony of bearing all mankind's evil, of being separated from his heavenly Father, who was also one with Isa Masih in a way no human brain could comprehend?

"Greater love has no man than this, that he lay down his life for his friends."

"This is how we know what love is: Isa Masih laid down his life for us."

Those words recorded by Isa's closest disciple John had become engraved onto Jamil's mind.

Isa laid down his life for me. Not in weakness and resignation and despair. Nor because someone took it from him. But of his own choice in a supreme act of strength and triumph and love.

The decision Jamil had made was no longer agonizing, but simple and inevitable. Positioning the flashlight so that it shone directly on his face, Jamil initiated the cell phone's video mode and began to speak.

46

If Steve had refrained from involving colleagues and friends in Jamil's rescue, he'd no such qualms about his present mission. "Phil, they've taken Amy. I'm going in after her."

The best thing about a teammate he'd worked with so long and closely was that the former Special Forces medic wasted no time asking who or where or why. "What do you need?"

"Best scenario, a chopper. And a pilot. Any chance Bones has Khalid's bird up and running?"

Like Phil, team mechanic/pilot Timothy "Bones" Bonefeole had been among the responders to that midnight break-in at Amy's compound as well as the later bombing. Both men thought highly of the aid worker's spunk and courage. So it was no surprise to hear an echo of Steve's own cold fury in Phil's response.

"We're loading the chopper now to fly Khalid up to Pul-e-Charki. He wants a fancy entrance on camera for that apostasy trial. We can pick you up once we've dropped him off. Just tell me where, what the parameters are, and how big a team you need."

The whoosh of relief leaving Steve's lungs told him exactly how much fear and anxiety he'd been tamping down. This was what it meant to have friends at your back. "No team. I don't want to drag Condor Security into this. I only need transport—and a distraction."

"Then you know where she's being held?" Phil expressed no surprise at Amy's abduction itself. Kidnapping for ransom had become a booming enterprise in Kabul. "You can't be crazy enough to be going in alone. You got any idea how many and who's responsible?"

"Oh, I know exactly who's responsible, and you're not going to believe it," Steve answered grimly. "This one calls for low profile, especially considering who's involved. I don't want anyone who doesn't already know Amy."

Steve turned off his headlights once he left the main route from Pul-e-Charki. No sense in alerting any watchful eyes of his trajectory. By the time he'd finished his arrangements, the compound where he'd left Amy was looming ahead. He took note of the Pajero still drawn up against the perimeter wall before his fist thundered on the metal gate. A panel slid sideways, a flashlight probing Steve's face before the gate opened to the middle-aged watchman Steve had seen earlier. At his back was an entire flock of women and children. An immediate relieved chorus rose. "Where is Miss Ameera?"

"She isn't here then?" Steve's reply was less question than confirmation. "Do you know when she left?"

A petite, dark-haired woman stepped up beside the chowkidar. "We thought at first she had gone because her vehicle was not here. But the children said you drove away in her vehicle. And yours is still here. We called and called, hoping perhaps she went for a walk and became lost. But if she heard us, she has not returned. We were making arrangements to go search for her."

"That won't be necessary. I know where she is. When I find her, I'll let you know. Or she will." Steve heard the rattle of the gate being barred and locked from inside as he headed back to the vehicles. He'd arranged a drop zone for Khalid's Mi-8 helicopter in a nearby field. But first he shone a flashlight into the abandoned Pajero. Amy's knapsack was all the confirmation he needed of Jamil's report. It held two items of interest. Amy's notebook computer. And a flat square wrapped in plastic sacking and duct tape. If this was the package Jamil had given Amy, she'd never opened it.

After slicing away the wrapping, Steve slid the disk he found inside into Amy's computer. By the time he'd watched the short video, Steve was gritting his teeth to curb rage. Not that he'd suspected Jamil any longer of lying, but there might have been confusion, miscommunication.

There was no misunderstanding the cold orders, then an aquiline profile illuminated by a flash of lightning. So Ismail was the enemy behind that suicide vest on the Ministry of Interior roof, the foiled counternarcotics summit bombing, the New Hope destruction, and presumably the sugar factory blast that had been the first attempt against Khalid's life.

Still unanswered was why. What could motivate a favored subordinate like Ismail to murder?

Though why hardly mattered now. The drone of a helicopter was audible approaching from downtown Kabul. Khalid, unless another of Pul-e-Charki's evening guests had their own private chopper. Steve hurried to finish his own preparations before driving back down the dirt track. The chopper's roar was heading his direction from Pul-e-Charki by the time Steve pulled up to the drop zone.

The iPhone rang. "We need those landing lights."

Steve switched on his headlights. Moments later, the helicopter descended, not touching ground, but low enough to stir up a cloud of dust. Switching off his headlights, Steve headed at a run toward the helicopter. The Mi-8's own running lights were off, but a slight limp with which a shadow swung down from the chopper's open side door identified Phil Myers.

"Ian's holding down the fort at Pul-e-Charki," Phil shouted into Steve's ear. "Bones spun Khalid a yarn about a fault in the running lights that needs checked out. So it's all yours. Go get your girl."

"You're the best." Steve shoved car keys into Phil's hands. "You can wait at that compound down the road. You'll find the Pajero and friendlies I mentioned. I'll call when it's clear to come pick us up."

"And if I don't hear from you? I still don't like this, Steve!"

"If you don't hear within the hour, feel free to storm Ismail's place with an entire ISAF battalion. But with Condor Security contracted to Khalid, and Ismail on his payroll, I'd hate to see trouble for you or anyone else on the CS team over this. I know Ismail's men, a bunch of mujahedeen leftovers. No discipline. Piece of cake."

Phil had no chance to argue further because Steve was already swinging himself aboard. Bones's helmet turned his way, a thumb rising in welcome. As Steve returned the gesture, the Mi-8 rose from its hover. Steve tightened the Velcro straps of body armor Phil had provided. Black and green skin paint already transformed rugged features to dappled shadows invisible a few feet away. He double-checked vest pockets and pistol belt before pulling up over his hips the nylon harness of a rappelling line. Tugging on thick gloves, Steve gave Bones another thumbs-up.

The Mi-8 had risen to make a high loop above the plateau. Now the helicopter reversed action, spiraling downward into a tightening circle that had as its center Ismail's compound. Bones was making no effort to elude attention, quite the contrary, and as the helicopter circled low around the compound, he turned on its running lights. The cacophony of engine, rotors, and flashing lights should by now have drawn any guard worth his salt to his feet. But while yellow radiance leaking from a shuttered top-floor window indicated occupancy, Steve spotted no movement along perimeter wall, balconies, or walkways.

Ismail's security team would seem far less concerned about attack from without than preventing escape from within.

The crash of the door flying open came far sooner than Amy had expected. It should have taken hours before the trial was over. Unless something else had gone wrong.

But it wasn't Ismail who entered the room. Amy swung her feet hastily from the bed as she recognized the guard whose sliced face left one eye milky-blind. Nor was he alone. Crowding through the door behind him were more of Ismail's militia than Amy had seen to date. A full half-dozen men.

As Amy stood, Farah scrambled to her side. Terror glinted in lake blue eyes, clenched the younger girl's teeth. Amy's own fear wobbled her awkward Dari as she demanded, "Leave this room at once! You have no right to be here. Your employer gave orders that we were not to be disturbed. That we were to be freed when this is over. How dare you disobey him like this!"

Rotted and broken teeth were in full display as the intruders exchanged amused grins. And though Amy searched for any yielding or compassion in those hard, bearded faces, she found none. It wasn't difficult to believe these men had all been mujahedeen, fighters so fierce and cruel that Soviet soldiers had preferred death to falling into their hands, whose raping and pillaging of the Afghan population had in protest swept the Taliban to power.

Their one-eyed leader stepped forward with a harsh laugh. "Free you? Are you so foolish? Do you think you above all can be released now to speak to other foreigners of what you have seen and heard this day? We have just received our orders. Ismail has sworn you will leave here undespoiled, not free. When word comes that all has gone as planned, we are to take you well away from here and slit your throats."

The leader's decayed grin widened. "But if Ismail vowed that you would be sent to the next world untouched, we did not. Why should we waste time and pleasure and two women who will soon be dead in any case?"

Already hysterical sobbing was coming from beside Amy. Groping sideways, Amy drew the other girl closer. She wouldn't have thought she'd ever be glad to see Ismail, but now she could wish desperately he was walking through the door. The other men surged forward. One reached past their leader to snatch at a stray blonde strand. Amy slapped the exploring hand away.

In response, the half-blind leader yanked Amy against him. A hand pulled off her headscarf. His companions murmured excitement as bright tresses spilled over shoulders and back. Then her captor ripped at Amy's ankle-length chapan, buttons flying as he tore it free. By standards of Amy's own culture, the tunic and pantaloons beneath were amply modest, but at hisses and greedily widened eyes, Amy felt suddenly naked.

The leader's scarred features were bending close, hands roaming intimately. Then unwashed breath claimed Amy's mouth. She could not suppress a moan of sheer, terrified revulsion.

"No! Don't hurt her! Leave her alone!" Farah's unrestrained tears had sounded so defeated that Amy was as taken by surprise as her captor when the younger girl sprang forward to pound on the guard's back. As he staggered under the force of Farah's fists and feet, her fingernails added new scratches to his facial scars.

But Amy's reprieve was as brief as it had been sudden. Capturing Farah's flailing frame, the militia leader lifted the girl from the ground, then threw her across the room. Farah slammed with a frighteningly loud thunk against a brassbound chest.

"Farah!" Amy would have run to the other girl if the mujahid leader hadn't snatched her close again. Blood streamed down scarred features as a hand tightened painfully on Amy's throat, his good eye wild with rage. Broken weeping across the room at least meant Farah was still alive.

"You filthy, vile little—" That Ismail's militia knew Farah's recent origins was clear from the stream of abusive phrases directed to the slumped form cowering against the chest. "You will be dealt with as the worthless criminal you are. But not before we have our pleasure."

A jerk of his head unleashed his companions toward the sobbing Farah. The militia leader's hand tightened further on Amy's throat, his grin made more ferocious by blood staining decayed teeth scarlet. The taste of absolute terror was metallic in Amy's mouth. She felt filthy and soiled under his groping in a way that would never scrub off.

Father God, where are you? I know you are powerful to save us. I thought I understood your plans. Steve would rescue Jamil. Ismail would release us when he didn't need us anymore. But this? How can you let this happen?

Words Jamil had once quoted so confidently rose to Amy's mind. *"The God we serve is able to save us . . . and he will rescue us from your hand, O king."*

Except that Amy knew the rest of that passage.

"But even if he does not—"

Even if he does not!

Had the comparatively privileged life of Amy's own cultural background, that wholeness for which she'd even felt guilty, led her to somehow assume she could count on miraculous deliverance from any serious harm? And yet God did not always so answer prayers. How many had surrendered their very lives for no other crime than following Isa Masih, Jesus Christ? Those three young men in a fiery furnace had spent their days serving the foreign king who'd destroyed their families and country. Countless women had endured such abuse as she now faced.

So why should Amy consider herself entitled to immunity from the anguish and pain she'd tended in so many others?

Father God, I do pray for a miracle to save us, if only to show Farah you truly love her. But if you have another choice, whatever you permit in my life, please let me not by cowardice or pleading or . . . or hate bring shame to your name!

Amy was so intent on blocking out terror and revulsion, she did not at first register deliverance when it came.

47

As Steve signaled Bones, the running lights abruptly went out again. Steve tossed a fast-rope rappel line out the open door. As the helicopter slowed to a near hover, Steve grabbed the rope with gloved hands. When the aircraft's insect-shaped shadow touched the villa's flat roof, Steve simply stepped out, the rope burning through his gloves with the speed of his descent. He hit the roof with bent knees, releasing the rope as he rolled to his feet. The helicopter banked off, line flapping. This time Steve did hear response. Shouts and running feet.

Creeping to the parapet, Steve looked downward. Ismail's lax perimeter watch was at last erupting outdoors. One. Two. Three. A fourth emerged onto a top-floor balcony. The Mi-8 circled twice more, running lights shifting repeatedly from on to off. By then Steve had crossed the roof to the far side, where a narrow concrete strip separated the villa from the side perimeter wall. Below, some distance from where Steve looked down, a fifth guard had emerged onto a second-floor balcony, his night vision destroyed by the flashing helicopter lights as he stared upward.

This side held what Steve had been looking—and listening—for. The generator's rumble came from a shed at the rear of the concrete strip. Where Amy and Jamil's sister might be within the compound, Steve didn't let himself consider right now. Lowering himself over the roof edge, he dropped lightly to a third-floor balcony. The guard didn't shift his gaze from the circling helicopter. Steve had dropped to a second-floor balcony before the running lights stopped their temperamental sputter. As the

Mi-8 banked toward Pul-e-Charki, the nearest balcony guard disappeared inside. That he'd evidenced no alarm had been anticipated—or at least hoped. Ismail's militia should be familiar with the private aircraft belonging to their own superior, Minister of Interior Khalid Sayef. If not, a military chopper in vicinity of Afghanistan's top-security prison, clearly checking out a problem with its electrical system, was hardly remarkable enough to rouse suspicion.

Nor was the next monkey wrench Steve was about to toss into this compound's gears.

By now Steve had dropped to the ground. He moved noiselessly along the side of the house to the shed. They hadn't even bothered with a lock. The stench of diesel fumes was choking as Steve played a pen flashlight over the generator's gears and hoses. Slapping the starter crank to its Off position would cut the electricity. But Steve wanted the generator out of commission. His flashlight beam brushed the rubber fuel hose. Perfect.

A knife from his belt spilled fuel across the shed floor even as Steve slammed a hand on the controls. Blackness was immediate. He slipped outside the shed and waited as angry shouts turned into running steps. A man-shaped silhouette appeared against the green glow of his NVGs. Unlike Pul-e-Charki security personnel, every man on this compound was at least complicit in holding hostage two young women. So Steve felt neither compunction nor pity in raising the M26 military-version Taser. The red dot of laser sighting played fleetingly over a torso. Then Steve fired. As two barbed darts hooked onto a woolen vest, fifty thousand volts crackled along the attached wires. The guard dropped without a sound.

Steve knew his weapon well enough to abandon caution in stepping close. The man was conscious but paralyzed, eyes wide open, his entire body shaking uncontrollably. Flexicuffs secured wrists and ankles, a third set twisting them behind the man's back. Duct tape across the mouth completed the immobilization. Steve shoved into place another air cartridge that provided the Taser's firing power as he sprinted along the side of the building. Reaching the far corner, Steve thrust his head around it cautiously.

Directly ahead was the main gate. To his right, steps led up to the front portico. This stood open, and someone had rounded up flashlight or lantern because a brightening glow from inside blazed white in the NVGs. Irritated swearing bespoke impatience that the generator hadn't resumed its roar, nor their comrade returned.

That wasn't all Steve heard. From somewhere deep inside the villa drifted female sobs, terror-filled and despairing. It took all Steve's control to retreat around the corner as the light—it proved to be a fluorescent lantern—emerged down the steps.

There were two of them. The first went down under the Taser's muffled pop. Steve was already rushing forward as the second whirled around. There'd been no time to load another air cartridge, so he used the Taser instead as a stun gun. Then Steve was slapping a new air cartridge in place as he raced, not indoors as every emotion yearned, but around the side of the building where the villa gave way to gardens and orchards. He couldn't leave adversaries loose at his back nor where they might stumble over their immobilized companions.

The top-floor balcony where he'd earlier seen a guard now stood empty. At ground level Steve spotted only one man standing on a veranda. The perp showed no impatience over the blackout. He was smoking a cigarette, its glowing ember a white-hot flicker through the NVGs. The man glanced down as a second dot of light danced across his chest.

Steve was getting good at this. Flexicuffs and duct tape went on with a speed that would have won a calf-roping contest. But Murphy's Law had been waiting overlong to strike. Steve caught a waft of burning tobacco before another white-hot flicker appeared in a doorway opening onto the veranda. This time the Taser's dual probes hit the doorframe as the smoker ducked inside.

Steve sprang after him. He had the advantage of being able to see while his quarry was slamming into walls as he ran. Steve's forearm slammed like an iron bar across the man's throat, the electrodes making an audible sizzle on flesh as Steve activated the Taser. But not before the guard's alarmed shouts echoed through the building. Somewhere above, that female sobbing broke off abruptly.

The hallway through which the two sentries had emerged to smoke opened into a sizable foyer with a wide staircase that curved to upper floors. Silence floating down the stairs was so complete, Steve could hear his own quickened heartbeat. He'd now put five perps out of commission, the exact number he'd counted from the rooftop. But he couldn't assume all Ismail's guards had emerged to watch that circling aircraft.

Easing another air cartridge into place, Steve stole up the stairs. But he was only halfway to the second-floor landing when he heard shallow, quick breathing from up the stairs. Steve froze. No human shape was in view, and even as Steve's NVGs probed the landing above him, that rush of air stopped as though the source was holding its breath.

Steve stilled his own breathing and waited. The instant he heard a whoosh of air leaving overtaxed lungs, he was racing up the stairs. The shape he'd expected was backed against the wall just to the left of the landing. Too close to deploy the Taser. Steve lunged forward, but he hadn't been quiet enough, and the bundle of cloth and flesh under his arm fought like a wildcat against his grip.

Then Steve caught sight of a much larger shape running into view at the top of the next flight of steps that led to the third floor. One hand carried an automatic weapon. A flashlight in the other blazed blinding fire in Steve's NVGs. Releasing his first captive, Steve whirled around.

But just as the Taser went up, so did the rifle.

Somewhere within Amy's reeling mind, she'd recorded the drone of an aircraft engine, a beat of rotors approaching, then receding. But military helicopters carrying out ISAF missions were common over Kabul. Only when the drone escalated to such a roar it must be directly overhead had that foul mouth jerked away, the brutal grip dropping from Amy's throat.

The militia leader was the first to race from the room. As his furious oaths and shouted orders initiated a stampede, Amy hurried to Farah's side. The other girl's headscarf and chapan had also been torn off, her tunic ripped open to the waist. She lay curled up in a fetal position, her low moans frightening Amy with their anguish.

"Farah, can you move? We must get out of here."

Despite the force of Farah's fall, Amy saw no blood. Reaching for the ripped chapan, she wrapped it around the younger girl. "Farah-jan, you were so brave to defend me like that. But now you must help me. I can't carry you alone. Can you at least sit up?"

Farah groaned as she pushed herself to a sitting position, clutching at her side. "I can move, but I do not think I can walk. Please, go, run. Allah, or perhaps your Isa, has heard your prayers. So save yourself. Me—the man is right. I am worthless and do not deserve to be saved. This is my fault for lying to you. And it has all been for nothing. If they will kill us though we do as Ismail asks, will they not kill Jamil too?"

Amy's every muscle yearned to race from the room before their captors returned. Instead, she put her arms around Farah. "Don't say that. If Ismail has betrayed us and Jamil too, it is his doing, not yours. And you are not worthless! The almighty Creator made you. Isa Masih, of whom you have dreamed, died for you. And if I have prayed, it was for your salvation, not just mine. I will not leave you."

Instead of calming Farah, Amy's words triggered a storm of weeping. As though to punctuate those despairing sobs, the lamp that was the room's only lighting blinked abruptly out. It wasn't just a dead lightbulb, because the open door through which the guards had burst from the room revealed total blackness in the corridor beyond as well. The generator that had rumbled in the background since Amy's arrival was now silent.

"Go, go!" Farah shoved Amy's hands away. "Please, if I must die for my transgressions, why should you die too? You can escape now as you came. But please go, lest you break my heart. Let me know you are delivered if I have not been able to save Jamil nor myself."

This time Amy did rise, but not before reaching over in the dark to kiss Farah on the cheek. The sudden blackness should have added more terror. Instead, a flame of excitement and wonder was licking through Amy's veins. "I think perhaps deliverance has come to both of us. Wait here for me, then, Farah-jan. I will not abandon you."

The younger girl was still sobbing with a hopeless desolation that tore at Amy's heart. But Amy didn't dare wait longer to comfort her. Who knew how long this hiatus of darkness would last before someone managed to power the generator back up.

Groping forward, Amy eased out into the corridor. Was the stairwell up which Ismail had marched her to the left or right? Already, Amy was shivering with cold in the silken material of tunic and drawstring pantaloons. And the drone of the helicopter was retreating into the distance. Had Amy been wrong?

But a reverberation of footsteps and angry cursing, then a faint glow that must be a flashlight or lantern, allowed Amy to position the stairwell to her right. At least some of the guards who'd gone to investigate the circling aircraft were back inside. If they were headed upstairs, Amy had little time to consider escape.

Amy slipped noiselessly to a banister that edged the third-floor landing. The layout of the stairwell permitted Amy to see clear down to the first-floor foyer, but only a small patch of tile was visible. In it stood two men, one holding a lantern, the other speaking into a hand radio. Even as Amy looked down, the one with a hand radio let out a curse, and the two men headed toward the front door.

Their departure returned Amy to pitch-darkness. More significantly, Ismail's men in the foyer meant Amy could not escape that way. But if she could get down to the second floor, perhaps she could find an opening onto a balcony. The drop to the garden would be far enough to turn an ankle, but Amy saw little other choice.

If Amy hesitated, it was because taking Farah's suggested exit out that rear orchard gate through which she'd been dragged meant conceding she'd been wrong about the chopper. If so, it was unlikely she could find help and return before Ismail's men carried out their threats against Farah's person or life. How could she abandon the other girl to save herself, even if Farah had begged her?

No, I can't leave Farah to go through this alone! She believed once that I'd abandoned her. I will not let her believe so again. Heavenly Father, I don't know what you have in mind for us, but whatever it is, let us leave here together or not at all. Let her see through my love just how great is your love for her.

The girl's weeping had ceased. Instead, Amy heard a quiet tap as though footsteps were crossing a floor in the darkness behind her. If Farah had recovered enough to walk, maybe they could both escape after all. If the power remained off. If the men stayed away just a little longer.

Too many ifs.

Then a yellow glimmer caught at Amy's peripheral vision. A flashlight beam was emerging from a room down the corridor. So not all Ismail's men had headed downstairs. This one must have stepped onto a balcony to check on that circling chopper. Amy caught a glimpse of scarred features, a milky eyeball. She retreated down the stairwell just as the flashlight beam played across the banister.

"Ahmed! Massoud! Where are you?"

Only the static of a hand radio answered. The two men in the foyer below had not come back into view. Was the militia leader's impatient demand addressed to them? Reaching the second-floor landing, Amy retreated until her back hit a wall. The flashlight was now probing the steps. Any sound would bring the man after Amy. But if Amy remained silent, he would likely head back to Farah. *What do I do, heavenly Father?*

A shout reverberated up the stairwell. If Amy didn't understand the Pashto phrases, she couldn't mistake alarm and anger before the male voice abruptly broke off. Overhead, the militia leader's furious demands elicited no response, and his flashlight winked out. Amy quieted her breathing by inhaling through her mouth. Below, neither voice nor movement nor light had succeeded that disrupted shout.

Then Amy heard it. Breathing as adrenaline-quickened as Amy's own. Stealthy footsteps moving unhesitatingly through the darkness toward the stairwell. Amy held her breath as they started up the steps.

Above her, the militia leader might be holding his own breath for all the sound he made. Had he after all caught sight of Amy as she'd ducked down the stairs? Had his last radio communication passed her location to the shouter below?

Or was it possible—?

Amy could hold her breath no longer. The reaction was immediate. A rush of footsteps up the stairs. The slam of a heavy body pinning Amy against the wall. A large, muscled arm wrapped her torso. Steel fingers muzzled the scream in her throat.

Furiously, instinctively, Amy fought back. With arms and body pinned, Amy couldn't struggle against that iron grip. But her feet were still free.

Her boot heel landed with a gratifying thud against a shin. From a muffled grunt, it had hurt.

Then Amy registered the faintest musk of cologne mingled with male perspiration, an abnormal rigidity that was body armor under her cheek, something indefinably familiar in the presence looming in the darkness above her. Abruptly as she'd lashed out, the fight and fury left Amy. As she grew still, the painful grip in which she stood eased fractionally, dropped away from her mouth. The name parting her lips emerged as quietly as the warm breath stirring the hair at her temple. "Steve!"

But Amy's surrender had come too late. Above them, the flashlight sprang to life. As its beam pinned two human shapes on the second-floor landing, the light threw into sharp relief a triumphant grin, an assault rifle. As Steve threw himself forward, an arm around Amy thrusting her behind him, the rat-tat-tat of gunfire broke the stillness of the stairwell.

48

"Please wake up! Oh, Steve, you have to wake up because we can't move you, and I don't know what to do!"

Steve opened reluctant eyelids to the ordinary white-gray glow of a fluorescent lantern. Its light glistened on tear-streaked female features that were vaguely familiar. But that soft pleading came from beside him. He turned his head. Long hair spilling from under a headscarf shimmered pale gold, and this time distressed, heart-shaped features were eminently familiar.

Amy Mallory.

With that identification, full recollection returned. A deep, shuddering breath wrung a groan from his lips. His chest felt as though he'd been hit by a battering ram. An acute pain as he turned his head explained a throbbing migraine. "I'm sorry, Amy. I should have had that last guy. What a screwup!"

He could taste the metallic saltiness of blood as his mouth twisted wryly. "So how long have I been out? What's the situation report? Where are Ismail's men?"

Amy was kneeling above Steve, so when she leaned forward, the flaxen fall of her hair brushed his cheek. "You've only been out a few minutes. And you were hardly a screwup. I think you must have got all Ismail's men because we haven't seen or heard any more since the one over there who shot you."

More cautiously this time, Steve turned his head again to take in a prone form lying nearby, hands, feet, and mouth bound with duct tape. The man was conscious, a single good eye glinting hate in the lantern light. Steve turned his head back to Amy. "Did I do that? Last I remember was him coming at me."

"Your stun gun thingy hit him just as he shot you." Amy indicated the Taser lying on the tile beside Steve. "You hit your head against the banister, and at first you weren't moving, so I thought—"

The quiver in her voice made clear what she'd thought. Blinking at a hand still resting against his body armor, Amy snatched it abruptly away. "But the bullets must have only hit your body armor because you weren't bleeding, just knocked out. I found your duct tape and used it to tie up the guard. By then Farah came." Amy indicated her young companion. "While you were unconscious, Farah and I checked to make sure there were no more guards. We counted five prisoners besides this one."

Steve took stock of his injuries. His top-of-the-line upper body armor had been worth every penny he'd paid because while questing fingers discovered three bullet impacts, none had broken skin, and if every rib still ached, cautious movement confirmed none were broken. The blood in his mouth proved only a bitten cheek lining, probably when his head had slammed into the banister. A lump on the back of his head was swelling rapidly, but probing fingers came away unbloodied. "And here I thought I was rescuing you. Sounds like you've been doing just fine without me."

"No, don't say that!" Amy shuddered. "They were going to kill us. If you hadn't come when you did, we'd be dead by now. Or wishing we were."

Steve's jaw went rigid at the revulsion in that last phrase. Only now was he taking in that while both women were properly cloaked in headscarves and chapans, the latter were ripped, duct tape holding them together across the front. He needed no further explanation of why the guards had been neglecting their perimeter watch. "Then let's call it a collaborative effort. And by the way—" Steve pushed himself to his feet and replaced the Taser on his belt before bending to scoop up the bound guard's weapon, though the movement forced another groan through his teeth—"how did you know it was me there in the dark?"

Even in the lantern's limited illumination, Steve could see pink flooding Amy's face. "I just knew. Not when I first heard the helicopter. But when the lights went off, and the guards never came back—well, it seemed like your sort of thing. When I first heard you on the stairs, I really did think you were one of the guards. But when you grabbed me . . ."

The pink deepened. "Ismail's guards don't wear body armor. Anyway, the bigger question is how you knew to come after Farah and me like this."

"Jamil told me." Though Steve spoke in English, Jamil's name drew a gasp from Amy's companion. Amy sucked in her own breath.

"Then you did reach him. Where is he?" Amy glanced around as though to find Jamil tucked into some shadowed corner.

"He wouldn't come with me. He said if Ismail found him gone before I got you out, it would put you in more danger. He was right, of course. But as soon as we get you out of here and safe, you can be sure I'll go back for him."

Steve had spoken roughly as though to banish horrified objections Amy hadn't even made. But the aid worker's expression in the lantern light held no recrimination, only concern, as she replied quietly, "Of course you will. Though right now we need to get you somewhere safe and let a professional look at that head injury."

Amy held up a small oblong. "I found my cell phone when we were searching the house. The guards upstairs were using it to make phone calls. Unfortunately, anyone I could call for help is a long drive away. Can you walk as far as the women's compound?"

"That won't be necessary." Steve dug out his own phone from a vest pocket. "I've got a ride waiting. But let's hurry! We need to be away from here before Ismail tries to reach his men and discovers there's no answer."

Steve did not allow the extent of his pain to show in his quick trot down the stairs as he punched in a speed-dial number. "Hey, Phil, I've got them both. All clear on this end. We'll be out front in two."

"On my way." Steve heard a car engine starting up. But when Phil spoke again, pleased approbation had given way to urgency. "At this end all is *not* clear. All is *not* clear. You've got hostiles heading your way!"

Steve was already stretching his long legs to a run, tossing over his shoulder to his two companions, "We've got to get out of here now."

Amy had grabbed Farah's hand. The two girls were tight on Steve's heels as he slammed open the front door and they raced down the steps. Steve could already hear the roar of an engine approaching the gate.

"There's another exit!" Amy gasped out behind Steve. "In the back through the orchard."

But once again it was too late. The compound gate was sliding sideways. Headlights pinned the three fugitives as a green police pickup breached the perimeter wall. If Steve were unhurt, he might have considered a last-ditch dash for that rear exit. But he could only brace himself dizzily as the pickup braked so violently, gravel sprayed his face. Neither did Steve attempt to raise either Taser or the rifle he'd purloined. Not with a dozen uniforms spilling from the pickup bed. The engine went dead, but headlights remained on. Then the driver stepped out.

Steve snarled recognition. "Ismail!"

The deputy minister strolled forward, but there was nothing casual about the pistol in his right hand. "When my security chief called to tell me of a circling helicopter, then loss of generator power, I knew it was no coincidence, but interference with my female guests. I should have considered it might be you, since your obsession with Ms. Mallory is not news to me. But how did she send word? I took every precaution."

Ismail sounded more admiring than angry. So long as the deputy minister did not find out who'd actually directed Steve here, opportunity still remained to go back after Jamil. If Steve could talk himself and his two companions out of here alive.

But it was Amy who spoke up, headlights outlining a raised chin and defiant expression. "Why does it matter how Mr. Wilson got here? You said you'd let Farah and me go if Jamil cooperated. Your men when they tried to rape us said that was a lie. That you'd given orders for us to be killed once the trial was over. Well, you're here now, so I'm guessing the trial's finished. Which means you must have realized Jamil will never do what you wish or give up his faith in Isa Masih, no matter what your threats. And since it's going to be even harder to hide two disappeared American citizens than one, especially a State Department hire like Mr. Wilson here, it seems the easiest solution for you as well as us would be just to let us go. After all, what can Farah or I really do to hurt you now? It would just be our word against yours."

Ismail's laughter held a note of hysteria. "Why do the infidels continue to underestimate me? Jamil has done exactly what I wished. And that is to die! Oh yes, if he is not dead yet, he will be any minute. And as a shaheed—a martyr. So all will know he was never truly a follower of Isa Masih but a foolish young man who tried before to assassinate his enemies and this time has succeeded."

The deputy minister had been speaking in English, so that only Steve and Amy could have understood. But now he held up a cell phone. Its speakerphone was turned up to high volume, the background sounds of a crowded room making low Dari commentary difficult to decipher. "The prisoner is approaching the judge. Qaderi is in place. Khalid is on the move. It must be now."

The miracle had not happened. No last-minute rescue had materialized. Jamil could only hope now his words would reach their intended audience.

He'd taken all possible precautions. Ground plastic casing and circuitry underfoot, then scooped the cell phone shards into the malodorous camouflage of his chamber pot. After stripping off his thigh bandage, he'd done the same with the tracking device. While he regretted destroying valuable instruments that were not his, he couldn't risk them being found on him.

The corridor guard had looked lethargically drowsy when he pushed open Jamil's cell door for a quartet of uniforms. The march that followed led through a gate into the administrative sector. The washing facility to which Jamil was taken was where he'd cleaned up for the Red Cross delegation. A full strip search confirmed Jamil's wisdom in divesting himself of tracker and phone.

He emerged to find his clothing gone. Waiting with a clean set were Ismail and the prison administrator. This time the weapon was even more ingenious than the last. No modified Army parka, but a set of heavy winter shalwar kameez topped with the thick, woolen vest poorer Afghans wore for warmth in winter. The material of drawstring pants and tunic was stiff with what Jamil knew had to be the explosive while the vest was abnormally padded and heavy, just like the Army parka Ismail had once draped around his shoulders in a bathroom, its lining, Jamil guessed, packed with the same shrapnel of stone, bone, and glass that had fooled metal detectors in that earlier bomb.

Jamil made no attempt to resist donning the prepared clothing items. Though Ismail did not approach him, he raised a cell phone. Jamil had no difficulty interpreting its message. Do as told, and the call would be made to free Ameera and Farah. If not . . .

Jamil's own silent plea as the bomb settled over his body did not vary. *As I once prayed to die and then to live, so I pray now only that I might not kill. I know that you, almighty Creator, who laid down your life as Isa Masih in my place and for my sin, are able to rescue me as you rescued your followers from the fiery furnace. Yet you have permitted many followers instead to lay down their lives that your love might be seen through their martyrdom. So I do not ask for rescue, but only for your will—and that I might not kill.*

His prayer seemed a hopeless one as the guard quartet returned to lead Jamil down more corridors. Were they aware of what Jamil carried on his body? Surely not, or they would hardly jostle so close. If Ismail's scheme succeeded, Jamil's escort would be the first blamed. If they survived. Or even if not. Knowing Ismail, Jamil had no doubt such a scapegoat was not incidental but deliberately planned.

Ismail and his companion had followed at a discreet distance until Jamil heard a cell phone ring. His escort halted during a brief, low-voiced discussion. A situation had arisen at Ismail's compound. Jamil's heartbeat quickened. He had no doubt who was behind this sudden emergency. Ameera and Farah's safety now rested in Steve Wilson's hands. All that remained was for Jamil to finish this.

Though Ismail hurried away, Jamil did not take it as a reprieve, since the prison administrator immediately gestured for the guards to prod Jamil forward. A gun barrel nudged Jamil through tall double doors.

When Jamil had faced his earlier hearing, this courtroom had been virtually empty. Now it was crowded with officials in Western suits or rich, embroidered chapans and turbans. An array of news cameras and caterpillar mikes curved around the wood-paneled walls. Behind the heavy, solid desk at the front sat no underling this time, but Minister of Justice Qaderi himself. Arrayed like a judges' panel on either side were his more prominent election rivals. Among them the man whose actions had set Jamil's feet upon the path leading to this place and time and predicament. Family friend, mujahedeen commander, minister of interior, Khalid Sayef.

The prison administrator had abandoned his party, pushing through the congestion toward the back of the courtroom. Was the detonator for the walking bomb that was now Jamil somewhere within his pockets? Whoever was pulling Jamil's strings would want to check visually that their weapon was in place before setting off the explosives.

Or was someone watching from elsewhere, perhaps through the eyes of one of those cameras? Ismail, even? Jamil could not let himself forget how that other bomb at the New Hope compound had been exploded from such an unexpected distance.

Jamil was more confused by Qaderi's presence. If he was right about the hand behind Ismail's actions, he'd have expected the minister of justice to arrange a tardy entrance. Instead Qaderi's position placed him directly in the line of fire.

Then Jamil took in the heavy construction of that desk, its solid, hardwood panel that shielded the minister's lower limbs and robes from indiscreet exposure. It offered a more substantial shield than body armor. Jamil had no idea how powerful the weapon he carried might be. If Qaderi held the detonator, he'd simply have to duck down while triggering the bomb. If his purpose was to take out Khalid and other main competitors while portraying Jamil as terrorist and assassin, the explosive radius of the bomb wouldn't need to be great. In fact, the prison administrator's presence at the rear of the room would indicate the opposite.

Jamil had no idea how much time might be left him. But as a gun barrel prodded him forward, he saw to his horror that Khalid had pushed himself to his feet, murmuring some comment to his neighbor before taking a step toward the door. As he'd done on that other occasion, Jamil remembered suddenly. Did the man have some internal sense of danger and preservation?

Whoever held the detonator would surely not let his target take another step away. And still Jamil spied no answer to his prayer. *Please, let me not kill!*

Then his eye fell on it. The two-sided barricade in the far front corner that formed a witness box for plaintiffs fortunate enough to be permitted live testimony. Waist-high, its panels were carved from the same rich, heavy hardwood as Qaderi's desk. Jamil could reach it in three strides. Which he dared delay no longer because Khalid had moved another pace toward the door.

Ameera, I will see you again. It will not be so long. Farah, my sweet princess, you will be well. Isa, into your hands I commend them.

One step.

Screams and shouts erupted across the courtroom as the audience witnessed the prisoner break away from his guards.

Two.

A rat-tat-tat of gunfire rose above screams with complete disregard for collateral danger to bystanders. Jamil staggered as searing pain ripped through a thigh, his shoulder. But he didn't slow.

Three.

Jamil was toppling over the barrier with a momentum made easier because spectators obstructing his progress had scrambled out of the way. He could no longer see Khalid's progress nor anything else. Then it didn't matter anymore. His torn, bleeding shoulder had just slammed into the tile flooring when the explosion ripped through him.

Jamil had expected the pain. What he had not expected was the joy. The light. Then a face whose eyes he recognized. Eyes that blazed with such love and welcome.

"If we are thrown into the blazing furnace, the God we serve is able to save us . . . But even if he does not—"

Oh, but you have, Isa Masih; you have!

I am free.

49

Even as the explosion rattled the cell phone's miniature speaker, a single crack of sound, distant enough for its timbre to be muffled, could be heard from the direction of Pul-e-Charki. His two companions' anguished cries matched the sharp twisting in Steve's own chest. Rushing forward, Jamil's sister sobbed against Amy's shoulder.

Ismail was speaking in English again. "I truly regret you chose to mix yourself in this, Willie. You were a good comrade and true warrior in those days we fought the Taliban together, though you are an infidel and will never see paradise. But you must understand now why you will all die, no matter what the complications."

Oh yes, Steve understood perfectly why Ismail couldn't permit his three prisoners to walk off this property. There was no further point in trying to persuade Ismail to let them go. Or in hiding Steve's own interaction with Jamil.

Aloud, Steve said evenly, "Then turning Jamil into a suicide bomber, not convincing him to recant his faith, was what you had in mind when you told Bolton you'd deal with the religious freedom issue before elections. Which you can't pull off so long as anyone's around to testify Jamil's martyrdom was rigged. You're ahead of me there, Ismail, because not in a million years would I have dreamed you'd pull a stunt like this. You've played the loyal follower so well that even seeing that video Jamil took of you, it's hard to believe you were behind all those attempts on Khalid's life.

"So how long have you been Qaderi's mole in Khalid's camp? Clear back to when you were fighting Tallies with Khalid while Qaderi was in exile? Then Khalid starts getting too powerful and in the way of Qaderi's own presidential ambitions, so he orders you to take him out?"

But the growing triumph in Ismail's sneer told Steve he'd gotten something very wrong even before the deputy minister leaned forward to hiss scornfully, "Did you believe Khalid dead? It is Qaderi who is dead right now along with others as Allah wills of those who seek to oppose Khalid. Khalid is very much alive, and now he will be the next president of Afghanistan. You fool, did you really think I would serve Qaderi above Khalid? or that any of this was done without his knowledge? On the contrary, Khalid planned all of this."

Ismail's continued flow of words held neither apology nor defiance, but pride. "Qaderi is a pious and upright son of Islam. But all his talk of reform makes enemies of the wealthy and powerful. Nor does he understand that Afghanistan can no longer exist without the outside world.

"Khalid, on the other hand, knows one must be pragmatic. After the Taliban, he was willing to retire from battle. But when the weakness and incompetence of Afghanistan's new rulers became apparent, he saw as did I that only the great mujahedeen commander Khalid Sayef had strength to restore peace and order to our nation. So he devised his course. First counternarcotics to acquire necessary funds. Then Ministry of Interior, where he could place his own followers into every province and police district before the next presidential election. And when that position was unjustly given to another, he took his own steps to amend that injustice."

"You're talking about the sugar factory bombing?" Steve had thought he was beyond being stunned by Ismail's revelations. "You're saying Khalid never was a target, but the one who planned it?"

"A brilliant strategy. Not only did Khalid receive at last the position he merited, but your own government greatly increased his prominence when they assigned their own warriors to protect him. Then Jamil came into our hands. It was Khalid who conceived a use for his former enemy."

Fanned out with their weapons fixed on Steve and the two women, the police uniforms looked bored at a conversation they couldn't understand.

Farah was weeping quietly, but Amy lowered her head so that only the silent tension of her body line told Steve how attentively she was listening.

Ismail spread his hands, palms up. "You know how that day ended. At first Khalid did not mind so much because even without Jamil's death, all turned out as he planned. The Americans and other Western leaders made clear they favored him in the elections. Qaderi—indeed, all the candidates—seemed little threat. Until Jamil so foolishly permitted himself to be arrested. If nothing else, for all he has done to destroy Khalid's plans, Jamil has earned the death he received."

Ismail dropped his arms. "But Khalid is never without a Plan B. Or rather I, for it was I who planned this checkmate. Tonight the statement of shaheed Jamil made before abandoning his mission will be broadcast. When the world hears from Jamil's own lips of his hatred for Khalid and desire to kill him, none will doubt tonight's intended target. And once Allah's favor is again made apparent by Khalid's miraculous escape from death, the Afghan people will gladly mark their ballots for him.

"As for your government and others, they will count themselves fortunate that Khalid and not Qaderi survived. They will send more aid because Khalid has both power and will to enforce peace. Nor will they look too closely at what he does to ensure that peace. Have they not already given up their foolish talk of democracy and Western liberties? And because Khalid will not interfere more than necessary to placate the mullahs in his people's personal lives, the West will declare him a progressive leader and be only thankful they can at last take their soldiers and go home."

Ismail was turning away. "But enough. You think I do not know you seek only to delay me?"

Not all the police uniforms had remained with their weapons on the prisoners because the guards Steve had immobilized were now emerging into the open, rubbing their wrists, expressions unfriendly as their glares landed on Steve. At Ismail's orders, the uniforms piled back into the pickup. One climbed into the driver's seat and began reversing out the gate. Steve was not happy to see them go. The deputy minister was only too clearly ridding himself of the outside witness those police uniforms offered.

Guards had retrieved fluorescent lanterns by the time departing head-lights plunged the front drive into darkness. The gate still stood open, and as the pickup raced away, its roar was challenged by another fast-approaching vehicle. *Please, God, don't let it be Phil driving into this ambush!*

But the twin beams shining through the open gate belonged to another police pickup. This time the pickup bed was empty, and only a single person stepped from the driver's seat. The official with white-striped brown beard Steve knew to be the Pul-e-Charki administrator. Steve didn't waste his breath appealing to the newcomer. His presence simply confirmed one more person who'd remained a staunch follower of Khalid while ostensibly on Qaderi's payroll. At least he could now guess how Ismail had once again managed to smuggle a rigged-to-blow Jamil into the heavily secured event this trial was supposed to be.

Ismail held up his cell phone as he switched to swift Dari. "We heard the explosion. Was it not a success? Or is Qaderi not after all among the dead?"

"There are no dead."

What Jamil's sister had been able to understand of Ismail's boastful English, Steve had no idea. But that she'd caught the Dari was clear by her sharp cry, drowning out Amy's own gasp. The prison administrator glanced toward the two women. "Except the prisoner, of course. He managed to throw himself behind a partition just as the bomb went off, perhaps in last-minute remorse. The presidential candidates thus spared are already praising Allah's mercy to the TV cameras."

The sag in Ismail's body was immediate, his triumphant sneer replaced by such a look of rage that his lips drew back in a snarl. The gun in his hand came up, and for a moment, Steve thought the deputy minister was going to shoot the bearer of the news he'd just received. Instead the gun swung toward the three captives on the front steps. "So Plan B has not been successful. Inshallah. There is always a Plan C. Meanwhile, it is time to clean up the loose ends."

Steve had already racked his own brain through Plans B, C, and the rest of the alphabet. If he launched himself at Ismail, he might get his fingers around that bony neck before he went down. But that left half a dozen weapons trained on the two girls.

So he did not move as Ismail's finger tightened on the trigger. At his side, he could see Amy's mouth moving silently. In prayer? Steve didn't close his eyes nor shift them from the small, round opening of that handgun muzzle even as he offered up his own prayer. *Father God, this is it. Into your hands I commit—*

But the gun barrel was dropping. Ismail swung around to the newcomer. "No, if the foreigners question, I must be able to say honestly that I had no part in their killing. I will return to Pul-e-Charki. You deal with them as soon as I am gone."

Handing his pistol to the prison administrator, Ismail headed toward the pickup. Steve tensed as the official hefted the gun. But he was not directing it toward his captives.

Steve almost let out a warning cry as the pistol rose. A crack of gunfire. Then Ismail slumped to the ground, the bullet entry point above the left ear.

Steve threw his arms out instinctively, little though he could do to protect his two companions. But the pistol was now lowered. At the official's curt order, the automatic rifles covering the prisoners were lowered as well. The Pul-e-Charki administrator looked meditatively down at Ismail's slumped body.

"It is truly sad that Minister of Interior Khalid's own deputy should be found to be involved in such evil. Not only the attempts on the minister's own life, but now this assault on foreign citizens. A full investigation will be made into all this man's activities in recent months."

He gave Steve a curt nod. "You and your companions are free to go."

Steve did not move, his eyes never leaving the smoking muzzle of the gun. It was Amy who stepped forward to ask uncertainly, "You mean, you're letting us leave?"

Bushy eyebrows shot high. "But of course. You are not under arrest. It has already been explained to me the crimes Ismail committed, not only against Minister Khalid but in keeping you and your companion prisoner here in his home. I am only glad I was able to arrive before this madman carried out his threats to kill you. That he would suggest I might help him in his crimes only demonstrates he was not in his right mind in all he has done tonight."

This time it was Steve who spoke up. "You're saying Ismail wasn't telling the truth when he accused Khalid of being behind all this?"

The prison administrator looked incredulous. "Of course not. Khalid is an honorable man. Have I not served him long and well myself? Would he be implicated in such crimes? No, if Ismail did not lie to cover up his real target, Khalid himself, then perhaps he was a fanatic who truly believed Afghanistan to be best served by impelling Khalid to power. In that he would be right. In either case, an investigation will clarify the man acted alone plotting with this Jamil, who blew himself up."

"And if we testify otherwise?"

At Amy's query, a glimmer of the same cold ferocity that had been on Ismail's face showed fleetingly in the official's expression. Steve automatically shifted to place his body between man and aid worker. But the Pul-e-Charki administrator relaxed, waving a negligent hand. "Testify as you like. Who will listen when all evidence points clearly to what has happened here this day? Khalid will be horrified when he finds out all this man has done, even as he rejoices to discover at last the traitor in his midst. That this has ended with no further loss of life except the two perpetrators is cause for more rejoicing. Now the Afghan people can turn to the important issues of the upcoming elections."

The official's expression was deadpan, but his tone held irony as he glanced down at the dead body spilling a scarlet flood across the gravel. "Perhaps Ismail should have remembered his own words. For every Plan B, would Khalid not also have in place a Plan C?"

50

The trek back to the AWR compound seemed endlessly longer than Amy's previous journey. Once he'd ordered their release, the Pul-e-Charki official ignored Ismail's three prisoners, leaving them free to stroll out the gate. But more headlights were now racing down the dirt track. Khalid's cleanup crew? Whatever the administrator's assurances, Steve must have had little faith in him because though he was swaying on his feet, he'd sharply vetoed having Phil drive into the armed camp for a pickup.

Instead, Amy took the lead across the open fields. That Steve offered no protest was a worrying indication of how much pain he must be battling. Farah no longer wept, stumbling after the other two in such a robotic daze, Amy feared she'd gone into shock. At least the moon had risen high over the mountain peaks, its silver light reflecting off the barren plain, so their steps were better lit than Amy's outward trek.

Phil, waiting impatiently at the vehicles with an M4 cradled in his hands, let out a furious stream of prose when he registered Steve's faltering steps and pain-drawn features. "You overgrown idiot, why didn't you tell me there were injuries? I'd have been over in a shot no matter what your op orders."

"Precisely why I didn't," Steve answered tersely. "Stop fussing; you're not my mother!"

Ignoring him, Phil dug a field medical kit out of the Pajero by the time juvenile lookouts on the compound wall brought Arif running to open the gate. The medic stripped off the upper body armor to confirm that neither the head injury nor bruises now purpling Steve's torso had broken skin, then forced down a dose of Demerol before permitting his friend to take another step.

Inside, the compound buzzed with agitated voices, and not only because of concerns over a missing Amy. As the group followed Arif across the compound grounds, Amy could hear the solar-powered radio blaring. Their juvenile escorts raced along the path ahead of them. "She's back! Ameera-jan is back! And she's brought Farah-jan with her!"

The compound's entire population was gathered around the radio in the communal salon. When Farah and Amy stepped into the light of a fluorescent lantern, their ripped clothing and tear-streaked, bruised faces drew outraged hisses and sympathetic exclamations, but no surprise. This was only too common a scenario in their lives. The wail with which Farah threw herself into her former housemates' arms, their fussing clucks and pats and hugs, answered the question of whether the girl would be welcomed back. And whether she'd be willing to stay.

Nor did the compound residents shy away from Steve and Phil, as might have been expected. Instead, they bustled around, pressing tea and supper's leftovers on their guests. As he'd promised, the foreign warrior had brought back their Ameera-jan and Farah too. Before Amy could react, she found herself seated, a warm cloak wrapped around her, chilled fingers pressed to a hot mug.

Only then did Najeeda raise the question on all their minds, gesturing toward the radio, still tuned to local news in the background. "Is it true what they are saying? that Jamil, who told us your beautiful stories, is dead? that he blew himself up trying to kill others?"

Beside Amy, tears streamed again down Farah's cheeks. The pain in Amy's own chest was so strong, she could only shake her head helplessly. Just then the news commentary shifted to a single voice speaking. The oldest boy, Enayat, exclaimed, "It is Jamil!"

Reaching over, he turned the volume all the way up. Enayat was right, Amy recognized immediately. But what were these words Jamil was speaking? Words shaking with venom and rage. Though she'd never actually heard one before, Amy knew what this had to be. A shaheed statement of intent, such as suicide bombers routinely videoed to be broadcast once they'd accomplished their mission of death.

This then was the threat to which Ismail had alluded. It must have been taped before the New Hope bombing and Jamil's own change of heart. But who would ever believe that? Even if Ismail had failed in his ultimate purpose, even if Khalid's competition was still alive, the world hearing these words would still believe Jamil was nothing more than a suicide bomber with hate and revenge in his heart. Even worse, so would these children to whom Jamil had been medic and role model and friend.

"Are you okay?" A large frame hunkered down in front of Amy, shielding her tears from the rest of the group. The Demerol must have taken effect because Steve was moving more easily. But his gray eyes darkened, his firm mouth twisted with pain that was not only from his injuries. "Amy, I haven't had a chance to say how sorry I am for your loss, you and Farah both. I failed you. You and Jamil."

"Don't say that!" Amy cried out. Even though she'd spoken English, her outburst had drawn curious eyes, so she dropped her voice to a fierce, urgent whisper. "You didn't fail us. You saved our lives. Jamil . . . there was nothing you could do. Ismail killed him—Ismail and Khalid. And God allowed it."

Amy wiped a quick hand across her eyes. "That's what I don't understand. When I thought we were going to die, when I'd resigned myself to dying, God heard my prayers and sent you to rescue us. I haven't even thanked you for that yet. But why did God bring rescue for Farah and me and not for Jamil? I'd so much rather he'd saved Jamil because now all Afghanistan—the whole world—believes Jamil to be a liar and murderer! How could God let those evil men win? let all Jamil's dreams and hopes for his country, the teachings and love of Isa he so wanted to share with them, be silenced like this?"

Jamil's voice was still speaking on the radio, but his words changed. Amy's head shot up.

"If you are hearing my words today, then I am no longer among the living. They will tell you I was a terrorist and murderer, seeking only revenge and death. They will even use words I once spoke long ago as proof. And they will not be lying. For such I was before I came to know the teachings and love of Isa Masih. From hate and vengeance against those who destroyed my family and corrupted my country, he changed my heart to love and forgiveness. Before I am silenced, I must tell you that Isa Masih is no prophet but the almighty Creator himself come in human body to show his love to his creation. He laid his life down freely as a sacrifice to pay the debt for my sins and yours. Where once I feared to die in my sins, I am no longer afraid because Isa's martyrdom has washed me clean and set me free."

Jamil's voice through the radio's tinny speakers held an unreal calm. "And now evil men believe they have triumphed in killing me, in attempting to force me to kill others. But it is not true. As Isa laid down his life on my behalf and yours, so I lay down my life freely for those I love. Long ago three followers of the almighty Creator were also threatened with death if they did not worship a pagan king's image. They chose instead to walk into a fiery furnace rather than deny their Creator. The Almighty sent an angel from heaven to deliver them. And the Almighty is strong enough to save me now. But even should he choose death for me this day, I will not turn away from following Isa Masih. Because he alone can change a heart of hate to love. He alone can heal Afghanistan.

"Oh, my people, this day listen to his words and his love. And, my sisters, my brother, whom I love, if we do not meet again in this lifetime, I will be waiting to greet you in paradise. 'This is how we know what love is: Isa Masih laid down his life for us.' 'Greater love has no one than this, that he lay down his life—'"

As though someone at the radio station had just realized what they'd been playing, the recording abruptly cut off. Steve looked dazed. "So that's why he wanted my cell phone! But how did he manage to have them play that instead of Ismail's original recording?"

"It doesn't matter," Amy said softly. "Look!"

Steve swiveled on his heels to take in what had brought wonder to Amy's eyes and heart. Every face illuminated by the scant lantern light held a similar expression of absorbed concentration, even children surely too young to understand what had just transpired. Seated beyond Steve, the compound's new chowkidar abruptly placed his teacup on the rug with a force that spilled it. Amy braced for an explosion. But Arif's weathered features held instead a baffled raptness as he shook his gray beard from side to side. "The words he speaks of Isa's love for all mankind, I remember such words when I was a very small child. Foreigners who took me from the streets, where I was starving, spoke of such things before the mullahs forbade them."

"Khalid isn't going to be too happy," Steve murmured incredulously against Amy's ear. "Or Qaderi and his mullah cohorts. Because somehow in the annals of eternity, I don't think this is going down as a failed mission after all."

"But I don't understand." Najeeda removed an arm from around Farah to look at the younger girl. "Is this the same Isa of whom you told us, Farah-jan, who healed the blind and fed the hungry? And why should he give up his life in martyrdom for us?"

On Farah's other side, Ameera stirred immediately. But before the foreign woman could speak, Farah rose to her feet. The pain in her heart still poured unchecked down her cheeks, but stirring within her breast was a growing flame of the joy and love she'd heard in her brother's voice. She bent first to hug Ameera, this woman not of her country, but who had become indeed a sister of her heart.

"Ameera-jan, I understand now all you told me of Isa, why my brother made such a choice. He does love me. So much that he laid down his life for me and you. As Isa loves me. And Jamil has kept his promise, for he has not left me alone, and one day we will be together again."

With confidence, Farah moved to the center of the crowded room. Turning off the radio, she settled herself on the rug. Neither Arif nor Masooda made any objection as her hands began to move gracefully. "I will tell you the story. You have already heard how the Almighty placed the first man and woman in a beautiful paradise until they disobeyed their Creator and were cast out. But the Almighty loved mankind too much to leave them in despair."

Isa took you to paradise, my brother, so it will be a while longer before we are again together. But he left me in your place. And I will carry forward your dream for Afghanistan; I will speak the words and love of Isa on your behalf so long as Isa permits.

Oh, my brother, I was so wrong!

Love is no illusion.

51

"You're looking for Amy? I'm afraid she's not here at the moment. She finished packing, said she was going to get a little air before heading to the airport." Becky Frazer gestured toward two suitcases sitting inside the door, the same Steve had once carried for Amy into this apartment. "I don't know if you're aware she's flying out on this evening's Indian Airlines run, New Delhi–Miami."

The nurse-practitioner lifted a cell phone. "I'm lining up her ride right now. I've got a clinic myself, unfortunately, and my driver's off for the rest day. But one of the international schoolteachers has visitors flying out. I'm hoping he's got room in his van."

"Don't bother." Steve shook his head. "I've got a Condor Security vehicle and driver on hand. We'll make sure she gets her flight."

"I sure appreciate that. And I know Amy will. You're welcome to wait here for her. Or if you'd like to go find her yourself, I saw her heading toward the vocational institute. Where we host the worship gathering. You might try the top floor. That's where I go to think."

An approving twinkle, the warmth of her smile drew Steve's own rare grin. "Thanks, I'll do just that."

The three-story brick cube that was the compound's main building had been abuzz with vocational students when Steve had been here last with John Atkins. But today was the Friday rest day, and the weekly worship gathering was scheduled elsewhere. Striding through empty, whitewashed salons, Steve headed up a concrete staircase. He had a good idea of the thinking spot to which Becky Frazer referred.

The top floor was divided into several large classrooms. The farthest looked out over the compound's front wall. Blast film covered the windows, part of Steve's security upgrade. Its tint allowed those inside to see out but prevented spying eyes from peering into the building. This top floor was high enough to offer a panoramic view of central Kabul, the twin minarets of the main mosque thrusting skyward like filigreed needles above the rooftops. In the distance, the snowcapped mountain peaks encircling the city were visible today through the smog.

At one of the windows stood a slim, still figure.

Steve hadn't seen Amy since they'd slipped away from Farah's storytelling last night. By then the Demerol was kicking in, and Phil had put his prosthesis down hard, pronouncing both Steve and Amy unfit to drive home. An edict simplified when Amy turned the Toyota Corolla's keys over to Arif, informing the delighted chowkidar that the vehicle was a final donation from New Hope. Steve's memory of the rest of the evening once they'd delivered Amy into Becky Frazer's comforting arms was hazy. But he'd woken this morning clear of head, if still sore, an impressive array of black and blue mottling his rib cage.

Amy hadn't noticed Steve's approach, her body tilted slightly forward to stare at the vista outside as though storing a memory she might never encounter again. Seizing the opportunity, Steve paused in the doorway to drink in the sight of her. Here alone behind tinted windows, she'd tossed aside chapan and headscarf, today's choice making a burgundy pool on the floor beside her. Perhaps for travel ease, she'd chosen to wear the matching thigh-length tunic over jeans, gold embroidery against burgundy silk glinting as brightly as the free spill of her hair. Along the cheekbone visible to Steve, judicious makeup did not completely obscure a bruise where one of Amy's captors had hit her across the face. But even as the sight of this roused fresh anger in Steve, he could wonder incredulously at his own blindness that he'd ever estimated this woman's attractiveness to hold more character than stereotypical beauty.

On the contrary, that tall, slim frame, the resolute, small chin and full mouth, possessed a beauty that went bone-deep. A warmth and passion that would remain undiminished, Steve recognized with a sudden ache in his chest, when the shimmer of gold had faded from that silken spill of hair and the graceful body was gnarled and bent with age.

Amy had once named it. The warming glow that gave her such beauty. That made such friends of hers as John and Ruth Atkins and Becky Frazer so attractive.

Love.

In turn, Steve had challenged Amy that change could only come to a culture when its own people were willing to change. And not only to change, but to lay down their own lives, instead of asking others—like, say, American soldiers—to bring about that change. An unlikely prospect, since what could possibly impel a hurting and bitter populace to change from rage to forgiveness, from violence to peace?

Amy, John Atkins, Jamil himself had thrown the answer into Steve's face until he could no longer dismiss it.

Once again, love.

Love of the almighty Creator of the universe stepping into a troubled planet in the human form of Isa Masih, Jesus Christ.

Love of Christ followers who would leave comfortable homes and lives to step into a troubled nation in some distant corner of the planet, pouring out their lives in service to a people who too often didn't even appreciate their sacrifice.

Love that could transform a terrorist and would-be suicide bomber into an itinerant health care worker willing to risk freedom and well-being to offer relief in the name of Isa Masih. And then in the end to lay down his life, no longer out of hate and vengeance but deliberate, willing sacrifice.

Was it really so simple?

Because if so, then what Amy had been doing all these months in Afghanistan, as well as her American nurse friend Becky Frazer, John and Ruth Atkins, and so many others within a community Steve had once written off as naive and misguided, was neither foolish nor futile, but a far more effective means of bringing about peace and lasting change than all the weapons and foreign aid handouts in ISAF's arsenal.

Oh, to be loved like that!

To love like that!

Steve had taken a step forward when Amy suddenly turned her head, offering a clear view of her expression. It held such desolation, such forlorn vulnerability, that Steve froze. He could guess whom she'd been thinking of to bring that look to her face. And why Amy had retreated here to this high aerie unaccompanied. She hadn't wanted to weigh down her friend and hostess with the intensity of her grief. So she'd come here for solitude to mourn.

Steve eased backward. He'd return to Becky's apartment to wait for Amy's return. Give her time to put on a smiling mask appropriate to spectators.

But Amy had continued to turn away from the window. As an unseeing gaze brushed his own tall frame, desolation flared into astonishment in hazel eyes. Her exclamation carried the same unhesitating recognition with which she'd breathed his name into the blackness of an unlit stair landing. "Steve!"

Amy took a quick step toward him as Steve moved forward into the room. "What are you doing here? I thought . . . I tried calling your phone this morning, but there was no answer. I ended up getting through to your team house. Someone named Cougar. He said you'd already packed and left, that it was all arranged to fly out today on some military flight. From what he said, I thought you'd be in the air already."

She paused briefly before adding with diffident hesitation. "It was no big deal. I just wanted to let you know I was leaving Kabul today. A Ministry of Interior official showed up here this morning with a revocation of my humanitarian visa. Said I had twenty-four hours to be out of Afghanistan or I'd be arrested as persona non grata. Fortunately they still had a few open seats on the evening New Delhi flight. This Cougar told me he'd pass word on to you."

"Yes, I got the same notice." Steve strolled farther into the room. "And Cougar did give me the message. Sorry about the phone. I was in meetings all morning. The kind where they confiscate such contact with the outside world as cell phones."

Always the medic, Phil had insisted on a visit to the embassy clinic that morning. Steve had headed immediately afterward to the deputy chief of mission's office. But discussions with Carl Bolton and a number of unnamed associates had not gone well.

The DCM had not questioned Steve's accounting of events. "We'd no inkling Ismail planned to go so far with this election crisis he'd hold an American citizen hostage. But we can hardly visit an overzealous subordinate's sins on a highly respected cabinet minister and presidential candidate. Yes, we've seen the video in question. Just one more headache to complicate these elections. How did the guy manage that from a Pul-e-Charki cell?"

Steve didn't bother enlightening him, and Bolton at least had the good sense not to probe too deeply as to just how Steve had uncovered Amy's hostage situation or managed to infiltrate a government official's well-guarded compound.

"But none of this changes our position," the DCM summarized definitively. "No, we certainly won't make public these accusations against Khalid. They wouldn't stand up in any U.S. court of law, much less over here."

So it still remained an even toss-up just which of a bad lot would pull off the elections in two weeks. Would it even matter?

To Steve's fury, Bolton had followed his dismissal with the intelligence that Steve's credentials to operate a State Department contract in Afghanistan had been revoked since the Ministry of Interior had found it necessary to cancel his visa. Khalid might prefer no more bodies littering his campaign. But it would seem he wasn't above using the Ministry of Interior's control over immigration to rid himself of inconvenient witnesses. In compensation, Bolton had with Machiavellian courtesy arranged a seat for Steve on the first ISAF cargo flight out.

Steve raised his shoulders now in a shrug. "I did have a military flight offered. But I chose to book my own. Indian Airlines. New Delhi–Miami. Leaving 6 p.m."

"But—that's the same flight I'm taking!" Amy broke off to eye Steve doubtfully. "I didn't even realize you had friends or family in Miami."

"No such luck. But Special Ops Command up at MacDill Air Force Base north of Miami has been after me to take a contract training Afghanistan-bound teams. I agreed to at least go up there and hear them out once I was done standing in for Phil over here. Which I am."

Was Steve's flight change really so easily explained? Amy schooled her face to composure as the security contractor closed the intervening gap between them. Like Amy, Steve had opted for more casual travel dress than his usual safari-style work clothes. But jeans and T-shirt did nothing to camouflage the powerfully muscled tall frame and wide shoulders. A watchful alertness that double-checked every corner of the room as he advanced into it. The lithe control of his stride that didn't project repose, but a coiled spring prepared to launch into action.

A dangerous man and a competent one.

A warrior.

But Amy's own observant survey had not missed as well a slight stiffness that might denote pain. The smallest wince when Steve turned his head too abruptly. And was that bandage wrapping Amy could make out under the thin T-shirt material?

Sharply Amy demanded, "Are you okay? I can see the bandages, so don't try to tell me you weren't hurt after all."

Reaching Amy, Steve pushed up sunglasses to expose keen gray eyes that crinkled at the corners in a faint smile but held as well the unreadable look at which the contractor was such an expert. "Couple cracked ribs. The doc insisted on taping them up. No big deal. I've gone into combat with worse."

A protracted silence followed. Amy filled it with a rush. "So are you going to take the job? The one in Florida."

"Have you heard anything further from your women's project?" Steve asked at the same instant. "Any fallout for Farah and the others from this?"

Steve's hesitation allowed Amy to be the first to answer. "Dr. Amrita called me this morning. Masooda had let her know what happened. She doesn't think there's going to be a problem. Even if Khalid knew about Farah, he doesn't know where she went from Ismail's compound. I talked to Farah too. After spending some time with Dr. Amrita and Masooda, she's made up her mind what she wants to do. Finish her education, then go to medical school like Jamil if funds can be found."

It had been difficult telling Farah that Amy was leaving Afghanistan immediately. But though Amy could hear tears in the girl's voice, she'd assured, "I will miss you, Ameera-jan. But I will never again be alone. And someday we will meet again."

Farah's cryptic wording indicated other listeners hovering near. But Amy understood the girl wasn't referencing her housemates. Farah too had encountered the freedom and love of Isa Masih that had transformed her brother.

"Medical school! Good for her. As to funds, maybe you can let your Dr. Amrita know a scholarship's available when Farah's ready for it. And money to cover any other need the girl might have."

Amy stared at Steve. "An entire scholarship to medical school? Even at local prices, that's a generous offer."

"I've got funds. I've been stashing away my contract pay for years. Can't think of a better use for it." The tall contractor shifted his body to stare out through the blast film before he went on. "Besides, I promised Jamil I'd look after his sister. And you as well. I didn't understand at the time why he was so urgent about it. But he must have already known what Ismail had in mind. And that I wasn't going to have opportunity to come back for him."

Steve dragged his gaze from the city skyline to Amy's face. "Your Jamil was a good man, a brave one. A man I'm proud to call my brother."

Tears stung Amy's eyes at the expression in the gray eyes, no longer unreadable but warm with a compassion and regret and sadness that caught her breath. Shakily she said, "I think he'd say the same about you. And I do appreciate your offer for Farah. But as for me, if you came here out of some feeling of obligation because you promised Jamil to keep an eye on me, it really wasn't necessary. A return phone call would have been just fine. Or even a text that you'd got my message."

Amy had thought she'd managed to keep hurt from her voice. But a hand running forcefully through Steve's dark curls conveyed exasperation. "I didn't come here out of obligation. I came because if we're on the same flight, it would be rather silly not to offer you a ride. And because

I wanted to see you. Did you really think I'd leave without even saying good-bye, checking out how you were doing?"

Amy raised her eyes to his. "To be honest, I don't know what I thought. Maybe that it was your polite way of making clear you wanted to put all this behind you. For which I couldn't blame you. I'm well aware of how much trouble all this has caused you."

"Trouble!" Steve dropped his hand from his hair, exasperation giving way to a wry twist of his mouth. "You bet it's been trouble! Any mission worth doing brings trouble. But I got into this of my own choice. Because I believed in the mission. Because I believed in you and Jamil. I only regret profoundly how it's all turned out. And that's something I couldn't say over the phone. I know how deeply you and Jamil loved each other, the hopes you had for a future together. I hope you believe me that if there were any way I could change what happened last night, bring Jamil back to you, I'd give anything, do anything, to make it happen."

There was no mistaking passionate sincerity and compassion. If only Amy could read what else that gray gaze held. "We both would. Which is maybe why God didn't leave it up to us. Because much though I'd wish to change it, you were so right that Jamil's death wasn't a failed mission. I don't know if you've heard what all's happened since Jamil's final recording went live. News channels all over Afghanistan and the Muslim world played it before the mullahs, and authorities started screaming. By then it was already all over YouTube."

Amy closed her eyes to evoke that dim recording as she'd watched it on Becky's computer, a thin, bearded face lit with unearthly peace in the weak gleam of a flashlight as Jamil spoke that final message of love and faith to a listening world.

"No one seems to know how Jamil got his message out, just that a shaheed confession purporting to prove Jamil wasn't a genuine apostate was delivered to Kabul's biggest TV station to be aired in conjunction with the trial. But Kareem works at that station, so I've no doubt he's the one who doctored that confession. I just hope he doesn't find himself in any trouble over it."

And that the young Afghan journalist would himself one day embrace the faith expressed in his friend's last message.

"I wouldn't worry," Steve reassured quietly. "Your journalist friend seems a competent young man. And with Ismail gone, who's to testify the original tape was different from what aired?"

"In any case, it's taken less than twenty-four hours for the video to be ranked as one of YouTube's top downloads, including all across the Muslim world. Qaderi, Ismail, and Khalid, even our own State Department, thought they could make Jamil and his faith conveniently go away. But he's already reaching more of the Afghan people and others around the world with the good news of love and hope and freedom in Isa Masih, Jesus Christ, through his death than in all his wandering as a healer or even in the lifetime he could have had. That old saying is as true as it has always been. The blood of the martyrs truly is the seed of the church."

Now it was Amy who turned her head away to gaze out through the blast film as she added quietly, "I do appreciate you coming here to say all this in person. There's a lot of questions I'd still like to ask, including the full story of what happened in Pul-e-Charki last night. But there's one misunderstanding I should clear up first. I did love Jamil. I do love him. I grieve his loss. But I was never *in* love with him. Not the way you implied."

The long frame beside her stiffened abruptly. "But . . . I'd always thought . . . Jamil said—"

"Yes, I know how Jamil felt about me. I tried to tell him the truth that last time I saw him. I love Jamil. As I love Farah. As I love the New Hope children. Enough to give my life for them. I've even battled with the fact that I should be *in* love with Jamil. He's such a wonderful person, and any woman would be privileged to be loved by him. And yet I somehow also knew God had another plan for Jamil's life that didn't include me. In time once Jamil was safely away from Pul-e-Charki, I knew he'd eventually come to that realization on his own. To be honest, I'd thought maybe he was even the man to show Farah that human love as well as God's love is no illusion. And I was right. But as her brother, not her husband. I was right too that God had another purpose for Jamil's life, if hardly what I had in mind. Jamil is my brother, my friend, and I'm looking forward to seeing him again one day. But I'm not mourning him. Not in the way you seem to think."

"So you're saying you were never in love with Jamil." Steve was suddenly closer to Amy than he had been. Close enough to make her heart race. Too close for her to look up and see his expression without turning her body to an even closer proximity. "But I saw your face when I walked in on you just now. If you weren't thinking of Jamil, who were you thinking of?"

Amy had her gaze fastened on a blue and yellow kite skittering in a zigzag above the apartment building across the street. With spring winds, kite season had returned to Kabul. But the tall man beside her was still quietly, implacably waiting, and Amy knew former Special Forces Master Sergeant Stephen Wilson too well by now to even consider he'd any plans of backing off before he got an answer. Swallowing, Amy with difficulty found her voice.

"Actually, I was thinking of you. I . . . You'd left once again without any good-bye. Or at least I thought you had. And . . . maybe I was being a little presumptuous, but whatever's been between us, however much trouble I've caused you, I'd come to consider you a friend. The first friend I really encountered in Afghanistan and maybe even the best. So I guess you caught me feeling a little sad I might never see you again to . . . to say good-bye properly and thank you for everything you've done."

Amy took a step back so she could turn to face Steve. "But you're here now. You've said good-bye and checked up on me like Jamil asked. So . . . so please don't feel any further obligation. My future's settled. If there's one thing all this has made clear to me, it's that I've found the mission to which I'm committing the rest of my life. My heart is with the Afghan people, not just a short-term project or two but for the long haul like John and Ruth and Becky. With this visa blacklist, I don't even know when I'll make it back into Afghanistan. But I know this is where God is calling me. I've promised my parents I'll spend some time with them in Miami. But I've already checked out an aid project that's helping Afghan refugees across the border in Tajikistan. And someday I will make it back into Afghanistan. Maybe by then Jamil's hopes for freedom there will have become a reality."

But Steve had closed the judicious gap she'd placed between them with a single stride. "Sounds like a mission worth fighting. Any chance you could use a partner? Because I made up my mind some time ago that I won't be taking that job offer. And from what I've seen, your profession could use a volunteer who's got some skills in security and crisis management."

Steve's offer was cool, matter-of-fact. But there was nothing either cool or matter-of-fact in the light flaming suddenly to gray eyes, the smile softening to tenderness. And something else that was making Amy's heart race even faster.

"A partner?" Amy echoed in a whisper. "Just . . . just what is it you're saying, Steve?"

"I'm saying I love you, Amy Mallory. I'm *in* love with you. I think I have been since the moment I saw you under that ridiculous burqa in the middle of a Kabul riot. Jamil knew that, if you didn't. Which is why he asked me to look after you for him. Bottom line, I too have finally found a mission worth committing the rest of my life to, if you think your humanitarian aid community can handle a roughneck like me. If necessary, I've already pledged myself to go this mission alone. But I'd sure rather go it together. Like your friends John and Ruth, I want to walk with you side by side through whatever years God gives us on this planet, work with you to share Christ's love wherever that takes us. So please tell me all your roundabout talk of friendship and thinking of me means you feel that way too. Do you love me, Amy Mallory? Are you *in* love with me?"

This time Amy didn't have to find her voice. Whatever Steve had glimpsed in widened hazel eyes and blazing smile was enough that his arms were suddenly tight around her. It was some minutes later when Amy found breath enough to speak again. "If you're not taking that job at MacDill, any chance you'd be interested in alternative plans for Miami? That is if you don't mind Cuban food and a rather large, overly extro-verted family that'll be irritatingly nosy about your intentions."

The firm mouth above hers curved to tender amusement. "I was count-ing on it."

Afternoon shadows had grown long through landing windows as Becky Frazer headed up the concrete staircase of the vocational institute. The

Condor Security driver had inquired impatiently about his passengers. *Better check on those two before they miss their flight.*

The nurse-practitioner had just reached the final flight of stairs when a sunbeam slanting through a window above threw into sharp relief the single silhouette of two people sitting close together on the top step. The couple was not embracing, only their shoulders touching as a quiet murmur of voices floated down the stairs. But there was somehow about those two close figures a oneness, a protective tenderness in the way the larger shape leaned toward his companion, a relaxed peace in the upward tilt of that slighter profile, that brought to Becky's mouth a smile that was both satisfied and wistful.

The nurse-practitioner headed back downstairs. The airport could wait a little longer.

Neither Becky Frazer nor the absorbed pair at the window could see or hear it, but somewhere far above, seated among that "great cloud of witnesses" the holy book describes as watching over brothers and sisters who have not yet finished the great race of faith, a friend and brother who'd recently crossed the finish line was offering his own thunderous applause.

EPILOGUE

Kandahar Province, Afghanistan

"Are you sure?" Omed's hand was on the wooden door leading from the dirt courtyard to the narrow lane beyond. But he turned back once more to where his wife stood, infant son in her arms, their other sons and daughters clustered around her long cloak.

Najia's long-lashed dark eyes could not completely banish apprehension, but beautiful, oval features enveloped by her winter scarf were resolute. "No, you are right, my husband. It is time. We have prayed about it."

"And if what happened to Jamil—?" Omed broke off, unable to finish. "I do not worry for myself but for you and the children, for my mother, and Moska and her children too. Is it right to place you all at risk?"

"If no other of our people has the courage of Jamil, how will Afghanistan ever be changed?" The gallantry with which Najia lifted her head, the gentle wisdom with which she spoke, were among many reasons Omed loved this small, young wife of his, a stranger when they'd married, but now so dear to him. "It is for our children you must do what the Almighty has placed within your heart. For their future, the future of our homeland. Do not fear for us. Whatever happens, Isa will care for us."

"If anything goes ill, we will meet in paradise. But I believe all will go well. Until the elections at least, the mullah will not wish to cause more trouble. And this town is filled with friends." Omed did not kiss his wife good-bye. It was not their way, not with the rest of the household gathered to watch. But his hand touched her cheek briefly, a smile in his eyes meeting her brave gaze reassuringly.

Then he was out the door, walking swiftly toward the town commons, where merchants were setting up stalls and unloading produce for today's rest-day market. Selecting a spot near the town well, Omed spread out his patu and seated himself cross-legged. Villagers and merchants alike drifted over as Omed opened the book his children were learning to read to him. Among them was Omed's brother-in-law Haroon, a silent burqa at his heels. The carpet workshop where his wife was now healed enough to work had closed for the rest day.

Though Omed could not read the graceful, swirling symbols and dots printed on the page his oldest son had marked for him, he'd committed to memory the words they spelled out. He spoke clearly enough to carry to the back of the gathering crowd. "In recent days, a good man, a healer, whose kind deeds have touched even our own village—"

Omed's brother-in-law stirred uneasily where he'd hunkered down to listen.

"—was arrested in our streets, tried, and put to death for no other crime than that he followed Islam's highly honored prophet, the great Healer, Isa Masih. I am no scholar, only a simple man who works with my hands, as all here know. But if a good man is willing to lay down his life as shaheed rather than deny the teachings and ways of this Isa, does it not seem that we, the Afghan people, should at least know what are these words for which he dared to die?"

Omed raised the book so that the entire crowd could see its open pages. "Into my hands has been granted possession of Isa's holy writings. So today let me share with you, my neighbors, my countrymen, the words of love and peace and life Isa has to say."

Lowering the volume to the woolen blanket, Omed began to recite slowly, measuredly:

"Blessed are the poor in spirit, for theirs is the kingdom of heaven.
Blessed are those who mourn, for they will be comforted.
Blessed are the meek, for they will inherit the earth.
Blessed are those who hunger and thirst for righteousness, for they will be filled."

A Conversation with the Author

What led you to write a story set in Afghanistan?
Like so many reading this interview, I believed the 2001 overthrow of Afghanistan's Taliban regime presaged new hope for freedom and peace in that region. Anyone who follows the news is aware that neither freedom nor peace has ever materialized. Instead today's headlines reflect rising violence, corruption, lawlessness, and despair. The signing of Afghanistan's new constitution establishing an Islamic republic under sharia law tolled a death knell for any hope of real democracy.

And yet so many players I've met in this drama—whether military, embassy, or humanitarian—have involved themselves for the most part with the best of intentions. As I came to know the region and love its people, I was left asking, if trillions of dollars in aid, all the weapons the West can bring to bear, and a lot of genuine goodwill aren't enough to bring about lasting peace and democracy, then what is the true source of freedom? Can outsiders ever truly purchase freedom for another culture or people? Searching for answers to that question birthed *Veiled Freedom* and its sequel, *Freedom's Stand*.

You have a firm grasp on the plight of the Afghan people, their politics, and their country. Your realistic writing has prompted government agencies to question you to determine how you've received classified information. How do you go about researching your stories with such accurate details?
Thoroughness is key. I can honestly say that if I missed a single tome dealing with Afghanistan's present or past, as well as Western involvement there, it wasn't on purpose. Add in my own sojourn in Afghanistan (I went deliberately under the radar), as well as extensive input from contacts on the ground who are real-life counterparts of my characters: Special Ops,

private security, humanitarian aid, Afghans, etc. Additional research tools like Google alerts, local news and blogs, security and embassy info coming out of Afghanistan kept me daily updated during the writing process.

Tell us about your own visits to Afghanistan. What did you experience there?

What I found most shocking was how little has changed, despite a decade of American and NATO occupation and trillions of aid dollars. People are still starving, beggars everywhere. After an initial freedom, most women are back in burqas. Mud-brick hovels are still the norm, while less than 6 percent of the country has electricity. Afghans express more concern over the corruption and brutality of local police and government officials than the Taliban, while Islamic sharia law trumps any pretense at freedom and human rights.

Not that all Afghans have failed to benefit. All over Afghanistan, partially finished aid projects from police stations and schools to power plants sit empty and crumbling from shoddy construction. But there are entire neighborhoods of brand-new turreted, gabled, and towered mansions built by the elite, who've profited from both the aid windfall and opium boom, too many of them government ministers.

What real-life situations or people in Afghanistan inspired this story?

Ironically, the real-life story that most inspired *Freedom's Stand* had not yet happened when I began writing it. Even as I answer these interview questions, Afghan father of six and amputee Sayed Mossa has now spent six months in a filthy Kabul prison cell, without legal representation or formal charges, enduring horrific abuse, for the sole crime of choosing faith in Jesus Christ. His arrest came after cell phone images of Sayed and other Afghans praying in Christ's name and being baptized were publicized. His situation reflects so closely the story of *Freedom's Stand*, I might have been reporting on it. In actuality, though Sayed's arrest came afterward, conditions on the ground were such that I knew it was only a matter of time before my fiction became reality.

The plight of Afghan women also inspired this story. If fictionalized, all events and bios I included are based on true-life experiences. Including some of my own. Riding a bike, for instance, with my hostess from their humanitarian compound to another a few blocks away, a faster, therefore safer, trip for expat women than walking. Though swaddled head to toe in headscarf and chapan despite intense summer heat, we drew the attention of Afghan male passersby. Their automatic reaction was not curiosity or even disdain for our daring to be on a bike, but to begin stoning us. My hostess was knocked from her bike, left with a serious knot on the head. The next day bike transport was placed out of bounds for the expat female personnel, one more small freedom lost. It was one of many lessons in what Afghan women experience every moment of every day—and they can't get on a plane and fly away!

My characters are themselves complete fiction. But they definitely reflect their many true-life counterparts I've come to know.

Some readers might think that your stories are anti-Afghanistan or anti-Muslim. How would you respond to that accusation?

On the contrary, it is because I have come to love so much the Afghan people that I find myself angry at the oppression and injustice I've witnessed there or under any other Islamic totalitarian regime. Whether Muslim, Christian, or any other religious belief, faith should be a matter of heart choice not government imposition. Women should have the right to live free of abuse and to have equal representation under the law. The poor and underprivileged should have equal access to justice and fair governance as those who can afford bribes. It is a misconception that Muslims do not want these things as much as any other human. Across the Islamic world, it is Muslims who are rising up to advocate for personal freedom. And it is Muslims who are being crushed by their own governments for those demands. I am as passionate about human rights and freedom for every Afghan and Muslim as for Christian believers thrown in prison for daring to exercise personal choice of faith.

When it comes to cultural differences, how should we distinguish between moral (or human rights) issues and traditional practices?

An excellent question without any black-and-white answer. Every individual may draw the line differently. But tradition and culture have too long been used as justification for unjust practices, whether slavery, abuse of women and minorities, government imposition of religion. Two scriptural principles that helped propel civil rights movements still offer the best guidelines: "Love your neighbor as yourself" (Mark 12:31) and "Do to others as you would have them do to you" (Luke 6:31).

What do you want readers to come away with after reading this story?
I would like readers to close this book with a better understanding of Afghanistan and the entire Muslim world and how vital and interconnected events there—especially such issues as freedom of worship, freedom of speech, and human rights—are to our own country's future and security. Even more so, I want every reader to understand what the only true source of freedom is. Bottom line, when enough individual hearts change from hate to love, cruelty to kindness, greed to selflessness, their society will be transformed as well. Change a heart, change a nation. And how does one change hearts? Hopefully, by the last page of *Freedom's Stand*, the reader will have an answer to that as well!

How can your readers help meet the needs—material, political, and spiritual—of people in Afghanistan? Where can they find more material on this subject?
They can help by raising their voices on issues of human rights and freedom of speech and worship, especially in countries receiving our tax dollars and military aid. Organizations like Open Doors and Voice of the Martyrs offer great resources on how to get involved. To donate, there are many wonderful humanitarian groups serving in Afghanistan. Unfortunately there are also less-reputable start-ups milking the aid bonanza. While security cautions do not permit me to offer specific recommendations here, longevity of service in Afghanistan and a trustworthy reputation as a nonprofit are two good qualifiers to consider. To learn more about Afghanistan itself, my own Web site and blog (www.jeanettewindle.com) has a list of recommended reading and other material.

Discussion Questions

1. In *Veiled Freedom*, where we first meet *Freedom's Stand* protagonists Jamil, Steve, and Amy, each is involved in a quest for freedom. Having found true freedom in Isa Masih, Jamil feels impelled to share this good news. How does his experience sharing this message differ from his expectations?

2. The humanitarian code dictates not getting personally involved. Amy finds herself balking at this. Is she right or wrong?

3. When Steve finally finds a mission he can believe in, it requires laying aside his own future hopes and ambitions. What does the phrase "living sacrifice" come to mean to Steve? to you?

4. The life story of Amy's young protégé Farah gradually unfolds throughout *Freedom's Stand*. How do you react to her story—and its reality for millions of women under Islamic totalitarian regimes?

5. In chapter 13, Amy struggles with seeing the Afghan children she loves leaving to an unknown future. How does she find peace to let them go? Into whose care does she find she can release them?

6. In *Freedom's Stand*, Steve starts off thinking aid work is just throwing away material resources. What changes his mind?

7. In chapter 20, Jamil's hopes that the teachings of Isa Masih will transform his people have been dashed. What does Amy remind him is the only true way transformation can come to a people or nation?

8. In chapter 32, Steve forcefully makes a point on his embassy's stand regarding freedom of faith in Afghanistan: "What won't happen is that the 'free West' can keep enjoying forever their own freedoms while tacitly conceding those are now considered optional for the rest of this planet." Do you agree with him or disagree? Is freedom of faith simply a cultural distinctive Western nations happen to enjoy or a basic human right?

9. How do other freedoms—whether of thought, speech, media, assembly, action—hinge on the fundamental right to choose freely one's own personal beliefs of heart and mind? Can a society really enjoy these other freedoms while prohibiting freedom of faith?

10. In reading of Isa Masih's voluntary death on the cross, Jamil ponders what could motivate any person to such willing martyrdom. In chapter 47, what does he finally recognize as the only true motivation?

11. In what different ways is love portrayed in this novel? Which aspects of love speak most directly to your life?

12. By the end of *Freedom's Stand*, Jamil, Amy, and Steve must each in turn make a stand involving sacrifice and love. What is the cost to each of these protagonists? the reward? In the end, which outweighs the other?

13. Jamil literally risks his life for the truth he has found. What causes or truths are you willing to take a stand for?

14. What can you do to raise a voice on freedom of faith issues? What should you do on an individual level? a church level? a government level?

Fires smolder endlessly below the dangerous surface of Guatemala City's municipal dump.

A politically relevant tale of international intrigue and God's redemptive beauty and hope.